ALL FOR NOTHING

Walter Kempowski

Translated from the German
by Anthea Bell

All for Nothing

GRANTA

Granta Publications, 12 Addison Avenue, London W11 4QR

First published in Great Britain by Granta Books 2015
This paperback edition published by Granta Books 2016

Original German edition first published in 2006
Alles Umsonst by Walter Kempowski
Copyright © 2006, Albrecht Knaus Verlag, Munich,
a division of Verlagsgruppe Random House GmbH, Munich, Germany

English translation copyright © Anthea Bell 2015

The rights of Walter Kempowski and of Anthea Bell to be identified
as the author and translator of this work respectively have been asserted by
them in accordance with the Copyright, Designs and Patents Act 1988

TRANSLATOR'S NOTE
The italicized quotations throughout the text of the book
are from a variety of sources, including such famous German
poets as Schiller, Goethe and Heine; folk songs; patriotic songs
and verses of the 20th century; popular songs of the early
part of the century and from films made
under the Nazi regime.

This book has been selected to receive financial
assistance from English PEN's PEN Translates programme,
supported by Arts Council England. English PEN exists to promote
literature and our understanding of it, to uphold writers' freedoms around
the world, to campaign against the persecution and imprisonment of
writers . . . free exchange
of ideas. www.englishpen.org

9 8 7 6 5 4 3 2 1

ISBN 978 1 84708 721 8
eISBN 978 1 84708 722 5

Typeset by M Rules

Printed and bound by CPI Group (UK) Ltd, Croydon, CR0 4YY

www.grantabooks.com

For Jörg

To save our souls from sin, dear Lord,
Our lives are all in vain.
Only Thy grace and Holy Word
Obliterate its stain.

Martin Luther (1524)

The Georgenhof

The Georgenhof estate was not far from Mitkau, a small town in East Prussia, and now, in winter, the Georgenhof, surrounded by old oaks, lay in the landscape like a black island in a white sea.

The estate was a small one. All the land apart from a remnant had been sold and the manor house was far from being a castle. It was built over two floors, crowned by a semicircular pediment with a battered metal finial in the shape of a spiked mace, the weapon also known as a morning star. The house stood behind an old stone wall that had once been painted yellow. It was now entirely overgrown by ivy in which the starlings nested in summer. Early in this January of 1945, the tiles on the roof were rattling in an icy wind that swept up fine snow from far away over the fields and against the estate buildings.

'You'll have to strip that ivy off some time,' the owners had been told. 'It'll eat all the plaster away.'

Rusty, discarded agricultural implements were propped against the crumbling stone wall, and scythes and rakes dangled from the tall black oaks. A harvest cart had collided with the farmyard gate long ago, and the gate had hung askew on its hinges ever since.

The home farm, with its stables, barns and a cottage, lay to one side of the manor house, a little way off. All that strangers driving along the road saw of the place was the main house. They wondered who lived there: why don't we just stop and say hello?

And then with a touch of envy they wondered: why don't we live in a house like that ourselves, a place that must be full of stories? Life is unfair, thought the passers-by.

NO THROUGH ROAD, said a notice on the big barn: no one was allowed to go into the park. Peace reigned behind the house and in the little park and the wood beyond it. There has to be a place where you feel you belong.

4.5 KM, said the whitewashed milestone on the road that ran past the house to Mitkau, leading to Elbing in the other direction.

Opposite the property, on the other side of the road, a housing development known as the Settlement – or in full, the Albert Leo Schlageter Settlement – had been built in the thirties. All the houses were exactly alike, neatly aligned, each with its shed, fence and a small garden. The families who lived here had names like Schmidt, Meyer, Schröder and Hirscheidt. They were what you might call ordinary people.

The name of the owners of the Georgenhof was von Globig. Katharina and Eberhard von Globig, members of the civil service aristocracy set up under Kaiser Wilhelm II, ennobled in 1905. The estate had been bought for good money by old Herr von Globig before the First World War, and more pastures and woodland had been added to it in times of prosperity. Young Herr von Globig had sold all the land – meadows, fields and pasture – except for a small remnant, investing the money in English steel shares, and he had also financed a Romanian rice-flour factory, which enabled the couple to lead a life that, if not exactly luxurious, was comfortable. They bought a Wanderer, a car owned by no one else in the district, and they drove it mainly to the south.

*

2

Now Eberhard von Globig was a *Sonderführer*, a special officer in the German army, and at war. The uniform suited him, including the white coat worn in summer, although its narrower shoulder-boards marked him out from the officers of the regular army as an administrator who had nothing to do with weapons.

His wife was famous as a languorous beauty, black-haired and blue-eyed. It was not least for her sake that friends and neighbours visited the Georgenhof from time to time in summer, to sit in the garden and feast their eyes on her: Lothar Sarkander, the mayor of Mitkau – stiff leg and duelling scars on his cheeks – Uncle Josef and his family from Albertsdorf, Dr Wagner the schoolmaster, a bachelor with a goatee beard and gold-rimmed glasses. His beard made him look like someone you felt you knew, and even strangers would pass the time of day with him in the street. He taught German and history to the older boys at the monastery school in Mitkau, with Latin as a subsidiary subject.

In the summer holidays Cousin Ernestine from Berlin sometimes came to visit with her children Elisabeth and Anita, who always loved to go riding, and would steal away into the house and eat the curds of sour milk standing on the kitchen windowsill, flies hovering over the dish. They liked the hay wains that swayed as they came down the path and they enjoyed looking for blueberries in the wood.

Now that it was wartime, the Berlin family came mainly to forage for supplies. They arrived with empty bags and went away with full ones.

The two Globigs had a son whom they had called Peter: thin face, curly fair hair. He was twelve years old, as quiet as his mother and as serious as his father.

Hair all over the place, mind all over the place too, people said

3

when they saw him, but the fact that his flyaway curly hair was blond made up for it.

His little sister Elfie had died of scarlet fever two years ago. Her room stood empty and untouched, her puppet theatre and the doll's house gathering dust. Her clothes still hung in the wardrobe adorned with painted flowers.

Also on the farm were Jago the dog and Zippus the tomcat, horses, cattle, pigs and a large flock of chickens, with Richard the rooster.

The Georgenhof even had a peacock, who kept himself to himself.

Katharina, the dark beauty dressed all in black, caressed her son's hair, and Peter had liked it when his quiet mother did that until recently, when he would ward off the caress with an energetic shake of his head. Katharina never spent a long time standing beside the boy. She left him alone, just as she herself liked to be.

Another family member was 'Auntie', a sinewy old spinster with a wart on her chin. She was always on the go, and in summer went around the house in a limp, washable dress. Now that it was cold, she wore a pair of man's trousers under the skirt of the dress and two cardigans over it. Since Eberhard had become a special officer 'in the field', although in fact he was behind the lines, she made sure that everything went smoothly at the Georgenhof. Nothing would have functioned without her. 'Nothing's easy,' she would say, and with that attitude she ran the whole show.

'You must keep the kitchen door closed!' she called to everyone in the house; she had said the same thing thousands of times before. 'There's a draught blowing right through the rooms,' meaning that you couldn't heat the place. She complained of the cold: why had she ended up here in East Prussia? Why, for heaven's sake, hadn't she gone to Würzburg when she still had the option?

She kept a handkerchief tucked into her sleeve, and put it to her red nose again and again. None of it was as easy as the others might think.

At the outbreak of war, the flow of money dried up: shares in English steel? A rice-flour factory in Romania? It was a good thing that Eberhard had his position in the army, for they couldn't have managed without the salary he drew. The few acres of land they still had, the three cows, three pigs and the poultry, provided something extra to eat, but they had to be looked after. Nothing would come of nothing.

Vladimir, a thoughtful Pole, and two cheerful Ukrainian women kept the farm going. The Ukrainians were stout Vera, and Sonya, a blonde girl with her hair braided and pinned up around her head. Crows circled over the oaks, and the 'dicky-birds' got their share on the bird tables, which were fairly regularly supplied with food in winter. 'Dicky-birds' was what Elfie, now two years dead, used to call them.

When more money had been coming in, the von Globigs had furnished a comfortable apartment on the first floor of the house, three rooms, a bathroom and a little kitchen. It had a warm, comfortable living room with a view of the park, where Katharina could write letters or read books. And when Eberhard came home they were undisturbed there. They could close the door and be on their own, as they put it. It meant that they didn't always have to sit down in the hall with Auntie, who had a finger in every pie and always thought she knew best. Auntie, who was always jumping up to fetch something, or staying put when that was more of a nuisance.

*

Now, in January 1945, the Christmas tree was still standing in the hall. Peter's godmother in Berlin had given him a microscope. He sat in the dimly lit hall at a table not far from the tree, which was dropping its needles. Looking down the tube of the microscope, he saw all kinds of things in great detail: salt crystals and flies' legs, a piece of string, the head of a match. He had placed a notebook beside him, and he noted his observations down in it. 'Thursday 8 January 1945: pin. Jagged edges to the point.'

He had wrapped his feet in a rug to keep the draughts away. It was always draughty in the hall, because the fireplace sucked in air, and the kitchen door was 'left open the whole time', as Auntie complained. Those Ukrainian women, she said, could never learn to close doors. Eberhard had found them in the east. Did they want to come to the great, powerful country of Germany, he had asked them in their village, did they want to see Berlin, with its cinemas and U-Bahn? And then they had landed here at the Georgenhof.

Peter moved the tube of his instrument up and down, and from time to time he put a ginger biscuit in his mouth.

'Well,' said Auntie as she hurried through the hall, 'working hard at your science, are you?' The snow really ought to be swept away from the entrance, she thought, but it's easier to do these things yourself than ask someone else. Besides, the boy was busily occupied, and who knew, maybe his passion for that instrument would bear fruit later. The university in Königsberg wasn't far away, was it? If Peter had been hanging around doing nothing, that would have been different.

'Leave him alone,' Katharina had said when Auntie complained that he didn't get out and about much.

When Peter had tired of the microscope, he stood at the window and watched the birds flying around at a loss because, once again, there was no food on the bird tables, and then he used his father's binoculars to look into the distance, although he wasn't really supposed to do that. The binoculars weren't a toy, he had been told, and it showed if you touched the lenses with greasy fingers, let alone adjusted the focus. 'Someone's been at my binoculars again,' von Globig would say when he came home – which was seldom enough – to the Georgenhof.

Peter looked over towards Mitkau, where the chimney of the brickworks could be seen next to the church tower. The school was closed because of the cold. 'Cold holidays' was a new expression. Young people could stay at home, but the Hitler Youth made sure that they were not idle. They had wanted to take Peter out of doors on a cold winter's day to shovel snow away from the big Mitkau crossroads. But Peter was suffering from one of his chills, which meant that he couldn't take part in that operation. 'It's his catarrh again,' said the members of the household.

Cold and coughs, however, didn't keep him from sliding down the little slope behind the house time and again on his toboggan. The sun was shining in front of the house, and it would have been even better to toboggan there, but he had been told not to because every now and then a car sped past.

He returned to his microscope. The dog Jago kept close to him, resting his muzzle on the boy's right foot, and the cat lay on Jago's coat.

What a wonderful picture, the household said, just see the cat lying on the big dog's back!

'What a delightful son you have,' said the visitors from Mitkau who liked to come to Georgenhof, although it meant a walk of an hour and a half. 'Such a pretty boy!' They arrived with empty bags and left with full ones.

Dr Wagner, that confirmed bachelor, dropped in quite often.

He was worried about the boy now that the monastery school was closed. When young people raced boisterously past him in its cloisters, he liked to buttonhole fair-haired Peter and ask, 'Well, my boy? Has your father written home again?' And now, with the school closed because of the cold weather, he was concerned for him.

In summer, when the weather was warm and fine, he and his third-year boys had gone strolling through the sea of golden grain crops and along the quiet little River Helge, which flowed through the countryside in great curves to left and right, willow trees growing beside it. The boys had stripped off their trousers and shirts and plunged into the dark water. Shouting at the tops of their voices, they would often run through the wood, ending up at the Georgenhof, where they were given strawberry-flavoured water and allowed to eat their sandwiches sitting on the grass in the park, like cheerful summer birds.

The schoolmaster would take his silver flute out of his pocket and play the tunes of folk songs, while Katharina listened from the house.

Now, in the cold winter of the sixth year of the war, Dr Wagner dropped in even more often than before, coming on foot in spite of the ice and snow, and he too was in the habit of arriving with an empty bag and going away with it full. He took apples home with him, or potatoes, and sometimes a swede, which in fact he paid for, because Auntie used to say, 'It doesn't grow for love.' She reckoned that a swede was worth ten pfennigs.

He enjoyed sitting with Katharina for a while if she put in an appearance. He would have liked to take her hand, but he had no real excuse for that. Auntie made a lot of noise when he visited, pulling open drawers and closing them again with a bang. The message she meant to convey was: there's always something to be done in a big household like this, even if it looks as if we're just idling our days away.

So Wagner was a little concerned for the boy, as he put it. He went to Peter's room with him and taught him things that had never been mentioned at school.

Binoculars and microscope? There was a little telescope in the physics lab of the monastery school. He could take it to the Georgenhof and look at the stars with the boy, couldn't he? No one would notice that it was missing, and then surely he could return it when everything was over?

Dr Wagner concerned himself with the boy for love, or at least he didn't ask fifty pfennigs for an hour's tutoring. He was happy with a few potatoes or half a head of cabbage.

2

The Political Economist

One dark evening the front doorbell rang. The man who had rung it was getting on in years, wore an unusual cap and walked on two crutches.

Vladimir, using his electric torch, had already spotted him wandering round the yard in the darkness, and the two Ukrainian women had stopped what they were doing to look out of the kitchen window, wondering who was approaching the house.

Jago had got to his feet, barking once or twice, and now the stranger stood in the doorway. The bell rang once more, and Katharina opened the door to him. Next moment the man was stalking past her and into the hall on his crutches, swinging his legs back and forth, accompanied at every step by Jago. He wore a green rustic jacket, with side pockets set at a slant, and black ear muffs. The ear flaps of his cap were held together with a looped piece of twine on top of his head. He had a leather strap round his body, and a heavy briefcase resembling an accordion hung from it.

He would just like to warm up a little, he told Katharina and Auntie, who was bringing in the supper-time soup at that very moment. Could he do that? No buses, no trains, the way was heavy going in this icy wind. He came from Elbing, he said, and had made his way here on foot from Harkunen. What a journey it was, too! Who'd have thought it? Fifteen kilometres, in this weather, and at this time of day.

He was bound for Mitkau, and had expected to find an inn

along his way, the Forest Lodge; it was marked on his map as a good place for family parties out on excursions.

And he had indeed passed it, but it was closed and the doors and windows bolted. There were strange folk in those parts and he'd heard confused scraps of all kinds of languages, Czech and Romanian.

Hands in their pockets, they had watched him go.

The man's name was Schünemann, and he had come a considerable distance by train, then he had been given a lift in a farmer's cart from Harkunen, and he had travelled the very last part of the way here on foot. In this snow, too!

All he wanted, he said, was to warm himself and take a little rest, and then he'd be off again. He'd find shelter for the night somewhere along the way, he said, looking around him.

Why on earth had he set off through the countryside at this time of the year? Going to Mitkau, of all places?

Katharina looked at the man. A visitor at this time of day? And the man looked back at her, not without interest. Good heavens, a woman like this hidden away in the country. She belonged somewhere else by rights. Berlin, Munich, Vienna!

He walked stiffly over to her, legs swinging back and forth, said that his name was Schünemann, he was an economist by profession, a political economist, and she wasn't to worry, he only wanted to rest and get his breath back.

'Ah, warmth!' he said, unhooking the briefcase from the strap over his shoulder and putting it down by the fireside seat. He unbuttoned his jacket and, now free of his crutches, went close to the fire and let his body soak up its warmth. Warmth! The dog Jago, wondering what the man might be seeing there in the fire, went to sit beside him, and wagged his tail briefly. The man might be all right.

Then the cat came along to find out what was going on.

The man sat in the chimney corner, lit a pipe and cursed the day when, at his father's persistent urging, he had decided to study political economy.

'If only I'd been a cabinet-maker,' he said, turning to Auntie. 'But a political economist, of all things!' he cried, calling on these people to bear witness to the course his life had taken.

Peter asked him what a political economist was.

'Hmm,' replied the man, 'it's not all that easy to explain. Now if I'd been a cabinet-maker instead . . .' Could he, he asked, take a quick look through that microscope? He thought that the lens wasn't properly adjusted.

He didn't like the silence in the east, he said – such extraordinary peace and quiet. He put his head on one side, as if listening, trying to catch some kind of sound, and because he didn't like the silence, he said he wasn't going on to Insterburg as he had originally intended; he would stay in Mitkau for a few days instead. And then back to Elbing as quickly as possible, and on again by way of Danzig to Hamburg, where a cousin of his lived. He was planning to take refuge with this cousin.

'Did you see the fires burning last night?' he asked Katharina, who put an oil lamp on the table – for there was yet another power cut – and sat down herself. After all, it was supper time.

Fires? She knew nothing about that . . . it was all so complicated. Anyone who ever spoke to Katharina found her a total blank. She had never heard of anything at all, she hadn't even guessed at it. 'She hasn't the faintest idea,' people said of her, 'but she's beautiful . . . very beautiful.' She was the most striking person present at any social gathering, although she hardly ever said a word.

What else could you say about her? She shut herself up in her own rooms, and heaven only knew what she did there. She read a lot, or rather she made her way through a great many mediocre books. Her reading matter could not be said to include Goethe and Lessing. As a girl she had been a bookseller's assistant, and since then it had been her habit to skim books; she did not attempt anything too difficult.

In any case, they had to eat now. The thermometer showed a temperature of minus sixteen degrees, and the barometer suggested that it would get even colder.

Perhaps they hesitated a little too long before asking the visitor to join them at the table, where the soup tureen was already standing, but then it was done: he was invited to take a few spoonfuls, whereupon he knocked out his pipe and came quickly closer, sat down, rubbed his hands, and repeated again and again that he only wanted to have a little rest and get his breath back.

He sat opposite Katharina and scrutinized her. A Mediterranean beauty in this bleak wilderness at the back of beyond? He thought of Anselm von Feuerbach, whose classical pictures everyone knew.

Katharina looked as if she wanted to say she couldn't help being out of place here. She was holding a key and toying with it; it was the key to her boudoir, which she always kept locked. It was shiny from her constant nervous fidgeting with it. No one else had any business up there.

He had set out without thinking it over properly; rumour said that the major roads would be checked after tomorrow, so he had slipped through just in time. And he had thought that a cart might give him a lift on the way, but the road had looked deserted – and not an inn anywhere in sight. He had already thought of the Forest Lodge: Lord, it is good for us to be here: if thou wilt, let us make here three tabernacles. Then, at the last minute, he had seen the manor house lying low behind the wall, under the black oak trees, and he had thought he could stop and rest here, warm himself up and then go on the last few kilometres to Mitkau.

He'd get there yet.

The Forest Lodge? Good heavens, yes, the Forest Lodge used to be a good place for an excursion; it had an outdoor café, ideal for families and school classes, the great forest was close to it, and beyond the forest the river, bordered by willows. But now the large windows offering such good views were boarded up. Now the Forest Lodge had become a hostel for foreign workers, Romanians, Czechs, Italians – folk described by the locals as scum. The Romanians never washed their feet, the Italians had already let the German people down in the First World War, and now they had gone and done it again. You couldn't trust such folk an inch.

The two Ukrainian women occasionally went down there, and stayed longer than was seemly.

The Georgenhof: there was something mysterious about the house. Who knows, he had thought, what's waiting for me there? And now here he was, sitting at this table with such nice, pleasant people. Best of all, although they had never set eyes on one another before, they were already on such familiar terms!

He hadn't expected to be so well entertained; they kept the old standards of hospitality going in this house.

He took some ration coupons out of his wallet to give them to Frau von Globig, but then offered them to Auntie instead, thinking she was more likely to be responsible for such matters. Katharina, her dark hair pinned up on top of her head, put her hand to the brooch that she wore. She seemed to be thinking: ration coupons . . . ? It was all so complicated.

'No, no, put those away again,' said Auntie, ladling out soup for him. Then she saw that they were coupons for men on leave and would not go out of date; they could be used anywhere and at any time, so she was happy to accept them after all.

'Who knows what may happen yet?'

Nothing was easy.

The man thanked her and said to himself: let's see how things go on. First to Mitkau, maybe straight on to Insterburg, and if not then Allenstein. Then back to Elbing as fast as he could go, from there to Danzig and on to Hamburg. And then on again south. But first to get this soup inside him, and he said repeatedly, 'Ah, delicious!', rubbing his hands as he kept a good eye on what was being tipped from the ladle and on to his plate. It was quite rich soup, and had a little meat swimming in it too.

It occurred to him, just in time, that it would be usual to say grace in a house like this. His parents had preserved that custom in his childhood. He remembered it to this day.

Busy Auntie, the fair-haired boy, blue-eyed Katharina with her mind elsewhere and a trace of soft down on her upper lip, and the tureen of good rich soup on the table.

Ding-dong, the grandfather clock struck, ding-dong.

The soup was hot. The political economist, who had studied at Göttingen University and lived for a long time in the mountainous Fichtelgebirge district of Bavaria, until he had had the silly idea of travelling in East Prussia, blew on his spoonful of soup, making the oil lamp flicker. He weighed up the soup spoon in his hand and said, 'So civilized!' Turning round, he showed the boy the hallmark; he had noticed at once that the spoon was sterling silver. 'Look, what does that say? Eighty per cent silver!' And he picked up Peter's soup spoon as well. 'Every one of these spoons made of eighty per cent silver! And the ladle, a wonderful piece . . . What do you think that's worth, my boy?'

The china, too! 'But that's – isn't that . . . ?' He could hardly turn the plate over here and now. However, as the soup was gradually spooned up a complete landscape was revealed, painted in blue. The boy hadn't noticed it before. Trees, a pool with cranes, a boat with a fisherman in it pulling his net out of the water.

Katharina thought of Berlin and Tauentzienstrasse, where she had bought this china during her engagement. The Georgenhof? she had thought. Perhaps they would always be entertaining guests there. *Many* guests? As far as she knew, people gave large parties on their country estates. In large halls, by candlelight?

So she had bought the dinner service for twenty-four guests. 'What on earth do you want with all that china?' her husband had asked when her dowry arrived at the Georgenhof after their wedding.

Katharina came from Berlin, and she had been to East Prussia only once before, to the Baltic seaside resort of Cranz, where she happened to meet Eberhard over coffee and cake. 'Rise high, O red-winged eagle!' the band on the beach had played. 'Hail, land of Brandenburg!' They had eaten Florentines, and Eberhard had smoked cigarettes in a well-worn meerschaum holder with a man and a woman carved on it. And in the evening they had danced the foxtrot in the seaside dance hall.

Silver? Fine china? The political economist was astonished to find all these precious things still in use, not hidden away long ago, or sent to Berlin or somewhere else. 'Suppose the Russians come?' And with all those foreigners just down the road. His nose was running, so he took out something that passed for a handkerchief, and it could be seen that he wore a diamond ring on his little finger.

'What do you think it'll be like here if things turn out bad?'

He did not exactly lick his spoon clean, but it was obvious that he would like a second helping, and Auntie picked up the tureen in both hands and poured the rest of its contents, splashing, into his plate.

Katharina laughed a little at that, but she wasn't sure whether she should. Mightn't Auntie take her laughter the wrong way?

How could you laugh at such a moment? How could you?

If things turn out bad? What did the man mean by that?

He meant the Russians now stationed on the border. They could strike at any time. 'And then it will be the worse for us!'

A bowl of apples was placed on the table, and the guest was invited to help himself from that, too. He praised the fragrant aroma of the fruit. Taking more coupons out of his wallet, he handed them over the table.

'O give thanks unto the Lord, for he is gracious, and his mercy endureth for ever.' This was the grace at the end of the meal, and he could wholeheartedly agree with it.

Ah, said the man, how he appreciated this! Family life! 'I suppose your husband is at the front?' With his well-manicured hands he peeled the apple he had been given. And when he had eaten it, he was given a second.

No, said Katharina, not at the front but far away; her husband was in Italy, and he had sent some lovely things home from there. Whenever he went away he phoned them at home.

'First he was in the east, now he's in Italy.'

'And these fruit plates!' cried Schünemann. Each was painted with different fruits, pleasingly arranged: bananas with black grapes and almonds; a grapefruit; black- and redcurrants; figs. He showed the boy how carefully the painting was executed, and told him what a pomegranate was.

Again and again, the man marvelled at the carelessness of keeping these plates and the silver cutlery in use – they should pack it all up, for heaven's sake! Including the fruit knives with their horn handles. That mob down the road weren't to be trusted an inch.

'If things turn out bad ...'

Who could tell what was going to happen? The Russians? Who knew? At the moment, he said, the front was deep in slumber, but that could change in no time at all. He had a funny feeling. He would be off to Mitkau tomorrow, he said, and then Insterburg, and back again as soon as possible. Perhaps he would visit Allenstein too. He did not say what his business was in Mitkau and Insterburg.

'Pack it all up!' he cried, as if he himself would be to blame if they didn't. Packing it in straw in a crate and burying it would be the best thing to do. Or sending the silver to Berlin, piece by piece, or Bavaria, or even better to Hamburg. Maybe he could ask his cousin, he said, perhaps he could store it all at his place?

Then he put a finger to his lips as if giving away a secret, and whispered that silver would always keep its worth. Send the larger items away, he advised, but maybe it would be better to keep the teaspoons. They could be used like coins. 'This is cash in hand!' As a refugee, he said, if you wanted to cross a river you could simply offer the ferryman a teaspoon. Silver! A man like that would grab it with both hands. Who wanted money in times like these?

Katharina rolled herself a cigarette, and Auntie took the dishes out to the kitchen. She had never looked so closely at the plates before. Silver? Send it away? It wasn't as easy as all that. They'd better wash the fruit plates themselves in future, instead of leaving them to the maids, who might fool around and drop them.

The two Ukrainians, Vera and Sonya, were screeching at each other in the kitchen. They quarrelled all day long, heaven knew what about. Or maybe they weren't quarrelling, it just sounded like a quarrel in their difficult language.

Or were they fighting over the Romanians in the Forest Lodge? There were strong men among the fellows there, Romanians, Czechs, Italians. You could hear them singing. If you passed their hostel you were bound to hear someone or other singing. And when the maids were in sight they pushed their caps back on their heads. The Italian had even put a feather in his.

Herr Schünemann looked at the portraits hanging in the hall. They were large and dark, pictures of dignified worthies from Potsdam and the Tuchola Forest area. Dignified worthies, even though no one knew for certain who they were.

Well, then. Berlin. Wilmersdorf?

When Wilmersdorf was mentioned, Katharina looked away. She had wanted to send Peter there at Christmas time – for who knew what might yet happen? – but the family in Wilmersdorf didn't want to have him.

The family in Berlin got in touch only when they wanted something. Potatoes, vegetables, they'd come to take all that year after year, even a goose for Christmas, but they didn't want the boy to stay with them. And maybe that was just as well, in view of the devastating attacks on the capital.

Last summer they'd sent their two daughters here, Elisabeth and Anita. The girls had spent such a nice holiday in the country.

'The Berlin family have broken off their relationship with us,' said Auntie. 'Broken it off once and for all.'

'I see,' said the political economist.

*

After supper he set out on a tour of the house, swinging himself nimbly up and down the hall on his crutches, even pushing the door to the next room open. Cold air blew in. It was the summer drawing room, built before the war, paid for with money from the sale of the landed properties, and never really used. Now it was full of chests and crates.

He went all round the ice-cold drawing room. 'What are those crates?' he asked, tapping one of them with his crutch, but then he let them be, closed the door and rejoined the others.

There was yet another room to be explored. Good heavens, a billiards room! A regular billiards table covered with green cloth. Card tables with polished surfaces by the window, and in the corner a sideboard with ornamental intarsia work on its doors. They probably kept wine and cigars in it.

The hunting trophies on the walls – horns, antlers, ranged side by side, and the stuffed head of a wild boar – had been old Globig's. There was even a lampshade made of intertwined antlers under the ceiling. Old Globig had been a great hunter; his triple-barrelled gun and his expensive repeating rifle still hung in a modern glass case that didn't look as if it belonged here.

Auntie kept close behind the man, following hard on his heels. After all, they didn't know each other. She explained that in the old days the gentlemen always used to smoke their cigars and play whist in here. 'But we'd better close the door now.'

And parties had been given in the summer drawing room, she said, not entirely accurately; the von Globigs had been going to give parties there, but then the war came, and now the drawing room was full of crates containing the worldly goods of the Berlin family members.

Auntie propelled the guest back into the hall, and he swung himself all round it on his crutches, looking at the Christmas tree now dropping its needles. He turned a corner of the rug over with his crutch. 'Genuine?'

Finally he looked at the cups stacked slantways in a small cabinet, opened its glass door and asked, 'May I?' He examined them one by one. Some had a landscape scene painted on them, with boys skating on the ice in the foreground. There were dead flies in many of the cups. Eberhard's meerschaum cigarette holder also lay here, rather stained, but interesting. Sepia photographs in ornate wire frames stood in front of the cups, photographs of grandfathers and grandmothers. The political economist asked who they were, and on getting no answer looked at Katharina, but she did not rise to her feet, she came no closer, she sat at the table smoking and playing with the matchbox.

Auntie went over and showed him the photo of a Tsarist officer of 1914, in a laced *litevka* uniform coat, holding a riding crop. There were all manner of stories about this officer. He was said to have been billeted at the Georgenhof when the Russians invaded in 1914, and he had the reputation of being a decent, well-educated man who spoke fluent French. The Globigs had much to thank him for; he had saved the manor house from being looted, and he had played billiards with them.

In the 1920s, unexpectedly, he had turned up here again, after escaping from the Soviets by way of Finland. He had looked down-at-heel, all his elegance gone, a fur cap on his head. He had pointed east, groaning, 'Oh dear, oh dear!' Then he had borrowed money and disappeared, leaving behind the fur cap; it was white, made of Persian lamb.

A photograph of the master of the house also stood on the folding flap of the casket; he was wearing a white uniform jacket with the Cross of Merit on the chest, although without swords. 'Is that your husband, ma'am?' cried Herr Schünemann to Katharina. Yes, she said, it was indeed her husband.

Eberhard von Globig was one of the specialists helping to keep supplies to the German population going, draining the resources of the eastern agricultural territories for the benefit of the Greater German Reich. This war was very different from the war of 1914–18, when the Germans had subsisted on turnips. This time bad feeling was not to be stirred up among the people unnecessarily; they would be allowed access to an adequate diet. Bread, butter, meat, whole freight trains full of melons. They came from the Ukraine, from Byelorussia – all kinds of good things were to be had there. Wheat, sunflower oil, who knows what else? But now it all lay in ruins, smoke rising from their fields.

Katharina remembered a pair of brightly painted wooden clogs that Eberhard had given her; folk art. She had never worn them.

'Ah, the Ukraine,' said Dr Schünemann to Katharina, with much meaning. 'It's as well that your husband is in Italy now. That, you know, is very, very good news.'

With expert fingers he felt the inside of the cabinet, fingering the little compartments. A secret drawer.

A secret drawer? Perhaps it contained golden guilders or Swiss francs? No, the secret compartment was empty.

Eberhard's latest letter lay beside his photograph, with a blue air-mail armed forces stamp on it. Schünemann picked up the letter and took it to the table, bringing the oil lamp closer to it. That stamp. Was he mistaken? A misprint? Was the right-hand wing of the plane shown on it disfigured by a notch? A deformity on the plate? No? Ah, well then, no. The shadow of his hands scurried over the walls as he held the letter close to the lamplight.

*

It was going a little too far to sniff the airmail letter. He was almost about to take it out of the envelope, but he caught himself in time. 'How can anyone be so inappropriate?' he said. 'But it's my passion, my enthusiasm . . .' He turned to Katharina again, and told her about people cast into transports of delight by collecting all kinds of things, old books, coins, and he even knew of murders committed by those who wanted to complete their collections. There was Master Tinius who killed a wealthy widow in Leipzig. All for a few old books.

He gesticulated with his crutch, and the firelight cast very strange shadows round the room.

The hunting trophies on the wall, ranged there side by side, they too were bound up with collecting and killing.

Katharina thought of the consignments of wheat that her husband had dispatched year after year, the freight trains of soil on its way from the Ukraine to Bavaria. A layer of humus sometimes a metre thick on those fertile plains, stripped off and sent to Bavaria in long convoys of railway trains.

Sometimes Eberhard had also managed to abstract something for the family's private use, brown sugar, for instance, several hundredweight of brown sugar.

And now he was in Italy, busily confiscating wine and olive oil to be sent away.

Katharina rose, her long limbs graceful, patting her hair into place as she stood up. Black jacket, black trousers, boots. She offered her guest a plate of ginger biscuits left over from Christmas.

Oh, not those, Auntie might well be thinking, those were the good ones, but she let it pass; after all, the guest was an academic.

'Are you a professor?' she asked.

'No, not a professor. I'm a political economist.' And he would rather have been a cabinet-maker, or a graphic artist.

*

The guest put the letter back and apologized for his indiscretion: when he saw stamps, he said, he forgot everything around him. He was a collector himself, he explained, his passion was philately, and this stamp, if he was not much mistaken ...

Reaching for his leather bag, he took out a stamp album packed among his underwear and his shirts. Leafing through it, he said he collected only the finest, only the best. Old German stamps were his special field. And he had bought this album in Harkunen yesterday morning. Now what's this, he had thought ...

He took a pair of tweezers out of his waistcoat pocket and explained the old-fashioned stamps in the album to the boy, most of them with numbers on them, but some with crowns and coats of arms. You could live well for a good month on the proceeds of selling *this* stamp, he said, pointing the tweezers at a stamp showing John of Saxony.

Mecklenburg, Prussia, Saxony: how pleasant it had been in the Germany of the past, and he spoke of when measurements were in ells, feet and miles, he spoke of post-coaches in which you travelled from country to country without needing a passport or visa, he spoke of kreuzers, guilders and shillings. And he even imitated the signal of the post-horn.

But sad to say, the Prussians had eliminated that wonderful variety, insisting on unity, unity, unity! That stamp with the head of Germania – could there be anything less imaginative? Germania in armour? Iron plates covering her breasts!

People would surely still be interested in the old colonial stamps after the war, he said, they would probably be worth a mint of money. A German New Guinea stamp. 'After the war,' he said, leafing through the album and sighing.

When you thought that the British had even considered giving the German colonies lost after Versailles back to Hitler ... but no.

*

Peter ran up to his room, fetched his Schaubek stamp album, held it out to the guest and pointed to individual stamps. Were these worth anything too? That made the gentleman laugh heartily: good heavens, my dear boy.

How old was Peter? Twelve? Just the age for it, you couldn't begin collecting too early. But really, these stamps were worth hardly anything.

'You have a great many stamps showing Hitler, my boy.' If the Russians came and saw *those* stamps, what would they say? Nothing but little portraits of Hitler. He wasn't so sure, he said, suddenly turning to Katharina, but 'Mightn't they burn the house down over your heads, dear lady?'

Then he told Peter, 'Go and get your paint box.' He asked for a basin of water, and set to work on the Hitler stamps, dabbing a spot of black paint on every face of Hitler. Peter had only to dab all those Hitler stamps with black paint and wash it off again after the war, then there would be no problems. But leaving the stamps as they were ... Suppose a Russian opens the album and sees the Führer grinning back at him a hundred times over?

The Russians? Would they be coming here? asked Auntie, putting the cups back in the cabinet neatly. At that moment it may indeed have occurred to her that such a thing was possible. After all, it was during the last war that she herself had come to the Georgenhof.

But the war of 1914–18 had been very different. Mankind had not been so excitable in those days. The outcome would probably be less civilized this time.

'We Germans are not children of melancholy,' said Schünemann, raising his eyebrows, hinting at things that no one in the house understood. But all fell silent, and the fire crackled.

*

Now the gentleman had an idea. He took the album that he had just bought cheap in Harkunen, weighed it up in his hand – and it was quite a heavy weight – and asked for an envelope. Then he took the stamps out of the album one by one, working very carefully, and put them in the envelope. 'There was I dragging that heavy album about with me, and this is much simpler.' Although, he added, it was a pity really.

Finally, holding a small brown stamp in his tweezers, he showed it to them, placed it on the table, held a magnifying glass above it and called the boy over. 'See that?' What did he mean, see that? What was there to see? He asked for an electric torch and held it over the indentations at the bottom left-hand corner of the stamp. 'Don't you see anything?'

Then he showed Peter how the indentations had been repaired. A single missing tooth had been completed. The paper, thin as it was already, had been planed down, and a tiny tooth from an entirely different stamp stuck in place. At this even the two women moved forward, Auntie on the left and Katharina on the right, saying that they would like to see it. And they urged Peter to fetch his microscope, saying that maybe the repair could be seen even more clearly under its lens.

This opportunity allowed the gentleman to notice that Katharina's breath smelt sweet, which was more than could be said of Auntie's.

The political economist, laughing quietly, talked about the skill of humanity in forging banknotes. Imitation ink, specially prepared paper . . . he still remembered how, as a child, he had once forged his father's signature on a 'blue letter' – one of those informing his parents that his work was not up to scratch, which had to be signed by a parent to show that it had been received. The signature had been accepted and no one had noticed anything wrong. And he was still alive to tell the tale. He had passed his final school examination, the Abitur, he had studied at university, all with great success. Sometimes he thought that perhaps some day he would be disgraced, just for forging his father's signature as a child.

It was a crazy notion of his father's for him to become a political economist. 'I ought to have been a cabinet-maker. Or a wood-turner . . . or something of that sort.'

Now he had put all the stamps in the envelope. What should he do with the empty album? It had an eagle with wings spread wide on the front cover. Put it on the fire? He went over to the hearth and looked at the logs that were crackling as they gave off their warmth.

He placed the empty album on top of them, and watched as the eagle slowly caught fire and then sank into ashes. Watching it disappear, like the Germany of the good old days.

After that, he put the envelope full of stamps in his briefcase, and said, 'Well, then . . .'

He had a great many banknotes in his briefcase.

The political economist prepared to leave, but they urged him to stay. Was he going away through the dark at this hour? Out of the question, they were not going to push him out into the darkness and the cold. The wind was howling round the house. And somewhere or other a solitary aeroplane could be heard. He could easily spend the night here on the sofa, they told him. That was only ordinary hospitality. How many people had spent a night in this house already? Or there was Elfie's room up on the first floor? But that was cold as ice just now.

Peter asked Herr Schünemann whether he could swing himself through the hall on his crutches – 'You must say *Dr* Schünemann, Peter,' said Auntie, '*Dr* Schünemann.' Then the gentleman made himself comfortable on the sofa. Katharina brought blankets for him, and pillows that he put under his head. The family stood around, asking whether he felt comfortable, and was there anything else that he needed? They said goodnight, and when he was alone at last the man wrapped himself in the blankets, and watched the fire on the hearth slowly dying down.

Was there a shop in Mitkau, he had asked, selling stamps to collectors? Yes, said Auntie, so far as she knew.

Next morning he had disappeared.

Katharina had been going to take him some breakfast. Of course there was nothing else missing, but the stamp had been torn off the army envelope sent from the front by the master of the house. The man hadn't been able to resist it. In return, several sheets of ration coupons were lying on the table.

'Think of that!' said Auntie. 'Just think of that!'

The door was open. He might at least have closed it.

And of course Jago the dog had seized his opportunity to go off again.

3

The Violinist

The next guest could be seen coming from far away, silhouetted against the horizon and crossing the fields, enveloped in swirling snow. Crows with ragged wings dived down on the fluttering figure. This visitor was a young woman, and she was pulling along a sledge with two suitcases on it. The sledge kept tipping over as she hauled it across the snow-covered clods of earth. She had difficulty standing upright in the violent gusts of wind, which blew the skirts of her coat apart, and it was some time before she finally reached the manor house that lay, like a last refuge, behind the black oaks. The young woman had a violin case on her back, and that, too, made the people from the Settlement stare at her.

She knocked the snow off her shoes, straightened her knitted cap with both hands, took a deep breath and opened the door of the house. Jago jumped up at her with a friendly welcome, and since no one else appeared she called 'Heil Hitler!' into the house.

She was petting the dog a little too boisterously, and the noise brought Auntie out of the kitchen, where the two Ukrainian girls were quarrelling again – couldn't they keep their voices down? A strange woman with a violin case in the middle of the hall? She had wiped her shoes, Auntie could see, but all the same. Peter came running downstairs, taking three steps at a time. A visitor!

Now Katharina appeared too, all in black: black trousers, black pullover, black boots, and an oval locket round her neck, gold with a diamond teardrop on it. She had just been lying down for a little rest, and was curious to discover what was going on.

The young woman, it turned out, came from Mitkau. Her name was Gisela Strietzel – 'I'm Gisela,' she introduced herself. She had been entertaining the wounded in field hospitals for weeks, and now she had to make her way to Allenstein. She had spent three days in Königsberg, three days in Insterburg and two days in Mitkau, playing music to grateful injured soldiers, whose arms and legs were encased in white bandages, while many had bandaged heads.

Now she had to get to Allenstein and spend a week there, and then at last she could go home to Danzig, where Papa was expecting her. But a bomb had hit the railway line, and the car that was supposed to be coming for her was delayed: no petrol. She didn't feel like hanging about, so she had borrowed a sledge for her suitcases and set off across country. Would it cost the earth? The sledge would have to be returned to the field hospital some time or other; that was another problem. Perhaps the kind folk here could help her?

After that she would have to find out how to get to Allenstein. This journey was giving her a hell of a time!

It remained a mystery why the young woman hadn't taken the ordinary road. Why had she struck out across country? 'I like to go my own way,' she said, and they had to accept that.

She took off her gloves, shoes and coat and undid the straps holding her cases to the sledge. The sledge itself could be left in the porch, which had a lock on it. The road had been busy for the last few days: an occasional cart packed high with luggage, while other travellers on the road were riding bicycles or wheeling babies' prams. All the traffic was going from east to west. And everyone could use a sledge these days.

*

It was obvious that she couldn't be sent straight out on the road again: a young woman who had been entertaining the wounded for weeks on end in field hospitals. A young woman putting her whole heart into giving pleasure to unfortunate men who had imagined a soldier's life as very different.

So that she would not be politely shown the door – looking after number one in these hard times – she opened one of the two suitcases and took out a 'front-line fighter's package for the great operation'. It had been given to her in Mitkau for her journey. Putting the package on the table, she opened it: chocolate, biscuits, cigarettes and glucose tablets. Katharina von Globig, Peter and Auntie watched. Peter got the glucose candy, and the can of airman's chocolate was pushed over to Auntie. Katharina immediately lit one of the cigarettes.

Was Peter a leader of the Pimpfs, the junior branch of the Hitler Youth, Fräulein Strietzel asked the boy. No, he wasn't, and it was difficult for her to understand that out here in the country they weren't so interested in service with the Hitler Youth and the Pimpfs. Out in the Settlement, yes – but not here. He had a cold? Was that any reason to hide behind the stove? What would our soldiers out in the snow and ice say about that?

The boy put a piece of glucose candy in his mouth, and Katharina drew on her cigarette. Fräulein Strietzel went over to the window to see whether the car might be coming after all, but it was getting darker and darker, and in the end they showed her the sofa near the fireplace where she could lie down and get a little rest; there was plenty of time before supper. She did lie down, and fell asleep at once. She did not wake up until Vladimir the Pole brought in firewood, dropped it on the floor beside her, and took his chance to get a look at the new guest. He put a hatchet beside the wood.

*

When the smell of fried potatoes rose to her nostrils, she was wide awake. She was surprised to see a Pole walking in and out, just like that. Didn't such people get above themselves if you gave them so much as an inch, allowing them liberties that they could only dream of out in the steppes? In fact, wasn't familiarity with them forbidden? Remember the massacre of Germans by the Poles in Bromberg, in 1939.

By the light of the oil lamp – there was a power cut again – they all had a plate of fried potatoes, pickles, and a slice of blood sausage, and the Globigs sat at the supper table and watched Fräulein Strietzel, who was a real artist, enjoying the meal. She had bad teeth, as they could all see.

It seemed strange to the young woman that they said grace before meals in this house; she scuffed her feet on the floor, listening. She wasn't going to bother with all that God-in-heaven stuff and say prayers, not she. Of course there was a higher power, Fate or Providence, whatever you liked to call it, and there was something like that to be sensed in music – but so far as she was concerned the church was just big business. At home, she said, they had a book of maxims from which her Papa would sometimes quote: Goethe, Schiller, Dietrich Eckhart. She asked Peter if he knew any good rhymes? *Itsy-bitsy spider, climbing up the spout. Down came the rain and washed poor spider out.*

She ate heartily, now and then pointing to the dark portraits on the walls with her fork. She didn't exactly describe them as daubs, but said they must date from the year dot. His Nibs of Nibs Castle, she expected. Then she asked if she could have another slice of blood sausage? She was terribly greedy, she said. It didn't occur to her to get her ration coupons out of her bag; she hadn't been asked for them in the field hospitals. In the field hospitals she had always been given second helpings, and no one asked for her coupons.

Over the stewed gooseberries, she told the Globigs about the new tanks that had moved into Mitkau. She had seen them for herself – here she clapped her hand to her mouth; should she be giving that away? – as well as the fabulous barricades being built there. Ivan the Russian would never get through those! Mitkau was becoming a regular fortress; there were experts at work, and the enemy would certainly break their teeth on the fortifications.

She described the present peace and quiet on the front line as a pause to take breath. At this moment the entire front was breathing in deeply, and the resulting silence might deceive many. Then, one day, it would let that breath out again, as if to sneeze, and the sound would be a great, vengeful roar. The enemy would be blown away like chaff on the wind.

Did they have any hunting guns in this house, she wondered, so that they could defend themselves if necessary?

Peter went to fetch the triple-barrelled gun, and showed her that if you had already fired the first barrel but had missed, you could still fire the other two at the same target.

Fräulein Gisela thought that was fantastic, and asked whether the guns at the front also had three barrels.

After supper, the fire on the hearth was stirred up again, and Fräulein Strietzel put her feet on a footstool. She talked about the wounded men in the Mitkau field hospital – 'the disabled', as she called them – the amputees, the crippled and the sick. There were even blinded men among them, a whole section of them. She described the kind nurses who took such good care of them. The poor lads had to be spoon-fed. And one of them was both blind and deaf. A few days ago a convoy of severely wounded men had arrived, and ought to have been sent straight on to the west, but once again the road was impassable.

Yesterday evening a variety show had been put on for the soldiers, with a conjuror, a juggler and two women stand-up comics telling jokes. And she had been the high point. She had brought an evening dress especially for such occasions, when she couldn't very well stand there playing the violin in trousers.

The wounded men in their ward – what a shattering sight. Many, many beds, ranged side by side, and oh, the way the men looked at her when she began to play. You could have heard a pin drop; the only sound had been a high, rhythmic groaning from the back parts of the building, but someone had managed to shut that noise up quickly. And when she raised her violin, put the bow to the strings and played the first note in that silence, a sigh had passed through the whole ward. You could hardly imagine a more grateful audience. Grown men in tears.

A blind man had been led forward; he had asked if he could just touch her hand. She would never in her life forget that moment.

Grown men in tears – she herself wept very easily, in the cinema, for instance. Not that she ever cried when playing the violin; that was more of a matter of technique, you left your feelings out of it. But the cinema was different. Had they seen *Friedemann Bach*, that wonderful film about J.S. Bach's eldest son? She had wept buckets watching it.

What times that young woman had behind her: eight appearances in only seven days. And she showed them her hands, covered with chilblains. Basins of hot and cold water were quickly brought so that she could bathe her hands in them alternately, and a tube of chilblain ointment, which was applied thickly. If something wasn't done at once, she would never be able to play the violin again. The chilblains would burst, and her finger joints would stiffen up.

Where did she come from? Where was she going? Danzig? Her father was a major in the Medical Corps, such a kind man. 'If there's anything more forceful than Fate, then it's the man who bears it steadfastly . . .' She spoke enthusiastically of the latest batch of young men called up – such splendid material, you could hardly believe it. Where were they coming from? Now it was those born in 1928 – the strength of the German people was inexhaustible. She looked at Peter, still too young, of course, but later he would be good material himself. When it came to the point he too would surely stand his ground.

Of the seven students in her violin class, five had already fallen, in Africa and Yugoslavia, at Stalingrad and in the Atlantic. Five brave young men. If the same toll of lives was taken in all the music colleges and conservatories in the country . . . oh, it would come to hundreds of young men. She spoke as if the enemy had set their sights on violinists in particular.

She did not mention the fact that later, when the war was over, that would be all the better for her professional opportunities. Then the time for women would come. They would have to fill the breach, that was obvious to her.

It was a long time since she had last heard from her fiancé. She wore a locket round her neck with his picture in it. She took it out and showed it to the three of them; they all had a look at it. A soldier in a tank, wearing a black beret. *O thou lovely Westerwald.* All kinds of things had been going on in the Ardennes. Now it was quiet there. Perhaps – with luck – he was in a prison camp. The Yanks treated their prisoners humanely. The main thing was not to fall into the hands of those subhuman Russians.

The remains of a four-leaved clover lay on the photograph in the locket; the young couple had seen it at the same time on his last leave. They had both bent to pick it together. It had been so funny.

She held her locket, for comparison, against Frau von Globig's, which was larger and heavier. What, she wondered, was in it? It had a small diamond teardrop on the outside.

Hail, land of Brandenburg.

After supper Auntie took the dishes out, and as she opened the door to the corridor the two maids could be heard screeching in the kitchen again.

'What's that?' asked Fräulein Gisela. Ukrainian women? Making such a racket? What did they think they were doing, screaming like that? If she had a say, there'd have been silence at once.

It was a mystery to her that such conduct was allowed in this house. A Pole and two Ukrainian women, all of them riff-raff? She looked from one to the other of her hosts, wondering if anyone was going to tell her why they let the domestic staff get away with it.

Eight o'clock. Peter ought really to go to bed, but he was allowed to stay up when Fräulein Strietzel took her violin out of its case. Her idea was to play something for her hosts, to thank them for the blood sausage.

The instrument had been in the wars itself: the fingerboard was attached to the body of the violin with an ordinary everyday screw. And as there was still no electric light, Auntie lit two candles to supplement the oil lamp. Then the sound of a serenade rang through the house, with sobbing effects and *sforzandi*, a moving and somehow familiar piece that the violinist had already played frequently in the field hospitals. It went straight to the heart of anyone hearing it, and once its haunting melody had entered their minds it took permanent root there.

*

The maids in the kitchen caught some of that sacred sound. They stopped screeching, stole out into the corridor, and listened close to the door.

Vladimir stood in the stable doorway, his letter P hanging crooked from his jacket, looking up at the glittering night sky. He too was thinking his own thoughts. Was the low rumbling sound in the east louder now? He'd better see to the horses.

It was a real private concert. Peter sat on the sofa beside his mother; he was on the left, Jago on the right, his mother in between them. The dog barked a couple of times, perhaps wondering whether to give free rein to his feelings and participate in this concert in his own way, but then he fell silent. The cat, who disliked high-pitched sounds, made his escape. They knew about Frederick the Great and his flute concerto at Sanssouci, the ladies of the Prussian court around him. Otto Gebühr had taken the part of *The Great King* in the film of that name.

If they had guessed that such a fine musician was coming to visit them, Uncle Josef could have come over from Albertsdorf with Aunt Hanna, or maybe even the mayor of Mitkau. On Midsummer's Day last year, long ago now, they had all gathered under the copper beech in the park, Eberhard, the Berlin family, Uncle Josef and his family too, to sing the lovely old songs. *Beside the well, beyond the gate / There stands a linden tree* . . . Dr Wagner had also been there, with his sinewy fingers. If he shaved off his goatee beard he would surely look much younger.

But this was not a mild midsummer's night, lit by glow-worms, with a bowl of punch and singing in unison. It was winter now, eighteen degrees below zero, with ice-cold stars sparkling in the black sky.

Was Katharina thinking of that midsummer's night herself?

Was she remembering how it had been said of her that she was no real good for anything, never lent a hand, didn't see where there was work to be done? Auntie had even told the two maids in the kitchen that Katharina had two left hands and lived only for the day. Lothar Sarkander had come over from Mitkau. He had been standing behind her that warm night, with one hand on her shoulder.

Katharina had stepped into the summer drawing room with him; the doors had been open, there had been climbing roses bearing a profusion of flowers on the fence to left and right. And Lothar Sarkander, mayor of Mitkau, had pointed to the little group outside on the lawn, saying, 'What a picture that is!'

He had a stiff leg, and duelling scars on one cheek.

Eberhard had been standing on the outskirts of the wood, grave and silent.

Fräulein Strietzel wondered aloud, lowering her instrument, whether she should stop. No, no, it was delightful, said Katharina, and took a cigarette. Fräulein Strietzel understood Katharina's present mood. *Immensee*, 'Bee Lake', based on Theodor Storm's story, and the water lilies in it. The film had just been shown at the Mitkau cinema. She raised her violin again and found her way back into the melodies; you should finish what you have begun.

Auntie, too, thought her own thoughts. She got to her feet and went back and forth; there were things lying about everywhere. Music was certainly beautiful, but she might as well take the opportunity of tidying up a bit. When was that Christmas tree going to be taken away? Was it to stand here for ever? Honestly, wasn't it enough to make you despair?

And since there were candles burning, surely she could put out the oil lamp.

*

Fräulein Strietzel played piece after piece: Handel's *Largo*, Heicken's *Serenade*. Now and then she went to the window and looked out into the dark night. After all, she had been told she would be collected and taken to Allenstein. She should have been there long ago. They were waiting for her.

Not a car on the road, nothing moving. What you promise, you should see through. She couldn't go on playing the violin here for ever.

The dark field outside was like a lake in the night.

It was quite late when there was knocking at the door. Not the car – never mind culture, petrol costs money, after all – but a soldier on foot, a lance corporal from the Mitkau field hospital. He hadn't shrunk from walking such a long way through the night to tell Fräulein Strietzel that she wouldn't be able to go any further tonight. Maybe tomorrow; they'd see. He had been going to phone, but there was no connection, so he had just come himself. He came from Bavaria, his name was Alfons Hofer, and he addressed the young woman standing in front of the fire on the hearth, violin in hand, as Fräulein Gisela. Looking at her like Jago when he was waiting to be fed. It was a miracle, he said, that he had found the manor house at all in the darkness. Nothing could freeze any worse now, he said, they'd have to let time take its course and see what happened.

Auntie heated some mulled wine for the man, made him liver sausage sandwiches, and the soldier told them how wonderful the variety show in the field hospital had been. They were all still talking about it, about the conjuror, of course, and the stand-up girl comics telling jokes – their act had been on the vulgar side, and why you had to wear such short skirts for telling jokes he didn't understand. The juggler tossing plates into the air, and then the high spot, of course – he addressed this part of his account to the Globigs – 'was her playing, Fräulein Gisela playing the violin'. The medical director of the hospital had emphasized that in his speech, he said, and all his comrades had been talking about it, saying again and again that they had never heard anything so delightful, they all agreed, they had all said the same. And it had been really special for him, he added, that *he* had been allowed to accompany her.

He sat down at the piano, and began to play something very lively, and although they had just been listening to serious classical music it turned out that Fräulein Strietzel had pieces quite different from serenades in her repertory. She played hits, old and new, sensitively accompanied by Alfons. They played all kinds of things, whatever came into their heads. 'Do you know this one?' 'How about this?'

The young man accompanied her, and the remarkable thing was that he played only with his left hand. His right arm had been amputated.

With you it was always so good,
It's incredibly hard to go now . . .

They played this song again and again, and then Auntie had an idea. She went into the billiards room, came back with a gramophone, and started it up. It immediately played the waltz song:

I'm dancing to heaven with you,
To the seventh heaven of love.

The young people couldn't resist. They danced round the table, followed by the dog, round and round it, dancing sometimes to the left, sometimes to the right, always just missing the Christmas tree. The lance corporal took the gentleman's part, and Fräulein Gisela, enchanted, danced in the circle of his arm – to think she could do that too, dance, and wasn't entirely devoted to melancholy. That was what she conveyed as they danced round and round. *A Lovely Night at the Ball: The Life and Loves of Tchaikovsky* – they knew that film, starring Zarah Leander. The fire on the hearth cast the shadows of the young people over the ancestral portraits on the wall, flickering over His Nibs of Nibs Castle, and Auntie poured more and more mulled wine until Fräulein Gisela's face was flushed red.

Then they danced over to the summer drawing room and its wide but ice-cold expanses, all white and gold. The windows looking out on the park were frozen, and against the wall stood a row of crates roughly cobbled together and containing all the worldly goods of the cousins in Berlin, who didn't want to lose their table linen and clothes at the last minute. In fact there was more room here for turning right and left.

Peter was asked if he had ever danced. 'Come here!' said Fräulein Strietzel, showing her bad teeth, and she grabbed the boy and gave him his orders: left, two, three; right, two, three. The boy took hold of her, very clumsily, and felt himself pressed close to her body, which was flat as a board with some protuberances, quite different from his mother's soft, warm body.

But it really was very cold in the drawing room, and then the air suddenly went out of the whole thing, like a balloon deflating, and they sat down by the fireside again. The gramophone was turned off.

Peter said he could go and get his microscope. What about looking at flies' legs under it? But no one pursued that idea any further.

Suddenly the ceiling light came on, and they rubbed their eyes. Where were they? What were they doing here?

'Bong!' went the grandfather clock. 'Bong!' And the clock in the billiards room went, 'Ding-ding-ding.'

Time for bed. 'Come along, Peter, it's late,' said Katharina. She took the boy's hand and said goodnight. Peter longed to know what had become of the soldier's amputated arm. Did you simply throw such things away?

Auntie sat where she was. Because now the question arose that it would soon be midnight. Could the soldier simply spend the night here?

Spend the night here? Two young people, full of life and energy, under the same roof? No, of course not, decided Auntie. And she began bustling about the place, putting chairs straight and waiting for someone to make a move.

And although the man had already taken off his boots, and kept saying that he didn't like the thought of the way back by night, in the snow, eighteen degrees below zero is definitely nippy, and he thought he'd drunk a little too much, they brought him his coat all the same. It was a case of retreat! The soldier wrote his army postal address on a piece of paper, so that Fräulein Strietzel could reach him at any time, and said he could take the sledge back to the field hospital with him. Then that problem would be dealt with.

Wouldn't he feel silly, a soldier pulling a child's sledge along? Oh, well, it was dark.

The soldier put his army scarf round his neck, had another liver sausage sandwich, and Fräulein Strietzel took him out into the cold and the darkness. It was some time before she came back, with snowflakes in her hair. The soldier carried a love token in his pocket, but Fräulein Strietzel had put it back there for him.

Perhaps they'd meet again some time? When she entertained the troops in Bavaria? Why not? People said Munich was a beautiful city.

Or after the war, she could simply visit Bavaria, and again why not? There'd be no problem in peacetime, would there?

Auntie herself thought there'd be no problem about going to Munich or anywhere else in peacetime. Maybe even Switzerland or Italy?

Perhaps she herself would see her own beautiful native Silesia again some day.

Fräulein Strietzel put the violin away and lay down on the sofa, and Auntie covered her up warmly with several blankets. Was there anything else she needed? A book, maybe, just in case? Something by Ernst Wiechert, who had been born near here? No, but thank you all the same, she told Auntie; then she'd have had to take her hands out from under the blankets.

If Fräulein Strietzel was not blissfully happy, she was content to be lying here in the warmth, looking at the flames and hearing the hissing, or sometimes it was more like rushing, that came from the fire. Like the voices of poor souls very far away.

Who'd have thought she could spend such a nice evening in this starchy aristocratic household? The soldier's name was Alfons Hofer, and why shouldn't they meet again some time? *Shed no tear, oh, shed no tear / the flower will bloom another year.* She sighed. A pity she hadn't unpacked her long dress; that would have put a finishing touch to the evening. That would have made it unforgettable.

She enticed the dog over, and he lay down on the floor beside her. It was pleasant for him, too, not to be alone at night in the dark hall. She looked at the flames on the hearth, and rubbed her itching knuckles. Dancing was banned, yes, dancing was banned for the German people, but did that count for private parties? Would she be in trouble if it came out that she had been dancing here? Had been dancing happily when there were soldiers fighting and bleeding to death?

She had better keep her mouth shut.

When you leave, say softly, 'See you!'
Not farewell and not adieu!
Words like that can only hurt.

Meanwhile, far away in Mitkau, the sirens howled, as they always did at this time of night. The population here was far from the firing line; the sirens meant nothing.

Next morning they all said goodbye. The reserved Katharina took the violinist in her arms, and Peter watched for a long time as she went away.

4

Auntie

Under her cardigans Auntie wore a limp dress, dark blue with small yellow flowers on it, now here, now there, as if they had been tipped at random out of a cornucopia. She had pinned a gold brooch on her dress. The brooch had golden arrows sticking out on all sides and a cornelian in the middle, and was a memento of her mother.

In the evening Auntie usually filled herself a hot-water bottle in the kitchen. Part of the stove acted as a boiler; it kept the water hot for a long time, and had done so today. The top of the stove had not been scoured; the maids had forgotten again, although she had reminded them heaven knew how many times. Auntie suspected that they had stolen off to the Polish carter's room. Plump Vera was particularly fond of flirting with the thoughtful Vladimir, and she didn't understand why he felt more attracted to slim Sonya. Sonya wound her braid round her head like a wreath, but her nose was always red.

Hadn't there been a pan with what was left of the fried potatoes standing on the stove? Auntie had fancied finishing them now, but someone else had got in ahead of her. And sugar had been spilt in the pantry – it crunched underfoot. Moreover, a sausage had gone missing yet again.

Auntie locked the door to the farmyard outside and hung up clean tea towels. Then she picked up the newspaper, tucked the hot-water bottle under her arm, listened at the door to the main hall – all was quiet, the violinist was already fast asleep – and climbed the stairs.

She also listened at Katharina's door. Was there any movement in there? Why did Katharina always lock herself in? Strange woman, she didn't suit Eberhard a bit, always so quiet, when a little cheerfulness would have done the poor boy good. On his last leave he had kept asking her: would you like to come to this or that with me? The answer had always been no. You couldn't really call her grumpy, just quiet and introspective, as if she had a heavy burden to bear. Or a great grief?

And yet she lacked for nothing. Did she?

The way Katharina always locked her door puzzled Auntie, making her wonder whether all that secrecy was intended for her. Anyone could have come into *her* room at any time. In fact she'd have welcomed anyone who walked in saying, 'Oh, Auntie, can I sit with you for a bit?' and then told her their troubles. Surely she, Auntie, could have understood everything.

But even Eberhard didn't always show his best side. He could be gruff and pedantic. It was those financial matters that caused trouble. The steel shares in England, the rice-flour factory in Romania – according to Eberhard, the managers were scoundrels to a man. Only his officer's salary kept the whole show on the road.

Auntie had the long, narrow gable room behind the pediment, with the now dilapidated finial of the spiked mace above it, and in keeping with the architecture of the whole house the ceiling was a tunnel vault.

Under the round window from which, in earlier times, the flag had been flown – first the black, white and red flag; then, of course, the swastika banner – there was a raised platform in the old style, divided from the rest of the room by a wooden rail. A desk and an old armchair stood on it. *When the spinning wheel purrs so softly / In Granny's room by the fire . . .* A crochet-work antimacassar on the back of the armchair kept the cover from getting greasy.

From this place, which she called her lookout post, she could see the new development, house beside house, all of them the same as each other. It was on the other side of the road, so you saw any cars driving by, and sometimes it was interesting to see what went on around those houses: children playing, women hanging out their washing, drunks staggering from place to place. Last year Peter had spoilt the look of the great oak outside the manor house by building a tree house in it.

'Do you have to do that, boy?' she had asked. But Eberhard had said, 'Leave him alone. He wants to be high up.'

If she leaned a little way forward she could also see the yard of the manor house, with its stables and the cottage near them. The Pole who joked with the maids more often than strictly necessary sawed up the firewood there.

Whenever she looked out of the window she counted the chickens and geese running round the yard. The milk cart came in the morning, and the bus, a clumsy-looking vehicle powered by wood gas, passed twice a day.

The poultry were kept in the big barn in this hard frost. Although the barn had been standing empty for years, there were still a few grains left lying around.

Sometimes the peacock looked round the corner. It was a long time since he last spread his tail.

There was never much traffic on the road: a bicycle, the milk cart twice a day, the bus to Mitkau. Now and then a car driving by.

Recently there had been occasional farm carts going west. Auntie had noticed more of them these last few days. Maybe they had better get the door to the yard repaired after all. Sometimes the carts rumbled past one after another, all piled high with household goods. There were isolated pedestrians as well, strange figures, coming from who knew where, going to heaven knew what destination.

Now and then foreign labourers from the Forest Lodge came into the yard to visit Vera and Sonya in the kitchen, although it was strictly forbidden. Auntie supposed they thought no one had noticed them. She suspected that the Ukrainian girls gave them something to eat in the kitchen. Goodness only knew why they weren't at work. Didn't these people have anything to do?

Odd characters came from Mitkau too, hands in their pockets; they didn't seem to mind the long walk. They appeared to be normal enough, if rather shady, and joined in when the men from the Forest Lodge sang songs, although sometimes they were perfectly quiet.

There were Czechs, Italians and Romanians among the labourers, and French and Dutch civilians. Foreigners, anyway. They all just lounged around, and the two Ukrainian maids often slunk off to join them, although there was plenty for them to do at the Georgenhof.

Vera and Sonya – never there when you needed them. Auntie had wondered whether to be stricter with them, but how was she to go about it? It was water off a duck's back to them.

Best to take no notice, someone had said. But suppose things turned out badly? You want to go carefully with those foreigners, that had been the advice, but it was now wearing thin. Who knew what might happen? She had heard it said that the foreigners carried knives under their jackets. One of the Czechs, a man with piercing eyes – he wore a peaked cap – had come as far as the yard recently. He had even been seen in the hall once, looking up the staircase. Vladimir had driven him out with his whip, but the man kept coming back, and one day he gave Vladimir a black eye.

Although Uncle Josef in Albertsdorf had advised them against mingling with these people, Katharina exchanged a few words with them now and then. There were amusing fellows with fine dark eyes among the Italians. One of them could even play the mandolin. They felt the cold here. The Frenchmen were more thoughtful; some of them were educated men, with families at home who supported them; they were schoolteachers and pastors, men who sometimes read a book. But others were pathetic souls with melancholy expressions on their faces.

'All this will be dealt with after the war,' Uncle Josef had said. 'We'll send them home then.'

When there was an opportunity, Katharina sought out the Italians, gave them cigarettes and engaged in friendly conversation with them, in their own language. She didn't actually say that she had visited southern Europe with the Wandervogel organization before the war, she merely dropped hints.

It was the Italians, poor bastards, who got treated worst everywhere – 'They let us down twice!' it was said. Katharina didn't share this poor opinion of them, since she had spent many happy times in the south long before the war. Those warm nights beside the sea, the singing of the fishermen – that was why she disliked the poor treatment of the Italians.

'*Venezia, comprende?*' she said to the Italians. And she thought of her husband, wearing his white uniform now in the hot south and procuring olive oil and wine for the troops. She had a vague idea that it wasn't always an easy process. He had written home saying that he expected promotion soon, and then he'd get a higher salary, thank God.

The housing development on the other side of the road had been given the name of the Albert Leo Schlageter Settlement when it was built in 1936, all the houses the same as each other, like toys taken out of their box and stood up side by side. People of no distinction lived here, keeping a goat, a pig, chickens and rabbits, and every house had its garden. Originally the development was to have been called the New Georgenhof. No one had asked Herr von Globig if he was happy with that name for the new housing estate.

However, the matter had been settled of its own accord before there were any disagreements; the authorities had decided to call the settlement after the heroic Freikorps man Schlageter, who had once spent a few days on holiday in these parts in the unhappy year of 1919. The resistance fighter Albert Leo Schlageter had faced the French, who shot him. In the middle of the development stood a granite stone engraved with the profile of the national martyr. When it was turned on, water flowed from this stone into a basin. Young people gathered around this fountain on summer evenings, singing songs in honour of the new regime. On hot days children paddled in the water. A man called Drygalski, who had joined the National Socialist Party in its early days, would chase them away. Now, in the cold of winter, the water feature was covered with boards.

Drygalski was a kind of deputy mayor of the housing development – at least, he put on the airs of a prominent personage who kept the peace, and he made a speech on Albert Leo Schlageter Day, or rather read it from a sheet of paper. It was this man who chased the children away from the water, because it wasn't proper for them to splash about in it. And if they still did, Drygalski felt it was his business to intervene. He had a good view of the place from his kitchen window, and he would knock on the pane with the knuckles of his fingers.

Why didn't they go through the wood to the little River Helge, where there was plenty of water? he asked them, but then the women were indignant. Did he really like the idea of the children running across the road, they asked, and who was there at the river to pull them out of the water if they looked like drowning?

Although the Globigs had opposed the building of the Albert Leo Schlageter Settlement in the year of the Olympic Games, it turned out to be a decidedly good thing for them. They had been able to sell a last tract of land, and the Georgenhof finally acquired a proper mains water supply.

But the old pond had been filled in – the romantic little pond where the ducks and the white geese used to swim, looking so ornamental. And of course the weeping willow, so romantic itself, had been chopped down. The pond had belonged to the Georgenhof from time immemorial. There was a heated exchange of letters with the head of the local district council, who said the pond had to go because it was a breeding ground for midges, and they couldn't have such a place in a clean new development where healthy people lived. Eberhard von Globig had produced old maps, the pond marked on them. It was so practical for watering the horses in summer! The ducks, heads under the water or upright and quacking, were a familiar local sight. They were caught and slaughtered in autumn.

The head of the local district council became insistent when Eberhard von Globig claimed that the pond really belonged to him. He and Drygalski put their heads together and set about devising a plan.

One evening Lothar Sarkander, the mayor of Mitkau, a man

with strict standards who had a stiff leg and duelling scars on his face, had come over in his steam-driven car for a private conversation with Eberhard von Globig; the two of them sometimes went hunting together. Sitting in the billiards room, Sarkander had talked about the new order of things, saying it would be better if Eberhard kept his mouth shut. Provoking people like Drygalski was not a good idea; they were in charge now.

Sarkander was invited to go shooting on the Georgenhof estate every year; it created good relations, and Katharina had once stood in the summer drawing room with him, looking at the park and the cheerful company lying in the grass there and drinking toasts. Long ago, she had even been to the seaside with him; that was in 1936, when Eberhard had to go to see to the horses at the Olympic Games in Berlin, leaving Katharina at home. She and Sarkander had been seen sitting in a beach hut drinking cocoa, Katharina in a broad-brimmed straw hat that surrounded her head like a halo, with her black hair flowing out from under it, he in white trousers, his stick between his legs. That was so many years ago that no one really knew anything about it. Or did they?

Well, she had to do something, that was the explanation. Eberhard had gone to Berlin, and she and the mayor of Mitkau had gone to the seaside.

If I'd known what I was missing,
If I'd known who I was kissing,
That midnight at the lido ...

Auntie's name was Helene Harnisch. She came from Silesia. Her gable room had flowered wallpaper and was full of mahogany furniture that came from Silesia too, a wardrobe, chairs, the plain desk, and a bed in which, said a family joke, a poet had surely died. Beside the desk hung a small pen-and-ink drawing of Hitler, the Führer and Chancellor of the Reich, with his tie featuring an eagle in a swastika, and underneath the picture his slanting signature with a slanting line under it.

Auntie sat down in her armchair, pushed the curtain aside and looked out into the night. Everything was plunged in the deepest darkness. Stars cold as ice sparkled in the sky; the moon had not yet risen. In spite of the wind and the freezing cold, the Hitler Youth had been marching round the housing development that morning: left, right, left, right. Drygalski had come stalking up and made a speech. The time to show what they could do was imminent, he told the boys, and he hoped he could rely on them when the moment came. He got them marching to Mitkau. There was plenty for young people to do there these days: carrying coal up from the cellar for the old folk, shovelling snow off the crossroads. They had come back late in the evening. Peter was supposed to have been with them, but he preferred looking through his microscope. He also had a nasty cold again.

Auntie kept the household accounts of the estate in the upper compartments of her old desk, which could be locked, and ever since Eberhard had been on active service she had dealt with the official correspondence there, because Katharina von Globig always forgot it, was easily discouraged, and looked so helpless, saying, 'Oh, my goodness, yes! I quite forgot.' In the end Auntie preferred to do everything herself.

She kept a bag of eucalyptus cough sweets for her bad throat in the desk, and sometimes gave Peter one, which he immediately threw away.

Her room smelt of ripe apples and dead mice, but it was comfortable, and Auntie called it her kingdom.

She liked sitting in the armchair at her desk, and looking down at the yard and the road and the housing development on the other side of it.

There was a fine old rug on the floor, and a lamp had been fitted at the desk. Its opaque glass shade was adorned with strings of green beads. When Eberhard von Globig came up here to complain to Auntie that there was nothing to be done about Katharina, his head knocked against it, and then the beads tinkled and the lampshade rocked, and took its time settling down.

A watercolour in a white frame hung over her bed, showing a white summerhouse with roses in intermingling colours clambering over it. It was a memento of her father's estate in Silesia. As a child she had liked sitting in that summerhouse when she was either unhappy or glad about something, with her left leg tucked under her, and there she and her girlfriends used to play at sending their dolls to school.

She had wanted to be a teacher, but that idea came to nothing. 'My beloved Silesia,' she used to say, and, 'Nothing's that easy.'

Her father's estate had been sold at auction in 1922, when everything was going downhill – the house and outbuildings, the woods and fields. A war profiteer who had made money out of others' misfortunes had lent her father money, again and again, and then the estate had had to be sold at the worst possible moment, and that monstrous man had stood by watching. The place was going to ruin, and the summerhouse had been demolished for no reason at all. They could easily have left it alone. The old gardener shed tears when he had to leave. As a little girl she used to stand on his wooden clogs while he did a bear-like dance round the circular flower bed with her.

She had been left with a few pieces of furniture and the picture above her bed.

*

A lute with ribbons on it hung beside the picture of the summerhouse; it reminded her of her youth. *There is no fairer land today* . . .

She herself had once played music to wounded men, in 1917, almost thirty years ago; she remembered the large white wimples of the Catholic nuns and the patients' striped pyjamas, and she too had been asked by a blind man whether he could touch her hand; it had been next to impossible to shake his own hand off. She had never heard anything of those men again. But the kindnesses she had shown them had surely not been given in vain.

Eberhard's last leave: they had sat under the copper beech in the garden in August, Uncle Josef had come over from Albertsdorf, and dear Hanna with the children; she had played the old songs of her youth on the lute, and everyone had sung along.

A summer's evening under the copper beech, drinking punch. Katharina had temporarily gone missing, and then she had come out of the summer drawing room with Sarkander, the mayor of Mitkau. And Eberhard had gone into the wood on his own to make sure that everything was all right. That had surprised her. As long as all that ago?

Auntie read the newspaper. One of the earpieces of her reading glasses was missing, and what she read was not reassuring. Something was brewing in the east. Who knew, perhaps they would have to leave this house, just as the old Globigs had left it in the First War.

She pulled out a large suitcase from under the bed. She had come to the Georgenhof with that suitcase all those years ago, and they had told her, 'You can have the gable room and make yourself useful.' That was over twenty years ago. And now, as the family joked, she was part of the fixtures and fittings. She got pocket money, had free board and lodging, and ran the whole place.

Opening the wardrobe, she took underclothes out of it and put them in the suitcase. Some of the garments were darned and mended, others had never been worn, and her handkerchiefs were still tied together with pink ribbons.

She took letters out of the desk and put them in the case as well, and photographs too. Then she closed the suitcase and pushed it back under the bed.

She sat down in her armchair. Had she forgotten anything?

The lute. She took the instrument off the wall and placed it beside the suitcase. There, now she was ready for anything.

Auntie poured herself a peppermint liqueur.

A single car drove fast along the road to Mitkau, followed by other cars and finally by trucks. Then came tanks, one after another, making the glass beads on the lampshade jingle. Then it was silent again.

Now she could hear the sirens from Mitkau, sounding an air-raid warning. The Globigs never reacted to that signal. What were they supposed to do? Get water ready and stand out in the yard in summer when there was a thunderstorm, yes, that was something else, but in an air raid? There was water in the cellar, but it was unusable. So what were they expected to do? Run into the woods? Yes, but not every night.

The sound of a solitary aeroplane was heard above the rooftops. The engine noise came closer and then went away again. Fiery signals like the Northern Lights fingered the black, starry sky. A searchlight groped through the darkness as well, and in the distance light anti-aircraft guns sent tracer fire into the sky. There were four explosions, one, two, three, four, and then the heavy Mitkau guns began firing. After that silence fell, and the solitary plane flew away, with its engine noise dying down. The bombs had fallen on Mitkau railway station; now it was burning, and rail travel would be disrupted again.

Auntie sat there for a little while longer as tongues of flame rose to the sky above Mitkau. She listened until at last the all clear sounded in the distance.

Then she drank her peppermint liqueur and went to bed. She didn't even hear another column of tanks rumbling past.

5

Peter

Peter was lying in bed. He had a feather bed on top of the mattress, a quilt on top of his blankets, and two pillows. A board lay across the bed with his books on it. Stories by Karl May. Back numbers of the humorous magazine *Flying Leaves*; he had found them in the attic. They contained caricatures of Sunday hunters, of students who were usually drunk, of young lieutenants who couldn't control their horses.

This evening he was reading the story of a shipwrecked sailor who hadn't given up, but went on and on paddling a raft until at last an island came into sight, and with it the prospect of safety.

He imagined lying in a cabin in a sailing ship – a cabin that smelt of tar – and the creak of the rigging. *The Wreck of the Palmyra*, he'd read that book and was still thinking about it. Never give up, that was the lesson it taught you.

Be the aim however high,
Youth will find a way . . .

Peter too had heard the air-raid warning in Mitkau and the four explosions: one, two, three, four. And he heard the tanks going east along the road. The whole house shook as they passed by, one after another. Big black shadows with sparks coming out of their exhausts, chains rattling, engines roaring. You didn't see them at all in daylight, and now you saw them only as outlines.

His room was next to Auntie's gable room. His model railway

had been set up on the floor since Christmas. Its rails ran in a circle, and it had a tin station building. Peter had extended the rails out into the corridor, passing through the cat flap, and there, too, they ran in a circle. When the train went out and came back a little later, he knelt down to watch it coming. Sometimes it stopped outside and had to be wound up. Now and then there were collisions when the cat insisted on squeezing through the flap at the same time as the train. A strange animal. No one really knew what went on in his head.

Model aircraft made of paper that Peter had cut out and stuck together hung beneath the sloping ceiling. German and English planes. A Vickers Wellington and a Spitfire, the Messerschmitt 109 and Richthofen's red triplane. That one didn't really fit with the others, which came from a very different time. But Peter had made it, so it might as well hang there. A slight draught of air from the window moved the models so that they touched gently. Peter sometimes shot at them with his air pistol, but he took care not to score any hits. It would have been a shame after he had spent so long working on them. They rocked slightly as the projectile passed by.

His microscope stood on the table. Looking at grains of salt and sugar crystals was all very well; he knew all about that now. Beside the instrument stood a preserving jar containing a decoction of hay; Peter wanted to observe the invisible life forms in the infusion, but so far it wasn't ripe enough. There was a whole world in there, Dr Wagner had said: birth and death, creatures eating and being eaten.

His father's binoculars lay on the windowsill. The microscope here, the binoculars there. When crows flew up from the oak tree he counted them. He also followed the V-shaped skein of wild geese in flight through his binoculars. Lately they had begun going north again. What did that mean, in the middle of winter?

> *If you fly south across the sea,*
> *Then what, ah what, will our fate be?*

He checked on his tree house several times a day to make sure it was all right. He also kept the Settlement under observation. Women taking long underpants frozen stiff off the line – that was a funny sight. He had never been interested in the children over there. He didn't know the boys, and he didn't want to know them. Football? They wouldn't have let him play with them even if he'd wanted to. For sport he had a rowing boat moored on the River Helge, and he sometimes went out and about on the river with it. The cows on the other bank came along to see what he was doing.

Peter never went over to the Settlement, and no one came over to see him. The road lay between them. And he would not have had a good time if he had ventured there. There were strong boys in the housing development who would have loved to pelt the young plutocrat with snowballs. Or might take him into the sweat lodge and refuse to let him out again. Auntie would certainly have opened her window to intervene.

The children had laid out a long slide there, and he would have liked to try it. Then Drygalski had come along with a bucket full of ashes and made it impossible to use the slide, which annoyed Peter, although it was none of his business.

When Peter did want to play outside at this time, he went down a small slope behind the house on his sledge, then pulled it up and came down the slope again. He had made a snowman as well, but no one had shown any interest in it.

'Lovely, dear, lovely,' his mother had said, hardly looking up from her book. The snowman bore a certain resemblance to the Führer and Chancellor of the Third Reich.

In summer, Peter often spent hours in his tree house, which he had fitted out as the cockpit of a plane: old alarm clocks did duty as parts of an instrument panel, a small wheel was the joystick, a tin can that he filled with water was a fuel container. At the front of his tree-house plane he had mounted the streamlined remains of a motorbike's sidecar. He was permanently flying west. Now, in winter, the snow collected inside his aircraft.

Dr Wagner came to the Georgenhof at three p.m. on the dot every afternoon to tutor Peter. Since he had never married, he was described as a confirmed bachelor. He had a small, pointed beard, and bags under his eyes, over which he wore gold-rimmed glasses. He also wore plus fours and black ear protectors, and now, in the cold winter weather, a fur-trimmed overcoat that had seen better days. Wagner taught history, with Latin as a subsidiary subject, and German language and literature. *We hear in ancient legends of many wondrous tales* ...

In spite of his advanced age, Dr Wagner still had to do war work, and he had had enough of working, he said, in his seventy years of life. Teaching German and history year after year, day after day. And when he was through with it, beginning all over again.

All the children in the monastery school, the milling crowds and the shouting in the venerable cloisters – and then there were his colleagues, all of them in a rut. Since the younger ones had been called up to go to the front, you could hardly ever have any useful conversation in the staff room.

The library was worth seeing. There had been some idea of sending it to Königsberg, in case the Russians came after all. But since the destruction of that city, the word had been: 'Thank God we didn't do it!'

When Wagner had got himself moved to that school, many, many years ago, it had been summer, the slanting rays of the sun had shone in through the windows with their pointed arches, beds of aromatic herbs had grown in the garden, and there were flowers everywhere: mallows, delphiniums, phloxes. The crooked, contorted cloisters, the refectory with its high ceiling – in summer it was wonderfully beautiful. The old medieval well still stood in the yard, with ivy climbing all over it. And he had been on good terms with his engaging young colleagues.

But now that old building was cold as ice, however much you tried to heat it. Those tall, damp rooms.

Instead of a Party symbol, Dr Wagner wore the ribbon of the Iron Cross, which, thank God, he had won in the Great War. With the help of that ribbon, membership of the People's Welfare Organization and the Reich Colonial League, along with occasional talks on air-raid precautions, he had been able to turn down suggestions that he might join the Party when advances were made to him by some of his colleagues, often at first, then less and less frequently, and now not at all. He had managed to keep out of it. Had he been able to pull strings of some kind in high places?

He could play the piano, and you heard him practising if you walked past his house. Sometimes he even sang as he played. 'I live a very quiet life,' he used to say. He lived this quiet life in Horst-Wessel-Strasse, next door to the tax office.

The school gates were closed now. Beds for old people who had been brought from Tilsit occupied the vaulted classrooms. And Dr Wagner was surplus to requirements. So he 'saw to Peter's education a little', as he put it – Peter being his favourite pupil, whom he had always liked. I'm not letting you go to the bad, he thought to himself. That thin face, fair curly hair, those serious eyes. Even if it meant walking four kilometres from Mitkau to the Georgenhof, four kilometres there and four kilometres back, he did not shrink from the daily journey on foot to see that all was well, to give the boy some coaching, arriving at three p.m. on the dot. I'm not letting you go to the bad! His father on active service, his mother so self-absorbed, those Ukrainian women in the house . . .

That's a very promising boy, he thought.

Dr Wagner had been seeing to Peter's education day after day since Christmas. He did not shrink from the long journey, he took it for granted, and moreover they always gave him a plate of bread and dripping. Something delicious to eat was welcome! Bread fried in dripping with apples and onions, and crisp crackling with it too. It wasn't so easy for a bachelor to manage these days. At least he sat in a warm room here. And the folk at the Georgenhof, it was obvious, knew how to appreciate Dr Wagner.

Although he himself was fond of animals, as he said, Jago the dog was not a friend of his. If you offered Jago some of the bread and dripping, he growled. And on Dr Wagner's evening visits to the kitchen – where he looked in for a minute, briefcase in hand, to say goodnight to the maids before going home – Jago even faced up to him, baring his teeth.

When he wanted to make sure all was well in the kitchen, he had sometimes found the maids holding the door shut against him on the inside. But Dr Wagner hadn't been born yesterday; he could take a joke.

Sometimes he calculated whether the calories he had taken on board at the Georgenhof made up for the calories he had asked his body to expend: four kilometres there and another four kilometres back, come wind or weather? And he dropped hints, but no one reacted to them.

There was a short cut, as he had finally discovered, and he used it now and then, but he kept it to himself.

So Dr Wagner duly turned up day after day, and he always had ways of interesting Peter in something. For instance, he liked to take Knaur's *Encyclopaedia* off the shelf and put the blade of a knife between the pages at random. Then he opened the book, which he described as a box full of treasures, and Peter had to read aloud what he found on the page chosen by pure chance. It was stichomancy, divination by opening a book at random, said Dr Wagner. Some people did it with the Bible. And whatever you found there, it was always interesting; you simply left out the uninteresting entries. 'Saffron milk cap, fungus, see *Lactarius deliciosus*', for instance. Then they talked about the riches of nature, the huge number of fungi in the world, edible and inedible, and how they were really parasites but were useful and many of them tasted good. Chanterelles, for instance, fried in butter. Or portobello mushrooms, also known as Paris mushrooms, considered a great delicacy and perfectly digestible if properly prepared.

Dr Wagner did not concern himself with the Bible. He had been prejudiced against the church since taking offence with someone in the 1920s. In his youth he had belonged to the Free Christian movement, whose members liked to meet in forests and turn to God under the crowns of the ancient trees. At the time the official church made stupid remarks about it, and withdrew from those who thought as he did, so he in turn withdrew from the church. At least that saved you the church tax.

*

A silver propelling pencil hung from his watch-chain, and he delicately pushed it out of its silver casing and back in again.

Sometimes he clenched his hand into a fist, sometimes he laid it flat on the table, always in a very correct manner. He wore a blue signet ring, its colour slightly faded in one place, probably from coming into contact with hot water.

His pointed beard could be stroked forward when opportunity offered, at thoughtful moments. It meant something like: I'm not sure you're right there. He never said, straight out, 'Oh, come off it!' or 'You couldn't be more mistaken!' or simply 'Nonsense!' He liked to leave things to chance. That was his method; he even let his pupils teach him; for instance, he got Peter to explain the model aircraft hanging from the ceiling to him, the difference between heavy bombers and dive-bombers, and the fact that the Wellington bomber has a turret from which the tail gunner cannot escape once the plane is burning. But Dr Wagner himself had actually seen the red triplane when Richthofen was flying it over the Somme – which Peter could hardly believe. Wagner imitated the high, thin sound of the MG gunfire, and with the flat of his hand he showed how Richthofen had manoeuvred his 'crate' at the time.

Unfortunately he kept treading on Peter's railway; several rails were flattened, and he had already played football with the station. 'Oh, my dear boy,' he had said. 'I'm so sorry. You have to bend it into shape like this . . .' and he had knelt down, with his creaking joints, to get it back into its proper state. He had had a model railway in his own childhood, although he had no idea what had become of it. It had been larger than Peter's. There had been papier-mâché passengers sitting in its open carriages, and the engine had boasted a tall chimney.

The hand-embroidered Christmas tablecloth, with swinging bells in red and fir tree branches in green, was still on the round table in Peter's room. It was here, at that table, that his broader education went on: textbooks lay open on it. 'What will flower indoors on tables and windowsills?' – a schematic depiction of plants and an atlas. Where is bauxite mined? A special map showed you, and you could find out how many locks there were in the Panama Canal. 'Life,' said Dr Wagner, 'is interesting from whatever angle you approach it.'

It was difficult to find the small town of Mitkau on the maps, but Königsberg stood out clearly. After all, Kant had lived in Königsberg. Kant had been a bachelor too, there's nothing special about it.

When the moment seemed propitious, Wagner had the boy doing mathematics. 'A cyclist goes from A to B ...' Straightforward enough in itself, the rule of three: what you have to put above the line, and what belongs under it, and then you abbreviate and multiply it. Perfectly simple, and yet Peter couldn't grasp it, however emphatically Dr Wagner pointed it out, however gently he brought his clenched fist down on the table. The boy just didn't grasp it.

In English: *I have washed, you have washed, he has washed.* To think that the British, such a cultivated nation, had razed a city like Königsberg to the ground. The cathedral. The inn called the Massacre. It was more than he could understand. His beloved Königsberg. Eating fried flounders in a little restaurant on the River Pregel, and the sirens sounding on the big ships in harbour there ...

Why hadn't he travelled the world before the war, Dr Wagner wondered, when it was still possible? He assumed that some day Peter would go where he could breathe the air of very different places.

Dr Wagner couldn't get the ships' sirens and the fried flounders out of his head. And crunchy golden-yellow fried potatoes. Such a simple dish in itself.

Of course Dr Wagner also told the boy what 'political economy' meant. He agreed that stamp-collecting was a good idea; those small stamps, he said, are like miniature stocks and shares. Collecting them was a good idea, yes, but *mending* them? Replacing a single indentation – he considered such a thing impossible, out of the question. Was it outright fraud? No, surely his imagination was running away with him, wasn't it? Well, said Dr Wagner, one must always stick to the truth. Stick to the truth, and be able to keep quiet about certain rumours that were now circulating. They originated with people who had an insight into what was going on, people who had seen developments in the east. Things so far-fetched that one really couldn't envisage them.

Collecting stamps and coins, yes, why not? Objects of value. Long after the paper mark has given up the ghost, said Dr Wagner, the stamps would still be here, unless they had been burnt . . .

Inflation – millions, billions? Difficult to understand and complicated to explain.

They looked up Budapest in the atlas, because that city was in the news. How far the Russians had advanced – alignments of the fronts in the course of disengagement – and where the Americans actually were. Why not stick pins into a map? The map in question was already hanging on the wall, although marked in the other direction to show how far the Germans had advanced east, in their military formations – their 'spearheads' and 'pockets'. It did not show where they were now. Whereas everyone knew where the Russians were at this moment. Not a hundred kilometres away.

Budapest was in Hungary, and some time or other it had

belonged to Austria and the Imperial and Royal monarchy. Long ago. A likeable place in itself.

The Emperor Waltz – Dr Wagner had seen that film.

Katharina sometimes sat at that table with them, however quiet and reserved she was. She would bring her cup of tea with her and sit down beside the neatly bearded teacher. She herself could still learn something here. Sometimes she even put on an afternoon dress, the kind she had worn in the old days. And if the sun shone into the room, making the ice flowers on the windows glitter, the cat would turn up too and settle down on Peter's bed with his paws tucked under him.

On occasion the conversation between the two grown-ups moved away into its own domain, going hither and thither, while Peter sat on the floor with his model railway and wound up the engine. As it went round the bend the carriages sometimes came off the rails.

'Not too fast, my boy, not too fast . . .'

To think that people who knew about the east had seen what was going on there now. Our good old German fatherland. For heaven's sake!

Katharina lit a cigarette and looked for Lake Garda on the map, trying to imagine what it would look like there now, and she thought of Venice and how she had stayed in a cold hotel with Eberhard, and it rained all day. Then she caught a chill below the waist on a gondola expedition, and came home with kidney trouble, and that was the end of that.

The plundering of Rome by the Vandals. The Italians in Forest Lodge, or were they Sicilians?

They were Catholic, anyway. A priest had once been to see

them. One of the Italians had fallen ill and died in the cold German Reich, where for all they knew there might still be wolves and aurochs keeping their distance, in inhospitable Germania. They could have wished him a different fate.

Dr Wagner was always talking to Katharina over the boy's head about the circumstances, those circumstances to which they were now exposed. He lowered his voice: the brickworks in Mitkau, the people who had to work there, prisoners in striped jackets. What would come of it all? 'Who'd have thought it?' There was nothing very strange about it if he touched this quiet woman's forearm now and then. Not when he had known her so long. But it didn't have to be like that.

'Will you be setting off westward too?' he asked sadly. Then he dropped hints, and cautiously framed the question of whether he might not be taken along with them on that journey. There would surely be room for him in the vehicle.

He could have gone into the Reich by rail, but when exactly should he do it? And when would the right moment come? Where exactly would he go? What reason would he give for such a journey?

Auntie had tried to make her own contribution to Peter's lessons. She had turned up with a folder full of pictures, 'Illustrations to Biblical History', and talked about the Saviour. But the seed fell on stony ground. The fact that the old German imperial crown bore a cross was beside the point. Here Dr Wagner joined in, mentioning the Christian west, and then talking to Auntie about Pastor Brahms in Mitkau, who was said to be most incautious, saying all kinds of wild things in his sermons – God is not mocked, and so on and so forth, instead of keeping his mouth shut. And then the words 'concentration camp' uttered in an undertone.

*

Dr Wagner's idea of making up riddles was a good one.

Cling to your dear, beloved fatherland ... could a syllabic riddle of some kind be based on that? Or *Horror stares from empty window frames*? Schiller, anyway, was eminently suitable for such things.

Magic squares of numbers – from left to right, from top to bottom, when you add them up you always get the same result. Strange, hard to understand. Were you supposed to be able to conjure up some kind of power like that? Cast a spell to banish misfortune? Dürer had put his mind to such things. Albrecht Dürer of Nuremberg, the beautiful city that now lay in ruins, like Königsberg and Hamburg, Frankfurt and Cologne.

Riddles were all very well, but Peter didn't understand why anyone would ask a riddle when you already knew what the outcome was going to be.

Well, said Dr Wagner, in dire straits you could always earn money from making up riddles. Five marks per riddle, perhaps?

Peter said that in that case they could simply copy them out of *Flying Leaves* and sell them, but that turned out to be the wrong approach. It led to a lecture of some length about the Ten Commandments, the iniquity of telling lies, and the fact that a good German boy must wash thoroughly, paying attention to his fingernails, wasn't that so? 'And always be cautious, my boy, that's a part of life.'

It seemed that one important question was whether adding a black mark to the stamps in his collection was or was not a good idea.

'Brig: a two-masted square-rigged ship ...'

He had seen many handsome sailing ships in Königsberg. Why hadn't he just gone away back then, when the whole world was still open to him?

But gone away where? That was the question. Where should they have gone?

Riddles: the great questions facing mankind. When Dr Wagner got around to discussing those, he leaned back and looked into the distance. Where do we come from? Where are we going? Those were questions that he had often asked himself during his seventy years of life, without ever coming a jot closer to the truth. Perhaps the meaning of life was that we must perfect whatever is our own potential? Strive for perfection, as Goethe understood that word.

Now, when he sits alone in his room, he often thinks of the good times, of home, of eating fried flounders with his mother beside the River Pregel. And he is sorry that he wasn't nicer to her.

'Time, time, you can never turn it back, my boy.' And he would stand up and look at the cuckoo clock, with its pendulum swinging quickly back and forth, left to right and vice versa, and the little door is already opening, and the cuckoo calls out of the clock whether you want to hear it or not.

So many things were a riddle to him. The differences between people – quite apart from the difference between man and woman. For instance, the difference between Germans and Russians. Germans, clean, industrious, honest; Russians, on the other hand, lazy, dirty, cruel? Then again, the other way round: Russians, kindly on principle, whereas Germans ... Recently there'd been much that was hard to understand, although here and now it was better not to talk about it. Things that, in themselves, were not at all necessary.

'Riddle', a good Germanic word, not for the great questions that face mankind, but for the little ones, often very simple matters. That too was part of a teacher's educational plan: it should show his pupil that some things are hard even for an adult to understand.

Of course, he didn't say so to Peter. He left it to the boy to come to his own conclusions, however wrong they might be.

As a scholar, Dr Wagner concentrated chiefly on German literature and the German language; he got Peter to recite poems, and marked the stresses and rhythm of the lines in his book of poetry with his silver pencil, as well as the place to pause and take a deep breath.

> From afár a glów, like a víllage on fíre,
> Reflécting on póols as the flámes burn hígher . . .

At his request, Peter wrote a long essay about the Georgenhof, entitled *My Home*. It took him days. He illustrated his experiences and events with pictures. Lightning and threatening storm clouds in the sky above a haywain, the cherry harvest, with Peter himself and the girl cousins from Berlin sitting in the cherry tree, and Auntie looking out of the window. She said that it is better to preserve the cherries in jars than tear them all off their stems and put them in your mouth right away.

He said in his essay that the estate had been only an adjunct to the old Georgenhof, whose ruins still lay in the forest. It was burnt down by the French in 1807 and never rebuilt. He poked around there quite often, although he wasn't allowed to play in the ruins; adders had been seen there, and the whole thing might collapse. All the same he went there now and then. He had already lured his cousins in and then scared them by calling out in a hollow, ghostly voice.

The Hitler Youth had once met by night in the part of the vaults still standing, holding smouldering torches and singing defiant songs.

> Comrades, arise and fight,
> We'll raise our banners higher!

There had been repercussions to this episode. The police had told the local Hitler Youth that it wouldn't do; a vaulted ruin like that could easily fall flat.

When Peter had finished his essay, Dr Wagner wrote *Good!* under it in red ink, and Auntie tied the pages together with a blue ribbon, which made them almost a book. He could give it to his father for his birthday. It lay on his desk, and Peter imagined his pleasure in receiving it. His father's birthday was in May. *In the merry, merry month of May.*

There was another room next to Peter's bedroom. It had been his little sister Elfie's room until she died two years ago.

Everything had been left as it was when she was alive: her doll's house, her puppet theatre. Even the knitted witch with a metre-long cord dangling from her stomach. Elfie's clothes still hung in the wardrobe, and until recently clean sheets had regularly been put on the bed. Her photograph lay on the pillow. She had had frizzy hair in braids, not fair like Peter's hair but raven-black.

When she died the cat went missing and didn't come back for three days.

What a pity, Peter sometimes thought when he was lying in bed. I could have knocked on the wall now, and then she would have knocked back.

6

Katharina

Since Eberhard had been called up, Katharina had been living in the 'refuge', as they both called their private little apartment. Auntie had begun looking in on her for afternoon coffee and a nice chat, talking about Silesia and what it had been like to be driven away from her old home – she had turned up every day to discuss the sorrows of this world. Every day from three to four. When it threatened to become an established habit, Katharina locked her door. 'I need time for myself,' she said. Not just for a few hours but for days and weeks. She always needed time for herself. We all live our own lives, and furthermore, as she had said all along, she was not a countrywoman, she'd have liked to be a bookseller. She had never heard about lime and nitrogen. As for milking cows – oh, for heaven's sake!

She was living in this comfortable little apartment, and Auntie had her own lovely room – sunshine all round!

Anyway, they ate meals together down in the big hall, and they could talk then.

The little apartment consisted of a living room, the bedroom and a study, with bookshelves supported on golden-bronze brackets lining the walls. The shelves held novels, side by side, and they had all been read, because Katharina had been a bookworm since childhood. As she always said, she had wanted to be a bookseller, not the mistress of an estate. And it was in a bookshop that Eberhard had seen her again in Berlin, where she and he were looking at one and the same book at ten one morning, and that, as it said in an account written to commemorate their wedding, was 'the book of life'.

She regularly got fresh supplies of books from Mitkau; they were the luxury she allowed herself. The bookseller there always had something extra for her as well. Konrad Muschler, Eckart von Naso, Ina Seidel. And also the Blue Books – pictorial volumes that she liked leafing through: *The Provinces of Germany* . . .

The study contained the little desk at which she wrote letters to her family in Berlin, telling them that she was fine, but how was all this going to end? Or to her husband in distant Italy. They had gone to Italy before the war in the brand-new Wanderer car, and now Eberhard had been there for months.

Photographs of her parents stood on the table, and a picture in oils of little Elfriede. It had been painted shortly before she was snatched away by scarlet fever in 1943, when no one was expecting any really serious childhood illness. She would be nearly eight years old now; Katharina was always working out her age.

Attached to the refuge was a conservatory that brought light into the little apartment. From there, you looked out over the flat roof of the summer drawing room and the terrace, and so to the park, the lawn surrounded by rhododendrons, and Auntie's green and white summerhouse. They had had it put up in 1936, when everything looked likely to improve. The village carpenter had put it together in three days for Auntie's birthday – it had been a great surprise. And it had been used only once.

Katharina liked to sit in the conservatory, looking down on the black forest that stood like a wall beyond the meadowland of the park. She often sat there with her friend Felicitas, who laughed so prettily, and chattered cheerfully – here you were undisturbed, yet somehow at the same time in the middle of nature.

Felicitas with her bright aquamarine pendant round her neck, and Katharina with her gold locket, both of them in the conservatory among cacti and geraniums.

Felicitas, blonde, a pretty little face with a pointed nose, was always so happy, and she made the more phlegmatic Katharina laugh with her stories. She managed to find something amusing in all her experiences – and there were a great many of them. She told her stories with a wealth of gestures, to Katharina, who could only marvel at her friend's imagination. Anyone standing down on the terrace could have heard every word spoken up here, and would have had something to laugh at.

The two friends laughed a great deal, but sometimes their mood was muted. Then they talked about Fritz from Frankfurt, who had had to go to Switzerland under cover of darkness, and other matters on Felicitas's mind.

There were a few matters that they never discussed; each of them kept those strictly to herself.

They toned one another down, the two friends – but then they got each other wound up and going again. Felicitas had a knack for that.

Now, in winter, they did not sit in the conservatory, but drank coffee in the comfortable little living room. Katharina had bought charming little armchairs for ladies. At Eberhard's insistence a painting of the Treptow observatory hung on the wall.

All kinds of postcards showing works of art hung beside the picture of the observatory: Dürer's portrait of his mother, Feuerbach's *Medea*.

*

In the middle of the apartment was a china figure on an old stand meant to hold flowers. The figure was entitled *Crouching Woman*, and Eberhard had bought it from the Royal Porcelain Manufactory in Berlin.

Felicitas was not visiting at the moment; she was pregnant, and in the cold wind on the slippery road she could easily have fallen. Katharina sat alone in her room, reading, or she made silhouettes out of black card, mostly of flowers and birds, and stuck them in an album devoted to the seasons of the year. When she had finished one of these works of art she lit herself a cigarette and sat back, pleased with herself.

Eberhard had travelled a great deal during this war: the good days in France, time spent in the proud country of Greece, and then the Ukraine, with its great fields of sunflowers. And wheat. Everything had turned out all right, although someone had put a mine in his bed in the Ukraine. And now Italy!

He had sent parcels home from everywhere, and Katharina sent much of their contents on to the family in Berlin. Weren't they getting anything at all there? 'We live on our ration cards,' they wrote, and Katharina felt sorry for them. Even in these last few years she had repeatedly gone to Berlin to help them out. And Berlin offered her what she missed at the Georgenhof: the theatre, concerts, the cinema as well – that wonderful film *Rembrandt*.

And then large, heavy packages containing books arrived at the Georgenhof.

But now the Russians were on the border – who'd have thought it? – and Katharina had withdrawn entirely into her refuge. The question was, might it not be better to go to Berlin, but Katharina shrank from the raids on the city. Furthermore, Eberhard had already sounded out the situation, and now people were saying, out loud, that in such times as these everyone ought to stay where they were.

Although, on the contrary, the Berlin family had contemplated moving to the Georgenhof and waiting there 'in peace and quiet to see what happened'. They had last all seen each other the week before Christmas, and tears had been shed when they parted. Elisabeth – a nice person, really, but it was not so easy with her deformed feet. Katharina hadn't ventured to ask Ernestine whether she could take Peter back with her. She would have been asked, 'Where would he sleep?' So she had left the subject alone.

Katharina had given her a fully grown goose for the Christmas holiday. Vladimir had looked as if he were wondering whether that was all right, and Auntie had to think how she could account for the fact that there was one goose less running about the farmyard. Would they get into trouble over that goose? After all, the poultry were counted. And maybe that ultra-Nazi Drygalski would find out? He seemed to have eyes everywhere. But after all, it could just as well have been the fox that got it.

It was a long time since Katharina had been bothered with any of the housekeeping. 'Is your aunt there?' was the question if she picked up the telephone after it had rung a dozen times, and she preferred it that way.

'Leave it, Kathi,' she had been told. 'Auntie will do it . . .' And she left it at that.

Even if she had wanted to see to something herself she wouldn't have been allowed to. 'She's a dreamer,' they said of her, 'she does everything wrong.' Some people would have called her eccentric, and felt sorry for Eberhard. It was hard luck to be landed with a woman like that, a woman who went out walking when other people were so overworked that they hardly knew whether they were coming or going. Who lay on the terrace in the sun when labourers were bathed in sweat as they mowed the rye. Who was always reading books, and had once been seen in the woods with a paint box sketching the old oaks overgrown with ivy, and the river with willows on its banks.

'Don't you ever go to see Elfie's grave?' Auntie had asked, and that had caused a rift between the two women that was never going to heal.

When she first came to the Georgenhof with Eberhard, her father-in-law had shown her the ruins of the old castle in the woods. The steps of the porch and the columns that had toppled over backwards. 'The French burnt the castle down just to warm their feet,' he had said. He had always liked calling her 'my little daughter' and putting his arms round her waist. Then he had a stroke, and for a long time he was bedridden, and only Katharina was allowed to plump up his pillows. She had sat at his bedside, both of them sighing. He had remembered her specially in his will: 'The fur cap, child, it's Persian lamb, you'll get that.' The white cap that the Russian officer had left behind, a lambskin cap.

The rest of the household left her in peace, but when the Ukrainian maids wanted to pour out their hearts they turned only to her. She even let them into her room. They wept out loud there, making as much noise as when they shouted at each other in the kitchen. Katharina had given them panties – darned, yes, but with plenty of wear left in them. And last summer she had even gone down to the River Helge with them to bathe. They had been seen down there laughing together, all three of them. And Katharina had found skirts and the jacket of a skirt suit to give the Ukrainians, who had nothing of their own. The check jacket that Katharina had worn in Cranz, back in the days of the seaside café on the Baltic. *Rise high, O red-winged eagle.* In that unique summer, with the boats setting their sails at a slant on the bright blue sea. Sonya wore the jacket now when she visited the foreign workers at the Forest Lodge, her wreath of blonde braids round her head.

There was a sequel to this outing to bathe in the little River Helge. Drygalski had appeared on the bank in his brown boots and called them back – or rather, told them to come out of the water, where they were shouting and splashing about. He had said there would be repercussions: bathing with foreign workers from the east? It had been a difficult time, but nothing came of it. The report had been summarily dismissed in Mitkau; Sarkander fixed that. After all, he pointed out, these women workers from the east had come to the German Reich of their own free will, and that had to be taken into account.

Katharina was still locking the door of her refuge, either from the inside or the outside, depending on where she happened to be, and she never let anyone else have the key. If someone knocked on her door she would ask, in tones of annoyance, 'Yes, what *is* it, then?' opening the door just a crack. Although she had no particular opinion on anything else, was always ready to give way and hardly knew what time of day it was, she was immovable on this point. A person must be allowed to be alone somewhere. After all, the house was large enough.

The only thing Auntie could do if she really needed to attract her attention was to go up to the attic and march back and forth above Katharina's room, stamping her feet until dust trickled down, disturbing her peace and quiet. But even then Katharina seldom stirred herself.

Usually Katharina lay on the bed, looking at the beautiful Madonnas in art books, or reading, or cutting silhouettes out of black card for her record of the cycle of the seasons. She did it, moreover, without drawing the outlines first. Felicitas marvelled at that, and told everyone.

Katharina liked to have a fruit bowl full of apples, such as the one that the political economist had admired, on the table. Here was the bowl of apples, there was the *Crouching Woman*, and on the wall hung Feuerbach's *Medea*.

Now and then radio music was heard coming from her room, the big Blaupunkt radio with the magic eye, and cigarette smoke wafted through the house. Was she lying on her bed again, reading?

Sometimes she stood inside her door, listening, to see if there was anyone outside eavesdropping.

'No one has any business here,' she said, and she set about cleaning the place herself, not that she usually lent a hand with any other housework. Sometimes she saw Peter here when he had done his homework; she found that a nuisance, and she boxed his ears with his exercise book if he hadn't been writing neatly, but otherwise she was easy-going with him. Historical dates? She didn't know any of those herself.

Just so long as he got a reasonably good report. 'Then you can do as you like,' she used to say, 'just so long as your report is reasonably good.' How else could they face his father? But since Dr Wagner the schoolmaster had taken his education in hand she had no more fears on that score.

'Isn't that a picture?' Lothar Sarkander had said when she was standing in the summer drawing room with him, watching the family picnicking in the park with cabbage white butterflies fluttering round them. It was so long ago now. Lothar Sarkander, the man with duelling scars on his cheek and the stiff leg; the man who made sure in Mitkau that the von Globig family lacked for nothing. He had wavy hair going slightly grey at the temples.

He had been standing beside her, pointing to the bright scene out there before them: the family sitting on the grass, the children in front of the dark, silent woods, and the white butterflies overhead. It had stuck in her memory; she couldn't forget it.

Eberhard would never have said such a thing. But the *Crouching Woman*? – It had been Eberhard who gave her the *Crouching Woman*. Or had he been making himself a present of the little sculpture?

Even the Ukrainian girls had gone up to the figure to touch it. Felicitas was always wondering out loud what it had cost. The Royal Porcelain Manufactory – it was even signed, wasn't it?

Unfortunately people from the housing development were always using the park as a short cut on their way to Mitkau, in spite of the notice saying NO THROUGH ROAD. Drygalski in particular took the short cut, treading heavily over the lawn and spitting into the rhododendrons to right and left. He used to pass the kitchen, turn into the park, look at his reflection in the windows of the summer drawing room, glance up at Katharina and then leave again on the other side. Now, in winter, the dark semicircle that he had trodden round the house disfigured the white blanket of snow.

Sometimes he could be heard in the kitchen scolding the maids, asking what they thought they were doing, and saying that he'd soon get them working, which was none of his business.

'Oh, never mind him!' Katharina had said when Auntie told her. 'I expect the man has troubles of his own.'

When she glanced at the thermometer in the conservatory, or opened the window to scatter birdseed in the little house for her feathered friends, Katharina looked down at the semicircle he had trodden. At the front of the house, Auntie looked at Peter's tree house, and Katharina looked down at the semicircle trodden in the pure white snow down below.

Frost-flowers formed a pattern on the windows, and the door was draped with green blankets to keep out the cold air.

In the living room, under the slope of the roof, there was a storage cubbyhole for luggage and bedclothes. This in itself spoiled the look of the room, so Katharina had placed a small artisan-made chest painted with flowers in front of it, and spread a cover over the chest.

Katharina kept the cubbyhole locked as well. It contained special provisions to which Eberhard had added from time to time: cigarettes above all, coffee and cocoa and soap too, soap from France when it couldn't be bought at all in the shops. There were also liqueurs, cognac, and seventeen bottles of Italian red wine, a Barolo Riserva.

The existence of this store of provisions was one of the reasons she kept her room locked. Someone could have sniffed out these illicit goods – tobacco, cocoa, soap?

When Eberhard had last been here, in autumn, his heavy heart full of gloomy thoughts, he had gone all over the house, into the main hall, the billiards room, the summer drawing room – and then he had drunk coffee up here with his wife, as he had done so often before, although as Auntie said, there was plenty of room downstairs, but, soon they wouldn't be seeing any more of each other. They had sat side by side whispering, while acorns pattered down on the roof of the summer drawing room. The English shares in steel and the rice-flour factory. The shares would be worth nothing now in the war, and as for the Romanians? A good thing he had his salary as a special officer; it would keep their heads above water.

'Scoundrels, all of them,' Eberhard had said. They had sat

beside the stand with the *Crouching Woman* on it, listening to music; music to accompany dreams. The eighteenth-century waltz from *Le Bal Paré*, was it? And *I know there'll be a miracle some day . . .* Had they held hands?

Eberhard had opened the door to the cubbyhole and crawled in to check the provisions. 'Mind you're always very careful,' he told Katharina, putting a cigarette in his father's charred meerschaum holder. He rubbed his boots shiny with a woollen cloth.

He often told her to 'Mind you're always very careful!' When he saw his wife he warned her, 'Mind you're careful, Kathi,' and she replied, 'Yes, and you too!' But there in Italy he was a long way from the firing line.

The question was whether he ought not to send his wife and son somewhere else, perhaps Lake Constance? That was what Eberhard asked himself, but he came to no conclusion. Things had been all right so far . . .

For some time Katharina had been listening to the BBC news. It was both alarming and encouraging. She listened lying on her bed – one hand on her locket, her mouth open – as she heard the news from over there, read in a calm, pleasant voice, matter-of-fact and entirely without malice. She turned the radio down very low. Who knew, Drygalski might be taking the short cut again to see whether the Ukrainian girls really were in the cottage where they ought to be at night, and not in the Forest Lodge with the foreigners there? That interested the man enormously, although it was none of his business.

There was something he didn't like about the Georgenhof, although everything seemed to be in order. His own wife was lying sick in their living room, which was also their kitchen. And the people here lived in the lap of luxury. To think that Frau von

Globig, that high and mighty lady, had asked him only once how his wife was.

Eberhard had advised his wife always to turn the radio back to the German news programme when she had been listening to the BBC. Better safe than sorry.

Now and then you could smell real coffee all over the house. Katharina was giving herself a treat upstairs.

7

Mitkau

On a cold winter's day, Katharina put on the Russian officer's Persian lamb cap, had the horse harnessed to the coach that still stood in the carriage house, and drove it to Mitkau. In the hot summer of 1931 the coachman Michels had brought her home from Mitkau railway station, a newly married bride, in that old-fashioned vehicle. Michels, so it was said, had been the first to fall in Poland. Her little bridal wreath still hung by the coach's olive-shaped back window.

It was cold, and the wind blew a dusting of fine snow over the icy road. Katharina had spread the fur rug over her knees, and the gelding – clip-clop, clip-clop – cheerfully drew the light weight along. The coach was child's play to the heavy horse, an animal of character who tried rolling his eyes to look back at anyone getting in.

Katharina liked to use the old vehicle for her drives into town, and she drove it herself. Michels had taught her how. She went into town once a week; it had become a habit of hers. 'I need it,' she said.

The little town of Mitkau, enclosed by a stout, sloping wall, lay on the River Helge, which wound its way through fields and meadows, its banks lined by willows. The arch of an iron bridge crossed the little river. That bridge had cost the community dear; the citizens had been paying for it since 1927, and it would be a burden on the municipal budget for many years to come.

*

Katharina was driving towards the tower of the town church. Even from a distance, you could see the green-painted arch of the bridge on your left, and straight ahead the tower of Mitkau church, with the gables of the town hall and the monastery. The chimney of the brickworks could be seen on the far right.

When the little town was to be immortalized on a stamp – a local man had won a medal in the javelin event at the Olympic Games, and Hitler had visited Mitkau twice – the Gauleiter had the bridge shown in the foreground of the design, with the church, the town hall and the monastery as subsidiary elements. The wording under the picture said GREATER GERMAN REICH. The enlarged design of the stamp had spent a long time in a glass case in the front room of the town hall. Anyone coming to the registry office there to collect ration cards, or permits for items in short supply, could look at the picture. Who'd have thought our little town would ever be on a stamp! But now, in January 1945, the glass case had been taken away, and no one talked about the stamp any more.

The Helge was only a small river, little more than a brook, winding its way through the landscape without any great drama. The monks had once used the stream to drive a watermill, but the millwheel had fallen into disrepair long ago. Boys skated on the river these days.

The Helge also flowed past the Georgenhof at a little distance. The Globigs always meant to take the rowing boat upstream to Mitkau. Going in the other direction would have been easier, letting yourself drift downstream to goodness knows where. Some time or other you would end up in the Vistula Lagoon. In summer you could sometimes cross to the other side of the little river dry-shod, and children jumped from stone to stone on their way to the monastery school instead of going the long way round over the bridge. At the moment, they could easily have gone sliding across the ice, but that wasn't necessary because school was closed. The classrooms were full of old people sitting with their hands folded. They had been brought from Tilsit in a closed van and were now sitting here waiting for something to happen. At Christmas there had been a big Christmas tree for them in the refectory, and a group from the Bund deutscher Mädel or BDM, the League of German Girls, had sung carols and served mulled wine and cake. There was a larger-than-life statue of St Christopher on the north side of the refectory, all that was left of the once lavish furnishings of the monastery.

The school used the refectory, with its slightly vaulted ceiling, as a hall and a gymnasium, and there the old people sat at long tables spooning up their soup.

Sometimes you saw the old people walking up and down the cloisters, past the tombstones. Sometimes the old men sat in the window bays playing cards, but that had stopped entirely now that, day after day, the thermometer showed such cold temperatures.

Katharina drove past the wreck of the railway station – its ruins, still smoking from the last air raid, were being cleared away by prisoners from the brickworks – and stopped outside the town hall. A fourteenth-century Gothic brick building, it did not feature in any art book, but it was pretty. It had a stepped Gothic gable sloping down to the marketplace, with an iron bar at the top to prevent it from falling. Outside the entrance there was a granite pillar, and the iron chain used to bind malefactors to it in the Middle Ages still hung from this pillar.

Katharina exchanged greetings with an elderly couple coming out of the town hall, and asked how they were. So-so, they said, thanking her; two sons missing in the east, and their daughter could never be left on her own because of her epileptic fits.

Boys from the Hitler Youth were clearing the snow in the street. An SA man had told them how to do it, and wondered what the point of the boys pelting each other with snowballs was. Could it be reconciled with the gravity of the situation?

A unit of reservists came marching along from the marketplace: old men in a varied assortment of uniforms with hats on their heads and long rifles on their backs. Their armbands proclaimed their membership of the Volkssturm.

Katharina spread her fur rug over the gelding's back, and the horse deposited a pile of dung on the fresh snow. His eyes followed the woman; with luck she wouldn't be in there too long.

She was carrying a dead hare wrapped in newspaper under her arm, a present for the mayor. Secretaries hurrying back and forth along the corridor passed the time of day with her; they all recognized her, and knew that she was a close friend of the mayor. Once, when Eberhard von Globig was still in charge of sugar factories in the Ukraine, a handsome present for the town had arrived, a consignment of raw sugar although Mitkau hadn't been due one. Wartime had made it possible to do many friends a good turn on the quiet.

So without first going to the reception room to announce her arrival, she knocked on the mayor's door, opened it and walked straight in.

The mayor, Lothar Sarkander, a man of upright bearing with duelling scars on his face and a stiff leg, sat at his desk under a picture of Hitler, cleaning his pistol. He looked overworked and anxious. A calm, thoughtful man, every inch the lawyer from head to toe. Salt and pepper hair neatly arranged, with the help of brilliantine, in many small waves above his thin face. Much of the grey in his hair had shown only recently. He had been a supporter of the new ideas from the first, but had now been 'healed' of them. Too late.

They did not bother with saying 'Heil Hitler'. Instead, Katharina put the hare on the mayoral desk, where it looked like a dead baby. Sarkander reassembled his pistol, put it away in the drawer and came round to the front of the desk. He knew about the hare coursing arranged on the Globig estate, since he had been asked for permission, and as he had immediately given it, a visitor from the Georgenhof bringing him his dues could be expected.

And there she was, Frau von Globig, Katharina, with her black hair and blue eyes, the ring with the coat of arms on her finger, the gold locket round her neck, her white Persian lamb cap on her head. Sarkander shook hands with her, then drew her to him and kissed her on the cheek, glancing at the dead hare. After that he asked after her husband: how was Eberhard doing in warm, distant Italy?

'You should be glad it's Italy, Kathi! He's well away from the firing line there.'

Sarkander may have wondered why he didn't maintain his friendship with this woman on a regular basis. But he was a decent man, and he had a wife and children.

They had stood in the summer drawing room, and the family had sat out on the lawn with Uncle Josef. The doors of the drawing room, looking out on the park, were wide open. 'What a picture,' he had said, pointing to the picnic. And what about the two of them there in the drawing room, strange to one another in their familiarity?

Hadn't Eberhard been there that day? Or had he only gone into the woods for a moment to clear his thoughts?

And they had both thought of that other, very secret matter of which so many other people were aware.

If I'd known what I was missing,
If I'd known who I was kissing,
That midnight at the lido . . .

On that one fine day at the seaside, she had worn a round hat like the sun on the back of her head, and hadn't he been all in white? The sea had lapped gently against the breakwaters, and there were lights on the fishing boats by night.

Eberhard had gone to Berlin and the Olympic Games, and he hadn't taken her with him. 'I'm sure you can understand that, can't you?' No, she hadn't been sure that she could. So she had gone to the seaside with Sarkander.

They sat down, and Katharina crossed her legs – she was wearing riding boots – and lit herself a cigarillo. The delightful summer parties at the Georgenhof . . . The telegraph connection to high places – Eberhard had always made sure that it worked well – was still working, in spite of telegraphic interference by people of Drygalski's kind, those proletarians. 'I'll get them yet!' he had told the mayor.

'Ah, well, Drygalski . . .' said Sarkander. 'Leave those folk alone.'

The two of them exchanged news, whispering to each other although there was no one else in the room. Last night's column of tanks, the ruined station, the prisoners in the brickworks . . . And they talked about the Russians on the border, where something unpleasant was brewing.

'To think it's come to this!'

Lothar Sarkander in his elegant suit, the Party symbol on his lapel, had moments of insight. He knew which way the wind was blowing.

Was it a good idea to keep Peter here? Sarkander asked, standing up and pacing up and down the room. Wouldn't it be better to send him to Berlin?

Wasn't it too late for that now?

Sarkander might have to go to Berlin on duty next week. He could take the boy with him, why not?

But didn't the Russians behave very decently at the end of the First War?

'We'll find ways and means to get the two of you to safety in good time,' he said. 'You can rely on that.' He put his hand on her shoulder, and she moved a little closer to him.

Then he fingered the blood-stained hare and sat down at the desk again, and the young woman went away feeling comforted. What she didn't know was that Sarkander had sent his wife and children away to Bamberg in the autumn.

Katharina went over to Gessner & Haupt's bookshop on the marketplace, where the bookseller gave her an art book, *German Cathedrals of the Middle Ages*. It was in the Blue Books series, a volume that she didn't yet have. She already possessed *Greek Sculptures*, *The Quiet Garden* and *Rembrandt's Self-Portraits*. If she kept her eyes open she'd be able to complete her collection.

The bookseller was feeling depressed. In spite of his stomach trouble he had been called up as a reservist. He had been told he must be ready, just in case, and if the sirens went three times he must go to such and such a meeting place. He must not leave Mitkau and they must be able to reach him at any moment. And if you hear the sirens going off three times, then put on your uniform and hurry to the meeting place.

And then what?

He was sixty-two years old, and this was not how he had imagined spending his old age.

The bell rang as she left the shop, and the bookseller watched her go. Those people are well off, he thought, taking a stomach pill. There was an open carton in his back room and he was filling it with rare books. The first editions of Lessing and Goethe had long ago been sent to safety.

Soldiers were hunched over hot drinks in the overheated Café Schlosser. Many had girls with them, who would sit with other soldiers when these had to move on.

Here Katharina met Herr Schünemann the political economist, who immediately swung himself over to her on his crutches, addressed her as 'dear lady', kissed her hand and so forth, greatly surprising the soldiers: such gallantries in the sixth year of the war?

By now Schünemann had been to Insterburg, he had visited the little stamp shop here, and had come away with good pickings: old German stamps, quantities of them! He opened his bag and showed her his new acquisitions one by one. What does she think of these? he asks, he would really like to know! His bad breath wafts round her. Katharina thought privately that the stamps were shabby specimens, but she supposed he might be right.

She leaned back, and Schünemann went on talking to her. 'When devaluation comes – and dear lady, what do you think this war is costing? – then these little things will rise in value enormously. I shall retrieve my entire fortune like this!' he said, with a mischievously boyish expression on his face, meant to show he was no fool.

Katharina thought of the army stamp that he had torn off its envelope on the quiet and taken away. She wondered how much that would be worth some day. Maybe Schünemann was thinking the same? He quickly paid for his coffee and swung himself away again on his crutches. Off to Allenstein! There were surely all kinds of things to be picked up there.

Katharina paid another visit to her cheerful friend Felicitas, who was always so funny, always so amusing, and told such good stories. There was a hare to be delivered there too. Her friend was heavily pregnant, and the meat would do her good.

The house was beyond the town wall. At the end of the road, with its many sharp turns, freezing prisoners were busy turning the Senthagener Tor into a tank barrier with tree trunks. Others were levering up paving stones to prepare one-man positions for reservists armed with single-shot anti-tank weapons. The earth was frozen solid. Digging holes in it was extremely difficult.

The two women greeted one another loudly, and even the canary sang for all it was worth. The hare was put in a pillowcase and hung in the kitchen window.

'Just so long as there's gas,' they said, for otherwise it couldn't be roasted. Pickled in vinegar, maybe? But there wasn't any vinegar either.

Felicitas had been lying on the sofa listening to the radio.

A señor and a lovely señorita
Went happily walking along by the sea . . .

A glass dish with crunchy oatflakes stood on the table, and Katharina was offered a green liqueur in a little pink glass.

Felicitas with her bright aquamarine pendant, and Katharina with her gold locket.

*

From the window, they could see the prisoners toiling away at the tree trunks, an old non-commissioned officer standing beside them with a long shotgun, hands in his pockets. He had wrapped a scarf round his head.

There were two kind of prisoners at work: Frenchmen in thick coats, and other prisoners in striped uniforms, with an SS man keeping special watch on them from the shelter of a doorway.

The Senthagener Tor, with its snow-capped battlements, looked rather snug. It reminded people of the Napoleonic Wars, when those who got away from the Grande Armée in 1812, hungry and freezing, asked to come into the town. Men from Württemberg and Bavaria had been welcomed in and given hot soup, but not the French. The French were turned away to go elsewhere. Generosity to a defeated enemy is all very well, but while they were still on top the French had gone on levying forced war contributions, had stabled their horses in the church and had burnt down the old Georgenhof castle. The people of Mitkau had not been able to forget that.

'What do you think?' asked Felicitas. 'Will the Russians really get to Mitkau?' And she ran her hands over her body, sighing.

It seemed to her incredible that the Russians could be interested in such an insignificant town as Mitkau. This was the back of beyond. And how was such a little place to be defended? She couldn't see what there was here to defend. The two women knew nothing about the ammunition depots along the Helge. Nor did they know that substitute units of the National Socialist Motor Corps were camping in the Forest Lodge.

Above the radio hung a photograph of Franz, her friend's husband, an attractive lieutenant, his cap with the lieutenant's cord round it sitting jauntily on his head. The radio was French; he had brought it back from France in the hot summer of 1940, and it was elegantly curved. It had a streamlined look, and was far more stylish than any German radio set.

One day you'll be back with me again,
One day you'll be true to me again . . .

Both women sighed repeatedly at the slow foxtrot being played. Felicitas put a shovelful of coke into the stove and stirred up the embers. Perhaps Franz would be standing at the door some day? Who could tell? He was in that wretched dump Graudenz, in a fortress where he had to deal with German shirkers and deserters. 'They'll all be shot, of course,' he had said. Felicitas could have visited him, but in a place like that where there wasn't even a cinema?

As for Eberhard in Italy ... nothing could happen to him there. 'You're lucky,' said Felicitas, and Katharina sighed deeply. Yes, she was really lucky.

The doorbell rang, and a girl came in. She saluted, Heil Hitler, bobbed a curtsy and asked if she could help with anything. Her hands were blue with cold. 'Oh, it's lovely and warm in here . . .'

The girl belonged to the 'Help for Mothers-to-Be' organization set up by the Party. Boys were sent to shovel snow and keep the main road clear; girls were to lend a hand to pregnant women.

Yes, she could fetch a bucket of coke, and here were the ration cards; could she buy bread, butter and sausage, and she was to count the change and make sure the shop didn't cut too much off the coupons.

Katharina said she had just been to see the mayor, but when she was about to say more her friend put a finger to her lips: *ssh!* She had a refugee family from Lithuania in the next room, on the other side of the sliding door, a woman and three children, and they were eavesdroppers! Lower-class people who had recently made themselves at home in the kitchen as well, using the good china and putting it away all anyhow.

'And you should see the loo!'

Their presence here, making themselves at home, treating the china roughly and failing to keep the lavatory clean, was all to do with the 'community of nations'. One must observe that, naturally, but not in a way like this. Felicitas suspected that these people had never used a proper toilet before. No doubt in the east they had a little shed outdoors.

At this moment the sirens howled. Felicitas put her hand to her belly and said, 'Oh, how it goes through one!' Would it be bad for the baby?

They both stood up at once, switched off the radio, covered up the canary, opened the window just a crack. 'We can't even talk in peace for a few minutes!'

The air-raid shelter in the cellar smelt of potatoes. It was a vaulted cellar; in earlier centuries the house had belonged to the Senthagener Tor, and in the past people under arrest had been put in here, vagrants and those who couldn't show any papers, dubious characters who had to be expelled from the town to take themselves somewhere else.

The rest of the household had already gathered in the cellar, the fat refugee woman with her screaming children – a group reminiscent of the work of the illustrator Heinrich Zille – a sick young man and a miserable old woman.

The French prisoners were crowding into the cellar as well. For them, it was a welcome opportunity to take time off work. The non-commissioned officer grumbled a bit that it wasn't really right, but he wasn't so keen on standing out in the snow himself, so they sat down and thawed out a bit.

The other prisoners, the ones in striped uniforms, had to stay outside.

The Frenchmen looked at the two women. So elegant, so lady-like? And the women tried to dredge up their French vocabulary. They knew how to say 'Good day' and 'I love you' in French, but that was all.

The refugee children looked at the prisoners with great interest, and were soon crowding round them. The brass buttons on their uniforms . . . The men put the children on their laps, which wasn't really right.

Did these Frenchmen have any idea that Napoleon had forced the people here to pay war contributions, and used St Mary's Church as a stable?

The sick young man sitting in the corner would probably have liked to stroke the children's hair as well, and he could have talked French to the Frenchmen. But was he to tell them that better times were coming? They knew that for themselves.

The non-commissioned officer's nose was dripping. He was absorbed in his own thoughts.

After the all clear went, there was tumult outside. The young man had gone out to the prisoners in striped uniforms and given them bread. This was intolerable! Did he know, he was asked, that they had committed serious offences? But for the presence of the Frenchmen it could have been a bad business.

Before Katharina went home she had to deliver a third hare, which was for the pastor. Eberhard had said so in writing. 'Don't forget the pastor; who knows what we may yet need him for?'

The pastor, whose name was Brahms, was a doctrinarian who

sometimes, when something like extra sausage was being considered, unexpectedly came out with very old-fashioned principles. When Elfriede died, in the winter of the scarlet fever, he had objected to a grave for her in the forest. And it had been difficult to make him change his mind. A solitary cross? A grave mound overgrown with flowers in the middle of the forest?

'It will soon be forgotten,' he had said. And, 'In death we are all equal,' and other such things. Lothar Sarkander had intervened and had made it possible.

When the German soldiers went to Poland in 1939, there had been some idea of Brahms giving them a blessing in a little service. Or at least those of them who wanted it. The organist had already looked out some sheet music.

No, that was not something he could do, the pastor had said. There was no provision for an ecclesiastical occasion of that kind in the evangelical state church, and he was not minded to strike out on his own. Someone would have had to make up a special liturgy for it.

It had been rather bold to say such a thing. Even the Party had asked about it. But no one really bore him a grudge. The church was the church and Pastor Brahms was thought of as fractious, and a fractious person was somehow very German. 'Here stand I, I can do no other . . .' Sarkander had pointed out that Martin Luther had also been a fractious man.

Katharina rang the doorbell of the parsonage and gave the pastor the hare, with a kind of bobbed curtsy. 'So here you are again for once?' said Brahms, feeling the dead hare with his thumbs and barely saying 'Thank you.' He had so much to do, he said, he was afraid he couldn't ask her in. Did she know that seven more men from Mitkau had fallen this week? He was sitting with their womenfolk, and there was no comfort. 'Only yesterday . . . but it's no use.' And then there was the additional burden of the old people in the monastery. How long, he wondered, would all this go on? These were intolerable circumstances.

Katharina went over to the church.

It was certainly icy cold inside, and Katharina didn't stay long. From the Globigs' traditional pew, which was usually empty, she had a good view of a likeness of Jonah which, as if miraculously, had survived Protestant iconoclasm. Jonah and the whale, an old fifteenth-century carving with some gilt still left on it. She had always liked Jonah's cheerful face as he waved a last goodbye to the whale. Eighteen side altars had suffered at the hands of the iconoclasts, hacked to pieces and burnt, and then the main altar had been unceremoniously chopped up for firewood by the French later. Only cheerful Jonah and his whale had survived. Not even the French had done anything to him.

Katharina threw a coin into the missionary box, a figure of a Moor who nodded his head in thanks. Old postage stamps wouldn't have done for him.

Out in the porch she almost bumped into the pastor again. He led her back into the chilly darkness. There was something else he wanted to say . . . and he took her further into the dark. He had something on his mind. He approached her purposefully, and then dropped hints, and finally came out with it. It was a question of giving a man shelter for a night – a refugee. Could that be done? It was mixed up with politics, so not a word to anyone. She could think it over at her leisure and then let him know.

One day you'll be back with me again,
One day you'll be true to me again . . .

On the way home Katharina thought of the *Crouching Woman*, and of Felicitas and the twilight hours spent in her own comfortable refuge. A strange man? For a night? Possibly one of those men in the striped uniforms?

She couldn't agree to it just like that. Shouldn't she ask Eberhard first? But – Italy? Wouldn't it take ages? Letters arrived six weeks after they were sent. And anyone could overhear a telephone call. 'Not a word to anyone,' Pastor Brahms had said. And through what hints was she to present Eberhard with the idea? A strange man?

On the other hand, shouldn't one help a stranger? Wasn't it her Christian duty?

Dr Wagner was already waiting in Horst-Wessel-Strasse, and she took him up in the coach. This time he had two bags with him. The gelding looked back intently as he got in.

Today he was going to show the boy something else, he said. He had brought some postcards of Greek art, youths throwing spears and bending bows. There is nothing sweeter than to die for your country, *dulce et decorum est pro patria mori*. They would have to study that proposition.

8

The Painter

Peter was sitting in his room watching the housing development through the telescope. House beside house, arranged in straight lines. An old woman with a bag came round the corner. She slips, and no one notices. Cars drive by on the road, women shake out their mattresses. She lies there and tries to get to her feet, like a horse that has fallen. Peter watched her lying by the roadside, he up here, she down there . . . how could he have gone to her aid?

After a while he was tired of watching. And when he looked again, the black heap of clothes that was the old woman had disappeared.

It was cold, because the stove wasn't drawing properly, and Peter would have liked to crawl into bed, but that wouldn't do, because Auntie had a way of suddenly flinging open the door to see that everything was all right, particularly when it was quiet up here in his room. It wouldn't have done for him to be lying in bed reading in broad daylight. So he sat at the window and drew shapes in the frost on the panes.

Around midday the sun came out, and Peter immediately left everything where it was and ran down to the yard, where flocks of sparrows flew up from the stable. He teased the Ukrainian maids, who finally hit out at him with the broom, and he threw the chickens some grain.

The rooster, a fiery red fowl with a blue tail, was called Richard, and he was Peter's friend. When Peter appeared the bird moved a little way aside, so that the hens couldn't see him, and then Peter bent down and held out a few grains of corn to him in the hollow of his hand. However well fed he was, the rooster would peck them up and nestle his head into Peter's hand. It was a friendship of equals.

Peter picked up a new-laid egg in the henhouse and tipped the contents down his throat. Auntie wouldn't have liked that either. You boil or fry eggs – it's disgusting to drink them from the shell raw. He also liked eating the sliced turnips that were thrown to the cattle.

The peacock was nowhere to be seen; he had moved into the furthest corner of the barn to get out of the cold. Even the corn that Peter was throwing to the chickens couldn't tempt him out. He sat high up in his corner and didn't move.

The dovecote was uninhabited, and all was still, bar the odd feather wafting around the opening through which the birds flew in and out. Only a few swallows nested in the dovecote. Old Herr von Globig had been a bird fancier. The peacock with his tail and his little crown, a turkey and his family. Geese. When he couldn't go hunting any more, pigeons had been his pleasure. He would lie on the terrace, offering them grain, and he was pleased when they came down to him, cooing and nodding their heads.

Pigeons: their heavy bodies, their elegant flight. Of course the old man had noticed that they didn't have nice natures; they were always friendly to him, but they would peck each other until they bled. 'Just like human beings,' he said, 'one of them tormenting another.'

He had tried to persuade his cousin Josef in Albertsdorf to get pigeons of his own. Then they could exchange news by pigeon post, he said, without paying for postage and packing. From the

Georgenhof to Albertsdorf and back. They could tie letters to the birds' legs. Pigeons have an extraordinary sense of direction.

But what kind of news, Josef asked, would they be exchanging? Anyway, what was the telephone for?

When the old gentleman died, the family got rid of the birds. On the housing estate, however, everyone who wanted pigeons could have them, and they flew in flocks, sometimes right and sometimes left, turning and wheeling in the air.

The cottage stood next to the big old barn that hadn't been in use since the sale of the landed property. Its lower floor was the laundry room-cum-kitchen, and the Ukrainian women slept on the top floor. You got to it by climbing a ladder. Peter liked teasing the women; he called them 'maid' until they hit out at him with the dishcloth. Sometimes he climbed up to their bedroom, where they kept their wooden chests and put their things tidily away in an empty cupboard. There were coloured postcards on the wall, depicting a prima ballerina in different ballet positions. He teased skinny Sonya rather more than stout Vera, who had a mysterious smell. Sonya smelt too, but her odour was not uninteresting. However, if she managed to get hold of him that was no fun at all. She hit out, and hard.

The two women argued. Sonya screeched, and Vera answered her back more calmly. Sometimes they both sang the melancholy songs of their native land together. Sonya took the soprano part in her high voice, Vera sang the lower part in a dark, velvety tone. They were probably remembering the sunflowers at home, and how they had volunteered to come to Germany, a stupid thing to do. Eberhard himself had found them and asked if they wouldn't like to go to Germany, saying that he could fix it. And their whole village had said: don't be silly, give it a go. Germany. A chance like this doesn't come along every day. You're not getting anywhere here. And their mothers had urged them to accept the offer, while Grandpa hummed and hawed. In fact it hadn't been such a stupid idea to go voluntarily after all, because a few weeks later they'd have been taken to Germany anyway, with no choice in the matter.

Now their native land was far away and the Red Army was back there. The two girls didn't know that their mothers had been deported under cover of night for collaborating with the enemy in the east. No letter had come through, no message – even pigeon post wouldn't have been any use. Now the girls were in a foreign land, quarrelling and singing. And when Peter annoyed Sonya she hit out really hard.

Sometimes Peter watched Vladimir the Pole feeding the horses. The two brown mares and the gelding; you had to be careful not to stick the pitchfork in the horses' legs when you were mucking out the stable. The smell of their fodder was appetizing: a mixture of oats and chaff. The gelding blew the chaff away before he began eating.

When Peter was smaller, he had been found one day sleeping beside the gelding in the bay. That huge animal, who liked to push uninvited guests up against the fence.

Only the heavy farm carts and the old coach stood in the carriage house now. All the other implements and vehicles had been sold when the family parted with its landed estates.

The coach looked like one of the horse-drawn cabs in Berlin, with leather upholstery, and carbide lanterns in brass holders to left and right of the coachman's box. The narrow wheels were covered with white rubber, and the little bridal wreath hung in the small, oval window. The coach belonged to the old inventory of the property, and had probably been there for ever, but the little wreath dated only from 1932. When the cousins from

Albertsdorf came over and played hide-and-seek, Peter slipped into the coach and it took them ages to find him. Stay put and don't move, that was the way to play the game.

Once Peter had shot at some crows with the air pistol. One of the birds dropped to the ground, but was still alive. It flapped its wings and went on living, until at last it lay dead. Then Vladimir came out of the cowshed and looked long and gravely at the boy.

If you were going to kill something you had to do it properly. From time to time Vladimir came along with the axe, picked up a chicken, and one blow was enough to kill it. None of the chickens strode past their comrades to save their lives, like the legendary medieval privateer Störtebecker after his beheading; there was no saving anyone's life here. Some time or other every chicken's turn came, and the axe went chop-chop. The cat, who otherwise kept out of the way, came running at the sound; he knew it meant something for him. He had a rightful claim to the head of the fowl.

When Peter looked to see if the tree house in the oak was still in good order and wondered whether to climb up to it and leave a stock of chopped turnips there, a farmer's cart stopped in the road, and a little man jumped down. The man said goodbye to the farmer who had given him a lift, walked round the manor house and came in through the back door to the kitchen, where the maids were quarrelling again. When they saw him they stopped shouting, and stared at him in silence.

The man in his long coat seemed rather strange. But when he had unwound the scarf wrapped round his head, he looked perfectly normal, indeed smart. He laughed and asked the Ukrainian girls, 'What are you shouting for? Surely things aren't as bad as all that?'

Then he addressed them as 'ladies' and asked whether he could warm himself up a bit.

They cleared him a place at the kitchen table, and even gave him a mug of hot milk and a piece of bread and honey.

Where had he come from? the women asked. Where was he going? He asked in return where did *they* come from? Where were *they* going? And when Auntie came along, with a brooch on her pullover and wrist-warmers on her wrists – where had he come from? Where was he going? – he stood up, told her his name and said he was an artist, a painter, and added that it was wonderful to be allowed to warm himself here in this traditional old kitchen, you didn't usually meet with such hospitality these days. To think he'd been offered milk and honey, he'd never known such a thing before. There was an almost biblical touch to it.

He came from Düsseldorf, he said, and he had been travelling through the German provinces for months, drawing 'what was left standing', as he put it. The mayor of Mitkau had given him a friendly welcome and let him do as he liked in his town. And it had also been the mayor who directed him to the Georgenhof, with its finial in the shape of a spiked mace, the morning-star type, set high above the gable room, telling him that nice people lived there.

Where had all this come from? Where would it all end? That was the question.

When he heard that Auntie was from Silesia, he said he knew Silesia like the back of his hand. He had been occupied for the last two years illustrating that great work *The German Provinces*, drawing the provincial buildings still standing. It was supported by the Party, he explained, and he had three extensive portfolios ready in Düsseldorf. He had begun his work in Swabia, then he had gone along the Weser, and so to Thuringia. And Silesia too. All that was already on record, now it was the turn of East

Prussia, in winter at that, but he was nearly finished. In the next few days he would continue his work with Allenstein, and then conclude it in Danzig.

He had been in Silesia a year and a half ago, in summer, when deep peace reigned there. All those pretty little churches. Where had all this come from? Where would it all end?

Königsberg was done for now, but he had turned to depicting that city and what remained of it. There was still a great deal he could put on record and he had been able to save so much for posterity. Burnt-out granaries, a flight of steps with a banister rail rising from the rubble, and of course the ruins of the cathedral and the castle. The British had done a thorough job, you couldn't deny that. A lovely city, but finished now.

And he had just left the little town of Mitkau, which was on the defensive.

He had been arrested there! He had been asked what he was doing, shut up in a filthy cell with six other men, and not so much as a plate of soup. Just for drawing the tank barrier outside the Senthagener Tor. As if he were a spy. They had tried to confiscate his drawings, he said. There'd been a lot of telephoning. The mayor had rescued him, with many apologies, and had even given him an auxiliary police officer.

Fancy shutting *him* up like a spy. In a cell with six other men. And shady characters they were, at that.

In Mitkau he had been interested in the tower of St Mary's Church from the south-east, a view not shown on any picture postcard. Pastor Brahms was an impressive man, a kind of Luther, but why hadn't he let him in? Standing four-square outside the parsonage, not even inviting him inside. Asking, 'What do you want?' instead of being friendly and letting him into the parsonage. It was the fault of the pastors themselves if they lost their congregations.

Once inside the church – which otherwise was rather bleak and gloomy – he had sketched the capitals of a few columns and some finials, and then the amusing carving of Jonah with his funny whale. Was there a photo of it? he wondered. You couldn't really draw something like that.

The artist had turned to the monastery as well, with its draughty cloisters and the refectory, crooked with age. Old people had been shuffling about in it, coughing and spitting. The refectory with its St Christopher and the cloisters.

He had drawn, from all sides, the marketplace with its uneven surface, the town hall and the cosy little houses round it. And the Smithy Inn, with its curving gable end. He didn't think the big bridge so interesting; the old wooden bridge with the Dutch curve to its central section would have been a more attractive subject. But it had had to give way to modern times. He had sketched it only to please the auxiliary police officer.

He had noticed it when sketching the tricky subject of the Senthagener Tor, when he was drawing the tree trunks lying diagonally in front of it.

He showed Auntie the sketchbook, as if it were evidence of his industry, and she identified the Mitkau buildings without any difficulty. The town walls, the Senthagener Tor – he'd never seen anything like it before – and the monastery with the doddery old folk in the cloisters. Why, soon that sort of thing, she said, would be on a par with Rembrandt.

But the refectory? The St Christopher? The columns with their capitals? The finials? She wasn't familiar with those. It had all been so different in her native Silesia. Much more appealing and cheerful than anything here.

And the gate? And what were those figures in the picture?

He had Mitkau in the can now, said the painter. Danzig would be the last great task he had set himself. He just had to visit Allenstein first, then go on to Danzig and maybe Elbing. Then he would pack everything up and go home 'to the Reich', as he put it, and then he would have a good sleep for once and see what else could be done with his wealth of material.

He was really interested in all that had happened to him here. Hours on end in prison, sharing a cell with six subhumans. For hours on end! Work-shy scum, mere rabble . . .

The Ukrainian maids were curious to see his art as well, and looked over his shoulder, but Auntie said, 'Come on, what's all this?' and they got back to work: peeling potatoes, washing the dishes, cleaning the mighty stove, both in front of it and behind it.

It was the kitchen range that made the painter reach for his crayon, a real traditional range – gigantic, and the Esse cooker. He immediately began sketching the range, and he also sketched the two maids at work near it. He paid most attention to plump Vera, drawing her in profile, whereupon Sonya ran off to the cottage to fetch her check jacket.

The painter then, for professional reasons, or so he said, asked about other architectural features of the house. The cellars? And was there anything else remarkable in some way or other, something worth illustrating?

The cellar could be dismissed without more ado, although it had old vaulting and the date 1605 on a coat of arms – but it was dark and damp there. Water came up over your feet in it. At most there was the spiral staircase. Who used to climb down all those steps? A manservant sent to fetch wine? Or the bailiff, carrying a lantern and propelling a thief caught stealing wood ahead of him? Did this place have a dungeon? Had poachers or tenant farmers late with their rent languished here under lock and key, behind bolts?

These days water dripped into the cellar, gurgling, and green mould was creeping up the walls.

He now knew what it was like to be locked up, said the painter. He would never forget those hours in the prison. Sharing a cell with six suspect characters, for hours on end. Work-shy scum, he repeated, the dregs of society. Bread as hard as a stone, that was all he'd been offered. His companions had fallen on it like animals. Uttering hoarse sounds.

Then he was taken on a tour of the manor house, which he called a castle. The billiard room, the ice-cold drawing room, white and gold with all those crates against the wall. And the hearth in the hall, with a fire already burning in it.

'A genuine fire!' he said, rubbing his hands.

Katharina was busy tending the fire, cutting shavings from the firewood stacked by the hearth with a small chopper. Her profile was outlined against the leaping flames. This was one of her bad days; on many days she looked so good that people said: Dazzling! Today she didn't look her best, and she knew it. She merely gave her guest a brief nod; he could see that she had a lot to do. Her long black hair was caught together simply with a slide. And when he began sketching her at once, she was reluctant and hid her face behind the dustpan.

The man stopped in front of the paintings. Paintings both large and small, all in gilt frames. They had been bought along with the estate in 1905. No one had ever shown any interest in them before, no one had taken them down and looked at them closely.

He passed over the pictures of horses hanging among all the

antlers that Eberhard liked so much in the billiards room, but a landscape with cows in the foreground, and the towers of Potsdam in the distance, that was something special. Such a work mouldering away here in East Prussia? He made a mental note that here, entirely unexpectedly, he had come upon a remarkable picture of Potsdam. It wasn't really right for it to be hanging in this house. He knew the Reich Curator of Art in Potsdam personally, he said, and he felt sure he would want to buy it at once.

That was all very interesting, but Katharina wondered why they would want to sell the picture. It's been hanging here for ever, she said.

Where did these things come from? Where would they end up?

Then he turned to the large, dark portraits: what about these monsters? he wondered. He took them carefully down from the wall, one by one, and stood them side by side. They were heavy – he mustn't drop one and break its frame. 'For goodness' sake!' said Auntie. 'I hope this will be all right!' What would Eberhard say?

The painter wiped the pictures with a duster, but nothing else came to light. They were portraits; you could hardly even make that out. And there was no inscription of any kind, no coat of arms, no signature. They could be portraits of anyone. Dead and gone, rotting away, worm-eaten.

He could investigate them more thoroughly, he said, given cotton wool and warm water. He would be glad to make himself useful in return for the delightful welcome he had found here, the hot milk and bread and honey.

Peter brought the painter cotton wool and water, and then he set to work on the pictures. He did it very gently, dabbing a little here and there, going very cautiously.

'This is very interesting,' he said, showing the grubby cotton-wool ball he was holding, 'but these people are all very, very ugly. You'll never find a buyer for their portraits.'

He cleaned their eyes; he enjoyed doing that. It was only from the eyes that he removed the dirt, and they shone out of the brown gravy colour, reminiscent of Rembrandt's palette, that surrounded them. Just as the gelding could roll his eyes right back when he thought something wasn't exactly as it should be, these old ladies and gentlemen now looked around them. Where, they seemed to be asking, where the devil were they? Waking from a century of slumber and studying their whereabouts.

The painter hung the pictures back on the wall. The old ladies and gentlemen were back where they belonged; no one was going to take an interest in them again in a hurry.

Auntie said she had another picture upstairs; would he like to see it? It came from her native Silesia.

Yes, he said, he would, but of course his time was limited; he couldn't stay here for long. However, he'd like to look at the picture. Auntie steered him upstairs into her domain and he stood in her room admiring the mahogany furniture. But as for the picture – the thing above her bed? A pavilion in a white frame? No, it wasn't worth more than a glance. Prettily painted, a watercolour, but probably the work of an amateur. Yes, the pavilion was attractive – the picture wasn't.

Before he left the room he pointed to the little picture of Hitler that Auntie had hung over her desk, inconspicuously executed in pen and ink, and said, 'You'd better take that down.' Then he positively lost his temper: didn't she know what sort of a fellow the man was? Hanging it up there! How can any thinking woman bear to have that Austrian looking her in the eye, day after day?

Has she ever seen the Mitkau brickworks, he asks. No? The men who work there? 'They don't have such a nice room as yours . . .' He had talked briefly to two of those poor bastards in the prison cell, had given them his bread. They'd fallen on it like animals.

And what, he asked, did she think the Russians would say when they set eyes on that picture?

He went over to the window and pointed to the housing estate. An intolerable sight, he said, houses all marching in step with each other.

That desk, however, was a beautiful piece of work. To think of it rotting away here.

When they went back out into the corridor, Katharina could be heard moving quickly about in her room. She closed the door and shot the bolt. She could do without the visitor looking in to make sure everything was all right with her.

Did he really think, asked Auntie when they were down in the hall again, that the Russians might come to Mitkau?

'Ah, well,' said the painter, laughing, no, he didn't think so, but all those tanks being sent out to ward them off – the Nazis wouldn't be doing it for no reason at all.

It sounded as if he were really saying: yes, they might come.

'Our men will throw them straight back to the Urals.'

The wind had died down, and the sun was shining strongly; thawing ice even dripped off the branches. He stepped out into the fresh air. *I must be gone, I cannot stay*, he said, quoting a folk song, and he immediately began sketching the battered finial in the shape of a spiked mace over the pediment. The oak and the tree house in it, the crooked door in the crumbling wall. He drew the castle that wasn't a castle so that it was framed by the crooked door. And the spiked mace, of the morning-star type, was at the very top, in the middle.

After that he drew the two Ukrainian women as they hurried off to the Forest Lodge to tell their friends about him, scarves wrapped round their head and shoulders. Vladimir was making a rope in a leisurely way. He had tied one end to the stable door and was working along its length, with strings hanging from his belt, as he worked them in.

Peter watched the artist recording all this for posterity. A pity he'd be taking the pictures away with him.

How lovely shines the morning star . . . he asked Peter if he knew that hymn. *Kindly, dearly . . .* The morning star is Venus. Sometimes you can see the planets in daylight, but in the evening Venus is the evening star. *O thou, my gracious evening star*, as the Young Pilgrims sing in *Tannhäuser*. Venus, yes . . .

Those who got hit on the head in the Middle Ages by the morning-star kind of spiked mace no doubt saw stars of a very different kind.

Finally the artist said, 'I'm off, then, my friend', and put away his sketch pad. He stopped one of the carts jolting by and went off.

Where had he come from? Where would he end up? It didn't matter. The main thing was, he was going away.

Peter was cross with himself; he wished he had told the artist about the ruins in the wood. The columns that had fallen over backwards would surely have interested the man. And now they were lost from the records for ever.

Maybe he would also have been interested in Peter's little sister's lonely grave in the woods? But Peter didn't think about that any more, no one did.

*

Auntie stood by the telephone. Should she or should she not? Could a man be allowed to travel the country stirring up discord? Calling Adolf Hitler 'that fellow'? Oughtn't everyone to be united behind the Führer? Particularly now.

Who did you call when everyone was to unite? Who was responsible? The Gestapo or the Criminal Investigation Department of the police force?

What was the Gestapo's phone number? The number of the police force was in the phone book. Would a call like that be handled discreetly? Would she have to appear in court?

The man was certainly over the hills and far away by now.

Perhaps she could ask Drygalski for advice, or Herr Serkander?

Katharina was sitting in her little room. Why did I go to see the pastor, she wondered, as if the devil were after me? The idea of taking in a total stranger! Then again, why didn't I just say no? If only Eberhard had been here, if she could have asked him . . .

She went back and forth through the argument in her head hour after hour. And other fears were added to these new ones: that daring visit to the seaside with Sarkander, the trip that had never become publicly known. Were there people who had some idea about it? Eberhard hadn't heard of it. Or had he? Had someone told him? There had been a certain coldness between them. Something had been lost.

Oh dear, is all our happiness gone?

She couldn't really picture the man whom the pastor had said she might be asked to shelter here. Maybe young, maybe old? Shabby in appearance, or with a pistol in his hand?

Very interesting, really. Who would have thought of having an experience like that? What strange times these were.

*

He could sleep in the cubbyhole off her room. She pushed the chest aside, opened the little door, stuffed all sorts of cushions and blankets inside and tried out the bed. Crawled in on all fours. It smelt of tobacco and chocolate in there.

Or perhaps the idea would fall through. Brahms might call and say: It's all over, dear lady, the man's already been captured. Or: We've thought of another solution.

She thought of the man she would be asked to shelter as a little like the painter downstairs. Small, sharp-witted, something of a scamp. Or was he a skeleton with dysentery?

No, she told herself, I won't let myself in for this.

She listened for sounds down below in the house. The man seemed to have left. She wouldn't have wanted him breaking into her boudoir here like some kind of art expert! Perhaps he would have admired the *Crouching Woman*?

She leafed through the album of silhouettes. What a good thing she hadn't shown him that; the man would probably have made derogatory remarks. She did those little pictures just for her own pleasure, and they were nothing to do with anyone else. But just suppose she had?

That picture the man had drawn of her, with the dustpan in front of her face? She'd have liked to see it, but now it was too late. Maybe that was the last time, she thought.

She took the shavings of wood and put them in the stove. The fire had gone out; she'd have to relight it.

9

Drygalski

Drygalski had once kept a shop, Groceries and General Stores, but the international economic crisis had finished him, and his shop had gone under the hammer, leaving him out on the street with his wife and family. He had gone hither and thither looking for work, hat in hand. Southern Germany, western Germany – no luck at all in Cologne, Görlitz, Bremerhaven, and then he had felt impelled to return to his original home, the beautiful province of East Prussia, where, as he put it, his cradle used to stand.

And it was there that the National Socialist Party had taken him on. He had found a berth in the Regional Homestead Office of the German Labour Front, the Party's own trade union organization, which replaced all former trade unions. He became head trustee of the local Labour Front, and made much of that title.

'I'm head trustee now,' he told his wife at the time, and she had breathed a sigh of relief. Things were looking up at last.

Head Trustee Drygalski of the Regional Homestead Office, Mitkau Branch, unemployed for a long time but now in a permanent position. He wore brown jackboots and a little moustache like Hitler's. The family's poverty-stricken existence had ended when the National Socialists came to power. There were still boxes full of exercise books and erasers in the attic of his house on the estate, and crates containing soap powder, nail brushes and floor-cloths from the bankrupt stock of his shop.

'What does he think he looks like?' said the Globigs, laughing behind the net curtains when he came down the road. 'Oh, do look, here he is again!' He strode along as if he had to carry a storm-tossed banner against the enemy, forging his way uphill through wind and weather, and the Globigs sat behind their net curtains laughing, and said he was a real bigwig.

It was Drygalski's great grief that he didn't have the aristocratic particle *von* in front of his surname. None of the research he carried out into his forebears showed that he was related in any way to the German polar scientist Erich von Drygalski, who had spent months in the Arctic, measuring the thickness of the ice and the direction of the wind. He had sent letters again and again to the scientist in Munich – it was only a small step from 'Drygalski' to 'von Drygalski' – might such a connection not be possible? None of his letters had been answered. Even a request to the Munich Regional Homestead Office for aid had borne no fruit, and there was no trace of a relationship in church registers either.

Drygalski had begun taking an interest in the wind and the weather himself; he had bought an anemometer, checked the temperature out of doors morning and evening, and tapped the barometer. In spite of the cold, he also wore his coat unbuttoned when he walked through the housing estate, letting it swing out behind him to show that he didn't mind the icy temperature at all. Although he had splayed toes and flat feet, he thought: We're a tough lot in this family. And when he met the foreign workers from the Forest Lodge, he drew air in sharply through his nose.

As head trustee of the German Labour Front on the Schlageter Settlement, he had been given a larger than usual corner property, Number 1 Ehrenstrasse, and now he felt responsible for the people who had moved there, for the young community beginning to form. The Albert Leo Schlageter Settlement – such a name pledged you to do what you could. He regularly went from house to house, collecting voluntary contributions for the Winter Aid organization – no one was to go cold and hungry – and he inspected the estate in summer to make sure that the gardens were free of weeds, and in winter to see whether snow had been swept away. Gates must be securely locked in the evening, not left open, wasn't that so? Or what would the place look like? Snowmen are fun, yes, but who needs one in front of every house? After a while they hang their heads and collapse . . .

So he went on his rounds every day, even if the dogs barked at him from one fence to the next.

The position of head trustee and the house on the corner plot – the Drygalskis might have felt well off now, but since their son had lost his young life in Poland the house was terribly empty. As a child the boy had liked to watch his father slicing sausage, had crawled up and down stairs on all fours, and later had slid down the banisters. In the new house, here in the Settlement, he used to sit in his room for hours, looking thoughtfully into the distance. Sunsets aroused enraptured thoughts in him, and he put them down on paper in rhyme. One day it had been discovered that he was writing poetry, and he'd had his face slapped. And now it was very quiet upstairs. No one went into the young man's room any more.

The Drygalskis' parlour, furnished with large chairs and a round coffee table, was kept for best; you never knew who might drop in at No. 1. The District Leader himself had come to see them once. In his office, Drygalski had a roll-top desk, a table with a typewriter and telephone on it, and a much-used sofa stood in the kitchen that was also a sitting room. Smooth covers were stretched over the twin beds in the bedroom. A picture of the couple's son, Egon Drygalski, hung above the beds. He had fallen in Poland, shot in the head as he stormed forward, and died at once. The picture had been copied by a comrade of his from his passport photograph, but the network of lines that had been drawn on the face to ensure that it bore some similarity to the dead man could still be seen; the artist hadn't been able to erase them completely. An ancient bunch of sweet woodruff was wedged into the pinewood picture frame, and was dusted once a month. A crucifix hung beside the picture, his wife insisted on that.

Drygalski didn't just make sure that all was well on the housing development; for years he had also been keeping the Globigs under observation. It was true that the centuries-old oaks of the Globig property warned the Schlageter Settlement, with its brand-new birch trees, to stay where it was, calling a halt to any further advance, as the mayor had said when laying the foundation stone of the Settlement, but what about that peculiar tree house in the branches of the oak, with sacks of some kind hanging out of it? And half a motorbike was balanced in front of the tree house, maybe even nailed to the trunk somehow? They let that boy have all the freedom he wanted; to be sure, he was a fair-haired Aryan, a real German boy, but he didn't turn up to do his Hitler Youth service, and his mother seemed somehow disengaged from the world; she should be called to order as a matter of urgency, but she never showed her face. He had no opportunity to tell her his opinion of her.

When he thought how he had shown *his* son what was what. He'd been hard on him, so hard that his wife had often asked if it was really necessary. Their son would run upstairs, howling, shut himself in his room and sob.

*

'Nothing matters to Frau von Globig,' Drygalski told his wife. 'She must get wind of things in advance. And just let me give her son a piece of my mind . . .'

Get wind of what things in advance? Since Herr Drygalski had been feeling better, his wife had been feeling worse, at first just hanging listlessly round the place – 'Pull yourself together, Lisa' – then lying down a good deal, and now bedridden. The doctor sometimes came with his bag, but he left shrugging his shoulders. Wasn't there anything to be done for her?

His son fallen at the front, his wife pining away, and now rats in the cellar, if he read those tracks correctly.

The Georgenhof over there, ivy climbing all over it, and the crooked spiked-mace finial askew above the gable – what would the people who drove past think of it? On one side of the road the neat, clean housing development, roof beside roof, all set out in straight lines, and opposite it the manor house, once painted yellow but now overgrown with ivy, and with grass hanging out of the gutter.

The courtyard wall needed repairing again, too. Romanticism is all very well and good, but a wall is a wall, and when there are cracks in it they have to be mended. And the implements that had been lying around for ever, a roller, harrows of some kind, all broken and decrepit. A rusty ploughshare – that symbol of a new era, rusty? And the yard gate hanging off a single hinge. If the gate stands open all the time, day and night, why does anyone need a wall?

He'd asked, Heil Hitler, couldn't those tools be given away as old iron, melted down to make tanks and cannon, and Auntie had said, 'We still need them all.' Had even added, 'What on earth are you thinking of?'

As for his own house, Drygalski kept it in good order. At least, if a door stuck, he repaired it at once. And he drew up a regular cropping plan every year for his garden behind the house: kohlrabi on the left, runner beans on the right. Fruit bushes along the fence; they needed pruning now. Nothing the matter but the rats. How to deal with them was still a puzzle.

There was something wrong with the gentry over the road. Putting out the swastika flag only when absolutely necessary, and then it was just a tiny little rag of a thing.

Drygalski kept looking over at the Georgenhof, the big house beyond the oak trees. It stood there like an island. When he was chopping wood behind his house he looked that way, or when he was feeding the rabbits. Even when he was getting his wife to drink soup he looked out of the window. She had been in bed for weeks, pale and suffering. He gave her oatmeal porridge, and had to be on the watch all the time in case she brought it up again. She hadn't left her bed for months.

Yes, when Drygalski plumped up his wife's pillows, he had a view of the grand property over there, the yellow house where Auntie sat at her window overlooking the road.

He could see the house and who went in and out of it from his desk, and when he telephoned, and from the kitchen stove as well. Even from the lavatory he could see it as he did up his trousers, and Auntie made sure to return his glances.

When Drygalski had to go into town he liked to take a short cut through the park, although it didn't get him anywhere much, so he had made it a habit to trample round the manor house. A notice on a cracked board said NO ENTRY, but surely these people didn't have the nerve to claim land for their sole use when they went walking for pleasure, did they? After all, the German forest was everyone's property. And he blew his nose extra loud into the rhododendrons to right and left. In summer he had once seen the whole tribe of them here as he stood with his hands in his pockets. They were picnicking on a rug spread on the grass, drinking punch, the uncle from Albertsdorf, aunts and children dressed in white all over the place. They had waved to him as if to annoy him on purpose.

He could always find a reason to prowl round the outside of the house. And now, in winter, he had trodden a semi-circular path through the snow behind it.

The women workers from the east, the Polish driver – their credentials had all been repeatedly checked, and there was nothing to be done about them. They wore the symbol marking them out as foreign workers, but they kept going off to the Forest Lodge to see the foreign riff-raff there, the Czechs, Italians and Romanians. 'They're hatching some kind of plot,' he told his wife. 'And they steal like magpies!' He took his pistol down from the wall and loaded it. The priest from Mitkau who never called on the Drygalskis, even though they were good Catholics, went in and out of the Georgenhof as he liked. What a nerve.

Last summer Eberhard von Globig, in his white uniform jacket with the Cross of Merit on his breast (the plain Cross of Merit, though, no additional swords), had gone riding through the housing estate as if to take a look at it, had said hello in a friendly way (in too friendly a way?), had watered his horse at the Schlageter Fountain, a good horse called Fellow that then had to be handed over for the war effort, and had bent down to Drygalski and asked how his wife was. (He had refused an invitation to come into the house.)

All the same, Eberhard von Globig had sent him a little bag of brown sugar and a canister of sunflower oil. 'Make your wife something good to eat.'

'You have to butter these people up,' Eberhard had told Katharina. 'Who knows what may happen?'

*

Now the Russians were on the border, the sirens howled every day, and the sound of pigs squealing in agony at their death rang through the housing development. People were slaughtering all their animals and packing up their possessions just in case, although it was strictly forbidden to think of flight. Carts stood behind the houses, carts large and small, weatherproofed with straw and roofing felt. Every crack was painted to keep bad weather out, too.

Suppose the Globigs were packing up as well? It would be a good moment to catch them at it, thought Drygalski. Then he could ask them whether by any chance they thought the Russians would get as far as Mitkau. Didn't they trust the German Wehrmacht? The Russians had been beaten back in the autumn, hadn't they?

The People's Comrades who had come from the east, from Tilsit, from Lithuania and Latvia, couldn't be asked whether they trusted the German Wehrmacht. They'd have given the right answer or none at all.

Drygalski asked his wife whether she needed anything, put his cap on and strode over to the Georgenhof. He found a pig hanging from a ladder while the Pole gutted it, with the girls lending him a hand. They stopped chattering at once when they saw the man from the Settlement coming. Brown jackboots and a Hitler moustache?

'Killing pigs, are we?' asked Drygalski, and he almost pinched blonde Sonya's cheek on a whim. Good healthy stock, she seemed.

He addressed Auntie, who was rendering lard in the kitchen. Heil Hitler, was she weighing everything accurately and handing it in to the authorities?

'Yes, yes,' she said, showing him a list with items crossed off it. 'It's all being delivered.'

He was offered a saucer of boiled pork; would he like to try it? Yes, he would. And he asked for some salt, went over to the Pole and watched for a while as joints of meat were thrown into various different tubs, to make sure he was doing it properly. He thought of his grocery shop, and the way he always sliced the ham so nicely on the slicing machine, and gave the children ends of sausage.

Jago the dog watched the Pole as well, taking an interest in his own way. The cat, as usual, made himself scarce. He knew he wouldn't be forgotten.

Drygalski examined the big farm cart standing in the farmyard, broad and heavy, and sure enough, its sides had already been reinforced, and it had been provided with a kind of roof. So they were already packing up here too, were they? But as he was holding his saucer of pork he refrained from asking more revealing questions.

Now that Fellow had been handed over for the war effort, the Globigs had only three horses left. Two for the big farm cart and the gelding for the coach, wasn't that so?

Auntie took this opportunity to tell him that a very strange painter had been here, the artist kind of painter, saying very odd things.

An artist? What for? Making a record of antiquities? Drawing architectural features of interest?

But then why hadn't the man been sent over to the Settlement to draw the Schlageter Fountain? Drygalski couldn't understand that. And he went once round the house and then back to the Settlement to look at the fountain, which was a really ornamental piece. The bronze plaque on it was turning slightly green. Thank heavens there were photographs of the monument; it was shown from all angles in the newspaper supplement *Mitkauer Land.* The photographer had gone to a great deal of trouble.

But fancy not telling the artist about the fountain – that really was too bad.

Dr Wagner too had turned up to join the pig-butchering party, in his warm walking coat, knitted gloves and black ear protectors. He had brought a small can with him and asked Auntie for some of the broth from the sausages. And as he stayed put and did not look as if he would be going away in a hurry, he got his broth and a little pork to go with it. He knocked his shoes together because he had cold feet. Nothing was easy.

Meanwhile Peter dragged the Christmas tree out of the hall and left it in front of the house. The tree, once covered with lights, had served its purpose. He should pour a little melted lard on the branches, said Dr Wagner. How happy the birds would be!

They climbed up to Peter's room, followed by the cat and the dog, to go on with his studies. They put some wood in the stove, and Katharina joined them.

German Cathedrals. She showed them the book and talked about the painter who had been here, drawing everything, every nook and cranny. Who had even taken an interest in the pictures in the hall and the rather decrepit finial with its spiked mace. How good that there are people who care about such things. Although . . . wouldn't photographs have been cheaper? Drawing pictures of everything was such a laborious way of going about it.

Wagner leafed through the book about German cathedrals. Ah, Speyer, ruined by the French ages ago; Worms, gutted like a pig. And now the air raids: so many already destroyed. Lübeck, Königsberg and Munich. Dr Wagner thought of all the other buildings now gone. Whole towns, bridges, museums with all their contents. Paintings. Valuable libraries perishing on the pyres of burning cities.

What a good thing there were people still trying to save what could yet be saved, at least in a small way.

Even beauty must die, though she rules men and gods alike.
Yet the adamant breast of Stygian Zeus she cannot sway.

So said Schiller. These terrorist gangsters couldn't tear the poetry in his head out of him, said Wagner. And with his silver pencil he marked those verses in Echtermeyer's anthology of German poetry that must be preserved for posterity. It would be a good idea to learn them by heart.

Then he recited several poems in a sing-song tone of voice, as old people did, his eyes filled with tears, and he buried his face in his hands, the brown marks of old age and large veins on the back of them, to sob into them. The fate of his fatherland moved him deeply, anyone could see.

Katharina pushed the plate of bread and sausage over to him. Her mind wasn't on what she was doing; she was thinking of something else entirely. It was as if she wanted to ask a question, but she couldn't bring out what was troubling her here and now. A mysterious guest was to be smuggled into the house. Today? Tomorrow? The day after tomorrow? Perhaps not at all. Smuggled into her room, to be more precise. But how was it to be done? She thought about it. She thought of those lines by Goethe:

where darkness through the thicket broke,
with countless sombre, baleful eyes.

For her to hide him, he would have to cross the hall – and that would be out of the question. Go up the creaking staircase? Past

Auntie's room? Auntie was always on the watch. What about Jago the dog?

Going through the kitchen wouldn't work, and in any case he'd have to pass the hall and the suspicious Jago, and then climb the creaking stairs. The more carefully you tried to slink up them the louder they would creak, the more secretly you went about it the more boisterous the dog would be.

The only possible way was to start from the park, scale the fence for the climbing roses, get into her conservatory and then into her room.

Perhaps he was an old man, and wouldn't make it here anyway. Then she'd be sorry, but it would be the doing of a higher power.

As evening drew in she put her white Persian lamb cap on and drove to Mitkau. She would have to speak to Brahms and see if the whole thing couldn't be called off at the last minute.

She took Dr Wagner with her. He held the little can of sausage broth between his knees. He looked sideways at her and was glad to see how boldly she handled the reins.

Like a white hand, the aurora borealis felt its way across the sky – whoosh – and an unusual roll of thunder could be heard. A winter thunderstorm?

A poem by Eichendorff went through Wagner's head as he sat beside the beautiful woman, holding his can of sausage broth in both hands.

Katharina had to show her identity card at the Senthagener Tor, and was asked what she wanted to do in the town. 'Ah, Frau von Globig. And who's this gentleman? Oh yes, Dr Wagner.'

A wooden barrier was pushed aside and she drove through the echoing gateway.

*

An icy wind swept clouds of snow ahead of it down the streets. Katharina thought: I could still go back. Just turn round and get into bed at home, hear nothing, see nothing. I could simply not go to see the pastor, he would wait and wait and then give up and tell himself: The lady changed her mind.

Her warm room, the books, the radio ... Why let herself in for daring ventures that were nothing to do with her?

She dropped the teacher in Horst-Wessel-Strasse, held his hand just a moment too long – he might take it for a budding interest in him. And then she tugged the bell pull of the parsonage, where Pastor Brahms was already waiting for her, his watch in his hand. The black bulk of the church stood next to the parsonage, where a load of snow was sliding off the roof.

He greeted her, looking up and down the road at the same time; a guest so late, with a horse and carriage! What would the neighbours think?

He asked her in, shaking her hand with one of his own and leading her in with the other – leading her into his dark, stuffy study.

There was a copying machine beside the wall; he had just been turning its handle.

Almost immediately he explained it all to her again in detail. Explained what it was about. It was a case of conveying a human being on the run, escaping pursuers, from one hiding place to another. It was a case of taking in an entirely unknown person of the male sex whose fate, fundamentally, was nothing to do with her. Goodness knew what he was supposed to have done.

It was a question of giving shelter, for a single night, to a human being who couldn't show his face at an inn. For just one night, so really only for a few hours, that was what it was about. And this was the night.

Did Pastor Brahms know whether the man was something to

do with the July plot, or a deserter? Or maybe even a communist, a man who had once broken the windows of the capitalist class and blasphemed against Our Redeemer? One of the Red Front? – Or a Jew? There were fugitives all over the country, passing through towns and forests, staying briefly in old factories and garden summerhouses, crouching in cellars and attics.

His informants had said, 'For God's sake help the man.' That was all, even Pastor Brahms knew no more. He too would be seeing the stranger for the first time tonight. And next morning the stranger would be sent on again somewhere else.

But nothing would be the same as before.

Be that as it might, she noticed a certain callous streak in the pastor. Katharina gave him a small sausage. He immediately cut a piece off it with his penknife and pushed it behind his gums like chewing tobacco. They were sitting in his dark study, the clock on the wall struck, and on the table lay a commentary on the Revelation of St John: I am Alpha and Omega, the beginning and the ending. Pastor Brahms was preparing a cycle of sermons on the end of time for the old people in the monastery; he preached on a different apocalyptic chapter every evening. 'And the heaven will open like a book . . .' The old, sick people there, brought from somewhere in the east, barely able to understand German, now side by side in the cold monastery; they had seen better days. Now they lay in the refectory, with the gentle curve of its vaulted ceiling above them, and the blue and gold stars in the vault.

Day after day he was preaching to the old people about the Day of Judgement, when all time ends and we go to the right or the left hand of God, and only then would it be seen who was found wanting and who would stand the test. To think that so many would be cast out into the fiery lake.

He said to Katharina, seeing her tremble and hesitate, 'It must be done, and today.'

What kind of a man would he be, she wondered, and would it be dangerous? Aren't there laws of some kind? And then there was her husband, what would he say when he found out that she was giving shelter to someone, to a *man*? In her room? Was he an officer, anyway? And was it really to be today?

'Listen,' said the pastor. 'Yes, it must be so.'

After she had said everything she was feeling, she suddenly added, 'Yes.' She was impelled to say yes, something in her said it. She would do it, take the man in, in God's name, and for a few seconds she became another person. Or perhaps she said yes only to get out of that dark room where the pastor sat in front of her, chewing her sausage.

He drew back the curtain over the darkened window and peered into the yard, penknife in hand, through a crack in the blackout material. He put his forefinger to his lips: a visit from Frau von Globig, who never usually came here, at this late hour? What would the neighbourhood think? Weren't the neighbours already on the watch? – Brahms had known there to be someone crouching beside the water butt in the yard to listen in on what he had to discuss with the members of his congregation. But surely no one would think of crouching in the yard at this time of night, when the temperature was fifteen degrees below zero.

'All right.' The pastor took out his handkerchief and blew his nose loudly. So now this woman joined the roster of those who were to save a human life. That life would be handed on from one of them to another. And it would be done this very night.

How people can rise above themselves. He'd preach a sermon

about that one day. Not yet, but the hour would come, and it would come soon, when he could announce that fact. When he could free himself of fear for his own life, like Abraham freeing the ram from the thicket.

Then they came to what he called the *procedere*. How and where was the man to be hidden?

Although Katharina had just said yes, listening to herself and not quite clear what it meant, it turned out that she had a good idea of how to smuggle a man into the manor house and hide him there, in spite of Auntie, the boy and the dog Jago. The Pole and the two Ukrainian girls mustn't notice anything either, and of course on no account must Herr Drygalski, that snoop who went tramping round the house almost every day, looking up to check the blackout at the windows.

She told the pastor how the stranger could get to the path that Drygalski had trodden in the park and climb the picket fence with roses growing over it.

Several times Brahms got confused by her account: *Round the house?* Through the park? *Climb the fence?* The question was whether the poor man would be able to climb the fence at all, was he strong enough? And, 'Trodden path?' asked the pastor. Where exactly was it? The description was very vague.

Katharina took the red pencil with which the pastor was annotating his Bible, found a piece of paper and did a sketch. Brahms put it on his desk. Then he thanked her, holding both her hands. So now let matters take their course.

When she had climbed up to the driver's box of the coach, the pastor stood in the road for a little longer. Was he going to shake himself and say, at the last minute, 'Oh, you know, I don't think we'll do this, we'll find another solution!' Because those who put themselves in harm's way may perish there.

No, he didn't say so.

The gelding looked back and tugged at the reins. How much longer would he have to wait? The animal was so cold that he too wanted to be back at the warm Georgenhof.

And as the pastor returned to his copier, Katharina drove away, clip-clop, the dark-haired woman in her white Persian lamb cap. She skirted the inside of the town wall, and branched off through the dark town itself. Should she look in on Felicitas, consult her? Pour out her heart? What would her friend say about this? That what she was doing was great? Felicitas could understand anything. Would she admire Katharina for her courage? But now, in her condition, she had other worries. And there was her husband in Graudenz, with all those deserters being shot every day.

Or Dr Wagner? Could she go over the whole thing with him, quietly? Wasn't he a very sensible man? And hadn't she given him bread and sausage? Couldn't she discuss matters with him? But the schoolmaster was in his own living room. He had warmed up the sausage broth and eaten a slice of bread and curd cheese with it. He was reading Livy. Perhaps he might venture on a new translation of the historian?

Katharina drove over the marketplace, past the Smithy Inn. The show at the cinema was just over, and people were streaming out, laughing and linking arms. The film had been *The White Dream* . . .

> *Riding on the merry-go-round*
> *With her feet above the ground,*
> *Isn't she a pretty sight?*
> *A skating star dressed all in white.*

The prison. The town hall. Might Lothar Sarkander still be at his office?

She drove past the church again. The desiccated bridal wreath swayed where it hung. Could she still back out? Yes, she could reverse the whole process. There was time for that.

Should she rush back into the parsonage to see Brahms, weeping, crying out, 'I can't do it!' Surely the man would understand? He might be relieved himself.

The pastor stopped what he was doing and listened. Was that woman coming back? No, it was too late for that now.

She was stopped again at the Senthagener Tor. She had to show her identity card once more. 'Oh yes, Frau von Globig – out and about in this cold weather?'

She didn't want to know if there was a man sitting in the back of the coach.

The church clock struck six. The pastor turned the handle of the copier: the stranger would soon be knocking at his door. So he must wait. He would send him on into the night, that was all agreed; he would feed him first, reassure him, and then send him on. The sketch of the Georgenhof lay on the table. Nothing could happen now.

Tomorrow evening, under cover of darkness, the man would come back again and then be sent on once more.

What were twenty-four hours?

And in future he could keep well out of such things, couldn't he?

The Georgenhof lay ahead, dark and menacing beneath the oak trees. Katharina got down from the coach and put her arm round the gelding's neck.

'Oh God,' she said out loud.

The horse put his ears back; everything was all right.

10

The Stranger

That evening Katharina sat in the hall with Peter and Auntie. The wind was blowing huge snowflakes round the house and whistling down the chimney.

Then it suddenly died down, and all was still. The Ukrainian maids were quiet. They had gone over to the Forest Lodge with little gifts from the pig-slaughtering party – tripe, chitterlings, kidneys – so that the lads there could share the sense of plenty up at the house. The girls didn't want them to go short. Probably they were already frying those delicacies, with the Romanian playing cheerful tunes on his accordion.

Katharina picked up a cloth and went from picture to picture, dusting the frames, then sat down again with the others, sighing. How much time did she have left? What business of hers was this man who was going to climb into the house? And why was he to do it? Whatever his troubles were, they were probably his own fault.

She could well understand, said Auntie, why Katharina was moping like that. Dear Eberhard so far away, and all the comings and goings of the last few days, all those people! Visitors had been arriving so thick and fast, it was about time to have peace and quiet in the house again.

She could really do with a glass of schnapps, added Auntie, and when she said that there was laughter. Auntie and schnapps! Well, why not after all that had been going on: the crazy stamp collector, the girl who played the violin, the painter yesterday? It would be good to sit back, have a rest and take things as they came.

On the other hand, she wouldn't really mind if someone knocked on the door now, and another guest arrived, bringing life into this place. Then they might hear what was going on in the outside world.

Auntie wondered whether to mention the strange hints that the painter had dropped. Did Katharina know that criminal things were going on in the brickworks, that he'd seen men beaten up there with his own eyes? A pitiful sight they had been.

And telling her to take down the picture of Hitler. What was the man thinking of?

Didn't you have to show something like that? If you didn't defend first principles everything went down the drain. Wasn't the Führer their ultimate prop and stay?

Katharina had heard about the brickworks too. From Felicitas's window she had seen the Senthagener Tor being barricaded in the cold. And her friend had told her about the men begging for food, but the SS man had sent them packing. Felicitas's husband knew such characters from Graudenz. He had said, 'You don't want to give such fellows anything, or you'll never be rid of them. Criminals to a man! They're like burs, brush them off in front and they'll cling to you behind. Anyway, it's forbidden. Give them anything and you're just storing up trouble for yourself!' Yes, Katharina had heard about the brickworks, but it was no business of hers, was it?

In a gloomy mood, Eberhard had once mentioned that all was not going well in the east. He had seen certain things when he went there on duty ... and if the wind turned, heaven knows, he'd said, what might come our way.

And now duty had landed him in Italy.

Katharina hadn't known that Auntie had a picture of Hitler in her room. His book *Mein Kampf* stood in the bookcase, still unread. Uncle Josef had said, 'The man's not as wrong as all that.'

Auntie definitely wanted a schnapps. Nothing was easy, as she always said. Katharina took a small bottle and two glasses out of the cupboard and poured some for both of them. Perhaps it would make her feel less like moping. Peter was given a glass of water, and they all drank a toast to each other.

The boy stirred up the fire on the hearth to burn so brightly that you might think the whole house would go up in flames.

Then Auntie picked up her lute and plucked out the songs of her youth on its strings, singing in her cracked voice. Ribbons hung from the instrument as mementos. Musical gatherings in Breslau. Her dear Silesia; she would never, ever forget her native land. She thought of the day when they were thrown out, and that money-grubber stood in the doorway, hands in his pocket, laughing scornfully. He'd even fired the gardener, saying he had no further use for him, and the gardener had a wife and child. She used to stand on top of his wooden clogs and dance round with him.

Beside the well, beyond the gate
There stands a linden tree.
How many a dream I've had of late,
How many sweet dreams of thee.

'Cheers!' she said, and the women poured themselves more schnapps. Katharina sighed deeply, which Auntie found some-how comical. They talked about people's dispositions, and how *she* always tended to take things lightly. And also, they said, work was a good medicine.

Katharina looked at the time. She got to her feet and walked up and down the room, then opened the door to the summer drawing room – '*Brr!* It's cold!' cried the other two.

The moon had risen, and its huge disc was standing behind the trees. Moonlight fell through the tall, narrow windows into the room.

She looked round, and felt as if she had never before seen the pictures in the wallpaper on which the moonlight fell. A couple with a flute and a mandolin, dancing children, a soldier with a girl on a rearing horse.

She looked at it all as if she had to impress it on her memory for the last time.

The flute concerto at Sanssouci – domestic music-making.

Eberhard had never been a man for going on holiday, the pleasures of dancing were not to his taste, and now there he was in Italy and must surely be doing something or other there. Perhaps there was a pretty child with him? One of those delicate, dark girls who put flowers in their hair? Who knew what was going on there at this hour of the evening?

She imagined Eberhard in a plainly furnished country inn, with a girl pouring wine for him. Perhaps he was telling her about the Georgenhof, and perhaps she didn't believe a word of it.

It was a long time ago since she had stood here with Lothar Sarkander. It had happened quite unexpectedly, in summer, when the doors of the drawing room looking out on the park had been standing open. They had seen the family sitting on the grass, and he had said, 'What a picture!'

Then there was that secret trip to the seaside.

They had been seen sitting in the beach hut, she wearing a broad-brimmed straw hat, he in a pair of white trousers.

Had Eberhard never heard about it?

She kicked the crates containing the worldly goods of the Berlin cousins and said, 'What a pity. We could have had lovely parties here. With dancing.'

Peter followed her and put on the light. A broad beam fell on the snow outside, and the magic was gone.

'For heaven's sake, the planes! The blackout! Suppose Drygalski sees it?' cried Auntie.

So they switched off the light, closed the drawing room door, and sat down in front of the hearth again.

Before Auntie could go back to playing her lute, Katharina went to the telephone and dialled Sarkander's number. Nine o'clock, it wasn't too late for that. She let the phone ring for a long time, but no one picked up the receiver. Just as well – what would she have said to him?

She went into the billiards room, took a board game out of the corner cupboard and put it on the table by the hearth: a polished ashwood board with maple intarsia work, and a little box containing the turned wooden figures that went with it, shepherds, shepherdesses, sheep. Did they all belong together?

'How do you play this?' she asked. But Auntie didn't know either. 'It looks like a very old game,' she said. You probably had to stand the pieces on the board, thought Katharina, setting them out at random.

There were three white dice in a leather cup, and Katharina shook the dice and cast them on the table. A one, a three and a five.

That made nine. Did it mean anything?

'*Nein* for no, perhaps?' said Auntie.

Well, the dice were cast anyway, thought Katharina. She sighed so heavily that Auntie laughed.

Heinrich, the carriage is breaking. Katharina thought of the story of the faithful coachman tacked on to the end of the Grimms' tale of the *Frog King*. But no, there wasn't any iron band around her own breast breaking. She breathed in deeply.

'You'll be all right,' said Auntie. 'If you ask me, you smoke too much.'

Katharina dropped a kiss on the tip of the boy's nose and said goodnight. Then she went to the kitchen to find things to eat. This could be a very long night.

When she opened her door upstairs, she briefly felt something like relief. Her little armchair, the table with the fruit plates, her books – it was all as usual.

But this was not a refuge for ever and ever; an adventure was going to take place here in the next hour, and it wouldn't be a game.

Katharina went into the conservatory and looked out. The moon was as small as a burning glass now, and its light cast the barred shadows of the oak branches on the snow.

Katharina lay down on the bed. She hadn't taken her boots off yet, and she looked through a photo album of the winding railway line over the St Gotthard Pass, with a view into the deep, rocky valley. She had always expected something to go wrong, but the railway made short work of the mountainous journey. Over there in Italy it had been raining. Sunshine here, rain there. And she had thought it was the other way round. Eberhard blinking in the sunlight. 'Got it wrong!' she had written in white ink under the photo.

*

She listened for sounds in the house. The others were going to bed now, too. Peter let the dog out briefly, then his door closed, and so did Auntie's.

Katharina listened for sounds in the house and for sounds outside. She didn't know that Auntie was standing at her own door, also listening, and looking through the keyhole, but everything was dark.

Katharina put the album aside. She was afraid. I am feeling naked fear, she thought, looking in the mirror. It was a feeling she had last had in her schooldays in Berlin, when her young girl's diary had been found. She had been going to write something in it, and it was gone.

Her wedding in the dark church. Until death do you part? Would she be able to last a whole lifetime with Eberhard? *Rise high, O red-winged eagle.*

Pastor Brahms hadn't smiled, he had been in deadly earnest. Until death do you part.

And that dream the night before the wedding. She had dreamt of Eberhard. He had been wearing long gloves, lady's gloves, and he had said, 'I must go and see to the cows now.'

She stood up again and went over to Peter's room. She never usually did that, but now she sat on his bed and looked round the little room. The model railway going through tunnels, socks and trousers on the floor, boots thrown around at random. Paper planes under the ceiling. What a poor little life!

The toy castle stood in the middle of the room, with knights behind its walls. The drawbridge was up.

Once she used to pray with the children every evening, as she remembered goodnight prayers from her own childhood, but when Elfie died the prayers had stopped. Now she would have liked to say one of those prayers for children with Peter . . . *the angels spread their wings, to you creation sings, O Jesus my sweet joy* . . . But it was no good. She neither folded her hands nor opened her mouth.

She had no words at her command, and magic spells wouldn't have been right. And she had never made the sign of the cross.

Should she take the boy to her own room with her? The way she used to in thunderstorms. And barricade everything in? She saw herself standing at the window with the three-barrelled shotgun, the boy beside her with a gun of his own, and they would defend themselves to the last.

She looked hard at herself, and the boy looked at her.

He didn't say, 'Is anything wrong?' or, 'What's up?' He looked at his mother in silence. How long would this last?

Finally she said, 'Goodnight,' and the word leapt out of her throat like a toad.

Katharina was afraid, but she was also a little proud of herself for saying yes to this adventure, and now she had to go through with it. No one had ever trusted her to do anything before, and no one would have thought what was going to happen now possible. Not she herself. Never in her life. She felt proud, but there was fear as well as her pride.

'Cold, naked fear,' she said out loud.

And it also occurred to her that what was about to happen was a lie. Was she really anxious to save a human being, or did she just want to prove that she thought herself capable of something? The wish to do something crazy, like that outing of hers with Lothar Sarkander. Would she have to tell Eberhard about that when all this was over?

And when would it all be over?

*

Everything was recorded in the photo album. Lake Garda – its waters had been smooth and green, with white boats on them. The street singers and the little café. Eberhard had written numbers down on his napkin and worked out, for her benefit, how wonderfully well money grew of its own accord in their account: the English shares, the percentages from Romania coming in. What a good thing they had given up farming . . . And they had discussed what to do with the money that increased as if of itself. Maybe they might even go to America on the SS *Bremen* some day?

Thank goodness they didn't have the estate hanging round their necks any more! Forty thousand acres – horses, tractors, maids, and the reapers from Poland every year.

Lake Garda. They had crossed to the other side in a boat, to the side that lay in shadow. And there was nothing at all going on there. But they'd had a lovely view of the sunny opposite side.

The words under the photograph were 'Eberhard as captain!' He was standing in the boat, shielding his eyes with his hand.

Then Eberhard had to put on uniform, and when gunfire was exchanged it meant the end of the English money, and the Romanians stopped paying. Instead his officer's salary came in, month after month.

He had sent wine and chocolate from France, and cigarettes from Greece. And brown sugar and sunflower oil from Russia.

The telephone on the desk; there was no one she could have talked to at the moment. 'Are you crazy?' Felicitas would have said. She couldn't expect understanding from that quarter. Or could she? Felicitas might even have laughed. 'Don't be daft!'

Perhaps she could have talked to Vladimir the Pole about it. But he was against communists and against Jews, and he certainly hadn't the faintest idea about the plot of 20 July. And then she'd have made herself vulnerable, dependent on his grace and favour. Then he'd have her in the hollow of his hand. He'd sit at the fireside and make the puppets dance.

What about Auntie? Could she go over to see her and say, 'Listen, there's something I have to tell you.'

Auntie had a picture of Hitler hanging in her room.

The idea of Drygalski occurred to her – why wasn't there anyone for her to confide in?

She wasn't afraid of Drygalski. She almost felt as if she'd be tricking him.

'We'll deal with this,' he might have said, protecting her from everything.

At this moment Drygalski was sitting at his sick wife's bedside, holding her hand. His wife, grey-faced, was staring at the ceiling.

He thought of their happy wedding, always so happy as they looked forward to it – they had imagined a boat trip to the valley in a folding boat, but nothing had come of that idea. Then they soon had their boy, and then Drygalski was always standing behind the counter, selling an eighth of a kilo of smoked sausage, hoping to get somewhere in life. He'd bought the new sausage-slicing machine – 'Will there be anything else?' – and then came the bankruptcy.

It hadn't been a profiteer who brought him down, but the taxman. He hadn't been up to dealing with the tax office.

They hadn't been angry there, they just kept looking at him and wondering whether he would manage to find something else.

And now came the refugees from the east, from Latvia and Estonia, singly or in groups, on foot, by rail or in horse-drawn carts. So far he had been able to find accommodation for them all. It had been possible to put them up in the Settlement; he had billeted them now here, now there. Everyone had to take in refugees. He had drawn up a plan so that he could supervise them. Refugees: there were some dubious characters among them who might appropriate stuff that wasn't theirs. Many of them never washed, or were always complaining. But there was also a fine old national tradition in those parts, people you could imagine in an engraving, upright and not to be intimidated. German blood that must be saved. The homeland spread its arms to take them in.

Some refugees would have to go to the Georgenhof too. It would be impossible to avoid that. It would be done tactfully. Perhaps suitable people would come along. Recently that retired judge and his wife had been here; they'd have suited the Globigs, but the judge hadn't hung around here for long, he had gone on again. Had taken a good breath of the local air and left. No one stayed here long. A few days, and then they were off again.

Drygalski held his wife's hand. Perhaps, he thought, I should read her something from the newspaper to distract her mind. But how was he to explain that the news now was of 'disengagement'? How was anyone to understand that?

It's a good thing, he also thought, that our son has already fallen, in Poland, or we would fear for him every day now.

He let go of his wife's hand. He must telephone Mitkau, find out if there were more coming from the east again tomorrow, and then go through the lists and think where to put them. Most stayed only a couple of days. There was constant coming and going.

On the stairs he hesitated for a moment. He went up to sit in his son's room, and looked out of the window. In the shadows cast by moonlight, he saw the long black lines of topsoil where the wind had swept the snow away.

In the Georgenhof, Katharina went to the door and put her ear to the keyhole. The dog barked; he heard the maids chattering as they came back from the pleasures of socializing. Should she bring them up here? Or go and sit with them? No, that wouldn't do. What would they want up here?

They down there, we up here – there was no sense of community.

She went into the conservatory, put out the light, drew the curtain aside and looked down at the darkness of the grounds; dark but illuminated by the snow. The semi-circular path trodden in the snow on the grass showed clearly.

She put a shawl round her shoulders. The cacti were wizened, the soil in which the plants grew was dry.

Big stars, tiny stars, sparkling and shining. The moon rose higher and higher. The branches of the oak trees rose in front of its primeval disc. The lines of a hand, lines of fate and lifelines.

The sound of a solitary aircraft moving over the night sky. The pilot would see the farms lying in the snow, the Georgenhof in the snow, the neat and tidy Settlement where every house was just like its neighbour, and Mitkau with its crooked streets.

Would he perhaps take the semi-circular path trodden down below as a signal, as a message, incomprehensible and mysterious?

Or perhaps he would see the solitary man stealing along now beside the road, a note in his hand. A man cursing himself.

Katharina stood at the window, pale in the moonlight. Who would he be?

A distinguished elderly gentleman who had been involved in

the July plot, an officer in civilian clothes, with duelling scars on his cheek? A gentleman of the old school, who had gone riding in the Grünewald Park in peacetime. Had fought in the First World War, in the Second World War, wounded three times. A man like that probably wouldn't be able to climb the picket fence. And would an officer then want to crawl into the cubbyhole on all fours?

A young officer would be welcome. *Two in a Big City* – that romantic film featured a young lieutenant, a blameless character, he has won the Iron Cross, he is passing through Berlin and drinks coffee with the girlfriend he's known for only three days. Katharina remembered the song in the film.

> *Two in the city who seem*
> *To be living a golden dream . . .*

Perhaps a young lieutenant who had deserted for some honourable reason? In trouble and on the run, that kind of thing can happen to young men. He just had time to throw on a civilian coat over his uniform and disappear into the darkness . . . on the run against his will, because at heart of course he was *for* the war. Had it all been for nothing? The columns of tanks, side by side and one after another, moving through the wheat fields of the east along a broad front, and the lieutenant himself standing in the turret of one of the tanks. Those had been the days!

Or perhaps a civilian would come, a man in a shabby suit? Wearing darned, fingerless gloves. Perhaps an artist who hadn't been able to keep his mouth shut. Or an organist. Someone who couldn't stand the killing any longer, who had confided in false friends and now had to save his skin. A man with a wife and children at home.

Or perhaps it would be someone seeking refuge who had been offered a different place to hide? In a different kind of case.

She sat down at the desk. For the first time in her life she wanted to write something that concerned only herself. But she couldn't think what to say. What did concern her? First she had to get this behind her, this experience that perhaps no one would believe later! And then she'd write it all down. Every detail. Her feelings, the suspense – yes, or disappointment, because perhaps it would all be quite different from anything she imagined.

She picked up her scissors and tried to cut a flower out of black paper, something she always did to calm herself down. But it turned into just a tangle of paper strips, and she threw it away.

Should she somehow or other get things ready? Do her hair? Light the candles in the candelabra? Katharina wiped the wash-basin in the bathroom clean – would there be any problems of hygiene? After all, a *man* here. And she kept crawling into the cubbyhole, fussing about the place, trying to make it more comfortable. She pushed the cigarettes, the cocoa and the Italian red wine, the seventeen bottles of Barolo Riserva, as far as she could to the back of the cubbyhole. 'That's something special,' Eberhard had said of the wine. 'We'll drink it when the war is over.'

Inside the cubbyhole she moved a suitcase in front of these secret treasures, and put another mattress on the makeshift bed. The man would be able to sleep there easily enough, wouldn't he? Just for one night. It was nice and warm beside the chimney. And definitely romantic. No one would find him here.

The cubbyhole could be locked. Maybe he should be locked inside it? So many questions to ask, so much to bear in mind.

*

Katharina listened to the news on the radio, softly, softly. The newsreader mentioned defensive battles in the west, disengagements, terror attacks. Not a word about the east. Not even on the BBC. But there was something in the air, you could feel it. The Russians would attack, a roaring horde demanding revenge! But when? Tomorrow? The day after tomorrow? In a week's time, two weeks' time? When? Must it be expected any day now?

> *This little song shall bind us two*
> *Together through all space and time,*
> *This little song from me tells you*
> *That I am yours and you are mine.*

The dog barked at around midnight – after walking up and down, Katharina had just sat down in the conservatory again. And when she was thinking, with relief: he won't be coming, he couldn't find the way, thank God it was all a false alarm – at that moment she heard the dog and saw a man on the semi-circular path. His shadow, cast in the moonlight, was like the hand of a clock pointing on the snow.

Katharina moved the cacti on the windowsill aside and opened the window. She flashed her electric torch once, twice. Then she heard someone climbing over the picket fence, which bent slightly under his weight. The dog was running around in the hall barking frantically. He never usually did that unless a rat scuttled past, or a hedgehog in summer.

Cautiously but nimbly the man climbed up to Katharina, and he was already swinging himself up to the windowsill and over it, bringing some snow with him. Then he was standing there on both feet. If he had fallen down to the garden it would all have been up. 'It was a thief,' she could have said. 'A thief in the night. No, I don't know the man.'

*

Katharina closed the window – cold air had come in – and he was already walking round her room. A small man, unshaven, with the black stubble of his beard showing and a bold expression on his face. 'Done it,' he said, putting his cap down on the *Crouching Woman*. He looked down at her black boots. And smiled: a woman wearing boots?

Then he showed her his hands; the thorns of the old roses on the fence had scratched and torn them until they were blood-stained.

Not an old gentleman, not a smart young lieutenant, not an organist. An ordinary but well-made man. He was wearing a rustic jacket, he had a kind of knapsack under his arm, and he brought the cold in with him. He stood in the middle of the room, listened to the dog barking downstairs and showed her his bleeding hands. Katharina fetched sticking plaster and a pair of scissors and put plasters on his injuries. As she did so, she felt his breath on her.

When the dog had calmed down at last, he walked round the room once more, checked the doors and windows, and then stationed himself by the stove.

His name was Erwin Hirsch, he was Jewish, he came from Berlin and he was cold. Yes, from Berlin, he was trying to get away to the Russians. He had almost been caught in Mitkau by the guards at the Senthagener Tor. Pastor Brahms hadn't warned him of that, hadn't said a word about the guards at the gate there.

It had almost been the end of him then. Obviously an unworldly man, that oddity the pastor . . . he'd had to haul himself up and over the wall, like Joshua's scouts getting into Jericho.

Then all the way here from Mitkau. It had taken over an hour, keeping to the side of the road, flinging himself into the ditch when any vehicle came along, so that no one would see him.

Katharina was shivering too, but not with cold. She stood looking at him, thinking: this is a nice mess.

The man didn't seem to mind the idea of sharing the room with a young woman. He had been through worse than that. Crouching in cellar cupboards, hiding in laundry troughs. He told her about it. He had been on the run for four years. But he didn't laugh at all his adventures. 'Imagine,' he whispered, and Katharina gave him cigarette after cigarette and was not surprised that he used the informal *du* pronoun in talking to her.

At that moment the telephone rang. They both jumped at the same time. It rang so loudly. An uncanny sound! The man flinched back, and Katharina picked up the receiver quickly, in case Auntie came running. 'What's going on? Is everything all right?'

The call came from General Command in Königsberg. A strange voice asked if that was Frau von Globig. 'You're on the phone? Wait a moment, please, don't hang up!' Then there was a click on the line, and Katharina heard her husband asking, from very far away, 'Is that you, Kathi? Can you hear me? Can you make out what I'm saying?' He was sitting over a glass of wine in his quarters high above Lake Garda, looking at the starry sky – 'Lake Garda, do you remember?' It was the head of the battalion's birthday ... 'Are you alone?' Now, he said, she was to listen very carefully. 'Pack your things at once and get away from there, understand? Get away, just leave everything ... First thing tomorrow morning ... The Russians are coming! You'd better go to Aunt Wilhelmine in Hamburg.'

And then the connection was broken.

'That was my husband,' said Katharina. 'How odd, as if he guessed something.' And then it all came pouring out of her:

Eberhard, always so formal, wooden, cold ... Things she had only felt, had never put into words, spilled out.

The stranger had turned pale, and he calmed down only gradually. 'That was my husband, he's in Italy,' Katharina said.

'Yes,' he said, 'these things happen in a marriage.' And whatever else he might have said, he kept it to himself.

Then he sat down at the table, and told all his own stories in a whisper: about Berlin, where he had spent months in hiding, and how he wanted to go and meet the Russians now. And Katharina gave him food and drink. Cold fried potatoes and blood sausage, which the man didn't really like. Katharina gave him an apple too; he turned it in his hands a couple of times, smiled and bit into it.

He sat on the chair where Eberhard had always sat. But Eberhard had never looked as if he were anything but a temporary presence in the room, smoking a cigarette in his meerschaum holder until he had finished it.

He told her long stories, the stories of his whole life, and he told them in order, firstly, secondly, thirdly. He had probably often told them before. At last he stopped, and Katharina showed him the cubbyhole, explaining that he could hide in it. He tried out the hiding place, the blankets and the mattress in it. 'Ah,' he said, 'like being back in one's mother's womb!' And he added, 'It smells nice ... there must be good things here.' Then he lay down at once.

It would have been freezing, but for the chimney above the hearth against which he could nestle. And the padding of blankets and pillows. Katharina had also put a bedside light in the cubbyhole, although they would have to be careful that not a glimmer of light got out under the tiles of the roof.

He made himself comfortable, with the blankets wrapped round him, and when Katharina closed the door he said, 'This reminds me of home. When we were children, we used to make ourselves caves in the bedclothes like this.'

Katharina lay down on her bed and listened. She could hear the pulse beating in her temples.

Then he turned in the cubbyhole and cleared his throat.

When at last all was quiet, she thought of Eberhard. Get away, just leave everything, he had said, and she was to go first thing tomorrow. How did he imagine she could do that? How could she just get up and go?

'Are you alone?' he had asked.

And the man in his hiding place thought of the dark days ahead of him. Really, there was no chance that he could make it.

I hope the end comes quickly, he thought.

11

A Single Day

It was a long time before the man crawled out of his cave next morning. Katharina sat in her armchair and listened, but there wasn't a sound from the cubbyhole. Now and then she thought he might be moving and turning over, and sometimes she heard his heavy breathing.

She took her jewel box out of her bedside locker and tried on rings. Should she wear her pearl necklace? She took off the locket that she usually wore all the time.

Switch on the radio? Better not; it would wake him. Or if he was already awake it would bring him out of his cave. Then he would be sitting here, and what was she going to do with him then?

All the long day ahead.

She leafed through an old magazine and listened.

The household was used to her reclusive existence. 'She's always sitting up there.' Now and then Auntie said she had two left hands, and didn't see work when it was staring her in the face. So it could happen that people never thought of her when there was something to be done. But now Katharina thought: I could lend a hand downstairs. She put the magazine down and stood up.

She wrote a note: 'Please be very quiet! I'll be back soon,' and left it outside the door of the cubbyhole. Then she left quickly, without a sound, in case he emerged from his cave and called out, 'Stop!' Perhaps he would be glad to be alone?

She came back once to close the bedside locker where she kept her jewellery, and went downstairs.

It was cold in the hall. The windows were open and Sonya was cleaning the room. Peter was sitting at the table looking through the microscope. He had put a drop of the water in which he had steeped hay under the lens and was looking for any kind of movement in it, but so far all was still and silent. The world had not been created yet, however much he turned the tube. He asked Sonya, who had done her hair in a braid wreathed round her head, to look through it too, but no, she couldn't see anything either.

'We have much bigger microscopes than that in the Ukraine,' she said as she went out.

Katharina wandered from room to room.

In the billiards room, which was cold, there were three balls lying on the table. She flicked one of them, and it rolled back from the side of the table and disappeared down a pocket.

She thought of putting away the china. The plates were all jumbled up against each other; she didn't see what to do about that.

The silver – she counted the teaspoons, and how strange, there were three too few. All of them neatly embedded in velvet side by side, but not the complete set! Surely she had bought china and cutlery for twenty-four guests at the shop in Tauentzienstrasse?

At this point Auntie joined her, and when she saw Katharina busy with the box of cutlery she cried, 'What are *you* doing here? What's the idea?' and took the box away from her.

'Some of the teaspoons missing?' She couldn't account for it either, but it was easy to lose small spoons like that; they could get swept into the rubbish bucket along with sauerkraut left on the side of the plate ... Maybe they were still somewhere in the kitchen?

Or perhaps the maids had gone off with them? But no, probably not; they must expect to be supervised.

Then she looked at Katharina and said, 'Why, you look like Faith, Hope and Charity – as if you'd danced the night away ...'

The peacock had died in the night. He had fallen off his perch and was lying on the floor. 'Shall I pull out some of his tail feathers? They'd make pretty decorations,' said Auntie.

And something else was new as well. 'Guess what – Drygalski has taken to peering in through the windows!' She had seen a trail of footsteps, said Auntie, leading from the path trodden in the snow to the drawing room. He had obviously been in the park and climbed up to the terrace – the trail was clearly visible. 'I swept it away at once, of course. One of these days he'll be climbing right up to your window.'

Katharina put her hand to her head. His footsteps in the snow! To think that hadn't occurred to her.

Peter was now looking at his own eye, reflected larger than life by the little mirror in the lens. 'You can see your own eye!' cried the boy. And when he wanted to show her how you could see your own eye looking huge through the microscope, she cried out, 'No!'

'What's the matter with you?' asked Auntie. 'Why are you so touchy?' And she got Peter to show her how you could see your own eye looking at you, looking straight back at you with a serious expression.

Katharina closed the window and sat down with the little cupboard, the photographs that stood on it and the cups. Was she supposed to throw all that away, break it? Wasn't this where

Eberhard always used to keep his meerschaum cigarette holder? She'd soon come upon it again ... She took out Eberhard's letters and sorted them into consecutive order. She didn't read them, she knew every line; she skimmed them, but occasional words jumped off the page at her. And their life together ran swiftly before her mind's eye. The early years, and how he had made life in the country pleasant for her. 'You should see this!' and so on, that was his style. She noticed how his handwriting changed in those few years from a childish hand to the writing of a man.

She remembered his habit of reading through letters for the last time when he had written them and correcting characters that he had set down too quickly. The dot of an 'i' here, the loop under a 'g' there, with his little finger crooked to one side. As if he had to approve what he had written. 'And behold, it was very good.'

Nothing was good. The English steel shares, the Romanian rice-flour factory – all the money was gone. So was the land. And a general would be driving around in their fine Wanderer car now.

It was like the Hans Christian Andersen story: 'Oh, my dearest Augustin, all's gone, gone, gone.'

All the same, somehow she felt: thank God. How could all those businesses have been run now? She hadn't the faintest idea.

She listened for any sounds upstairs. Suppose the stranger, entirely misunderstanding the situation, were to open the door of her room and appear at the top of the stairs? He hadn't thought of the footprints either.

She must be more careful.

'I felt a hot thrill of alarm run down my spine,' that was how she would tell the story later. 'The man hadn't even removed his trail after him!'

Later, when it was all over.

*

Among the letters she found postcards from Berlin, the Olympic Games of 1936. Eberhard had gone on his own because of the horses, and she had ventured on that trip to the seaside with Lothar Sarkander. The Isabelle Hotel. They had gone for a long walk up and down the beach. He had held her hand, which he shouldn't really have done, and it was late.

She put the postcards with the letters. 'It's a pity you can't be here too,' Eberhard had written from Berlin.

Should she write to him now? Everything all right here? It's all fine here. Guess what, the peacock has died. Or should she phone Sarkander, remind him of that one lovely day? He had been so different from Eberhard.

No, it was a tacit agreement between them; that day would not be mentioned.

Auntie came in again with a handful of peacock feathers. She stuck them behind the ancestral portraits. Better like that or like this?

She offered Katharina one for her apartment upstairs. 'This is the best one, shall I take it up for you?'

And once again Katharina cried, 'No!' louder than necessary.

Didn't peacock feathers bring bad luck? She remembered old Globig, who had always thought so much of that bird, and how, when Eberhard had introduced her to his father as his brand-new bride, he had always embraced her in a special way in the evening. And later, when he was confined to his bed, he would reach for her.

Katharina did the letters up in a bundle and put them in the little cabinet. She joined the maids in the kitchen and watched them, much to their surprise; they weren't used to having her come into the kitchen and watch them at work. Sonya was stirring a pan of soup, Vera was ironing the laundry.

Three teaspoons missing? Should there be a search? Should the cottage be turned upside down? But surely it all came to the same thing in the end.

Should the police be called?

The maids felt awkward when Katharina was with them, and tried to get her to go away.

Katharina herself didn't know what she was doing in the kitchen, either.

She thought of the man upstairs.

I'll grit my teeth, thought Katharina. After all, it was only for this one day. He would be going back to Mitkau in the night, and Pastor Brahms would send him on somewhere else. She had to get through the day and half a night.

'The worst of it was,' she would tell Felicitas later, 'that I couldn't tell a soul about it. No one was to know.' How surprised Uncle Josef would be, and the cousin in Berlin!

It was all rather exciting really.

Now the Ukrainian maids were beginning to sing in their high voices. What on earth was that song? Was it calling on freedom fighters? No, they were singing:

> *One of the ancient lays*
> *Leaves me so sad at heart.*
> *A legend of bygone days*
> *From my mind will not depart.*

Heinrich Heine; she had learnt that song herself at school.

Eberhard had found the two girls on his last leave, telling them they were to support his wife, but they'd have done that anyway, because Katharina was a gentle soul. There had never been a quarrel, she had given the maids clothes that she didn't wear any more, and she sometimes gave Vladimir the Pole tobacco.

The slaps that Eberhard gave the maids in their first year were another matter. 'You have to be strict with these people from the start,' he had said, and she was sure they had not forgotten it. Yet the maids had come of their own free will, so why slap them? At the time he had thought he must take a firm line, that was it.

Vladimir was standing in the yard chopping wood. He had been chopping wood for weeks on end, and stacking it up neatly like a rampart.

He still wore his military coat and square cap. A letter was embroidered on his jacket: P for Pole. White on a purple background.

He had been there when the Russians invaded Poland in 1939, and the Soviet soldiers had picked him up to transport him elsewhere. A woman neighbour had given him away; without a word, she had pointed to the cellar to show them that a Polish soldier was hiding there. At the last minute, however, he had managed to get away, and then he had ended up in German hands. A German motorbike had been coming towards him, and the men on it had taken him to the nearest prison camp.

Vladimir would have liked to tell people how the Russians had driven his comrades into a pit and shot them there, but he kept that to himself. He had once told the Czech in the Forest Lodge, and it had been a very bad idea. Since then he and the Czech had been at daggers drawn.

He had been given the job of distributing food in the German prison camp, and then he had gone to the Globigs, and he immediately found himself the man in charge of the yard. Eberhard had not slapped him about.

Vladimir did his work, and all was well.

He had a pair of glasses mended with sticking plaster which he put on when he wanted to read the Bible, for Vladimir was a devout man. Now and then the priest looked in and talked to him; they whispered behind the stable door. Once the priest had brought him a letter from Poland. Yes, his family were still alive, just across the border, but out of reach.

For days Vladimir had been reinforcing the big cart with planks. He had realized that they would soon be on the road. The Russians had been driven out of the East Prussian governmental district of Gumbinnen last autumn only with difficulty; that was sixty kilometres away as the crow flies. The terrible pictures of the massacre there for which they were responsible had been in all the newspapers. And that had been only a prelude; they would be back.

Vladimir chopped wood and the Ukrainian maids sang. Auntie hung up the sausages in the larder in order of size. 'There'll be fewer and fewer,' she said out loud. 'And the apples must be turned or they'll get rotten places on them.'

Then Dr Wagner dropped in, knocked the snow off his shoes, said 'Good day' and commandeered Peter. 'Irregular verbs today, my boy,' he said. 'Come along upstairs with me.' Dr Wagner could have used some apples, but no one offered him any this time. 'What are those peacock feathers doing?' he asked. 'Dear lady, don't you know they bring bad luck?' Katharina threw them away at once.

She climbed the stairs, stopped outside her door and listened. All was still. And when she was about to unlock the door, she realized that it wasn't locked, only latched!

Her guest was standing right in front of her, by the stove. He had been turning his jacket pockets inside out and knocking the dust out of them into the coal scuttle.

162

'Are you afraid?' he whispered.

He seemed slightly embarrassed. He was short but well made, with the coarse black stubble of a wiry beard on his chin. Pale. A Jew? He was not what Katharina had expected a Jew to look like; this man didn't resemble the phenotypical Jews in the caricatures. Black hair, and the nice lines round his eyes – were they twinkling at her? Encouraging her to cheer up. What was going to happen? Or was he thinking of something else? When he had turned out his jacket pockets, it was his trouser pockets next. Then he said, 'It will soon be over,' as if he had to comfort her.

No, she wasn't just afraid – she was terrified to the bone! Leaving the door unlocked. Why? So as not to lock him in?

He'd hardly slept at all, he said, not a wink, because of the aromas in the cubbyhole. Chocolate, tobacco! He supposed it was some kind of treasury. It reminded him of his aunt's general stores with the bell inside the shop door.

And now, at last, he could wash. At this time of day no one would notice the sound of running water; it could have been Katharina. He spent ages washing, and then shaved with Eberhard's razor.

Katharina found one of Eberhard's shirts, woollen underpants and socks, and handed them round the bathroom door to him. 'Ah,' he said, 'clean underwear!' She gave him the pullover that Eberhard wore for gardening, too, with EvG embroidered on it.

Washed, clean and freshly shaven, he finally sat down at the table. Bread, eggs, butter and sausage. Such delicacies, he said, he could hardly even remember what they were called. He ate it all, chewing sometimes on one side of his mouth, sometimes on the other, and showed Katharina his teeth – 'Here, at the back on the left!' – he had pulled the molar out himself.

*

163

His long sleep, the food, his shaven face. There was only the hair growing wildly in the nape of his neck. Katharina wondered whether she should cut it for him.

He kept helping himself to the 'delicacies', as he called them. 'Such delicacies!' They lived in the lap of luxury here! 'I don't suppose there's anything hot I could have?'

Pastor Brahms, he told her, hadn't even let him rinse his fingers. A piece of bread put into his hand, and off he had to go. 'No one in Germany thinks of anyone but himself, it's egotism writ large. He wouldn't even shake hands with me.'

Then he told her about all his escapes, going from hiding place to hiding place, for in Germany everyone thought only of himself. More out of fear, he added, than love of the fatherland. And he began whispering his stories again, his firstly, secondly, thirdly.

Before long the man was telling her about terrible things far to the east, and Katharina heard these incredible tales for the first time, in every detail. She knew nothing about those operations, people being taken away, transports. Or did she? Hadn't Felicitas dropped hints; mysterious stories that she hadn't really understood?

And Eberhard, on his last leave, telling her to be sensible? He had been in the Latvian city of Libau, and he knew about things that had happened there; Katharina was to keep it all to herself, for heaven's sake.

Things that you couldn't even imagine.

'I'm glad that the administrative centre there has been closed down,' Eberhard had said, even though the place was flowing with milk and honey.

The stranger kept telling her about such things, and meanwhile he looked out of the window and listened at the door.

He had marked places on the floorboards which didn't creak,

and he walked up and down with great strides as if he were step-
ping over large puddles, while he ran through the misfortunes of
his life. His narrative was like the way he moved from one floorboard to another, bit by bit, long or short, always carefully
picking his way, and accompanying his progress by mime and
gesture, as he went over all that had happened to him.

He had been all right in the old days. He had been a bookbinder,
restoring damaged books in the state library, but they had fired
him overnight. He had been able to do a little more work as best
he could in a cellar, but that came to an end as well.

His wife and children. The archivist had come over to him one
day and said, 'I'm afraid it's reached the point where we can't keep
you on any longer.' Had put a hand on his shoulder. 'Dear Herr
Hirsch, we have nothing against you personally . . .' And then he
had given him another few days of work down in the cellar, but
that was it. Fired overnight. He had had to give back his bookbinder's tools.

Then he told the story, again and again, of all that had happened
to him, telling it in short bursts, rhythmically, and his account
had something anecdotal about it; it was shaped dramatically,
with the aid of accents and effective gestures. He'd had enough
of it, he told Katharina, looking her in the face, he'd absolutely
had enough of it.

He told some of it twice or three times. Katharina had already
heard this or that before.
 Three years in different hiding places, and so on, and so on,
sometimes weeks in one place, sometimes only days. Attics, cellars. And days on foot, walking from one part of a city to another.
Sitting in the cinema. He told these stories over and over again,

and he had noted clearly the different kinds of reception he got. Hard-hearted, unfeeling specimens of humanity . . .

His wife! His children!

Yes, thought Katharina, but there were also people who helped you, my friend. Meanwhile she listened – *ssh!* – to hear whether Auntie was busy in the attic overhead.

His wife. 'Why did I have to go and marry a Jew?' she had said, forgetting the good years, abusing him and complaining. She even talked about the Führer. And then she had left him, went away with the children and everything else. 'I'll have the sheet out from under you,' she had said. 'Why did I have to marry a Jew?' And when he was going to caress the children, she had cried, 'Don't you touch them!' They were half-Jews. It wasn't so simple.

The boys had been dreadfully sad because they couldn't join the Hitler Youth.

While Katharina was still wondering how she could have failed to lock the door, he kept saying he hadn't slept a wink all night. The mice made him nervous, scurrying about, squeaking and scratching. He hadn't dared to yawn for fear one might get into his mouth.

There was a hole in the roof where the icy wind blew through, and the gap was right above his head. Katharina handed him some knitting wool so that he could stop the gap up, but he proved very clumsy. 'How do I do it?' He could repair old sixteenth-century folio volumes, but not a gap in the roof. Katharina crawled into the cubbyhole herself and stopped up the hole. It wouldn't have taken much for him to follow her.

When she crawled out again on all fours, they both laughed, it seemed to them so comical.

Then he told her more about the cellars and attics where he had hidden, and about his wife.

'It's my own fault. My father warned me: mind you don't marry a shiksa, he said.'

At one point he raised his head and looked straight at Katharina. 'I wonder when the Russians will finally arrive. How much longer will it be?'

What kept the Red Army from striking a blow? They bent over a map, and realized that the Red Army was less than a hundred kilometres away, ready for the final leap.

Should he wait for them or go to meet them? That was the question. But in this cold weather?

'If I'd stayed in Berlin . . .'

Go to meet the Russians? Put his hands up, saying, 'I'm a Jew!' But suppose they made short work of him, called him a spy and shot him. Or said, 'A Jew? So what? Anyone can say that, and we have enough Jews of our own.'

To take his mind off it, Katharina told him about her travels, about Lake Garda – and Italy.

He had once been to Italy too, to Venice. How strange! So had Eberhard and Katharina. They had seen Goebbels, all in white, coming out of St Mark's Basilica, and so had the stranger. They must all have been standing quite close.

Why hadn't he stayed in Italy? he asked himself, striking his forehead. And Katharina too thought: why didn't we stay there, following the English steel shares, or go to Romania while there was still time? But of course the rice-flour factory had failed dismally and nothing more was heard or seen of it, and they'd have been stuck in Romania.

Then they had to keep quiet, because they could hear Vladimir talking to the maids in the yard. They were fetching in wood and laughing. Then they whispered to each other. Were they looking up at Katharina's window? The Ukrainian girls must be amused, too, to think that Drygalski had taken to eavesdropping at the drawing room door, as Auntie had told them.

They themselves were presumably discussing whether to wait here, or whether it would be better to go to meet the Red Army.

When all was finally quiet out there, the man said, 'If I had . . . if I were . . .'

And Katharina thought: if he were . . .

They studied the map, their heads close, looking to see how far away the border was and where the Russians might be.

Meanwhile the stranger picked up the Blue Book of *German Cathedrals*, which was lying on the table. Ah, the Germans, he said, their glory days are over.

He went to the bookshelves – supported by gilded bronze brackets – and took out individual books. Stefan Zweig? She'd better not be caught with that, he said. He put the book down beside *German Cathedrals*. He found a book by Jakob Wassermann too, *The Little Gooseboy*. Katharina had had no idea that those two writers were Jewish.

Should she show him her silhouettes? Or the photograph albums? She didn't address him by the informal *du* pronoun, she said 'Herr Hirsch' to her guest, and told him she must go down or her absence would be noticed.

'That's fine, Frau von Globig,' he said. 'That's fine.' And he spoke in a way that suggested it was ridiculous for her to be a *von*, with the noble particle in her name.

She left him alone. Locked the door *twice*, click click, and left him behind to wander between her two rooms, going over his memories.

She put on her white Persian lamb cap and went out into the woods.

I must pass the time, she thought, and not hear any more terrible secrets or endless stories of his wife and children.

The question was, had Auntie noticed her locking the door *twice*, click click? Would she ask why?

Katharina walked to the bank of the little River Helge. The ice lay smooth and grey before her. The wind whistled round her ears. Carrion crows cawed overhead. Distorted willows stood on the bank. There was the big bridge in the distance. The stranger would have to avoid that as he went on his way. It would probably be guarded. Crossing the ice would be safer, he'd be just a little dark dot on the grey ice.

Wood lay stacked in cubic metres on the bank. It ought to have been carted away in autumn, but now it was dwindling. She saw that the boat hadn't been hauled in, and now it was stuck in the ice, rotting. Everything goes to rack and ruin when there's no man in the house, she thought.

She walked along the icy bank. The wind blew into her face. It would be good to go on and on, she thought, to go away and never come back again.

On the way home she passed little Elfriede's grave. She cast it a quick glance. The idea had been to put an obelisk on the grave and later redesign the park round it, but that had never been done. Pastor Brahms had been right when he had reservations. Why not lay the child to rest in the community's graveyard, where everyone else was buried? he had asked. 'Do you want extras? Old Herr von Globig lies here as well.'

She stopped, and her thoughts went back in time. Eberhard had pushed the child away when she put her arms round his neck.

'What a picture!' Sarkander had said in the drawing room. And then she also remembered that Lothar Sarkander had once stood by the grave, and didn't notice that she had seen him.

She made a little detour. She mustn't get back to the man up there too soon. The ruins of the old castle were covered with snow. No fugitive could have hidden in the rubble that filled its vaults.

She would have liked to talk to the people in the Forest Lodge. One of them was an Italian. She'd never looked closely at those people. Perhaps there were educated men among them. But none of them were here of their own free will, and they must be lonely, without any women at all.

She'd never noticed much.

Now the Czech came out of the back door, the man with his leather cap, and he was alarmed to see Katharina. He was on his way to fetch timber from the wood, meaning to steal it. Katharina greeted him and made a gesture, as if to say: Help yourself.

The Czech was not friendly. He had made his way into the manor house once, and Vladimir had chased him out.

He was welcome to get himself wood, Katharina told him.

That's what he was doing anyway, he said, as she might imagine.

Katharina looked at the time. She would have liked to talk to the man for longer, but he set to work at once, breaking off branches. Should she help him?

On the way back she met Drygalski. He was going into the woods too, and he practically ran into her arms.

'Going for a walk?' he asked. 'Isn't it too cold for you?' And he looked behind her to see whether, Heil Hitler, she was alone or in company. Frau von Globig had never walked in this part of the grounds. Was she out to catch timber thieves?

Was Drygalski here to help himself as well? That was the question. But the woods were here for everyone, surely. Did he have his eye on the neatly stacked timber on the river bank?

Had she been visiting Elfriede's grave? He still remembered the child so well. A little ray of sunshine.

'Your dear daughter, Frau von Globig,' he said, 'and our son.'

As she walked back to the yard with Drygalski, unintentionally keeping in step with him, Katharina clearly saw a pale face up at the window of her conservatory. And she thought of the footsteps in the snow that Auntie had swept away, without noticing that they went in only one direction.

But how on earth had she herself managed to forget to lock the door?

Her guest had crawled into the cubbyhole and was asleep. Katharina kept quiet, and time passed.

The books by Stefan Zweig and Jakob Wassermann lay on the table. The stranger had put Heine's *Book of Songs* on top of the pile, an old-fashioned edition bound in red leather, tooled in gold. He had laid it right across the other books, as if to say: Now *this* was a writer . . . you should hold on to him.

When darkness fell he crawled out. He had been stocking up on sleep, he said, and now he must think of saying goodbye.

They sat at the table, with a glow like fire on the horizon, and a rumbling that rose and fell again in the distance.

Then Katharina packed him some food; half a sausage, bread. She also brought herself to part with two packets of cigarettes and a chocolate bar.

Before climbing up on the windowsill, he stroked Katharina's cheek briefly once with the back of his closed hand. But he didn't say thank you. He took his cap off the *Crouching Woman* and sat on the windowsill. Would they ever meet again? Would their paths cross once more some day?

'Good luck, Herr Hirsch,' said Katharina, and the man swung himself out.

With relief, she watched him climbing down. But she also thought: what a pity.

Would he wave to her again? Yes, he waved from the path trodden in the snow. Where would events take him? Pastor Brahms would probably fix it somehow.

Katharina cleaned the washbasin, where black stubble still lingered, and flushed the lavatory. While she was about it she also disposed of the fingernail clippings that lay on the rim of the basin.

She tried stalking across the room as he had done, from one safe floorboard to another.

Herr Hirsch might have said thank you, she thought, it would hardly have tarnished his crown. She wouldn't be telling Eberhard about this. Well, maybe later, after the war, when it was all over. 'Just think what happened . . .'

She picked up the shaving brush that the man had used in two fingers and threw it away. Then she went to the door and locked it again. Just in case.

After that she turned the radio on. It was playing hit songs, and she tossed her boots aside and danced from one room to the other.

She had done it! She had brought off her daring venture, although no one would ever have thought her capable of it.

I'd give away all that I have
For one sweet, blissful night,

But I won't let you take my heart
Until the mood is right.

That night she crawled into the cubbyhole. The paper wrapping of an opened chocolate bar lay on the mattress, so the man had helped himself.

She switched on the bedside lamp and muffled herself up in blankets. Tiles on the roof clattered, and a thin breath of cold air met her face. This must be how explorers felt in the eternal ice.

12

The Offensive

It broke out in the east that same night. A constant rumbling just beyond the horizon, and the sky lit up brightly. It wasn't like the bombardment of Königsberg. Then, it had been possible to make out individual explosions far away in the distance. This was a never-ending roar that could be heard even if you covered your ears. A thousand cannon were being fired; no doubt about it, this was the attack.

On the radio, they were saying that the Red Army had embarked on its offensive. But none of those subhuman brutes from the east, said the commentator, would ever set foot on German soil, they could be sure of that. He also mentioned the Lord God. But surely a note of ugly laughter coming from somewhere was to be heard above or even within these words of comfort and reassurance, so calmly read over the radio. 'Watch out, you German women and girls, now we'll pay you back!' cried a croaking voice, and there was more ugly laughter in the background. 'We'll break your pride!' Then came the usual radio signal: *Be true and honest all your days . . .*

Then *Merriment in the Morning*, a programme of cheerful songs:

> *Don't look here*
> *Don't look there,*
> *Just look straight ahead!*

Auntie came out of her room in her dressing gown. She knocked on Katharina's door. Could Katharina hear all that rumbling and those explosions too?

'Yes,' said Katharina, she could hear them.

'Get away first thing in the morning!' Eberhard had said. And she told Auntie, 'We'd probably better get moving.'

Auntie looked at her as she had never done before. Was it possible that she had woken from her world of dreams?

Auntie went downstairs to the hall and walked up and down. Open the doors or close them, that was the question. Take suitcases down? Jago went with her, up and down, sticking close to her side. She went out of the house, too, listened in case she had been wrong, and came back in again. Brought down her suitcases, all neatly labelled and tied up with string as well, put them in the middle of the hall and sat down on them. Now she was armed for anything that might happen.

Yes, they'd better get moving. But how, and when? Nothing was easy.

At last Katharina herself came downstairs, yawning and with her hair untidy, and they sat side by side, while the collection of cups in the little cupboard clinked. They'd have to pack now. She personally, said Auntie, had packed long ago.

Katharina said, 'Not just yet. Why not wait and see first?' After all, the main packing was done. It was all on the cart, Vladimir had seen to that. The question was whether to take some of those things off the cart again and replace them with others.

Vladimir was summoned. Was everything ready? And should they take this and that, what did he think?

Maybe they should drive the cart a few hundred metres to make sure nothing fell off?

Yes, it was all packed and stowed on the cart, covered with tarpaulin and fastened down with straps and ropes, but some items could still be exchanged for others. Perhaps Eberhard's suits weren't vitally important? After all, he had his uniform. But bed linen and underwear . . .

The maids too came running into the cold, dark hall, where they really had no business, and looked inquiringly at Auntie. Did she hear all that rumbling and crashing? Yes, she did, and so did Katharina. So the offensive had begun. Should the maids be glad of it? They drew up chairs and sat down with the two women. They all had their mouths slightly open so that they could hear better, and they sat together with their shoulders hunched. It was still early in the day. They might wait and see what happened. The Prussians weren't about to shoot them.

Finally Peter also joined them, with a scarf round his neck because his tonsils were still swollen. Should he be dosed with Ems Salts or Formamint? Auntie still had a stock of eucalyptus pastilles, and she gave him some of those.

He was wondering whether to pack up his railway. The castle? The microscope? He had tucked his air pistol into his belt.

The fire on the hearth wouldn't catch, however hard Peter blew the bellows to get fresh air to it.

The women sat together shivering and listening. Vera was praying quietly. Vladimir went out again to see if anything else needed fastening down more firmly.

'We won't start,' said Auntie, 'until we're told to. Peter, tidy up your room, and you girls go back to the kitchen!' Wouldn't they need a permit?

'Is anything wrong with you?' Auntie asked Katharina, who was staring into space. 'You look so different today! So young!' No, there was nothing wrong with Katharina. She scratched her head. She was surprised by herself. A strange man had camped in her room. It had all happened so quickly, her adventure. Was it really over? Or would there be a sequel? Would some part of it stick to her?

To think it had been so easy.

It was all unreal and like a phantom, thought Katharina.

She stood at the window. Day was breaking, and there were all manner of things to be seen out there: people in the Settlement were standing in the street, listening, and telling one another about the thunder and lightning in the distance.

The road was busier now. Occasional motorbikes rattled past the Georgenhof – and there! A German Wehrmacht jeep raced along the snow-covered road. It skidded off the bend and fell down the slope to the Settlement. There was a general in it, and he died at once. Peter saw it happen through his father's binoculars. He'd never seen a general before, with the red braid on his trousers, and now he was actually looking at a dead one. A moment ago the general had been shouting at his driver: go on, faster, drive faster! Imagine not being with his men today, of all days, and then the jeep had turned a somersault and he was lying flat and . . . dead?

The driver and the front-seat passenger carried the dead general into a house in the Settlement, one of them holding his wobbling head steady. He'd been awarded the German Cross in gold. The women of the Settlement gathered outside the house, in fact entire families joined the crowd, and the foreign workers from the Forest Lodge came to see the dead general as well.

Drygalski shooed the foreign workers away. Really, it was the limit – such people wanting to feast their eyes on a dead German general. And he asked the women from the Settlement if they didn't have anything better to do.

The question was: now what? Where did you bury a general? Maybe he should be taken home to where he came from?

And was it a hero's death that he had died?

Furthermore, what would the troops ahead of them do without their leader? But surely there was more than one general?

Drygalski telephoned the office of the Party organization in Mitkau. But the Party wasn't responsible, nor was the local headquarters, nor were the police. A pack of Hitler Youth boys arrived, but they weren't allowed to see the dead general, however many of them gathered in front of the house where he lay. Drygalski made a little speech to them. He said they were being put to the test and must prove their mettle, and he gave them instructions: they were to march to Mitkau and report for duty there. There was plenty for young Germans to do these days. Once they had reported for duty everything else would follow. At last a car came to collect the body. The women folded their hands when invited to do so, and Drygalski the head trustee gave the Hitler salute with his arm outstretched.

The rumbling beyond the horizon, the way the ground shook. A noise of pounding and shaking, and you could tell some of the particularly violent explosions apart from one another. How many kilometres away was the front? A hundred and fifty? A hundred? Fifty? Still far off, anyway, but not as far off as all that.

And now a line of ambulances was coming along from Mitkau, driving slowly by, bearing the red cross depicted large and broad on their roofs and doors, one after another. The field hospital in Mitkau was being evacuated. A few horse-drawn carts were also trying to make their way along. And from time to time, dispatch riders raced towards them on their fast motorbikes.

Stand firm! Stand firm in the rising storm . . .

A solitary soldier fell out of the long column of ambulances and medical personnel.

It was the one-handed pianist who had played hit songs so well at the Georgenhof with the violinist, only a few days ago, believe it or not.

He came over to the house, stopped and clicked his heels. He was just calling in quickly, he said, to see if they were all right. And was Fräulein Strietzel still here? If so it would be a good idea for her to leave with them; he was sure that could be fixed.

No, they told him, the violinist wasn't there any longer; she must be in Allenstein by now. Or had she gone on somewhere else?

The soldier wore a Red Cross armband, and while cart after cart took the wounded away he told the women how wonderfully well organized it all was. The order had come to evacuate at once, and the severely wounded and those who had just had operations were immediately carried out of the local hospital, although medical instruments had to be left behind. The new and only recently installed X-ray equipment, for instance. Did the ladies have any idea, he asked, how much one of those devices cost?

He would never forget the few hours he had spent here, he assured them again, that evening at the Georgenhof. Then he bowed to Katharina and said, 'Make sure you get away from here – you still have time.'

He turned to leave, and then came back again. He had one more question, he said; did they still have any of that fantastic liver sausage that he remembered? Now that everything was going down the drain . . . Yes, they did have some of it left, and some was cut off for him.

He waved back to them from the road with his one hand, jumped into the nearest ambulance and was gone. What a nice man!

*

The thunder of the guns was still coming from away on the horizon in the afternoon, but they couldn't sit about in the hall for ever; there were things yet to be done. Maybe the curtains should be washed before they left, and the whole place thoroughly cleaned?

In spite of the general confusion, Dr Wagner had ventured to steal out of the town. Mitkau was teeming like an ant heap, everyone rushing round trying to escape, to get away . . . Not so fast, that had always been his motto; you don't want to eat your food as hot as it comes out of the oven. Despite the snow, he had managed to get through to the Georgenhof. And here he was, sitting with Peter at the table, his glasses in need of cleaning, the ribbon of the Iron Cross on his lapel, eating bread and sausage. He had a right to be here, he was doing his duty. The school might be closed, but he was giving a German boy private coaching. No one could stop him doing that.

He was too old to be a reservist in the Volkssturm, although he still felt really young.

He had just been showing Peter what the barrage of drumfire meant; he had drummed on the table with all ten fingers, bringing the ball of his hand down on the table-top now and then to represent the heavy artillery. A soldier had to run about and double back like a hare. He had taken off his jacket and rolled up his shirtsleeve to show his bare arm, and the long scar running down it. He had got that at the battle on the Chemin des Dames ridge in 1916. Your best chance was to jump into a brand-new crater, because where a shell has gone off once another isn't so likely to strike in the same place. He explained terms like *increased firing range* and *break in firing*, and the expression *battle of matériel* was also mentioned. And, he added, not every bullet hits the mark.

The small atlas was lying on the table. They looked up the Chemin des Dames ridge, and then they tried to work out where the roar of the cannon was coming from. It must be up here somewhere.

Then the front door of the house opened, and in strode Drygalski, making more noise than necessary as he passed the startled Jago, marched straight into the hall, and shouted up the stairs, 'Hello, is there anyone here?' The dog's hind paws slipped from under him as he scrabbled on the floor in his fright. Heil Hitler!

What were all those suitcases doing in the middle of the hall, he asked. 'Were you ladies thinking of going away?'

He had had a dead general taken away – yes, it was all thanks to him – he'd been doing all the things that no one else thought of, he'd been on the phone for hours, shouting and keeping everything in order.

Now he set about climbing the stairs to Katharina, who leaned over the banisters with the key in her hand and asked – Heil Hitler! – 'What is it?'

Auntie too opened her door. She had been busy sorting out her magazines, putting them neatly together in bundles and tying them up with string – ten years' worth of issues, they were valuable items. What was going on, she wanted to know, Heil Hitler. Peter looked out of his room as well.

Drygalski hurried upstairs, stumbled over Peter's clockwork railway in the darkness of the corridor, cried, 'What sort of housekeeping is this?' and kicked the carriages of the toy train out of the way. 'It's a positive pigsty!'

He brought the news that a married couple from the east had to be accommodated, which meant they were being billeted on the Globigs – 'And at once! You have plenty of space here.'

The couple would be arriving with bag and baggage this afternoon, a room must be cleared for them. 'And at once!' Drygalski repeated. You couldn't very well put such people up in a cowshed.

He took an official order out of his pocket and showed it. 'In case of non-compliance . . .' and so on. Then he got them to show him Elfriede's room, which had been standing empty for two years.

The doll's house, with its furniture nicely arranged, the puppet theatre with Kasper, Death and the Devil lying over the front of it, even the knitted witch was there with a string a metre long coming out of her stomach. Above the door hung a white-framed picture of brownies with nothing on, holding up a sheaf of flowers.

And on the wall above the bed was an engraving of the Saviour with the caption, 'SUFFER THE LITTLE CHILDREN TO COME UNTO ME', MARK 10 VERSE 14. He was patting the little children's cheeks, while the grown-ups stood thoughtfully to one side. It had been inherited from Elfriede's grandparents.

Her clothes were in the wardrobe, underwear and jumpers, her little dresses and the black knitted jacket with the green yoke and the silver buttons that she had wanted so much. Moths flew out of the clothes.

The bed was made up with white sheets and blankets, and there was a photograph of the dead child on the pillow, showing her with her crinkly hair in braids and her hands folded round a bunch of lilies of the valley.

The room was large enough, said Drygalski, pulling back the curtains and opening the window to let the good fresh air in for once. They must be nice to the comrades billeted here, he told Auntie and Katharina, they'd had some bad experiences.

*

He stood at the window for a while listening to the rumbling. Behind him, Auntie and Katharina were listening too. But as usual, smoke was rising from every chimney in the Settlement. You could even see people sweeping the snow away. All was neat and tidy.

What kind of people were being billeted on them, Auntie asked, and how much rent could they ask?

That infuriated Drygalski, who shouted something about the national community, and took the most impossible tone.

'Rent? What's got into your head? These people have lost everything!'

It was a pity the railway line had been damaged, or they could have been sent straight on into the Reich. That could easily have been organized if the line was still intact.

Now Dr Wagner the teacher also came out of Peter's room and joined them.

Was the front going to hold? he asked the head trustee. And at that moment the background noise in the east grew louder; it could have been because of a gust of wind intensifying the sound of the detonations.

'What are *you* doing here?' shouted Drygalski. Calmly sitting here in the warmth, while all hell was let loose outside. This sort of thing wouldn't do.

Dr Wagner pointed to the east, and ventured to ask the head trustee for advice: he had experience of the World War from the Chemin des Dames ridge, he said, but all the same he'd like to know more precisely. If he wasn't much mistaken, then what they were hearing was drumfire, wasn't it? But from the German guns or the guns of the Red Army, that was the question.

They all stood listening, as people used to listen to the Führer's speeches, but the schoolmaster's question remained unanswered.

The aircraft flying over the house were German, anyway. They'd show the Russians a thing or two. Drygalski almost felt like waving his cap to them.

Drygalski closed the meeting. He turned to go and see round the rest of the house; he had to see Katharina's room, he said.

'It's private,' she said, pushing past him and shutting herself into it.

Drygalski was about to go downstairs again, but then he said no, he must insist. He hammered on the door, and Katharina was obliged to let him in. Her bed was still unmade.

'Aha!' said Drygalski, shaking his head. He didn't put up with unmade beds at home.

'This is a real self-contained apartment! A bedroom, a living room and *another* room as well? That's just wonderful! And a toilet of its own?' Then if necessary the boy could move in with her, and so could Auntie! If more room was needed, then people just had to squeeze up together.

His eye fell on the books lying on the table. Heinrich Heine? Stefan Zweig? Surely Heine had been Jewish? Well, this was all very, very interesting.

'*German Cathedrals*, however . . .' And he picked up the book of pictures and held it out to Dr Wagner, who had come up behind him. 'Now *this* is the kind of thing you should be teaching!' he cried.

Dr Wagner wanted to see Katharina's apartment too, and this was a good opportunity. He stood on tiptoe. Wasn't that an open tube of tablets lying on the table? He managed to get a glimpse of the *Crouching Woman*; a female figure, naked? Her attitude was unnatural. The *Medea* on the wall was very different from this distorted figure on her plinth.

This woman lived very comfortably, Dr Wagner thought. Little armchairs, a plate with a pattern of fruit, and with apples on it. A pretty conservatory, with the cold, clear sunlight flooding in. He thought of his own dark apartment in Mitkau, in Horst-Wessel-Strasse, where there were always farm carts going by on their way to the abattoir and so forth. Now he saw what a lovely place Katharina had, and he thought: some people have everything.

Of course he lived comfortably, with his study, which might be dark but was spacious, the dining room with the seascape over the sideboard, the smoking room and the bedroom. There was even another little room looking out on the back yard. His mother had died in that room, and a hyacinth vase was still there with a dead hyacinth in it. The water in the vase must be full of plankton. All very nice, but farm carts frequently drove past – often there was no bearing it.

And here everything had its unique style. Orange shutters! Why hadn't he thought of having orange shutters? She had a view of the park too.

Drygalski went downstairs again and looked at the summer drawing room – impossible to heat, he assumed, and crammed with crates and boxes. Also, as Auntie commented, 'You can't get it properly blacked out.' He glanced at the billiards room, nudged one of the balls, which nudged another, and that one struck a third. Was Drygalski a man who never missed his mark?

He inspected the hall as if he were going to put chalk marks on the furniture ready for an auction sale.

Aha, pictures. 'Are those your distinguished ancestors?'

The ancestors looked back with their eyes wide open. Ancestors who might well have upheld good German values all their days.

Straw could be spread in the hall for a large contingent, he said thoughtfully, accommodation still had to be found for the inmates of the Tilsit orphanage. Here, however, Auntie was quick to get her word in. 'But the toilets,' she said. 'There aren't nearly enough of them for so many people.' And those that they did have, she added, were stopped up all the time. She blamed the Ukrainian maids.

Drygalski stood thinking right in the middle of the hall, under the candelabra made of antlers, wondering whether the summer drawing room couldn't be made fit for use somehow or other, and the hall and the billiards room too, and the women stood round him thinking of ways to prevent it, and watching him as he stood there thinking. There was no denying it, the head trustee had bow legs.

It was a funny thing, said Drygalski, how the general hadn't fallen fighting among his men but had died in a car accident. And now of all times, when the red tide was catching fire, such a man would be hard to replace. He, Drygalski, hadn't been able to save his life, but in a way he had saved his death. It was *he* who had seen to having him carried into a house. And who had told his wife in Hamburg. Seven children!

The driver, he said, would certainly be called to account. It might have been better for him if he had died with the general.

He wanted to see the cellar, did he? It dated from 1605. There was nothing to be done with the cellar, where water stood ankle-deep. It should have been possible to drain it long ago. Grudging hospitality if ever he'd seen it! That was the aristocracy for you.

He was still standing in the hall, beside the suitcases packed ready to leave, and the rumbling rose and fell again. He thought of his own wife, and what to do about her when it all got really serious. There was the Globigs' farm cart standing in the yard – couldn't a bedstead be loaded up on a cart like that for his wife? It was enormous! A few crates and boxes could be taken off to make space. After all, human beings came first, didn't they?

*

When Drygalski finally left – Heil Hitler! – the whole household heaved a sigh of relief. He said that when Peter was better and the swelling of his tonsils had gone down he must report to the Hitler Youth, and 'right away' at that.

The dog Jago curled up again, although his ears were pricked, and Auntie bent over her suitcases – really, nothing was easy – and only then took them back upstairs to her room.

Katharina shut herself up in her apartment. Only once she had locked the door behind her did her hair stand on end. 'It was all hanging by a thread,' she said out loud. Suppose Drygalski had come a day earlier and found the Jew here! Then it all would have been up for her. What providence that the man had moved on in the night. He had left even before the sounds from the front began. Where was he now? she wondered. Might he, in the end, come back again? Flung back by the rampart of fire as if by a hedge full of thorns.

She threw herself on her bed.

The daring venture was over. Or would there be a sequel? Would something of it cling to her?

Katharina took her tube of tablets off the bedside table. She swallowed one, and soon she felt all right.

'It was all hanging by a thread.'

At that moment Uncle Josef telephoned from Albertsdorf. He held the receiver out of the window and asked if she heard that? Did she know what it meant?

He advised her to set out at once. They themselves would probably stay in Albertsdorf, what with their three daughters and Hanna with her bad hip ... she couldn't be expected to take flight. 'I don't suppose the Russians will tear our heads off.'

Katharina immediately took another tablet from the tube. Set off with bag and baggage? Take flight?

13

The Baron

So that afternoon Elfriede's room was taken over by a baron from the Baltic and his wife, with Hitler Youth boys carrying their cases for them. Heil Hitler. The doll's house and the puppet theatre could stay, said the couple, they wouldn't be in the way. However, the baron asked whether the little girl had died two years ago in *this* bed, and he took the portrait photograph of her dead body off the pillow and pressed it into Auntie's hand. Didn't she feel that, somehow, it had now served its purpose?

The baroness, meanwhile, knelt down in front of the puppet theatre, pulled the curtain up and let it down, and arranged the puppets inside it. 'Ah, the Devil!' she said. 'He's always one of them.'

She arranged the chairs in the doll's house properly. There was a round table, and a gentleman lounging in an armchair. He had been lounging in it for a long time.

The baron sat in an armchair and watched his wife. So skilful! So clever! Energetic, that was the word for her. His wife got things done, and she wasn't to be easily deterred. She pushed the sofa over to stand beside the bed. The bed would be for her husband, she would sleep on the sofa, that was somehow or other taken for granted.

'I don't mind a bit.'

The only thing was that the bed could do with clean sheets, and then there would be nothing left to wish for. They hoped the bedclothes didn't date back two years, and the sheet wasn't a winding sheet?

The baron, who was not one of the landed aristocracy, but had been an accountant in a pharmaceuticals factory, acted as if he were an old friend of the family. 'We'll do fine,' he said, and left his wife to go on fixing things. He wanted to have a look round and see where they had ended up. He went from room to room, suggesting that the old wing chair might look better somewhere else, and the cabinet could be moved to opposite its present position. He called Katharina 'dear lady', and when appropriate he kissed her hand in the old-fashioned way. He picked up the cat, and that animal, who usually ran like the wind from human beings, nestled in his arms.

The black parrot that the couple had brought with them was a great attraction for the household. You mustn't get over familiar with the bird, or he pecked. Sometimes he spread his wings, first the right wing, then the left wing, and sometimes he called out 'Lora!' occasionally adding, 'You old sow!' He looked calmly at the cat. The cat looked back at the parrot with his paws tucked under him. They'd wait and see how things turned out. Take it easy was the right approach. The cat didn't like it that the parrot was given walnuts, not that the cat fancied them himself. The baron kept the walnuts in his jacket pocket, and he cracked them against each other, two by two.

A parrot? The maids kept coming out of the kitchen to look at him. They'd never seen such a thing before: a parrot! They reached for him, but he just looked sideways at them. And of course, they claimed, there were much bigger parrots than that in their native land.

'Oh, go on with you, get back to work!' said Auntie.

The baron's wife went round the house singing, chattering away to the maids in their own language and going out to see the horses: the huge gelding and the two fast bays. Peter showed her the dead peacock. He couldn't be buried yet because the ground was frozen hard, so for now they left him on the dung heap. He showed her the chickens and the rooster, told her how trusting the rooster was, and how he understood every word. And Vladimir had a long conversation with her, heaven knows what about.

When she went back into the house, he touched his cap lightly. He knew how to behave with aristocracy.

The baron walked in the grounds for a while, breathing in the air as if it were particularly healthy. This place shows no real sense of design, he told Peter, who was accompanying him. The river! Now that should be included somehow. And with his stick he drew a plan in the snow for the way he saw the grounds redesigned.

Apparently there were ruins of some kind here. 'Have you noticed them? Just sort of lying around?' A broad avenue could be laid out, leading to the ruins, and a teahouse by the river, wouldn't that be good? Some people never thought of such things, obvious as they were.

The baron had brought a very heavy suitcase with him, and never let it out of his sight. It contained material about his native city. He had collected everything to do with it: pictorial views both very old and brand new; brochures; books; menus. Photographs (the church of St Nicholas taken from every angle, the gabled town hall in the marketplace). He had all these things in his suitcase. It also contained his family papers; he could trace his forebears back over many centuries. His ancestors had come from Germany and had sought the protection of the Tsarina, who appreciated good German enterprise at the time. To return to the German Reich now seemed the obvious course.

He showed Peter some of this material, explaining the difference between a family tree and a line of descent.

He also showed Peter a kind of chronicle of his native city; he himself had written it and it was full of the life of the old days. *What Once Was Ours* was the title of the manuscript, and he had devoted every free minute to it in recent years. He described the customs of the country's merchants, who used to eat swan as well as other things at their banquets, and mentioned the introduction of traction engines on the great landed estates.

'All gone, all gone!' he cried as he walked in the grounds. The baroness asked Peter not to run his toy railway along the corridor because it disturbed her husband; maybe it would be best if he put it away, and Peter immediately did as she asked.

The baron, whose first name was Eduard, sat in his room, his chilly fingers sorting out his papers. Thank God he had put them in the suitcase at the last moment. He sorted them first by one method, then by another, and he wrote down his final impressions of his native city. Nothing, for God's sake, must be forgotten, and he licked his pencil, crooking his little finger with its signet ring as he wrote. Its fingernail, like the nails of his other fingers, was manicured. The generations with all their ups and downs ... who knew when they would see their native land again? Someone had to write down all the good and bad things that happened, and now terrible things were certainly going on and must be set down in the record for all time.

He must also give a faithful account of what had been done, again and again, to the people of the Baltic states. Recruited in the time of the Tsars, then massacred by the Bolshevists. And now the Germans had wreaked havoc. All of it should be, must be put on record without reservations. He felt it was his personal responsibility to do that, to bear witness for future generations in his entertaining way.

*

There was a brochure on one of the bookshelves, dating from Eberhard's time as a member of the Wandervogel, the German youth organization for ramblers. It bore the title *Roads and Footpaths in the Baltic States: A Hiker's Handbook*. It had pictures of avenues and secluded paths, small pools that looked enchanted, and large erratic boulders under the birch trees. At the back there was a large map that could be unfolded.

What a treasure! The baron assumed that Katharina would give it to him, since he had lost his native land, and the little booklet must be a matter of indifference to her. However, Katharina folded up the map and took the brochure into her room with her.

He placed the armchair close to the stove, and then he sat there, with the cat beside him, sorting his papers out. The parrot in his cage looked as if he was playing a waiting game. He saw everything that went on.

Now and then the baron stood up to go over to the window, holding the cat in his arms, and looked down at the road, which was busy with traffic. When would they get away from here? he wondered; this place was a trap.

The wind shook the window frame – or was it the detonations?

Sometimes the baron summoned slender Sonya and showed her, too, what an interesting chronicle he was writing, and asked in her language for a cup of coffee, and was there any of that honey left? Some bread and honey would go down well now. As a man from the Baltic states he spoke Russian, and he spoke it as elegantly as if it were French. Sonya stared when he asked her so politely, and then, sitting as he was, flung his arms round her knees and laughed in a friendly manner, showing his gold teeth. He was old, there was no denying it, but a cheerful heart beat in his breast.

Could she bring him some hot water, he asked, and then his wife knelt down in front of him and cut his toenails one by one.

Peter showed the baron his history of the Georgenhof, the project suggested to him by Dr Wagner. It said *Good!* in red ink at the end.

A very nice concoction too, said the baron. But Peter should look at this: he himself had already written a hundred and sixty-four pages, and had left the eighteenth century behind.

He would probably have spoken at even greater length on this subject if Dr Wagner hadn't come in from the room next door and told the boy, 'Come along now, we'll carry on with our studies. You're in the baron's way.'

He had been wondering whether they should read Goethe's *Hermann und Dorothea* together. It would be very suitable just now, dealing with refugees as it did.

The baron had also said that he, the schoolmaster, should remove the blue ribbon from his get-up; it had no kind of connection with Peter's essay. And he had asked the boy to bring him Katharina's little booklet, *Roads and Footpaths in the Baltic States: A Hiker's Handbook*, for another brief glance, because he wanted to look something up in it.

Then the baron locked the door, put the cat, who was arching his back, down on the floor and counted his money. The signet ring was on his finger. He had drawn all his money out of the bank while he still could, although friends had asked him whether he thought that was right. He was keeping it on his person, in an inside pocket of his coat. Nothing could happen to him now.

They met in the hall that evening, with Jago the dog, the cat and the parrot. Flames burnt high on the hearth. Dr Wagner was invited to join them too. Where had they all come from? Where would they end up? The baron, who immediately sat down in Eberhard's usual chair, told them about his historical work and how far he could trace his ancestors back. His wife came up behind him and brushed dandruff off the collar of his jacket.

Dr Wagner had ancestors himself, but somehow they didn't qualify for discussion. He might have a goatee beard, but the baron kept a real monocle in a waistcoat pocket lined with flannel. He used it when he wanted to get a hearing. The schoolmaster couldn't compete with that. Auntie's Silesia was all very well, but not in the same class as the baron's native city.

His beloved Königsberg, said Dr Wagner, stroking his goatee beard. Eating fried flounders in a little restaurant on the River Pregel . . . and hearing the foghorns on the big ships blowing in the harbour . . .

Then the baron took out his monocle and scrutinized the schoolmaster, and the subject was back on the correct lines again. Flounders were nothing to an ox roasted on the spit. Oxen had been spit-roasted in his native city. Swans were eaten there as well in the old days, and peacocks too! You couldn't imagine such a thing today.

'Oh, stone the crows!' said Dr Wagner out loud and quite distinctly, and after that there was silence for a while.

He had once seen the German crown prince in Cranz, said the baron, before the war. He was very slender and all in white. The spa band had played waltzes, and the crown prince was surrounded by young ladies on a white yacht. 'A real greyhound of a man!' said the baron. Katharina von Globig, sitting on the sofa beside the baroness, had no particular connection with crown princes, but as a native of Berlin she didn't like to hear the baron call the crown prince a greyhound. As for Cranz itself, that Baltic seaside resort, she had her own thoughts about it. *Rise high, thou red-winged eagle.* They had eaten cod, still blood-stained, and there had been an unemptied chamber pot under the bed. She thought of the charred meerschaum cigarette holder and how stingy Eberhard had been with the tip. They followed the cod with apple tart and whipped cream, and he had quickly put one of the small coins back in his pocket before the waiter came.

While the men were concerned with each other, the baroness admired Katharina, her black hair and her blue eyes. She even asked to see her hands. What beautiful hands she had! That made Katharina think of the bookbinder's scratched hands that she had dressed with sticking plaster. She wondered whether to invite this woman up to her own room. You couldn't really talk here in front of the fire in the hearth. Women are so different. The baron's wife had probably heard the stories that he was telling with relish many times before. But she was considerate of her husband, and didn't let it show.

There was another kind of disturbance in the house that night. At first the Globigs couldn't believe their ears, but as reflected light flashed over the dark sky, the baron's voice could be heard, clear and distinct. 'You old sow!' he said, and feudal aristocrat though he might be, he obviously meant his young wife. What she replied was more like a howl. And her husband repeated, loud and clear, 'You old sow!' Then there was a lot of noise, and coming and going, until Auntie knocked on the wall, hesitantly at first and then very hard, whereupon all was silent.

14

The Refugees

The wind whistled from the west, it howled round the house and rattled the decrepit roof. Its noise almost drowned out the drum-fire. Was this cup, people wondered, to pass them by? But no, the rumbling went on.

A cold, harsh, icy rain fell on the oak trees. And then came the great trek. Only a few separate carts at first, each on its own, then more densely, one behind another. You could see them from a distance, passing over the bridge in an endless file with tarpaulins fluttering; they drove through Mitkau, they drove through the Senthagener Tor and past the Georgenhof. Columns of carts keeping close together, from manorial estates, with one trek leader on horseback in front. They had put the names of their villages in front of the carts so that they wouldn't lose each other. And there were single vehicles, some comfortable, some wretched. Farm carts crammed with all they could hold, and here and there even a car with a spare can of petrol fixed to the back of it.

They moved quietly; all you heard was the creaking of the wheels and the 'Gee up!' and 'Whoa!' of the drivers, most of them women. On top of the carts were little huts, solidly constructed or hastily knocked together, covered with roofing felt or rugs. Bundles of hay for the horses hung from cords under the carts. Young girls on foot, leading children by the hand. And dogs ran along under the axles of the carts. There were a few pedestrians with rucksacks or children's sledges. They kept their heads bent. Their coat collars were turned up. Bicycles, babies' prams, handcarts.

Where had anything like it ever been seen?

Was it an illusion, or was Herr Schünemann the political economist hurrying about among all those vehicles on his crutches? Did he raise one of them in greeting? His bag was buckled over his back on a strap.

Next day Dr Wagner and the Baltic baron were seen standing by the billiards table, smoking and making conversation in a very correct way. The baron in his check suit, Wagner wearing his third tie, with the little order on his lapel. The round stove, which dated back to the nineteenth century, gave a certain amount of warmth. They wrote down their scores on the *beelyar* table, as the baron pronounced it, and leaned on their cues. Sometimes they stood by the ice-encrusted window, and breathed on the ice to make a little hole and look through it at the march of the Ten Thousand, as Wagner the schoolmaster called the long line of refugees. Xenophon, he added, said that traitors were buried alive. The two gentlemen took turns blowing their cigarette smoke into the air in a criss-cross pattern, and sometimes out of their nostrils. It looked like the vapour that came hissing from the noses of the horses out there.

Sometimes they counted the vehicles: there went a column of three hundred carts! It was like France in 1940, when the Belgians fled before the Germans.

The baron had been in Paris long ago, and he talked about it now. Bugs in the hotels, and filthy lavatories. Indescribable! The French were real pigs, all across the board. Every last one of them. And incidentally, the young women weren't as free and easy as a foreigner might assume. It wasn't a case of anything goes; you could come up against a brick wall; they were all hell-bent on marriage. All those risqué stories people told, not a word of truth in them. And yet, said the baron, he remembered the spring of 1932 ... 'I could tell you a thing or two ...'

Wagner had also been in France, in the First War, making his way along muddy trenches without a thought in his head about coquettish French girls. But as a student he and his friend Fritjof had visited Italian cemeteries, quoting Caesar – *Gallia omnis est divisa in parte tres*, all Gaul is divided into three parts – and found that in spite of studying Latin for all those semesters they couldn't read the funerary inscriptions. That bothered him to this day, although he had long ago decided to make a joke of it. Fritjof – that cheerful, sunburnt young man, powerful and supple, and then he had fallen fighting.

Birth and death – an everlasting sea ...

Ah yes, Goethe ... he must have left his tiny copy of *Faust* somewhere. When he volunteered in 1914 it had gone into the field with him. Where was it now? He'd take it again if he had to join this great train of refugees. Would he himself have to leave his native land? No, not a bit of it ... or not yet, anyway.

'In the First War we softened up the Russians too.'

Head Trustee Drygalski was standing at the roadside, making sure that everything was done properly. He kept careful check lists, and got the leaders of the trek to show him their permits; yes, they could move on, place of origin, destination, number of horses pulling the cart. Sometimes he climbed up on the carts to make sure there wasn't a soldier hidden among the household goods. And he told refugees where to go; every house had to take some in, individuals or whole families. It was only for a day or two, three at the most, as no one stayed any longer. It all had to be managed correctly, and Drygalski was the man for that.

Now and then he went home to see how his wife was. He added wood to the glowing embers in the stove, straightened her bedclothes, put a glass of water within reach.

He couldn't take in any refugees with his sick wife, and his office was needed for all those files and for telephoning. The roll-top desk against the wall, the table with the telephone on it.

There was one young girl who had no one in the wide world left. Had she said her name was Käte, or was it Gerda? She had plump red cheeks. Drygalski showed her the attic room and its beautiful view to the north, the Georgenhof and the wide fields to the west, now covered with snow. The wind blew over them. And cart after cart was now going along the road. This had been his son's room, years ago now, he told the girl. Fallen in Poland. The table at which he had prepared for the Technical College still stood by the wall. There was a folder of sketches in the drawer; no one had ever looked at them again. Also drawings of designs to improve the Albert Leo Schlageter Settlement. And an idea for an inauguration pageant; Drygalski had never known it existed.

The refugee girl wore Hitler Youth ski pants under a flowered skirt, and a pre-war quilted coat which had probably been her mother's. She had lost track of her own people at the very beginning of their flight, when she went into a farmhouse to ask for a little milk, and the carts from her village had gone on without waiting for her.

She nodded when Drygalski suggested staying here for the time being. She could make herself useful, he said, cook, wash the dishes, keep the house nice and so on. They were a little community now, he said, and she must always keep the front door closed. And look after his wife, wash her, spoon soup into her now and then.

A flushing toilet and a room to herself, the girl had probably never had it so good. At home she'd have been sharing a bed with her little sister.

Peter climbed into his tree house, with the instrument panel and the steering wheel, and watched the trek. The long line came from far away in the east, and wound on like a huge S into the white landscape, moving towards the hazy sun.

The foreign workers were also watching, standing at the roadside. They were pointing out to each other what the vehicles were, and wondered what would become of them – and hey, look at that one!

Of course Drygalski had to intervene. Gloating over German misfortune wasn't to be tolerated. But these people refused to disperse; they hardly even took their hands out of their pockets.

'Don't you have anything to do?'

No, they said, not here. For these foreigners the long line of refugees was a sign of hope. They smiled at each other: soon we'll be going home. Drygalski had no power over them. Or did he? Maybe he could still get the better of them somehow? Search the Forest Lodge and see what came to light. He telephoned the Labour Office; did the people there know that this riff-raff were standing about in the road, doing nothing?

He put in an appearance at the Georgenhof, sometimes he even looked in several times a day to make sure all was as it should be there. Heil Hitler. He had to, in his official capacity, although nothing there had changed. He talked to Auntie, and she agreed with him. Nothing was easy! But they all had to pull together. He told Auntie what a responsibility his was, he didn't know whether he was on his head or his heels, and he wiped the sweat from his brow, even though he was cold. In a casual manner, he gave Auntie a permit to go away on the trek herself, because she had always been so understanding.

He also made a note of the floor space still available in the big house; who could tell how things were going to turn out? The Settlement was full of refugees, every house there had guests, but the Georgenhof – the place was enormous, were things as they ought to be? There must be plenty of room left. That icy drawing room with the crates from Berlin standing there. No one could be expected to put up with it. 'When is that stuff going to be collected?'

Auntie understood everything, and spoke politely to him. She didn't think that large numbers of people could be accommodated at the Georgenhof. And to prove her goodwill, she told him about the painter who had spoken of the Führer in derogatory terms.

She also mentioned the Forest Lodge to Drygalski. It had once been a hotel, hadn't it? She was sure plenty of people could be put up there. Only the side wing had been cleared for the foreign workers, and there was nothing to be done about that. But what about the dance floor and all the hotel bedrooms?

Drygalski had thought of that for himself, of course, but the registration office of the National Socialist Motor Corps was in control of the Forest Lodge. So there was nothing to be done about that either; they had stored spare parts in the former hotel, bicycle bells and car horns. It all had to be put somewhere: wheel rims and transmission systems. The pennants and the parts to build spectators' stands from the last races held in the Mitkau area were stored there too. The banners saying *Start* and *Finish* had been kept since the summer of 1939, and after the war there would be racing again. Mitkau had never yet won the Reich championship, but maybe after the war? If not, it would be a real shame.

Drygalski telephoned the regional authority, where they saw his point, but said that at the moment there was no alternative.

Where living space was concerned, Drygalski was ruthless; after all, higher things were at stake, and something must be done at once. He had to find shelter for people without a roof over their heads, people who were cold and hungry. This was the time for the national community to prove its worth.

Peter must clear his room; he would sleep up in the private apartment with his mother, that was the simplest solution, and the little room there immediately suggested such a conclusion. Surely it was the most natural thing in the world for mother and son to be housed together?

Yes, the next refugees to turn up would be accommodated in the boy's room. Were there more bedsteads anywhere? It wouldn't be possible to occupy the attic; snow came drifting in through the gaps between the roof tiles. Auntie carefully folded up the permit that Drygalski had made out for her and kept it safe.

When Drygalski thought of his own home now it warmed his heart. The girl was a quick learner. Who knew, maybe she'd call him *Father* some day? Or more likely *Grandpa*? Well, never mind. He would look after this child whose parents had disappeared. Everything would be easier to bear now, with her to keep the house nice and clean, and get soup into his wife, and if necessary wash her and so on. How had he managed all this time on his own?

It felt special to come home in the evening, stretch out his legs under the table in the warm kitchen, supper on the table. What a pleasant sight to see the young creature, with her plump cheeks, standing by the stove. Drygalski felt like lingering in the kitchen with her for a little longer, but then he had to go out into the cold again and check the carts driving by.

Perhaps he could find something sweet in Mitkau, as a treat for the child?

Dr Wagner visited every day. He was not to be deprived of his chance to get the boy to practise his vocabulary, and teach him geography, for instance where Heidelberg is, with its famous castle 'destroyed by the French, remember that, my boy!' And Lake Constance, that wonderful expanse of water; it was once frozen right over, and a man on horseback rode to the opposite bank entirely unaware that he was riding over ice. Tipped over backwards – and crash! Was he dead?

Or there was that other story, of the miner who suffocated underground, and was dug out decades later, fresh and young as ever with rosy cheeks, and by then his widow was old as the hills.

It was a pleasant little party that assembled in the evenings; the Baltic baron and his wife, Dr Wagner, Katharina, that quiet, thoughtful beauty, and Auntie, who was no fool and was well able to contribute to the conversation. They sat by the fire, telling stories, arguing, whispering. It was as if they had known each other for ever and would always stick together.

Sticking together, that was the order of the day. The baron in his check suit looked as if he were wearing a fur muffler in the evenings, for as soon as he appeared the cat would come running, although usually the baron was already carrying him in his arms.

On these evenings Auntie put on a special dress, hurried into the kitchen and came back with a jar of morello cherries which they passed around, helping themselves from it amid laughter. His dear city of Königsberg, said the schoolmaster as he remembered sitting in a little restaurant on the River Pregel, eating fried flounders and hearing the foghorns of the big ships in the harbour . . .

The baron fixed his monocle in his eye again and again, thinking of the summer of 1936, the little house in Dünaburg and his young wife jumping into the water from the landing stage. The lake was like liquid silver.

For his part, Wagner recollected a bicycling tour with his mother in the Weser Uplands. She was long dead now.

'Didn't you ever think of marrying?' asked the baron.

'Well,' said Dr Wagner, 'you know how it is. First I kept putting it off, then it was too late.' And he thought of an expedition with his boys as they ran about wildly, jumping over the bonfire.

He also thought of the First War, and the trenches. It had sometimes been quite romantic there. He thought of the young, and their wonderful bodies, wonderful even if disfigured by their scars. He set about rolling up his sleeve to show the marks left by his own wound.

At the beginning of the war, Dr Wagner told the party, he had received some marvellous letters from his pupils. They had been written on the heights of the Acropolis, in Denmark, from the Caucasus and Burgundy. The flow had dried up now. He had heard less and less from his boys since Stalingrad. But he had kept them all in a folder, and he read them now and then. He intended to add photos of the boys to their letters, and it would be like a memorial to the dead. And after the war he would publish the whole thing in memory of the young blood that had been shed.

Katharina sat to one side on the sofa, with the baroness. In her black pullover and black trousers, you could hardly make her out in the darkness. Now and then the glowing end of her cigarette shone. And the baroness looked surreptitiously at her; maybe she could make a friend here? Help to polish her nails or comb that heavy dark hair? She moved closer to Katharina, but Katharina withdrew. She needed her freedom.

Under the large old pictures of ancestors who were not the Globigs' ancestors at all, they sat together. And the ancestors looked down at the company with their bright eyes. Were they surprised?

Dr Wagner raised his glass and said:

You happy eyes
Whatever you saw
Whatever it was
May it be as of yore.

'Yes,' said Auntie. 'That's good . . . who wrote it?'

They were all sitting by the hearth, the women, the baron with the parrot and the cat, and Peter, keeping quiet. He was still too young to be allowed to join in the conversation, but he could be there, and he listened to it all. Was he proud, he was asked, to bear such a great name?

The baron read aloud from his history of his birthplace, when and by whom the city had been founded and then, getting more interesting, how the Russians had wreaked havoc when they occupied the Baltic states in 1919, stabbed the city councillors and threw their bodies down a well. He smoked a very special pipe as he told this tale, Peter had never seen a pipe like that before. Or a suit patterned with such large checks either.

Wagner the schoolmaster, wearing his third tie, his head propped on his left hand, stroking his goatee beard the wrong way with his bony fingers, listened to the baron's stories, not exactly spellbound, but with interest. He hadn't known how efficiently the German Freikorps fighting bands had cleared the place out. There had been no shilly-shallying; they had driven the Reds away.

Was the baron going to revise his narrative? asked Dr Wagner; he thought it needed a finishing touch here and there.

'No,' said the baron. 'What I've written, I have written.'

Dr Wagner still had the poems of his youth in his desk in Mitkau. Why not give the company a taste of one or another of them on an evening such as this? Yes, why not?

The flames on the hearth flickered over the circle, making its members' eyes shine. The bottle of Barolo brought out by Katharina had something to do with that. They even took the old glasses out of the cupboard for it.

The parrot put his head under his wing, the cat lay on the baron's lap. It made you think of Boccaccio and Dante. They had sat by the fire telling stories too, hadn't they?

Late at night they lowered their voices to a whisper. The subject of conversation was the Jews.

'They'll take their revenge . . .'

'I don't think much of those fellows, but . . .'

'Oh well, forget it . . .'

Who'd have thought it could be so cosy at the Georgenhof? They'd think of that later on. A pity, really, that Eberhard wasn't here. Where was he now? Was he thinking of the Georgenhof? Of Katharina and his son, Peter?

Finally Dr Wagner played the first movement of the 'Moonlight Sonata' as he had never played it before, followed by another piece of a very different kind, and his audience quite forgot to ask what it was.

Wagner with his crooked back and his third tie under his goatee beard. He had never played that piece to them before. It must come from his last happy times. Summer days in the Harz Mountains. Winter days with his mother. Autumn with the leaves turning colour. The circular walk below the town walls, a fine view of the countryside.

The baron, who usually just cleared his throat while Dr Wagner was playing the piano, asked whether he would play that piece again. But Wagner had already closed the piano lid.

15

A Teacher

The next day, the Baltic couple left. The baron told Auntie how much he admired her for her thoughtfulness and all her busy activity, addressing her by name. 'Frau Harnisch,' he said, 'you are a very industrious woman,' and he patted her on her bony back. He kissed Katharina's hand several times, with feeling, and lightly stroked Peter, who was with them, on the cheek. 'Look after your mother, won't you?' And he waved to the ancestors on the wall, whose wide eyes followed everything that was going on.

Then he went into the kitchen and spoke to the two maids at some length. Was he appealing to them? Telling them they must take good care of their dear mistress and always stick together? The conversation probably went something like that. He gave them five marks each, and they thanked him, bobbing a little curtsy.

He even drew slender Sonya close to him for a moment.

'Lora!' screeched the parrot. 'You old sow!'

Dr Wagner the schoolmaster was already at the front door. And as cart after cart went by down on the road, to the background noise of guns rumbling on the horizon – *Goodnight, dear mother, goodnight* – the two of them shook hands, man to man. Don't come to grief at the last moment, keep your chin up and so forth. And here's an address in Wuppertal, commit it to memory, we can get in touch that way when all this is over.

The baron had certain plans; he knew exactly what he wanted to do, and so did his wife. They hoped to go as far west as possible. Bremen, perhaps, why not? Somewhere in the country there, maybe.

Dr Wagner had no concrete ideas yet. *I surge like the sea, restlessly swaying.* Lao-Tse said something like that. He would let himself drift, he wouldn't do anything by force, he would work calmly and with composure towards his own fulfilment. With a sweeping gesture, he indicated the East Prussian countryside at his feet and the snake-like line of refugees boring into it. Mustn't put one's hand into the spokes of the wheel of Fortune. Thank God, he had to say, that his mother was dead already. Gone at the right time. Those dear old people had been a luckier generation.

The Baltic couple had hardly gone out into the road, rucksacks on their backs, the suitcase beside them and carrying the parrot cage, when a car swerved out of the column and stopped. Did they want a lift? They certainly did! 'Then in you get!' said the driver. Although that suitcase, a heavy great thing – it would surely break the axle! – would have to be left behind. 'Sorry.' And they had to get a move on, they didn't have much time, couldn't wait around in the road.

What was to be done with the heavy suitcase? All those chronicles, and the half-finished manuscript? Should they leave it at the manor house until better times came? Think of all the things that might happen . . . Hadn't tanks driven by only last night on their way to the front? So the baroness dragged the case back up the bank beside the road and into the house again. Wagner, still standing in the doorway, took it into his own keeping; yes, he'd do what he could, he'd care for the suitcase like the apple of his eye, they could depend on that.

Should they extract the manuscript about the baron's native city? Wasn't it right at the top? But the cheerful driver was hooting his horn. The man even got out and walked round his car to help them in. Stood beside the car door until they were properly settled.

The baron waved grandly to the foreign workers standing side by side on the terrace of the Forest Lodge, following these farewells with watchful eyes. Wasn't that like a kind of salute? And off they went.

The Globigs were sad to see the baron and his wife leave. Those quiet evenings by the fire had been so comfortable; such cultivated people, it had been like getting a new lease of life. They would happily have kept the couple here for ever. Even Auntie sighed heavily; it was true, she had indeed done a lot of hard work in her life, the baron was right about that. He had hit the nail on the head. And she put on an apron: there was a lot of dust to be removed from the tops of cupboards. Peter held the ladder steady for her. It all had to be left neat and clean if by any chance they themselves were to go away from the Georgenhof.

There was a great deal of telephoning next day. Uncle Josef in Albertsdorf said, 'What, Baltic Germans? All those people were crazy.' And he added, 'A baron? Well, yes, if it was true – You'd better stay at home. We're all staying here, leaving now is the worst thing to do.' In addition, said Uncle Josef, he *couldn't* leave, because the whole house was full of people, people from God knew where, thieving like magpies. Thank God none of them were from the Baltic.

And yes, another column of tanks had gone by in the night, he thought they were Waffen-SS. They'd soon fix things. Hitler wasn't fool enough to let the Russians into the country. He might let them in just a little way, but then he'd pull the strings of the sack closed and trap them.

*

Go to Berlin after all? The Globigs discussed this idea over and over again. Go to Wilmersdorf? Katharina made long, detailed phone calls to her cousin. The Globigs had always sent the Berlin cousins such lovely presents, always when they were least expecting it. For Anita's confirmation, and the goose just before Christmas. And they'd had Elisabeth staying here for months on end when she was about to start medical studies and prepare for her first exam. The children had come to stay for ages in the holidays, riding the horses like mad. Hadn't they crossed themselves three times when they left, as you do on entering and leaving a church?

In particular, the possibility of sending the boy at least to Berlin was the subject of much discussion. But when it was brought up, they said in Berlin, 'Yes, but how do you think we could manage it? When Elisabeth is still having such trouble with her feet? Two operations, and she still isn't better. And where would he sleep? And then he'd have to go to school here, and Hitler Youth service . . .' It was all very difficult, and somehow or other it was out of the question.

Auntie asked what, for heaven's sake, was to be done with all those crates that had been standing around in the drawing room for months and months. No one here could take responsibility for them, did the Berlin cousins realize that?

To this the Berlin cousins replied that they were good solid crates, what could go wrong? They had put an inventory of contents at the top of each, and a copy of the inventory had been deposited with the Berlin cousins' lawyer so that there could be no misunderstanding.

Then they asked if perhaps the crates couldn't be sent back to Berlin by horse-drawn cart. A single load should be enough to do it. They knew that no trains could leave Mitkau now, but a horse-drawn cart could surely get through? All their table linen and bed linen were there, along with underclothes, suits, dresses. And the family silver!

They had even packed up the family Bible in one of the crates. Who would ever have guessed that things would come to this? That Bible dated back to the seventeenth century, too.

'Inventory of contents?' said Auntie. 'Well, you certainly find what people are really like in times of need.' And she held the telephone receiver out of the window, so that even in Berlin they could hear what was going on: the wind was blowing the sound of rumbling here from the east, and it was distinctly audible.

'Are you still on the line?' someone asked at the other end.

Those cousins weren't living in the real world! Depositing copies of the inventories with their lawyer. You could only laugh. All their table linen and bed linen? Underclothes? Suits and dresses? The silver! – Auntie stood thoughtfully in front of the crates and wondered what else might be in them. Cognac, maybe? Nothing was easy, was it? For goodness' sake, it was hundreds of kilometres from Mitkau to Berlin by horse-drawn cart. The horses would fall down dead!

Anyway, the big farm cart was already loaded up with their own possessions. Vladimir had stacked them neatly, crates and boxes and suitcases, all tied up with clothes lines. He had even seen that the horses had been shod with winter shoes. No one would have thought the man could be trusted to do all that. In the evening he sat in the kitchen reading the Bible. They'd made the mistake of assuming that everyone from the east was the same. 'Polish economy' – it was a synonym for bad management and disorder. He'd even managed to fit the big milk cans in. Why? Well, because they were full of dripping and flour and sugar.

New refugees arrived: a village schoolteacher called Hesse, who kept shaking, and his wife, Helga (Heil Hitler), with their two boys, whom they had called Eckbert and Ingomar.

Peter had to clear his room for them, as instructed by Drygalski, and move in with his mother. Before leaving his own room, he shot down the paper planes with his air pistol. The Wellington, the Spitfire and the Messerschmitt 109. They sailed to the floor one after another. Then he opened the window, set fire to them and let them sail out towards the tree house. True to life, they crash-landed in the yard. He packed his railway up in cartons, pushed the castle into a corner, and took the microscope with him. There was something moving now in the liquid where he had steeped some hay. Tiny animalcules were floundering about there. Would they get bigger? Would there be no room in the end for anything else on the glass plate under the lens?

The refugees stood in the hall with their luggage, looking lost, and didn't move from the spot. Goodness, what a huge place! Is it, they wondered, some kind of castle?

'And who keeps it all clean?' they asked Auntie.

They had been on the road for ever and a day, or rather three days, leaving everything behind. The teacher had left his collection of Stone Age artefacts from the village behind: his stone axes, scrapers and blades. All neatly numbered. His wife had left her pretty garden, where she grew dahlias every year, stocks, hollyhocks, phlox, systematically laid out in order of rotation and their requirements for light and shade.

The man looked damaged. That was because he had suffered a stroke three years ago. He mentioned it at once, telling them how one morning at breakfast, thinking nothing of it, he had slumped sideways with his mouth distorted.

'And I thought he was joking!' said his wife.

He wore glasses with strong lenses, and a Party symbol, and looked more like the grandfather than the father of his two sons, who both had glasses as well.

His wife, on the other hand, gave a vigorous impression. She had white hair combed back, held in place by a tortoiseshell hoop.

She pulled her husband's hair back from his forehead – had a lash fallen into his eye to make him blink like that? – cleaned the inside of his ears and straightened his tie. Yes, he had collapsed, said the man, and thought it was nothing much at first, but it was a stroke. And his wife had thought he was joking.

'Well, that's enough complaining of our troubles,' she cried. Even before she had taken her coat off she was going from pot plant to pot plant, nipping something off here, adjusting something there. And then – was it imagination, or did the flowers really breathe more freely for her care of them? Had they been waiting for a loving hand so long?

She took their ration cards out of her handbag and was about to give them to Katharina; she expected they'd have to eat here, she said, and she was happy to peel potatoes any time. There wasn't a grocer's shop anywhere near; they must have had to foot it to Mitkau for any extra little thing, and it was an icy road to walk.

'No, never mind the cards,' said Katharina. 'Keep them.' But just then Auntie came along. 'Ration cards? Of course . . .' They weren't a charitable institution, she pointed out. Two adults, two children? The baron had always helped himself with a lavish hand, and then he liked to go to the kitchen and find something to nibble from time to time. She didn't want that happening again. He never so much as mentioned the coupons. Ration cards? He didn't even know what they were.

'Well, you'd better come upstairs,' said Auntie.

Auntie showed them Peter's room. They'd soon feel at home there, she said. A bedstead was brought down from the attic, and mattresses, and the beds were made up with clean sheets. 'You'll be comfortable here with us,' said Auntie.

The boys were put in Elfie's room, where they immediately began playing with the puppet theatre, by which they meant bashing the puppets together and pulling the curtain up and down until the strings working it broke. Peter asked if they would like to see his little animalcules under the microscope, but they wouldn't. They took an interest in the *Crouching Woman*, though, and although they wore thick glasses they scrutinized her closely, going *woo-hoo-hoo!*

The teacher's wife went to the kitchen to ask if her husband could have a hot-water bottle. 'Oh, what a wonderful stove you have!' she exclaimed, and said she'd like to make dumplings on it. And look at all those copper pots and pans, arranged in order of size. She would really enjoy polishing them up with Sidol metal cleaner. Wonderful! How she would like to be in charge of a wonderful kitchen like this some day. The maids were pleased with her enthusiasm, and even felt a little proud of the kitchen, which they had never examined very closely, and acted as if it all belonged to them, but when the good woman was about to open the larder door, there was Auntie suddenly standing in the way.

So the teacher's wife hurried back up to him. He was already impatient, wondering where she was. 'Helga!' He took the hot-water bottle and asked her to push the chair over to the window for him. 'Where've you been all this time?' He held his hands behind his ears, the better to hear what excuse she could give.

They settled in. The Hesses had only a rucksack each and a few other oddments. It had all happened so fast. 'My stone axes!'

wailed Herr Hesse. 'My scrapers!' He had been obliged to leave all those things behind.

It worried his wife to find that the Georgenhof was a real landed estate, even if a dilapidated one. And she whispered in Katharina's ear, *Do you own the estate?* and wondered aloud whether they didn't want to leave at once. The Reds made short work of landowners, killing them on the spot. Junkers, the old-established landed gentry, were a thorn in their flesh. The Globigs might do better to get away while there was still time, pack everything and leave, preferably tomorrow.

She herself was uneasy, too: how long would she and her family be hanging around here? They had been told that someone would let them know. Outside on the road, cart followed cart, and they were stuck in this place.

Drygalski (Heil Hitler) gave the Hesses a hand moving in; he had nothing special to do at the moment. The lines of refugees came from the east of their own accord, and went on to the west of their own accord too. There was no need for him to do anything about it. He was prowling round Katharina as if he wanted to tell her something, and Katharina didn't like it. When she looked at his brown jackboots, she wondered where he had been in them.

Drygalski carried Peter's box of books, and the carton containing his railway and his tin soldiers, over to her apartment with his own hands. And his coats and jackets too; he handled every one of them and asked whether this or that garment was still needed. Couldn't some of these things be given to all those refugees?

Strange: that little chest in Katharina's bedroom. Hadn't it been somewhere else in the house before?

Perhaps it would be better to move the *Crouching Woman* out

of the field of vision? Was it a good idea for the boy to be looking at it all the time? The ancestral portraits downstairs, this
Crouching Woman up here ... they didn't really go together. He
didn't know that the artist who had created so sensuous and frank
a figure of a crouching woman was a Party comrade and had
access to Hitler – no, Drygalski had no idea of that.

Peter bounced on his parents' beds. Drygalski, standing in the
doorway, watched him. He looked at the boy: blond, with a thin
face, a real German boy, who would certainly soon be defending
his native Germany, gun in hand, when the going got tough, just
as his own son had done when he fell in Poland.

'How old are you? Twelve?' Yes, a little too soon for him to be
rushing into the thick of the fighting. And he had swollen tonsils at the moment, you had to take swollen tonsils seriously. His
son had also been blond, but he had never bounced on beds.

Drygalski switched Katharina's radio on; it was tuned to
Copenhagen. But it was forbidden to listen to foreign radio sta-
tions. The news in Danish? Weren't there plenty of German
transmitters; did she have to listen in to Copenhagen? However,
German soldiers were marching through the streets of
Copenhagen, weren't they? They were sitting in Danish cafés
eating whipped cream, and that was a fact. There was even a
Danish Waffen-SS, fighting shoulder by shoulder with their
German comrades against the Bolshevists. Danes, Dutch, French,
Slovakians, even Russians! Ukrainians! Cossacks! Man beside
man! All Europe had risen against the Red Peril. The forces
would hold together with an iron will.

And it was the same here. It was obvious that the Globigs were
welcoming refugees, that was to their credit.

But if someone tunes her radio to a Danish station, wasn't it
to be assumed that she might listen to the BBC now and then
too? Perhaps by accident. Copenhagen, it wasn't so far from the

BBC. Drygalski couldn't make up his mind. He'd better report it to the district leader and ask for orders.

Shouldn't she be honest, asked Drygalski, and admit that she listened in to the BBC now and then?

Katharina pushed the little chest in front of the cubbyhole again and sniffed. Tobacco? Chocolate? No, there was no smell of either.

The head trustee liked the conservatory. What a wonderful view! Everything perfect. It must be glorious in summer, even if it looked bleak now, of course. He glanced down at the path he had trodden in the snow, and was surprised by the regularity of the semicircle. As if it had been drawn with a pair of compasses. Frau Hesse, who had made her way into Katharina's conservatory with him, was looking critically at the cacti and flowering plants. What a sad sight they were. Dusty, with dead flies everywhere. They all urgently needed repotting.

Drygalski was about to say what a fine group the Globig family had been, sitting on the grass in summer drinking coffee. So peaceful and contented. Had that been before the war? He didn't say it was a picture.

'I suppose you've never used the arbour?' he asked.

But Katharina was guiding him towards the door. Was there anything else?

Unfortunately he'd had bad luck with his refugee girl, he said as he was going out. In herself, she was pretty and neat and a willing worker. A nice girl, she could have had whatever she wanted from him. He'd thought of offering her a home for ever. But she'd been overcome by lust! All of a sudden, lying in wait for him, following him down to the cellar and so on. Rotten through and through. He'd had to do something about that, of course. The hussy had been turned out on the street, immediately. He made short work of that kind of thing. A pity, really; otherwise she was a nice girl, trim and neat. He'd have liked to keep her.

'That girl could have asked me for anything ...' It had been sad to see her standing in the road all alone. But his wife, sick as she was, might have got wind of something, and that would have been terrible.

Sick, shaky Herr Hesse was lurking in the corridor to speak to the head trustee. Heil Hitler, his name was Hesse and he had been a Party member since 1939. He told Drygalski the symptoms of his stroke, how it had happened and what he had felt about it. His wife had told him that his mouth had been slanting right down. And at first she had thought he was only joking. 'If it hadn't been for my wife!' he cried, and then he asked himself and Herr Drygalski, 'What are we supposed to be doing here? We have a referral certificate for Danzig, but the railway line to Danzig isn't open.' What did he think they should do now? He supposed there was nothing for them to do here, and he couldn't very well just stand at the roadside.

Drygalski said, 'We'll find out.' There was some kind of reception camp in Danzig providing medical care, and that would solve it all. As he said so, he was wondering whether there was really any such camp, and if so whether it would be the place for his own constantly ailing wife. It was to be assumed that such a place did exist; the Party would surely splash out on such things.

Herr Hesse wasn't letting go of Drygalski so easily. There was something else on his mind, he said: his collection of old Germanic artefacts – couldn't a car be sent to collect them from the Hesses' apartment? Irreplaceable old stone axes and scrapers. Maybe a troop of Hitler Youth lads, ready for anything, could be sent?

'What did you say?' he asked.

But Drygalski hadn't said anything. He was pursuing his own train of thought.

The Hesses stood at their window, watching the procession of refugees go by, and they realized that they could feel the floor shaking. Frau Hesse told her husband, 'I think you'd better lie down and get some rest.'

'I should at least have brought the stone axe with me,' he said, adding that he would always blame himself for leaving it behind. 'The one with the hole in it . . .'

'But why worry?' said his wife. 'The Party will lock it all up and keep it safe until we can come back.'

It was unthinkable for them to stand at the roadside and hope to get a lift at once, as the baron and his wife had done. No one would stop for them. But Drygalski would sort it all out.

However, now to eat. Supper's ready! Supper's ready! The Hesses, sitting in a corner, half rose to their feet: did that mean them too? Yes, it did. 'Of course,' said Auntie, and she let their boys bang the brass gong hanging from the wall, with a brass elephant holding it in his trunk. Herr Hesse carefully wiped his plate and spoon on the tablecloth, and then started spooning soup into his mouth. They served chicken soup at home with baked egg garnish, said the village schoolteacher as he slurped. The globules of fat on top of his soup seemed to interest him. Was he actually counting them?

Peter showed the Hesse boys the hallmarks on the soup spoons. And the pattern on the plates: the pond where cranes stood, and the boat with a fisherman just bringing in his net from the water.

Hesse looked at his wife. How, he wondered, was he ever going to stand it if there was all this chattering at table? Could anyone tell him that? Children have to be seen and not heard, that was a good saying.

If he had opened his mouth during meals as a child, his father would have smacked him in the face.

Then he told everyone what it had felt like when he slumped sideways. It's all over now, he had thought. He told his story to everyone sitting at the table, and to his wife and children who, after all, had been there at the time. It was his wife who had got on her bike and cycled straight off to the local doctor, who arrived just in time to save him. His wife could tell them all about that, completing her husband's account of the incident. And then he, in turn, confirmed all that she said. Imagine if he had been alone at home! That could have happened, couldn't it?

It was now three years ago that he had collapsed. The day was marked in red on the calendar. Suppose he had lost his powers of speech, or been left disabled? And then what would have become of his stone axes?

The two boys were a little younger than Peter, and were quick on the uptake. Eckbert and Ingomar. You could see them imitating their father's dragging footsteps as he went along the corridor. He'd probably smacked them round the face often enough in the past, when he still had his full health and strength.

Peter took them all round the house, and yes, they were definitely quick on the uptake. They were not interested in the tiny creatures to be seen through his microscope, but they hammered away on the piano, they banged the gong and they got the gramophone working. *Si, si, si, give me a penny . . .* They took a good look at the damp cellar, where there were gurgling sounds – could wicked criminals once have been chained to the walls here, waiting to be executed? Peter locked the cellar door behind the two boys, rattled the keys, and let them stew in their own juice in the dark for a while.

There were walnuts laid out to dry in the attic. The boys explored the huge old wardrobes up there. A hussar's shako dating from imperial times? Peter's mother's wedding dress. A collapsible top hat.

They played dressing-up games, and couldn't understand why Katharina suddenly burst into tears as Peter came downstairs in her wedding dress, with Eckbert in Eberhard's top hat.

The coach was standing out in the yard now too. Vladimir had got it out of the carriage house and stuffed straw into any gaps, draught-proofing the window in its door. Peter sat in it to see what it felt like. It was very comfortable. He looked forward to driving away with his mother in the coach, going to the west. How much longer must he wait? The two Hesse boys scrambled in beside him, and they agreed that it was very comfortable.

'Stay where you are and don't move!'

They rode down the little slope behind the house on the sledge again and again. Then, after playing for a while, they took the sledge round to the front of the house and rode down the slope to the road. The drivers of the carts trotting past along the road hit out at them with their whips. A car stopped. Were the boys out of their minds? Playing with a sledge in serious times like these, riding all the way down to the road? They could easily have an accident.

Peter took the boys to the chicken run and showed them how friendly the old rooster was. They climbed up to the hayloft in the big barn and fooled around in the hay. One of the boys nearly fell through the trapdoor in the loft to the floor below.

'Don't tell my father,' said his brother, 'or he'll get slapped again.'

They climbed to the Ukrainian maids' bedroom in the cottage, too, but the maids sent them packing. Peter saw at once that the girls had all kinds of things in their room that hadn't been there before. He wondered whether those crates in the summer drawing room were still intact.

The Hesse boys shouted 'Polack!' at Vladimir, who grabbed them and gave them a hiding, hitting harder than was necessary. It was to be hoped that Drygalski hadn't seen that. German boys being chastised by a man of inferior race.

Was it just chance that the Pole brought the Hesse family damp wood for their stove that evening?

They ran through the forest, past the ruins of the castle and down to the river, where the old boat lay in the ice. They slid across the river to the opposite bank, and watched the long line of refugees trekking over the bridge.

They also went to see the foreign workers in the Forest Lodge. They slept in bunk beds, and it was rather cramped. The Czech wanted to kick the three boys out, but the others were friendly to them. They asked how strong they were and felt their muscles. The Romanian taught them to smoke, and showed them a conjuring trick: how to make money disappear when it had been lying on the table only a moment ago. Marcello the Italian sang them a Neapolitan song, accompanying himself on the mandolin. He had covered the walls with pictures of naked girls. The *Crouching Woman* couldn't compete with those girls.

The Czech carved them wooden daggers, and showed them how to cut someone's throat with a knife.

Romania? No, they had no idea where it was.

The boys' dearest wish would have been to sleep over with the foreign men one night, but of course they weren't allowed to.

Best of all would be to stay with them; go away with them and have adventures.

They brought the foreign workers a peacock feather, which was readily accepted. All they'd needed was a peacock feather, said the men, and now the place was really comfortable.

Of course the boys explored the whole of the Forest Lodge: the panelled dining room with a one-legged grand piano in the corner; the terrace where hotel guests used to drink their coffee; the rooms used by the National Socialist Motor Corps to store spare parts. Peter appropriated a shiny metal bar there, just the thing for the aircraft in his tree house.

Auntie was surprised to find that the hens had stopped laying. The inmates of the Forest Lodge, however, had plenty of eggs.

'Let me smell your breath,' the village schoolteacher's wife told her boys. 'You haven't been smoking, have you?'

Did they know how unhealthy it was to smoke?

The teacher threw back the blanket under which he was keeping himself warm, and scolded his family. Why didn't his wife keep a better eye on the boys? For heaven's sake, he had been telling them for years that they were forbidden to smoke, and now all rules could be broken. Next thing anyone knew they'd be going round with a bottle of schnapps.

Peter climbed up to his tree house with the other boys and fitted the shiny bar in place. He could fix a rear-view mirror to it, but he'd better forget about a horn.

They watched the great trek go on from up in the tree: occasional people on foot; horse-drawn carts piled high with possessions. People on bicycles, others pulling sledges. They counted the carts, but stopped when they got to two hundred.

They also saw a procession of prisoners go by, coming from the brickworks, wearing striped coats and wooden clogs. Sad figures dragging themselves along. They were guarded to left and right by soldiers with rifles at the ready.

The pale face of frail Herr Hesse appeared at his upstairs window. He was watching the prisoners go by too. He cleaned his teeth with a wooden toothpick, and then knocked on the windowpane to let the boys know they must get down from that tree house at once. What did they think they were doing? They'd break all their bones, and then there'd be trouble. Wasn't it enough that he, their father, had almost died, and without any advance warning? Those men in striped coats – they must be antisocial characters. Heaven knew what laws they had broken.

His wife was looking round the outside of the place. She walked once round the house, and then she wondered: why no garden, with such a large property?

'Don't you have a garden?' she asked.

'We have a park,' replied Auntie.

'Yes, but such a huge plot of land, and no garden?' And Frau Hesse talked about her dahlias, the begonias – their tubers would be rotting in the cellar now – and the vegetables she used to grow. Broad beans! Green peas! Leeks! There were rakes, scythes and spades hanging from the stable wall. How she would love to lay out a garden here in spring. Ah, in spring . . . ?

Frau Hesse, who had once been on a first-aid course run by the National Socialist Nurses' Association, noticed that Peter had something wrong with his throat. 'Come here for a moment,' she told him, and she looked down his throat, massaged his larynx and gave him some drops to take. Lo and behold, his tonsils weren't swollen any more next morning.

'That woman practises witchcraft!' said Auntie. She wasn't entirely happy with the way Frau Hesse changed the positions of flowering pot plants in the hall, put the cacti in the dark and what looked like dry twigs of some kind in water in a preserving jar, saying that then they would flower again. Auntie was about to put everything back in its old place, but somehow or other the new arrangement did look better, and made the dark hall seem friendlier. Especially when the sun shone in.

As for Peter's catarrh, now bewitched away, perhaps that wasn't such a good idea. What were they going to tell Drygalski when he came looking for Hitler Youth boys to help out somewhere?

Katharina and the teacher's wife got on well. They sat together. Frau Hesse took her good blouse out of her rucksack, and her wool and linen skirt, and Katharina put on the silver brooch that she had brought back from Italy. They played games of patience. First down in the hall, then they moved up to Katharina's room, and locked the door. There were always people going in and out of the hall, and all of them left the doors open. Upstairs they could be undisturbed.

'Helga!' called Herr Hesse. 'Where are you?' But there was no answer, even when he put his hands behind his ears. Helga was sitting on the other side of a locked door with Frau von Globig, playing cards. Then they stopped playing cards and talked about what women talk about, sitting together on their own. Katharina opened her wardrobe, and Frau Hesse enjoyed a fashion show: Katharina's pleated skirt, and all those hats. Katharina would have liked to tell the teacher's wife her secret. It was on the tip of her tongue to say, 'Just imagine, a man spent the night in that cubby hole! He climbed over the rose fence.' But she didn't, she kept it strictly to herself. What had happened here must remain a secret, and she would take it to the grave if necessary.

'Helga!' called Herr Hesse. 'Where are you?' He felt cold, and that couldn't be good for him.

The boys were nowhere to be seen. They had gone off to visit the foreign workers again. So he had to get up himself and move his chair closer to the stove. It was a mystery to him why that stove wouldn't draw. If he had another stroke it would be his wife's fault. Looking in the mirror, he drew his mouth down on one side so it looked as it had on that Sunday morning when he hadn't known what was about to happen. .

He had once made a Stone Age loom with his schoolchildren, and the man from the education authority had praised it. Heavens, how many years ago was that? It was all so far in the past. He thought of teacher training college, and how he and his friends used to climb over the wall at night. It had been summer, and the girls sat in front of their houses. The students joked with them, and then climbed the wall by night. He used to wear his hat tilted sideways on his head in those days.

There was no singing in the kitchen. The maids were quiet, and did their work in silence. When Auntie came in to see if everything was all right, Vera went over and asked if she could have a word with her.

'What, here and now?' said Auntie. But then she went upstairs to the maids' room with that mature young woman, who had volunteered to come to Germany from the distant Ukraine and glean experience far from the sunflower fields of her native land, and she sat down in the chair by the window.

'What is it?'

At first Vera shed copious tears, and then, wringing her hands, told Auntie that she was going to have a baby. What was she to do?

'A baby?' said Auntie. 'How did that happen? And now of all times!' What, she asked Vera, did she think of doing about it? That was exactly what Vera wanted Auntie to tell her. But Auntie had no idea either.

She couldn't find out whether one of the foreign workers in the Forest Lodge was to blame for this misfortune – the Czech, or Marcello the cheerful Italian? Or could it be Vladimir? No, surely not the upright and honest Pole. The Czech? He always looked so venomous, and once he had even made his way into the house. Auntie felt sure he carried a sharp knife. He was capable of anything.

Well, whether it was a Czech, a Pole or an Italian, at least it wasn't a case of racial defilement. And Vera wasn't giving any information; she just went on crying.

Frau Hesse was asked for advice, since she had cured Peter's tonsils, but her medical knowledge wasn't up to something like this. She could have relieved a sprained ankle with a criss-cross bandage, or put a dressing on a cut finger, but she didn't meddle with unwanted pregnancies. The Nazi nurses had not discussed the subject. After all, it was wonderful to bring another human being into the world, so why try to prevent it?

She advised Vera to avoid lifting heavy weights, and not to jump off a stool for fear of suffering a miscarriage.

After that, Vera could be heard all over the house jumping off stools wherever and whenever she had the opportunity.

Perhaps, said Auntie, St John's wort would help? But where would you get St John's wort in midwinter? And what was it supposed to do, or not to do?

Frau Hesse played patience with Katharina, whispered to the Ukrainian maids, and made her husband dumplings, in return for which, and weak as he was, he tickled her under the chin, even though, as he said, the dumplings tasted of Sidol metal cleaner.

When Frau Hesse heard of the problems of the Drygalski household, she put on her hat and went over there to talk to Drygalski's wife. Heil Hitler. A woman in the prime of life, lying in bed? She spent a long time explaining why she had to pull herself together. Otherwise her husband might start looking elsewhere. She talked about the Drygalskis' lovely house, and admired the way they had furnished it. And she pointed to the picture of their son, who had fallen fighting, and who she thought looked like Peter, and also to the crucifix – where did that come from?

And, wonderful to relate, fresh blood began circulating in the woman's veins. She sat up in bed and asked for a mirror. Next morning she was down in the kitchen, frying her husband two eggs and bacon for breakfast.

A woman must fight to keep her man, Frau Hesse had whispered, adding that Frau Drygalski, with her mischievous expression, still looked pretty good. Wouldn't it be worth cultivating it? Why didn't she get up and give her husband a mischievous smile now and then? And so Frau Drygalski did.

Drygalski was almost ready to fall on his knees before such a miracle. But as he ate the eggs she had fried him, he also began feeling furious. How did this come to happen all of a sudden? Had she, perhaps, not been so sick after all? Could she have been frying him eggs every day, and sometimes giving him smoked sausage with green cabbage? There he had been, slaving away and worrying about her. Mollycoddling her to her heart's content. And he'd almost landed himself with a problem in the shape of that girl, what was her name? She'd had a sudden fit of lasciviousness – she'd flung her arms round him in the cellar doorway, pressing her body close to his.

Drygalski walked round his house and spat in the bushes. No. He had let himself be fooled, and he wasn't taking that sort of thing.

By the fire in the evening, in the pleasant company which the Hesses must of course be invited to join, Hesse the village teacher told Dr Wagner the schoolmaster how nice he had always been to the village children. He had always tried to be gentle, although of course a teacher must also be strict, and then he went on to the story of how he had suffered that stroke on a Sunday, of all days. Without any advance warning, in the morning at breakfast.

'At first we thought nothing much of it,' said the teacher's wife, 'but when I saw saliva running from his mouth . . .' Then she thought: no, this won't do! And she had cycled straight off to the doctor. Now he sat there with his hands folded in his lap. She had wrapped a blanket round his legs, which had no strength left in them. And in the past he had been able to swing round in a circle on the horizontal bars in the gym, and perform a straddle vault over the horse.

Ah, his beloved Königsberg, said Dr Wagner. Eating fried flounders in a little restaurant on the River Pregel . . . and hearing the foghorns of the big ships in harbour going *wooo-wooo-wooo*. He had brought his poems with him, why not offer to read them? Sitting by the fire declaiming poetry was conviviality in the old style. The dog and the cat in front of the life-giving fire, and children listening with their eyes wide.

He was civil to the new guest, who after all was, in a way, his colleague, and the man's wife was very nice as well, in her skirt of hand-woven russet-red wool and linen. But when the man went on and on, yet again, about his stroke, Dr Wagner cast up his eyes to heaven, and then his glance met Katharina's. He was unaware that the village teacher also cast up his eyes to heaven, if for a different reason. This was all I needed, thought Herr Hesse, a specialist in higher education who prides himself on writing poetry.

So Wagner left his poems in his pocket. Anyway, he had brought the telescope from school, where it was standing around unused. As nothing had come of the poetry idea, he went outside into the open air with the boy to look at the stars. But the sky was overcast.

'Close the door!' the village teacher called after him.

*

Wagner said goodnight. These days it was better to be at home within your own four walls. He tried it: he tried carrying Katharina's hand to his lips, as the baron had done again and again. But she withdrew it with an expression of distaste.

He left the telescope at the Georgenhof. He couldn't very well keep taking it back and forth.

On the way home he thought of Katharina – he would have liked to read her his poems, up in her boudoir, at her feet, so to speak, as they did in the old days. He would have liked to read her one in particular, the most successful one. He had given it to his mother on Mother's Day. *Caput mortuum* . . . To think that it was women who bear all the sorrow in the world. God, how long ago was it that his mother had died? That kindly woman.

Although he could not see the stars, he was sure that a benevolent father protected him. The thunder in the distance suited his mood. The Twilight of the Gods! There was something grand in that idea.

Suppose people of some kind were billeted on him, in his own apartment? The thought filled him with anxiety.

That night Katharina lay on her bed fully clothed, listening to the distant rumbling. She felt the ground shake when there were explosions, and the glasses beside the washbasin clinked softly. She must talk to someone, but who? Pastor Brahms? Ask him whether everything was all right? Should she leave first thing tomorrow? Get away from any possible consequences of what she had done?

It was difficult to reach Lothar Sarkander these days; when Katharina phoned she was always told that he wasn't there. And anyway, what did she think he could have said?

'As you can imagine,' they told her in his office, 'the mayor has his hands full at the moment.' That wasn't the way they used to speak to her.

Katharina opened the cubbyhole. Why had she let herself in for that adventure? And then again: why hadn't she kept the man there? If you start something you should see it through. But she had been glad to be rid of him, that was the truth.

16

Police

Next morning there was a phone call from the police in Mitkau. Katharina was still in bed when the phone rang. They had picked up a man in the monastery courtyard – a Jew! – and after denying it for a long time he had admitted being hidden by her at the Georgenhof. Was it true?

Soon after that the mayor rang. Lothar Sarkander, whom she'd been unable to reach for so long, would you believe it? This time he didn't want to talk about the old days, he said not a word about the summer drawing room. He came straight to the point. For God's sake ... he had heard ... they'd been in touch with him ... 'How could you, Kathi?'

The police had already been to see him, he whispered into the receiver. The pastor had been taken away.

'How could you let yourself in for something like that ...? You must have known that these people walk over dead bodies!'

A note had been found on the man, a sketch showing the way to what was clearly the Georgenhof ... 'It's criminal to put anything down on paper! How could you be so naïve?'

The sketch had been put in front of the man, and he'd had to admit everything. Yes; he'd tried talking his way out of it, but the sketch was conclusive.

At midday, to the sound of fierce barking from Jago, a police detective turned up; a quiet, mournful man in a leather coat. He drove right up to the house in a steam-driven car, and left it outside the front door. Heil Hitler. Everyone was sitting at the table round a steaming tureen of soup. The Hesses, Auntie and Dr Wagner too. Katharina was calmly serving out the soup, which she never usually did.

When Wagner discovered that the newcomer was a police detective, he put down his spoon and pushed his soup plate aside. He thought it would be better not to get in the way here, but go back to Mitkau at once, even though he had only just arrived. Things that were none of his business were coming to light. He put the poems that he had been going to give Katharina back into his pocket, and strode vigorously away. He did not take the direct road back, which was icy; he didn't want a fall and a broken hip at this late date. Standing erect, and without hesitating, he walked towards the stream of horse-drawn carts.

'Is it much further?' a little girl asked him. Much further to where? He shrugged his shoulders.

The company round the table had risen to their feet, and the Ukrainian maids came out of the kitchen. The police officer had a photograph. He held it in front of Katharina's nose and asked if she knew the man in it. He had admitted to being hidden by her in some kind of cubbyhole on the first floor here. 'Is there such a cubbyhole in this house? On the first floor? And did you know that the man is a Jew?'

Auntie stood up as well, and looked at the photo. So did the two Ukrainian girls, who were curious too. Did Katharina know the man, and what was all this about a cubbyhole?

The Hesses also came forward. 'How? What?' asked the teacher. 'What's going on?' Had the time come at last? Had permission to leave come through?

'Eckbert! Ingomar!'

Were they finally to be off on their travels?

*

Drygalski turned up as well, Heil Hitler. He left the front door open and cold air blew in. He too wanted to see the photograph. The officer had already put it away, but he brought it out again. Drygalski examined the photo, and asked Katharina whether she knew the man. 'Do you recognize this man?' He himself had never set eyes on him, although he knew this area so well. Auntie didn't know him either.

Yes, Katharina had seen the man. She said so, loud and clear.

Well, said Drygalski, he'd thought as much, he knew there was something wrong here. He stood there four-square in his brown jackboots, legs apart, and he wished he had a riding crop in his right hand so that he could tap it against the shaft of his boot. They could pull the wool over your eyes for a while, but then it all comes out. You needed a sixth sense, that was the trick of it. 'I knew there was something fishy going on,' he told the police detective. He'd always known there was something wrong here.

Now the detective had to view the scene of the crime. The entire party began to move, a cavalcade climbing up to the first floor. Drygalski went upstairs first, saying that he knew his way around this place. So Drygalski was in the lead, but what with the narrow staircase and the darkness, the police officer soon overtook him. The Hesses followed, and so did the maids from the kitchen, still holding their dishcloths.

Katharina came up the stairs last of all, holding the banister rail. She wasn't in such a hurry.

The whole pack of them stood at the top, watching her climb the stairs slowly, step by step. She produced the key, and the door was unlocked. On view were the unmade bed, a tube of tablets and an open bottle of wine on the bedside table. Had some kind of unnatural vice been practised here? The *Crouching Woman*, just look at that. For heaven's sake!

*

The police officer stood in the middle of the room and looked round. No doubt about it, this was Frau von Globig's bedroom. Next door was the living room of the apartment, and beyond that the room with her books in it, and now her son's as well. Gilded bronze brackets supporting the bookshelves.

He opened the conservatory window and looked down at the fence. 'So he climbed the fence on his way here? Yes, he still had scratches on his hands; they'd been carefully dressed with sticking plaster.' When it's a matter of life or death, yes, anyone would climb a fence.

Drygalski pushed forward and looked down at the park himself, saw the semi-circular path he had trodden in the snow. He said he knew all about it; it had always seemed to him strange. When he was assessing the vacant living space, that little chest had been somewhere else entirely . . .

Was all this about the cubbyhole true? asked the detective. Surely there was some mistake? Oh no, there wasn't. A cubbyhole . . . ?

Drygalski got down on his knees and pushed himself, breathing heavily, into the hole. A mattress. Pillows, blankets? And here was a bedside lamp. A lamp in a cubbyhole? Then he began rooting about under the sloping roof like a boar scenting truffles, and said, 'Here!' Packets of tobacco, cigarettes – he even brought the bottles of wine rolling out. 'Look, Italian wine!'

'So if it comes from Italy . . .' he told the police officer accusingly. And the police officer saw it all.

Katharina was standing beside the *Crouching Woman,* underneath the indoor palm. Auntie was in the doorway, along with the Hesses and the two maids from the kitchen. Herr Hesse was saying, loud and clear, that he too had always thought it odd – all that locking of doors, and he thought he had heard the radio on more often than was normal, in the middle of the night at that. He mentioned his stroke, the difficulty his handicap gave him, how badly he needed peace and quiet. He had no feeling on the left, and he sometimes felt so strange. It was thanks to his wife that he was still on his own two feet. She'd told him she saw saliva dripping from his mouth, and then she knew what had happened to him.

Drygalski joined the interrogation. The police officer was a little too polite for his liking, with that conciliating smile. Shouldn't the woman be questioned rather more sharply? Harbouring a Jewish fellow from who knew where? Yes, where did he come from? Was there a whole gang of them to be discovered? Had Jews been going in and out of this house for weeks? Laughing heartily at the German nation's struggle for survival, eating and drinking their fill? Barolo Riserva, Giacomo Borgogno. 'And you gave the man your hand, did you? Did you? Perhaps at the same moment as a German soldier was sacrificing his life at the front?'

He looked at the unmade bed. 'It's disgusting!' A German woman screwing a Jew. 'Wouldn't you call that disgusting, inspector?'

And what, he would like to know, was her blameless husband up to? There he was in Italy, basking in the sun, while the German Reich fought for its very existence.

'It can't be any coincidence that he happens to be in Italy now!'

He took Eberhard's photo off the bedside table and threw it on the bed. It lay there, with the opened bottle of wine on the bedside table too, and all those people standing in the doorway, wondering what would happen now.

That, of course, was as clear as day.

The police officer didn't like this turn of events. He had really meant to begin by giving Katharina messages from Felicitas, who sent her love, and approach the matter slowly and indirectly, investigating according to his own ideas of the case.

He looked at the label on the wine bottle and picked up the tube of tablets. Then he closed the conservatory window and examined the book on *German Cathedrals*. It was almost as if he wanted to console Katharina. Perhaps it wasn't as bad as all that? 'We don't bite anyone's head off...' He preferred to make inquiries in peace and calm. Maybe that fellow had made it all up? However, if the Jew had climbed the fence, and crawled into the cubbyhole... And there was the sketch, neatly drawn in red pencil. By Katharina herself?

He took a booklet off the shelf. Its title was *What We Have Lost*, and there was a picture of Strasbourg Cathedral on the cover. An inscription to Katharina ran, 'Never forget.' And the writer had added, 'All for nothing.'

Katharina was standing by the doorpost. Drygalski avoided her eyes. He looked at all that tobacco and chocolate, at everything he had brought out of the cubbyhole. Delicacies that she had been giving to the Jew. He would have to take those luxury goods and give them to the old and infirm, that was obvious. He'd been meaning for some time to go to the monastery and make sure all was well there.

He switched on the radio. The BBC? No, all you could hear was the time signal of the German Shipping Forecast, followed by the Wehrmacht report, read slowly enough to be written down for the benefit of those who couldn't follow the broadcast easily.

There was no more to be found here. They all turned round and went down to the hall together. Herr Hesse withdrew to his room, saying it was high time for him to take his drops.

Going downstairs, the police detective held Katharina's elbow gently in two fingers, but he stayed beside her. 'How could you do such a thing, Frau von Globig ... sheltering a Jew?' he whispered to her. 'Did your husband know? A Jew!' Her husband in Italy would have to be questioned; a telex had already been sent. He would surely be interested to know that the man had been wearing a tennis pullover of his; they had worked that out from the monogram EvG. He would certainly think this or that about it. This or that? What actually had been going on here?

It was possible that she might be confronted with the pastor; they'd already had to lock him up.

'Helping a Jew ... what a thing to do, what made you take it into your head? If it had been an ordinary criminal ...'

'It was only one night,' said Katharina.

Her door on the first floor was wide open now.

The police officer looked round the hall again for a while, examined the contents of the little cabinet – and all the letters in it that would have to be read. The ornamental cups, the wire frame with the photo of the Tsarist officer ... all very strange. The landed gentry lived in a world of their own.

Peter had not gone upstairs with the others. He could hear what was going on anyway. He stood by the billiards table, rolling balls against the cushion.

The hunting trophies, horns and antlers lined up side by side, the stuffed wild boar's head, all dating from the time of old Herr von Globig.

Katharina took off her locket and placed it in the dish on the fireside table. She put on her coat and the white Persian lamb cap. With her arms round Peter, she looked gravely at him. Was it going to take long?

'Will she be back soon?' Auntie asked the police officer, speaking as if Katharina had already left.

Jago the dog snapped at the officer's hand.

'Get away,' he said, wiping his hand.

The foreign workers were standing on the terrace of the Forest Lodge. The Czech in his leather cap, the Italian with his Badoglio hat, the Romanian with toothache. They were smiling. Did these people take pleasure in the misfortunes of others? They looked behind them and called to their friends to come out; there was something worth seeing here.

When Katharina was already in the car, Auntie came running after her, saying, 'The key, Katharina! You won't be needing it any more now.'

At the last minute, Vera gave her some bread and sausage. She knew what it was like to be taken away and not have so much as a bit of bread with you.

The car drove off, and the ancestors in the hall stared after it.

The Hesse family clustered round Drygalski. If only they'd left long ago. They asked the head trustee whether they would be able to leave tomorrow.

'Why not?' said Drygalski. 'What are you waiting for?'

'But won't we have to be questioned?' asked the teacher. Since he had not done anything wrong, he would have liked to be questioned. 'And the official permit? Has the official permit arrived?'

'I wish we hadn't come here,' said his wife. But it had been the doing of a higher power. Drygalski himself had told them to move in.

'I'll tell you something,' said Drygalski, who was still searching cupboards, 'it will be best for you to go out into the road at once and get away from here. At once, do you hear me? At once.'

Then he himself left, to go and tell his wife the news of this extraordinary incident.

That day his wife was wearing a white blouse, and the brooch that her husband had given her in Braunlage. She had heated the stove well, and there was good soup in the old style on the table. He could give her a bar of chocolate now, but he didn't; he ate it himself.

She was astonished by the news, and praised her husband. But – Frau von Globig arrested? And she said, very loud and clear, 'Poor woman, she didn't deserve that!' Then Drygalski slammed the door.

Meanwhile horse-drawn carts were driving into the yard of the Georgenhof. The leader of their trek held a permit under Auntie's nose saying that they could stay the night there.

Women and children jumped down from the carts and streamed into the house, asking whether there was somewhere they could wash. Grave-faced men negotiated with Vladimir over grease for the axles of their carts.

The horses were taken out of the shafts and put in the big barn, breathing heavily. The cows being led behind the carts on halters got under cover too. Pedigree cattle of the finest breeds! They were bleeding around their hooves. The teacher's wife mixed water and vinegar, ointment and other ingredients in a bucket and washed their feet.

Peter was standing in the hall. His mother's white fur cap. So a strange man had been staying with his mother. He'd never have expected her to do anything like that.

He felt a little proud of her for doing it.

He met the Pole in the stables. Did the man put a hand on his shoulder, draw him close for comfort? No, he shook his head.

The two Ukrainian maids told the people who had come to stay the night what had happened here. Sonya said she wouldn't have thought the lady of the house could be so brave. But fancy running such risks for a lousy Jew. The women cried, and kept telling stories of all the things that had happened to them. It was a long time since they'd had chocolate to eat.

'We'll leave in the night,' said Vladimir. He was talking to Vera.

There was rumbling and pounding beyond the red horizon, and now and then louder music struck up.

17

Setting Out

See, good sirs, the watchman's light.
The hour of twelve has struck tonight.
May you and your fraternity,
Good sirs, think of eternity.

At midnight Auntie said, 'Let's be off.' She looked at her wrist-watch, as one does on New Year's Eve.

Should they wait for Katharina to come back? Who knew when that might be? Sarkander had said it could take a long time. 'A very long time. You needn't wait for her, you'd better leave at once. We'll look after her if she comes back again.'

Frau Hesse also advised them to leave, saying that if they could, they would go themselves – but four of them, and still no travel permit?

She too said, 'If Frau von Globig turns up we'll look after her.'

Auntie had phoned Uncle Josef, and he had said, 'Yes, that's fine, all of you come here. We have plenty of room. We're not leaving, we're all staying here. We'll be glad to see you; families should stick together in these times.'

No further mention was made of Katharina's fate. Uncle Josef had heard from other sources that she was under arrest in Mitkau. There was no need to discuss these things on the telephone. However, he said, 'Poor Kathi,' although he had always had reservations about her. Poor Eberhard, more like. 'Well, you come to Albertsdorf and rest for a bit. You can find out more news of her from here.'

Dear good Josef! Now at least they had an immediate destination before their eyes, and they knew what to do next. One way and another, they'd never done justice to Josef. He was a good sort really.

'How could she do this to us?' Auntie said to Frau Hesse. 'A Jew! Dragging us all down with her!' And she said to Peter, 'We're not abandoning your mother, you mustn't think that. She can join us any time if they let her out of prison. On her own she'll get through more easily. And she'll want us to go now . . . Sheltering a Jew, how could she do it? Dragging us all down with her! Now, let's get a move on or she'll bring us even more bad luck.'

She had heard of being an accessory after the fact, which was a crime – would that accusation be made now?

Peter wore two pairs of trousers, one on top of the other, shirts and pullovers, two or three of each. He cleaned his shoes, and Vladimir put the two bays between the shafts of the farm cart and harnessed the gelding up to the coach. Auntie was also wearing several layers of clothes. She had drawn money out of the bank in Mitkau weeks ago, gradually, 500 marks at a time, and she stuffed it into her pockets. It represented the working capital of the estate. In the end the bank clerk took to winking at her. He may have been thinking: this woman wasn't born yesterday.

They left the Georgenhof at midnight; Auntie thought they would make better progress by night. Vladimir agreed with her. Whatever happened they must stick together now. They were sensible people.

Vladimir had a sore finger. Frau Hesse put ointment on it and bandaged it carefully.

One last time, they went from room to room – all clean and neat – and then they left the house.

We go into the world so wide,
We can no longer stay;
With many thousands at our side
We also march away.

Auntie drove the coach; she knew how to handle the gelding. And the gelding hardly looked behind him at all, because he in his turn knew Auntie. It was child's play for the huge animal to pull such a light vehicle.

She had considered leaving the coach behind. There should be some space left on the big cart. And what would that old-fashioned coach look like among all the farm carts? Perhaps people would laugh: taking to the road in a coach?

But then Auntie decided to drive the coach herself, to get on the box, take the reins and release the brake. She had learnt to drive a carriage in her Silesian childhood. It had been a donkey cart then; a photo showed her and her three sisters, all of them in white, in the donkey cart. They hadn't driven the donkey up and down the park very often; the animal had had a mind of his own.

She put on a soldier's cap and wound a scarf round her neck. The gelding shook the reins straight and rolled his eyes; yes, everything was in place. He was a good horse, you could rely on him any time. Auntie had only to say 'Gee up!' and click her tongue, and he was moving on.

Auntie didn't trust herself to drive the heavy cart drawn by two horses; the reins got tangled up, and it wasn't easy. She couldn't deal with that. But they had Vladimir to drive the cart, the good-natured Pole who had proved his worth in so many situations.

Vladimir was wearing his square military cap, and Vera sat beside him in her quilted jacket and felt boots, with the wooden suitcase that she had brought from the Ukraine with her; she hadn't acquired many more possessions in all those years. From now on the two of them would stay together, for ever and a day. After all, something was growing inside her belly.

Sonya had changed her mind and was staying behind. She had braided her hair that day and put on the check jacket. She would rather wait quietly for the Russians, she said. She would look after everything: the dog, the cat, and she would lend the Hesses a hand. Everything else would sort itself out. After all, there was Katharina to be reckoned with, she told Auntie, as if Auntie hadn't thought of that.

'Perhaps she'll appear on the scene again one day,' said Frau Hesse. 'Things often don't turn out as we expect. And it would be terrible for her to come back to an empty house!'

She was impatient because Drygalski still hadn't brought them a travel permit.

Auntie placed herself and the coach at the head of the family procession, and then they set off into the darkness.

Unfortunately the first thing went wrong as she drove out of the yard. The glass pane in the left-hand door of the coach broke because the door was hanging off its hinges. Why hadn't they had it repaired? But there was nothing to be done about that now. Peter put a sheaf of straw and a suitcase in front of the window. Now he could see only out of the right-hand side of the coach, but that was enough for him.

The heavy cart followed, creaking and groaning, with all those crates and boxes, and the milk cans filled to the brim with dripping, sugar and flour under the tarpaulin. The feather beds, Katharina's dresses and Eberhard's uniforms were also part of the load. They wanted to press on; they ought to make good progress overnight, when the road was almost clear. Vladimir had spread a stout tarpaulin over everything in the farm cart and tied it well down. Vladimir was a capable man in any situation.

You got a reassuring feeling from Vladimir. He could be trusted.

Sonya took a few steps after the little convoy, but then she turned back. Jago followed for a short way as well before turning round. He too had changed his mind. Go off into the unknown? And where was his mistress? She couldn't be left in the lurch.

There was no sign at all of the cat. The crows didn't fly up either; they sat in the oak tree, looking as if they were shrugging their shoulders, and the dog went into the house.

Auntie didn't look back. The road led slightly downhill here and she had to brake a little, not too hard or the coach might fall to pieces . . . And behind them the Georgenhof disappeared, a dark silhouette in front of the reddish horizon.

Auntie did not look back, and no one watched her go. Even the foreign workers in the Forest Lodge, who usually took an interest in everything, didn't lift the curtain. They could sleep peacefully all night.

Auntie was well muffled up, with her soldier's cap on her head and her legs in a driver's sack to keep them warm, and bundles of straw to right and left. And the gelding was such a good-tempered animal. She took a sip from her flask. But then she felt afraid of the icy wind and the darkness on the road. Thank God the moon was shining, and the snow had settled, so you could get some idea of where you were.

*

Peter burrowed into the straw. The air was cold, but bearable. He had the binoculars round his neck, the air pistol in his belt, his microscope and Auntie's bags and suitcases beside him. Her lute lay on top of her bags. He had played hide-and-seek in the dark with the Albertsdorf cousins – stay where you are and don't move! He looked forward to seeing the Albertsdorf cousins.

Auntie was sitting at the very front, and Peter stared through the oval back window of the coach, past the dried-up wreath of flowers and out at the road behind. He saw the two bay horses following, pulling the heavy farm cart, and he could make out the figures of Vladimir and Vera on the box.

The ice-cold sky was full of sparkling stars, and their wheels crunched as they drove over the frozen snow, with the red horizon behind them. The distant rumbling had slackened off slightly during the last few days. Could Mother be coming after all? that was the question. Was she running after the cart shouting *stop, stop! Why are you going away without me?*

The trees and bushes at the side of the road; the tracks in the snow. They went along at a jog-trot pace. And then they saw someone else's cart ahead, visible as a black mound against the snow. They had nearly caught up with it and could move into the road behind it. It kept driving straight ahead; they had only to keep an eye on it and nothing could go wrong.

First to reach Uncle Josef in Albertsdorf. Then they'd see. Everything could be discussed with Josef. Rather a strange man, but on the whole his heart was in the right place. He didn't have an easy time of it, with his wife's bad hip.

Auntie had a plan; she would first go in the direction of Elbing and then turn north to the Frisches Haff, the zone of brackish water just inland of the Bay of Danzig. She was going to discuss that with Josef. Hanni had a good head on her shoulders too.

But weren't the Russians already in Elbing?

Hour after hour they drove on at an easy pace. It began to snow
in thick flakes that drifted back and forth in the wind like a curtain, ruffling up as they fell to the ground. The ditches beside the
road were full of snow, and you could hardly make out where
they began and the road ended. It was a strain, keeping your eyes
fixed on the cart in front. Peter joined Auntie on the box, and
when the gelding slipped he shouted, 'Gee up!'

Sometimes a vehicle came towards them; a truck with dipped
headlights, a motorbike, once even a tank. To make room for the
tank, the cart ahead of them moved a little way aside, and then
it slipped into the ditch.

Should they stop and help?

Peter was going to jump down, but Auntie said, 'No, we must
keep going. We don't have time to stop now.'

Peter saw small figures crawling out of the cart, their shadows
enormous in the light of their electric torches, and then it was all
dark again.

Vladimir stopped to help the people in the ditch and stayed
behind for a while. Auntie drove slowly on and finally stopped.
Johannsen's old mill should be somewhere near here. In clear
weather you could see it from the Georgenhof, so they would be
able to see the Georgenhof from the mill.

Soon Vladimir was behind them again, having helped the other
cart back on the road.

The longer they drove, the more carts joined the road from left
and right. Auntie was now following a trailer with rubber tyres
on its wheels and cat's eyes at the back of it. If you briefly flashed
a torch at them, they shone red in the darkness.

The first light of dawn was showing; Vladimir closed the distance between their two vehicles so that no one else could come

in between them. If they were separated they might never find each other again.

A solitary aircraft flew overhead. Did the pilot have a light on in his plane? Was his thumb hovering over the button to release his bombs? Was his machine gun trained on the road below?

Around now, Katharina was lying on her straw mattress in a cold police cell. She couldn't sleep; she had spread her coat and two blankets over her. A guard was doing his rounds in the yard. He shone a light on the windows, and when it reached her cell the shadow of the bars fell on the wall. She thought of a film in which there was a woman in prison, like her, with barred shadows cast on the walls.

But this wasn't a film. The key turned in the lock, and she had to get up and go with the man who came to fetch her. Flights of iron steps, barred doors. Then she was sitting on a hard chair in a warm interrogation room. The officer there sat at his desk signing files.

At last he turned to her. She was asked whether it was true that she had given shelter to a Jew, and was shown the drawing with the arrow on it saying Georgenhof, and the instructions to the man to climb the fence. She had admitted all this already, and it had been written down.

The police officer said that this was very, very serious, and he would like to know whether the man had made approaches to her in her room. Had she known he was a Jew? Then he delivered a long lecture about the children of Israel, describing them as filthy blowflies and a pack of criminals.

She couldn't deny anything, and making excuses seemed a bad idea. She said she hadn't guessed that; she hadn't known anything about a Jew. She'd thought, oh, she didn't know what. And she wondered, she said, whether she would have given the man shelter if she had known he was a Jew. Yes, she said that, and she asked the police officer if he really thought that she would have sheltered a Jew if she'd known who was being sent to her?

'Well, who did you think he could be? A deserter, perhaps? Or an enemy of the state?' He didn't quite like to say that that would have been even worse.

She thought of Pastor Brahms and his persuasions. He had made her do it, she said. Would she have thought of such a thing of her own accord? With her husband at the front . . .

'At the front?' said the police officer. 'Sitting in a cushy job in Italy, that's where he is.' Then he became insistent, and wanted to know whether matters had gone any further up in her room. Had there been anything in the way of racial defilement? 'Did you drink alcohol? You had quite a nice little stock of it . . . Did he touch you? Did he make advances? Stand up!'

At last another officer came into the room. It was the man who had brought her here. He was taking her back to her cell. There was coffee that had gone cold in the cell, and a piece of bread. She longed to say, 'Stay here, stay here with me for a little while.' But he had already closed and locked the door.

The two vehicles from the Georgenhof went on. Hours later, they passed a crossroads. The signpost said ALBERTSDORF 7 KILOME-TRES. So they turned right. They could rest once they reached Uncle Josef's house, they'd be at home there. Maybe news from Katharina had already reached Albertsdorf? They could discuss it all with Josef, and then they'd decide what to do next. We'll go on to the Frisches Haff, thought Auntie. First we'll go towards Elbing and then turn off for the Frisches Haff.

Uncle Josef had always spoken brusquely to her; well, that was just his way. When he came to the Georgenhof, alone on business, or on a Sunday with his whole family, he used to say hello to her, but that was all.

They reached Albertsdorf when the sun had risen. There was a heavy chain on the gate of the yard. Even though they had said they were coming, the whole place seemed to be locked up. The family must be sleeping late.

Vladimir got out of the blankets in which he had wrapped himself and opened the gate. The farmyard dog immediately went for him, but he used his whip and soon made it respect him.

The whole yard was full of other people's carts. Some of them were being made ready to go on.

'There's no room left here,' said the strangers, who didn't know that the newcomers were part of the family.

Finally they left the two vehicles beside the silo, one to the right and one to the left of it. The stables were already full of horses, but there was just enough space for the gelding and the two bays to fit in. Vladimir mixed oats and chaff, and gave the animals water.

Then he fetched Vera, and the two of them settled down in the hay along with some French POWs. It was very romantic in there by the light of the lantern. Vladimir got a bottle of vermouth that didn't really belong to him out of the cart, and pulled the tarpaulin covering it tightly over the contents again. Then they all drank vermouth, even the man guarding the POWs. After all, he was only human.

Auntie knocked at the front door of the house. Peter walked all round it, but everything was locked up. It was some time before anyone came to let them in. And no one welcomed them with open arms . . . 'There you are at last, my dears!' Nor was there a fire crackling in the hearth and a table laid for them. All the reception they got was a basic shrug of the shoulders.

Yes, the whole family had already left, they heard. Even though they'd said they were staying, they had left! It was lucky that Frau Schneidereit, staying behind to look after the house, even recognized Auntie. A visitor so early in the morning?

Grudgingly, she let them in. They were offered no more than a hot cup of tea and a piece of bread spread with onion-flavoured curd cheese. They would rest briefly, decided Auntie, and then go on.

Yes, they heard, Uncle Josef had already left. Immediately after Auntie's phone call from the Georgenhof he had slammed the receiver back on its stand and called to the household, 'The Globigs are coming. That's the last straw.'

It was the phone call that sent them off, as Frau Schneidereit now revealed. Uncle Josef had left with his family, bag and baggage – seven carts piled high with their possessions.

'Quick, quick, quick, children! We're leaving too,' he had called. After hesitating for weeks, saying they'd wait and see, now he couldn't get on the road fast enough. There were papers to be burnt on the dung heap, everyone to be chivvied along, the carts so overloaded that the horses could hardly move. The carts couldn't get out of the yard, so the horses had to be whipped all the way out to the road.

Uncle Josef had not left Auntie a letter on the table. Most of the doors were locked, and the beds had been stripped.

So Auntie curled up on a sofa, and Peter lay down in his cousins' room. They hadn't left a letter either.

Three doll's houses stood in the corner, one for each of the girls so that they wouldn't quarrel. And a picture of the three cousins hung over them, painted by the artist who had also done the picture of Elfie that hung in Katharina's room.

While they were resting, the other refugees harnessed up their horses and left the yard one after another.

*

Auntie wanted to leave at midday. All the strangers' carts had left the yard by then; they would be well along the road by now. Vladimir crawled out of the hay; the French prisoners had left as well.

Vladimir immediately saw that Vera's wooden suitcase was missing. The tarpaulin over the cart was untouched, so far as he could tell, but the wooden suitcase had gone! He went on looking for it. It had been on the driver's box, but it was not there now. He couldn't believe it.

Vera couldn't grasp it either. She didn't exactly strike up a howl of woe, but she cried floods of tears. All her possessions stolen. The pictures of her parents. All of it was gone.

Vladimir went round shouting, saying what he would do to the thief if he laid hands on him, shouting into Auntie's face in Polish. He'd slit the man open! Put out his eyes! He'd stopped in the middle of the night to help others when they fell into the ditch, and now someone had stolen Vera's suitcase.

'If I can lay hands on the bastard!' said Vladimir, uttering terrible curses in his own tongue, while Vera went on crying quietly.

A little later, they too set out. Cart was following cart on the road to Elbing, wheels crunching over the snow. They tried to thread their way into the long line of vehicles, Auntie first.

It took them some time to push in and join the cavalcade. They had to let whole village communities go first, until at last an old man stopped his horses. He pointed to them with his whip, indicating that they could go in front of him, and hurry up about it. No time to be lost. He must be wondering about the strange coach standing at the crossroads. Perhaps it reminded him of the old days? With a coat of arms on its door – had that made him let them go first?

But when Vladimir drove the heavy cart forward, drivers were already cracking their whips behind him. 'What's going on up ahead there?' After all, people wanted to stick together; the line of carts was strictly organized. If the people in them lost sight of each other here, it was all over.

Meanwhile, at the Georgenhof, Sonya took possession of the keys. She opened the door to the Czech and asked the Hesses how much longer they thought of staying, because she for one wasn't providing any more food. Drygalski had to be fetched to sort it out. Did she know, he asked Sonya, that he could send her packing in no time, along with her boyfriend? Right, she'd better get back to the cottage, at once too, or there'd be trouble. The Czech had already made himself scarce.

18

Resting

They reached the little town of Harkunen towards evening. Cart after cart stood all along both sides of the high street, one after another, and women sitting on cushions looked out of the windows. You had to think a long way back to remember when there were last such crowds here, and that was when Hitler came through to celebrate the special day of the Gau, the local district. Kaiser Wilhelm had once been received in Harkunen with garlands and girls dressed in white.

Auntie drove the coach into the fully occupied football field, part of a sports complex, and stopped in front of a goal. The Bund deutscher Mädel, the League of German Girls, were running a soup kitchen. Vladimir drove the heavily laden farm cart into a side street.

'We'll leave again at five in the morning,' Auntie told Vladimir. 'And mind nothing else gets stolen!'

'Right, five in the morning,' he said, and told her not to worry.

'We'll wait here for you,' said Auntie. 'In this football field. Come here at five in the morning, and then we'll go on. Five on the dot!'

Party officials were going from cart to cart, Heil Hitler, with forms to be filled in. They were asking all these people if they needed anything, whether everything was in order. There was considerable confusion on the football field, but people were managing; they'd make it somehow. On the whole everyone was reasonable. Complaining was kept within bounds.

The Party stewards found fault with Auntie's coach because it was blocking access to the field. Hadn't she been allotted a place to park in conformity with the rules? No, she had not been allotted a place, she had simply parked the coach where it was.

'That won't do. People can't act just as they like here.'

Even in this situation, unusual as it was, you couldn't do just as you liked; even here you had to follow rules. Otherwise everything would end in unimaginable chaos.

'Surely you realize that!'

So she moved the coach again, and the Party steward went ahead and directed her to a place in the lee of the wind, at the side of the gymnasium of the sports complex. He probably felt sorry for the coach – such an old-fashioned vehicle. But it had a coat of arms on the door, and that meant something, after all.

Auntie thanked him for showing her where to go, and she said 'Heil Hitler!' She added, 'There's a farm cart in the third street on the right with a Pole and a Ukrainian woman in it. They're with us, if anything happens.' She said 'Heil Hitler' again, and the Party man put his hand to the peak of his cap; he knew what was what now. The only question was whether, at five in the morning, Vladimir would realize that they were not in the same place. Peter stationed himself in front of the goal, with the binoculars dangling from his neck and the air pistol in his belt, but he couldn't stand there for ever.

'Why are you hanging around here, boy?' he was asked.

'We'll tell your friend Vladimir where to look when he turns up in the morning,' someone told him. 'Trust us for that!'

As chance would have it, a young war widow from Mitkau was fetching soup at the same time as Auntie. They didn't know each other, they'd never met before, but both were from Mitkau. That kind of thing creates a bond.

The young woman had made a spontaneous decision to get on her horse and ride away, leaving everything behind just as it was. She had nothing with her but a small bundle. She had the Iron Cross awarded to her husband who had fallen at Demyansk in a bag round her neck. She showed the Iron Cross to everyone, and said that she had ridden away because there was a whiff of Russians in the air.

Then she mounted her horse again and rode off. She couldn't stand it here any more. 'Perhaps I'll get through yet,' she said.

Meanwhile Peter went into the town: it had a long high street, a marketplace and a church. Sure enough, their big farm cart was standing in the third street on the right, and the two bay horses swished their tails when they saw him. Peter told Vladimir that they weren't in front of the goalposts any more, but outside the gymnasium. Then he went in search of a pharmacy, because he had left his toothbrush behind. There must surely be a pharmacy somewhere here.

He asked local people where he could find a pharmacy. The local people looked different from those on the trek, who were now described as refugees. The local people went to their offices carrying briefcases, and there were ladies wearing hats sitting in a café. They were friendly and gave Peter information. One lady took a fancy to him, and accompanied him to the pharmacy. Did he think, she asked, that the Russians would get as far as this? She was so worried, she didn't know what to do.

'Are you all on your own?'

Peter would have liked to tell her about his mother, who had been taken away, but she might yet come back . . .

People were queuing outside the pharmacy – Heil Hitler – and it was some time before he could buy his toothbrush. He also bought some toothpowder and a cake of soap. You were really supposed to be on a list of regular customers to do that, but the pharmacist made an exception for him because he was a refugee. He also bought a bag of Italian liquorice, which cost five pfennigs and tasted nice.

He was sure to be all right now.

'Close the door!' called the pharmacist.

He'd have to hide the liquorice from Auntie. He was squandering money when he bought it.

Old-fashioned gravestones in the shape of crosses stood crooked in the churchyard beside the little whitewashed church, and there were new wooden crosses there too. A man came along with a bundle; it was a dead child. The pastor arrived and said, 'Leave the body there, and I'll see to it later.' Then he turned back and asked for the child's name, wrote it on a piece of paper and put his note with the bundle.

The bundle lay there in the draughty church porch, and the note blew away.

In the church, someone was trying to play the organ, which was out of tune.

Eternity, O mighty word,
Running my heart through like a sword,
Beginning without end . . .

Peter looked at the crooked crosses. Did the dead lying under them have crooked legs, like Christ in the Mitkau church, whose feet crossed at the ankles? Were Elfie's feet crossed like that in her grave, or were they lying side by side, straight?

Dead bodies sweat. Had someone washed her feet with warm water? Had her whole body been washed with a warm sponge?

Had her hair been brushed for the last time and plaited into braids?

> *Eternity, great is my grief,*
> *I know not where, with my belief*
> *In God, my thoughts to send.*

He couldn't remember now what his little sister had looked like. No stone had been placed on her grave. Plenty of time for that, they had said. But no stone on her grave? No name, nothing?

They had buried her with a bunch of lilies of the valley in her hands.

Who would ever come looking for her?

There was a bar outside the church, the stumps of two linden trees in front of it. They sold weak beer in the bar. Two men staggered across the street with a drunk between them. They were refugees too, speaking so broad a dialect that Peter couldn't understand it.

The woman who had taken him to the pharmacy met him again, and this time she couldn't restrain herself. 'Poor boy,' she said. 'Going around here all by yourself? Don't you have anyone left in the world?' And she invited him to go home with her, saying she had some cake that she thought he would like.

She lived up two flights of stairs, in an apartment looking down into a back yard. The clock on her wall chimed, ding-dong ding-dong, with the hands pointing to four. Then Peter was sitting on an old green sofa trimmed with tassels, eating cake and telling long stories of all that had happened to him. His village – 'you wouldn't know it,' he said – had been captured overnight by the Russians, and he had taken refuge in the woodshed with the Russians outside, sort of hunched figures brown as earth. They were scurrying past, and he huddled into a corner and didn't move. His heart was in his mouth!

The woman listened, fascinated. So he went on and on about the hunched, brown figures of the Russians scurrying past, and the screaming of the women. And in the night, he said, he had crawled through the snow at a temperature of minus twenty-five degrees until he finally reached the German lines, where an officer congratulated him in person.

Here the old grandpa from next door joined them, and made doubtful noises over Peter's stories as he listened. So then it was time – 'Oh, my word! I must be going!' – for Peter to make himself scarce. 'His unit', he said, 'was waiting for him, and he showed his air pistol. The woman gave him a book about the World War, saying she was sure it would interest him. It contained old-fashioned pictures of old-fashioned soldiers. The book, she said, had belonged to her son, who was now a prisoner in Karelia. 'Hmm,' said the old man. 'Hmm. Figures as brown as earth?'

Perhaps the boy's stories were true.

At the same time, the telephone was ringing at the Georgenhof. The Hesses had lit a fire in the hall and were sitting comfortably beside it. It was the teacher who finally picked up the receiver and shouted, 'What?' down it. 'What did you say? General Command?' There was a rushing sound far away, a distant voice; he couldn't make anything out. Frau Hesse took the receiver from her husband, but she couldn't understand what the voice was saying either, except that it was Eberhard von Globig beside Lake Garda, trying to get in touch with his wife. 'Er – Herr von Globig . . .' said Frau Hesse – for a brief moment the curtain of interference was lifted – 'your wife isn't here any more . . . we don't know . . .' But that was as far as she could get. And what should she have told him? There was one more croaked phrase . . . 'In the cellar . . .' and that was the end of the call.

What did he mean was in the cellar? Frau Hesse took an electric torch and went down the cellar steps. There was water at the bottom of them, nothing else in sight.

At midday Lothar Sarkander turned up. Heil Hitler. No, he wouldn't sit down. This was just a flying visit. He walked round the room, looking at everything. He had sat here so often: the billiards room to one side of it, the hearth. He opened the door of the summer drawing room as well; frost glittered inside it. He stood there for a moment looking out at the silent, melancholy park, and then he slowly climbed the stairs to the first floor. So this was where Katharina had lived. And was that the daughter's room opposite? Elfie. Was the photo that used to lie on the pillow still there? He opened the wardrobe where the little girl's clothes were still hanging.

The Hesse boys were standing in the doorway behind him. When he picked up the knitted witch they looked at each other. Was this man allowed simply to nick it? Would that have to be reported to Herr Drygalski?

He hadn't been able to find out any more about Katharina. So far as he knew, she must still be in the police cells in Königsberger Strasse. Probably with all sorts of rag, tag and bobtail, whores, termagants, beggar women. Thank God, said Frau Hesse, they'd given her something to take from here at the last minute: bread and dripping, sausage.

'Good,' said Sarkander, and the duelling scar on his cheek twitched.

Pastor Brahms, he said, had been taken away. Apparently he had belonged to an underground association. Sarkander lowered his voice to a whisper. An operation on a major scale. He'd probably end up shorter by a head.

'Oh, don't say . . . !' exclaimed Frau Hesse, cupping her chin in her hand. 'But Frau von Globig? I mean, she's innocent really. I'm sure she just slipped into it by accident.'

'They'll certainly lean on her hard.'

He would ask Wagner to try to get more supplies to her, said Sarkander, and then he left with his stiff-legged gait.

Drygalski also dropped in. Heil Hitler. It wasn't news to him that the Globigs had left. They ought to have gone long before, and then none of that business with the Jew would have happened.

He himself had made out a permit for the whole household to leave, days ago, but Auntie wouldn't hear of going.

What interested him was the fate of all those crates standing in the drawing room. Surely sequestration of property was the penalty for sheltering a Jew? Maybe he had better find out just what was in them.

Was Sonya going to get uppity again? Should he dispose of her?

Quietly going about it, he took a quick look at Katharina's apartment, just to check up on it, but there was nothing more to find. He crawled into the cubbyhole, but there was no chocolate any more, and the tobacco was gone as well.

He took the shotguns with him to give them to the Volkssturm reservists. However, he couldn't find any ammunition for them.

At three in the afternoon, 'the usual time', as he said, Dr Wagner arrived.

'What, all of them gone without a word?' he asked. Hadn't they left a letter behind? Nothing! 'After all, we were friends,' he said.

He sat down with the Hesses up in Peter's former room. He had talked to the boy so often here. They had read Goethe together – Goethe writing about the moon. *Filling woods and vales again with her misty light* . . . No, it hadn't been a waste of time; they had made the most of it.

He would happily have gone with the Globig party, but he supposed there wouldn't have been room on their cart for an extra passenger. He'd been literally left standing. Well, they'd all have to wait and see what happened.

He for one hadn't gone haring off! *He* hadn't left the Globigs in the lurch! That was a comfort.

Frau Hesse said, 'We'll be leaving too as soon as our permit comes. Somehow or other we'll get away from here.' Yes, Drygalski had already told her to start at once, but he hadn't given her a piece of paper to take with them, that was the snag. If they were stopped and their credentials were checked, then they'd be at a loss.

She had borrowed Katharina's radio set; she could take it back to her room any time.

I'll whistle at your window
Tootle-tootle-too,
And softly, softly, softly
Then I'll creep in with you.

'What does it say on the news?' asked Wagner. But when Herr Hesse was about to tell him he waved him away. What kind of news could there be now?

There was nothing to interest him here any more. Where was the telescope? Shouldn't he take it back? Had he left it in unreliable hands? It had disappeared, it was no use looking for it now.

The Hesse boys had fallen eagerly on Peter's model railway. They sent the trains speeding round the curved track.

Sonya was standing in the kitchen, the Czech with the leather cap standing in the yard. No, she said when Wagner asked for bread and sausage for him to take for Katharina, no, she couldn't help him. It was none of her business. The Globigs had taken everything with them. She locked the kitchen door. Katharina wasn't her responsibility.

The cellar fascinated Herr Hesse. He wouldn't leave it alone. 'There's nothing down there,' his wife had said, but that couldn't be true. He summoned all his energy to get to the bottom of the puzzle. After all, as a young man he'd been able to swing round in a circle on the horizontal bar and straddle the horse, hadn't he? So he roused himself and went down the cellar steps, carrying the electric torch. He took off his shoes and rolled up his trouser legs. Down the spiral staircase, climb into the water, go along the passage – it was vaulted, and longer than he had expected. A date: 1605. Was there wine stored here?

'Oh, do come back out!' called his wife. Her voice echoed. 'I'm sure this isn't a good idea. All that cold water!' She kept the boys back when they wanted to investigate the cellar as well. 'Do you want to catch your death?'

Herr Hesse explored the place thoroughly, but there was nothing there. No wine, not anything at all. Just as his wife had said. The end of the passage was bricked up. An escape route from the old days? Did it lead to the ruins of the castle?

The water here had been stagnant for a long time, the floor of the passage was smooth and slippery – there! Hesse lost his footing and fell into the water. He was about to call to the boys and his wife – 'Helga!' But it was all over. Did he think of stocks, hollyhocks and phloxes at this, the last moment of his life? Or all his Stone Age axes and scrapers? His mouth contorted, he gurgled for a moment, a few bubbles rose to the surface, and then all was still and the water extinguished the electric torch.

19

Vladimir

Next morning Auntie waited in vain for the Pole. Five on the dot, she had said, but there was no sign of Vladimir. Peter went from cart to cart; vehicles were already leaving the football field one by one. He was looking for the Pole. Then he kept a lookout from the coach, standing on the driver's box, like a general taking the salute at a military parade, up above the murmuring crowd assembled here, with the light of electric torches and stable lanterns flashing over it.

Surely the Pole must come round the corner soon? Auntie too was asking herself that question. Was he taking his time, stringing them along? He'd be sorry for this, no doubt about it – a man who had been so well off with the Globigs! Fancy making them wait now. She sent Peter off in search of him, but he couldn't find Vladimir. He couldn't find the cart, he couldn't find Vladimir, and there was no sign of Vera either.

Perhaps Vladimir had gone to see a doctor about his injured finger? Was the hangnail infected? That could be nasty – but finding a doctor at this early hour?

He asked the woman at the soup kitchen – Heil Hitler! – whether a man wearing a square Polish cap had been there, and he also asked the Party official who made sure everything was in order.

Some children having a snowball fight asked if he wanted to join in. No, they hadn't seen a Pole with a square cap either.

Perhaps, it was suggested, the Pole hadn't been allowed on the football field because he was a foreigner?

'Yes, imagine letting those fellows run around as they like,' said the Party man. 'Such people can't be trusted for a moment.'

It seemed to him strange for anyone from the east to be trusted. In fact he thought he'd have to find out whether that was legal. He'd come back later and look into the matter carefully.

Peter returned to Auntie. 'I can't find him anywhere.'

'This is impossible,' said Auntie. 'I'll go and look for him myself . . .' And then the answer occurred to her. 'Of course, he doesn't own a watch! He can't tell when it's five o'clock!'

But even that got them no further; and after all, you could hear the clock striking in the church tower everywhere. Finally Auntie put on her rubber overshoes and set out herself, and she easily found the third street on the right where Vladimir had left the cart. A pile of horse dung marked the place, and that was all. The cart itself was nowhere to be seen.

She combed the streets of the little town, every nook and cranny of them, but in vain. And when she got back to the football field, where carts were steadily leaving – the gelding was already looking round for her – there was still no Vladimir. Well, he might have been here.

No doubt about it, however, Vladimir had gone.

It was clear: the Pole had gone on by himself to who knew where? The man had left them in the lurch. Wanted to go off on his own, with his lover, perhaps to make his way to his native Poland? Get his little lambs into safety and begin a new life? But how could he get back to Poland, with Russians all over the place?

Auntie went to see the mayor of the town – Heil Hitler! – but his office was closed. She went from there to the police, Heil Hitler, but they were no use either. The police were busy dealing with drunks who were staggering about in the road. Auntie would have to wait until daylight hours began, and then they'd turn to her complaint. They really couldn't look at the matter now. On the way back she cast another glance at the third street on the right. Still nothing to be seen. There was another cart now where theirs had been, with strangers using the space.

She went to the Party official who ruled over the football field, and he advised her to report to the police next morning. That, he said, was essential. She must report to the police. 'They'll find that Polack.'

How irresponsible, letting those foreigners wander round freely. To think that such things were allowed.

Now she must feed the gelding, and the fodder for him was on Vladimir's cart. What was she to give the poor animal? It was all on Vladimir's cart: Eberhard's suits, the bed linen, the milk cans of dripping, their underclothes!

The oats!

Then Auntie saw a bale of hay hanging from the back of the coach. It had not been there before. So Vladimir had at least left that, he had thought of the gelding. And he had even left a sack of oats tied to the coach too. He'd thought of the horse before making off. No one, after all, is bad through and through . . .

He had probably moved the fodder in Albertsdorf, at Uncle Josef's house. When no one yet suspected him of anything bad. So he'd already planned everything ahead at that point.

'Who'd believe it?' cried Auntie, and her hands were shaking. 'We're none of us a match for such people.'

She began thinking of all the stuff packed on the big cart, now lost for ever! Their clothes! The table linen! The silver . . . all the silver! The beds, the milk cans full of dripping and sugar. The photographs! And all the business documents of the Georgenhof. Although not the English steel shares, and the agreements with the Romanian rice-flour factory. Auntie had put those in her handbag.

It was odd that the sack of oats was stamped with the name of Albertsdorf. So that was where Vladimir had organized his operation? Or to say it straight out, his theft. Nothing was easy!

She asked the gelding what he thought of Vladimir abandoning them. She would have liked to shed tears, leaning against the horse's neck. But the gelding swished his tail and rolled his eyes. He might well be thinking: now what? Is the old girl going to make a nuisance of herself?

Peter was sitting in their reserves of straw, while snow came in through the broken window. He was trying to put separate flakes under the lens of his microscope – playing a game of catch with the ice crystals – but it was no use. Any flakes that he caught melted at once.

They were allowed to wash in the gymnasium – Heil Hitler. Hot water was ladled out from the soup kitchen's supply. Where gymnasts used to straddle the apparatus, swinging up and sideways over the bars, people from the National Socialist People's Welfare now stood keeping things in order. There were nurses available as well. Heil Hitler. Vladimir's injured finger could easily have been treated here. But he'd had ideas of his own.

The refugees sat at long tables, and were given coffee. There were not so many as on the day before. A number had gone on again at first light. But others were arriving, tired and frozen. And soon the football field was full again.

Some carts were even coming back from the way Auntie had meant to take, towards Elbing. The police had made them turn round because there was no way back to the Reich now.

*

A Party official went from table to table, Heil Hitler, saying com-
forting things to the refugees. Just as Pastor Brahms used to go
from one to another member of his congregation at the mission
party in Mitkau, the Party official too placed his hand on the
refugees' shoulders. Heil Hitler. He spoke words of comfort. The
chaos would soon die down. Ways and means would be found.
He was acting just like Pastor Brahms, who at this moment was
in a single cell in Königsberg with two bolts on the door. He had
a black eye; his right eye was badly bruised.

When at last it was eight o'clock, Auntie went back to the police.
Heil Hitler. She had to wait, of course; there was a long line of
people in search of advice. When her turn finally came, she was
treated in a friendly way. A middle-aged police officer even
offered her a chair. And then – 'Von Globig? Von Globig of the
Georgenhof?' – it turned out that he knew Eberhard. He had met
Herr von Globig in the course of a delicate case that he didn't
want to talk about here, but the gentleman had given him great
support, and it must be acknowledged.

Auntie showed all her papers. Besides signing her permit to
leave, Drygalski had written underneath, 'This woman should be
given every assistance.' That had a good effect, and the officer
said, 'We'll get the Pole, you can rely on that.' The case would go
straight to the front of the queue, he promised, and he would
phone the nearest towns and villages to alert the local authorities:
a Pole with a square cap might be coming through on a green
farm cart, and had a corpulent woman with him, a worker from
the east. They were to stop the man, arrest him at once and get
the cart to safety. Heil Hitler!

Auntie signed the record of their conversation, and then she
told the police officer, who really had other things to do, about
all the stuff packed on the cart: the clothes! The bed linen! The
silver – *all* the silver! After a while people waiting in the long line

behind her began to call out, asking what was going on in front there. 'This could take all day!'

Auntie added that the Pole could also be identified by his finger. 'The forefinger of his right hand is bandaged,' she said, and the officer jotted that down.

Meanwhile Peter had got up again and was wandering along the high street, past the carts lined up there, large and small, heavy and light. Single carts left to go back on the road, others were just arriving and were glad to get a good place. There was much lively coming and going. Refugee women went from house to house, asking whether they could wash somewhere, and Hitler Youth boys shovelled snow aside.

Perhaps he might yet find Vladimir, Peter thought. It was possible that he might simply have moved the cart somewhere else. But the air pistol wasn't likely to impress him much.

Or he might find Uncle Josef. He must surely be here somewhere. Perhaps the cousins would suddenly cross his path. Hello, how did you get here? In his mind, Peter was going through all the questions he would ask them. Why they hadn't waited for him, and so on and so forth, and he would tell them he was very disappointed in them.

He heard piano music in the town café. Peter had never been inside a café, but he went in, pushing aside the massive curtain that kept out draughts, Heil Hitler, and in the stuffy warmth, among soldiers of all kinds and women in hats, he saw the one-armed man sitting at the piano.

When you leave, say softly, 'See you!'
Not farewell and not adieu!
Words like that can only hurt.

*

No question about it, this was Lance Corporal Hofer from Munich.

Peter put a hand on his shoulder, and the soldier stopped playing at once and went to sit at a table with him.

'Peter! What a coincidence!'

He had been supposed to organize bandages and distilled water for the field hospital that had moved on long ago, and now that he had all the stuff together he should have been out on the road, following the hospital. People were waiting for him. But – 'You know how it is. When I see a piano I just can't resist. And are you travelling with your crazy old auntie?' he asked Peter, who didn't like that description. He thought that Auntie was all right, really.

Almost at once, Hofer asked whether Peter had heard anything of the violinist. 'I wonder what's become of her?' said the soldier. 'She planned to go to Allenstein, but the Russians have been there for some time now ... I'm afraid she'll be dead. The Russians don't beat about the bush; her violin won't have done her much good there.'

Then he told Peter, who at his age had no idea of such things, that the young woman had had her charms, was amazingly affectionate and so on and so forth, and he even said she had jumped 'straight into bed' with the medical superintendent in Mitkau.

'Wildly sexy!' was his verdict.

Then he gave Peter advice about women and how to win them over. He himself, said Hofer, could win any woman over, and wouldn't hold it against his young wife in Munich if she found a replacement for him some day.

'What use is life if you don't enjoy it?'

Then he told Peter how much at home he'd felt in the Georgenhof, the fire in the hearth, the summer drawing room ... and he described all sorts of things that Peter had no idea of. He mentioned a chamber organ, crystal chandeliers and endless suites of rooms . . . which all sounded very nice, but surprised Peter. What was the man talking about? A chamber organ at the Georgenhof?

Hofer also mentioned the Ukrainian girls. He described Vera as 'that fatso' and Sonya as a 'pert little hussy'. Sonya with her hair braided round her head and her red nose, yes, he'd have liked to play games with her . . .

'But at heart they're all the same.' And Vladimir had gone off with the cart? That was typical. 'These eastern folk steal like magpies.'

Then he took a charred meerschaum cigarette holder out of his pocket – you could see a man and a woman carved on it – and lit a cigarette. He told Peter about his time in Poland, about Warsaw and its dark side streets. And about lice and fleas.

Peter didn't bring out the story of the hunched figures as brown as earth here, and how he had crawled through the snow. While Hofer spoke of bumping someone off and putting another 'away', he looked out of the window at the street. Suppose Dr Wagner came past now? Not understanding but interested in everything. The moon, *filling woods and vales again with her misty light* . . . Were they all going to come by in procession out there? One after another. The stamp collector, swinging himself along on his crutches. Drygalski with his heavy tread – *Be proud; I bear the banner*; his father in his white uniform; and a troop of prisoners with his mother in the middle of them. All carrying, with difficulty, a huge chain.

Then he thought of the coloured picture on the door of Elfie's room, and the naked brownies holding up a garland of flowers. Not a chain, it had been made of flowers.

By this time Hofer had put the meerschaum cigarette holder back in his pocket, and was sitting at the piano again and playing something jazzy with his left hand. He went on until a man said Heil Hitler, and asked him if, in these hard times, it was right for the street to be full of all those refugee carts, while he sat here playing 'nigger jazz'.

The man had a glass eye. He had been sitting at the back of the room for some time, shaking his head.

And he asked Peter what he thought he was doing here; sitting in a café, when he couldn't be more than twelve. The Hitler Youth would have something to say about that; they'd sort him out.

Is that what German young people are like these days, he asked the others in the café who were clinking their coffee cups, is that what the young are like when their native land is fighting for survival?

Then Hofer stood up – Heil Hitler – and the man saw that he had only one arm. And Hofer closed the piano and asked the man what *he* thought he was doing here, sitting behind the stove in a nice warm room far from the firing line. He should be at the front, and so on. He dismissed any protests, asked the waiter for his bill, took his wallet out of his pocket and opened it as the one-armed did, with thumb and forefinger. He was surprised, he said to the ladies in hats sitting around, that a wounded man wasn't allowed to have the slightest pleasure.

Peter wanted to help him open the wallet. But Hofer wouldn't let him, and paid two marks fifty for his beer and Peter's helping of mousse. 'Good thing I don't have a stomach wound,' he said, and he hastily wrote down his military address for Peter, just in case, using a beer mat and a silver propelling pencil. The pencil seemed familiar to Peter as well.

Then Hofer cried, 'Tally ho!' and disappeared past the heavy curtain. A shame to have spoilt his little pleasures.

Peter went to the barber next to the café for a haircut. 'Heil Hitler,' he said, but the barber was a Dutchman and did not respond.

'Want a shave as well?' asked the barber. He meant it as a joke, because there was only a little down on Peter's cheeks. He whistled a patriotic melody that sounded like a folk song.

The haircut cost fifty pfennigs, and the price would have been agreed quickly if Peter hadn't started talking about the figures as brown as earth who had run past his hiding place, keeping low, and that made the barber thoughtful. He snapped his scissors in the air and looked at Peter in the mirror. Well, to think that a young fellow like him had done so much already! And he was wondering what would happen when Peter got home. Wouldn't he be called to account for himself? Now here was he, the barber, he'd come to Germany voluntarily to cut the Huns' hair for them.

He brushed Peter's collar and said, in English, 'So long!'

Outside the door the man with the glass eye was waiting for him. 'I had a son like you,' he said. 'Mind you don't squander your life!'

This time it was Auntie who was late. There had been all kinds of things available in the shops, and she had bought washing powder off the ration.

And when she was shopping she had met a nice man who helped her, and then she had chatted to him for a while. He came from Silesia, so he was a countryman of hers. The world is all a village, really.

'Thank goodness you're here, my boy. Don't you go and get lost as well.'

The Silesian had a slight disability, and dragged his left leg a little when he walked, but that didn't matter. There are good souls everywhere.

Then Auntie sat in the coach with Peter, and they made themselves comfortable and had a bite to eat. There were so many good souls looking at them, with their good faces staring through the windowpanes, that Auntie drew the curtain.

Then she wrote a postcard to the people left at the Georgenhof, saying that she hadn't found Uncle Josef, and she was now on the way to the Frisches Haff. 'What do you think, Vladimir has gone off! Love to Katharina!' she added, feeling very brave, and hoping that this message wouldn't get her into difficulty.

She wrote a postcard to the Berlin cousins, pointing out that no one could now guarantee the safety of the crates left at the Georgenhof. Why hadn't they taken them away long ago?

She was also going to write to Eberhard, military postal address number so and so. She started several times, but how could she tell him that they had left the Georgenhof? And say what had happened to Katharina? Better not send the card yet, she thought, better wait and see how it turned out.

Katharina was sitting in a cell by herself, as if it were a waiting room. She was wearing her heavy coat and her white fur cap. She had put her feet on a stool, and she was twiddling her thumbs. She watched her breath rising; it was cold in the cell.

A bit of grey sky could be seen outside the grey windowpanes. She had already tried standing on the stool to look out of the window at the marketplace, the church on the other side of it and the old town hall. If she had seen Sarkander she'd have waved, but Sarkander wouldn't have seen her. Did he know she was in here?

Didn't other prisoners look out of the window too; wasn't everyone hoping for something?

Not many words had been wasted on her case. The police officer had kept showing her the note with the sketch of the way to the Georgenhof on it, and she had nodded.

'Well now,' the officer had said, 'this is serious, Frau von Globig.' And he asked, 'What did you think you were doing? And you also listened to foreign radio stations.'

He had stopped asking about any incidents of racial defilement between Katharina and the Jew. The whole thing, he thought, was so unedifying that he began to fear for his own skin.

Far away in Italy, Eberhard had already been repeatedly questioned. His superior officer had talked to him seriously for a long time. First just the two of them were present, then the commanding officer joined them. Heil Hitler.

'Your wife gave shelter to a Jew, is that correct?' And, 'So you supported the enemy by holding shares in English steel?' That was a grave accusation; he should expect demotion. And he could wave goodbye to his officer's salary.

A Jew hidden in her room?

Eberhard did some calculations, and realized that it must have been on the evening when he was drinking wine with that little Italian girl.

After the war, when all this was over, he might go back to Italy. What about the Georgenhof? Get the estate back into good shape and forget it! What about this business with the Jew? The dust could settle on that as well.

There was something else on Eberhard's mind. Katharina, and the way she had avoided his kiss when they said goodbye. What sort of woman doesn't even give her husband a goodbye kiss on the cheek?

Get the gate of the yard and the morning-star finial repaired. Put his life in order, those would be his priorities.

20

The Old People

Next day Auntie went to the police again. She'd had about enough of this, she told Peter, and the friendly police officer had had enough of her.

She wondered whether Vladimir might come back after all. Perhaps there had been a mistake of some kind? Perhaps he had thought he was acting for the best?

'If that's so, I'll keep quiet about it,' said Auntie. Everyone can do somthing stupid now and then. 'D you hear me, Peter? If he comes back we'll say no more about it.'

Although her curses couldn't simply be withdrawn.

When Auntie's new acquaintance, the limping Silesian, came to see them he stabled the gelding, who was still inclined to turn his head behind him, in the fire station. The horse could even be locked in there. The Silesian told the people there that it was all right, and even brought in some straw. The man had all kinds of connections. He might even be able to get his new friends a room, he said. But that wasn't necessary; if they'd wanted a room they might as well have stayed at the Georgen-hof. They didn't intend to put down roots here, they wanted to move further on.

He turned up for breakfast in the morning, saying it was only natural for friends to keep company in these hard times. He listened calmly to the full story of the loss of the farm cart, and he helped to repack the suitcases in the coach. There was a lot of useless stuff to be sorted out — away with all those summer clothes!

It was ridiculous to be carting them around in the middle of winter.

'But what will we do in summer? Although heaven only knows where we'll be when summer comes.'

'You'll have been home again long ago next summer,' said the gentleman. But Auntie wasn't so sure of that. She thought she would never see the Georgenhof again. She didn't *want* to see the Georgenhof again. Hadn't she sacrificed over twenty years of her life to the place, more or less? And all for nothing. She hadn't been paid a proper salary; what she got was more like pocket money. Nor had anyone ever stuck social security stamps into a booklet for her: life insurance or a funeral benefit fund. She had no savings under her mattress.

She had been an outsider all her life. Back when she had been turned out of her parental home by Raffke, who stood in the road with a nasty look on his face. In those days she might have trained to be a teacher. She'd always enjoyed playing schools in the garden arbour. But no one had helped her except for old Globig. You'll come to us, he had said, and so she did. It felt like being liberated. However, no salary, just some money put down now and then for her, and a muff or knitted gloves at Christmas.

And later, when Eberhard had bought that wonderful car, the Wanderer, dark blue with a split windscreen . . . couldn't he have taken her for a drive in it some time?

'See what a lovely car we have, Auntie,' he might have said, hooting the horn as they drove out of the gate. Going south, to the sea, into the mountains! She'd have liked to go to Italy, too.

The Silesian told her how he'd love to taste Silesian ham again. He brought a jar of pickled gherkins with him; delicious. Pickled in the Silesian style. And he bought Peter a bowl of ersatz honey. It tasted extremely sweet and surely wasn't good for his teeth. You couldn't eat much of it.

Wouldn't he like to sell his microscope, asked the Silesian, or swap it? And he gave Peter a couple of rifle bullets, all polished and shiny. There were Polish, Belgian and German bullets too. They were made of copper and brass; one even had an eyelet at the back so that you could hang it round your neck.

Peter would have liked to make a collection of such bullets, and the Silesian promised to get him some more. 'I know a man who can get hold of them in return for a bit of ham.' He had a whole cupboard full of them, said the Silesian. He even asked whether Peter would like to have a Finnish dagger. Would it come in useful?

The ration coupons for soldiers on leave that the political economist had given Auntie at the Georgenhof turned out to be invaluable for buying bread. Five or six sheets of them! At the time Auntie had been going to turn down the political economist's offer, but when he still held them out to her, smiling, she had readily accepted. The man hadn't said where he came by them. They looked brand new, and a little different from ordinary coupons.

They were very welcome now.

One time the baker looked at the coupons rather more closely, and Auntie realized that there was something wrong with them. After that she was more careful, sending Peter or the Silesian gentleman to buy bread, and always from a different baker. The baker at the post office was the least suspicious; he was a good-tempered fat man with a red face. His name was Bartels, and he was known as 'the post-office baker'. He had hung the certificate qualifying him as a master baker over the door in a golden frame. He tore off as many coupons as necessary with his thumb, and then pushed the warm, fragrant bread over the counter. He even took an interest in his customers – where did they come from? Where were they going? – and Peter told him stories about the

Russians, hunched figures as brown as earth, who had stormed past him, keeping low.

Peter went up and down the high street, past the rows of carts. Perhaps Vladimir had come back, and would be standing here as if nothing had happened. I'm sorry, it was like this . . .

A farmer took a pee under his cart, where else could he do it? People moved aside a bit.

There was no piano music coming from the town café now. The place was being aired. An officer wearing the Knight's Cross went in. Heil Hitler. He came straight out again; he had probably thought he could sit in the warm and drink coffee, but all the windows were open to let fresh air in.

A man had been awarded the Knight's Cross for annihilating a Russian detachment by pressing boldly forward with the tanks in the armed wedge formation, and now he couldn't get a coffee here?

He had unbuttoned his coat so that everyone could see his medal.

Peter was in luck. The officer spoke to him. 'Boy, is there another café anywhere in this dump?'

Peter would have liked to go to the restaurant at the railway station with the officer, but the bearer of the Knight's Cross didn't want his company. He wanted to sit in a café listening to piano music and smoking a cigarette, perhaps being approached by a young lady who would ask him where he won the Cross. Then he would buy her a slice of rye-flour tart and ask whether she knew her way round this town, and what she did with herself all day.

He'd heard that there was music in this café – and now they were airing the place!

*

The Dutch barber stood in the doorway of his shop, snapping his scissors in the air. Perhaps he was thinking of the hunched figures, keeping low, as brown as earth, who had run past Peter in his stories. And Peter had heard screaming women, had he? Or perhaps the barber was thinking of his village at home in the Netherlands, where they had given him funny looks last time he went back on holiday.

His friend Jan was lucky. He wouldn't be considered a collaborator. He had spent a couple of days in prison for grinning when he'd been told he wasn't allowed to give the Hitler salute. He had it in writing, too! That would make a difference one of these days.

In the stationer's shop they sold puzzle books, the right size to go by military post. They were for soldiers at the front, sitting in their trenches and waiting for the enemy. The booklets had titles like *Clever Dick* and *Mastermind*. You could buy stamp albums there as well, and stamps in clear film envelopes, neatly sorted like the scores of the card game Skat. A hundred and fifty stamps for one Reichsmark. Austrian Republic and Danzig Free State stamps, used and unused. General Government of Poland stamps consisting almost entirely of the postmark.

Peter thought of buying a stamp album, and held it for so long that the salesgirl got impatient. Herr Schünemann had advised him to invest his money in stamps.

But in the end he didn't, because he could see that the assortments of stamps included some with the picture of the Führer on them.

The pharmacy was sold out of liquorice. Heil Hitler!

'Haven't you been here before?' asked the pharmacist. He thought it was odd that a boy who was a stranger to the town came wanting to buy liquorice twice running, when the stuff was sold out.

'I'm a refugee,' said Peter. He seemed to himself abandoned and all alone as he said that, and in fact it was the first time he had done so. The pharmacist thought that was sad, and opened up his display case to see if there was a little bag of Italian liquorice left there after all.

Looking through the shop window, Peter saw Auntie walking down the other side of the street with the Silesian gentleman. Auntie in her black hat, wearing her muff and her rubber over-shoes, the gentleman limping slightly. Which of them was supporting the other? Had the Silesian taken Auntie's arm?

The first cartloads of old people arrived from Mitkau. They were being evacuated from the monastery. The old folk were trans-ported in open horse-drawn carts, sitting on straw packed well round them. They were nodding their heads, as if in time to cheerful tunes played on a concertina. They had never thought they would have to go on the road again in their old age, with can-nulas sticking out of them like hedgehog prickles, with colostomy bags and devices for getting air into their thoracic cavities. They were bad on their feet and had trouble with their waterworks.

It hadn't been so bad in Mitkau; they had got used to the place. Why, they thought, can't people leave us in peace?

They were surely thinking, too, of their pretty home town of Tilsit. It used to be so nice, sitting outside their houses in summer, watching horses being ridden down to the river to drink.

Perhaps their evacuation had gone wrong?

The sun had always been shining in Tilsit. There were always sunflowers in Tilsit growing beside the fences.

The locals lined the streets as the carts of old folk arrived one by one. No one called out 'Heil.' Good heavens, what a sad load of poor old people. Coughing and spitting. They hadn't imagined that the evening of their days would be like this. What, wondered the spectators, will happen to us when we're old and weak? And the local old folk in the church care home, hearing that they were to have new arrivals, were wondering: when will they take *us* away? Lord, let me know the number of my days . . .

And many of the passers-by were probably thinking: terrible! Wouldn't it be a mercy to put these sick people out of their misery? Useless mouths to be fed, lives not worth living. The expression *vegetables fit for the graveyard* did the rounds.

Doctors in white coats arrived. Heil Hitler. Nothing had been prepared, nothing was organized. Should the seats be ripped out of the cinema? No, there were objections to that. The cinema was still needed; people needed something to take their minds off the present. They wanted to see a film to entertain them and make them laugh wholeheartedly.

> *What will our lives be now, dear heart?*
> *Happy or sad, say the powers above?*
> *What course does our life take, must we part?*
> *Or may we yet come to the land of love?*

They would have to call on the school; plenty of room there. The headmaster wrung his hands, and jubilant children ran down the street.

The local pastor put in an appearance, standing in his church porch like the post-office baker standing outside his shop, and sure enough he was needed: some of those taken out of the carts were dead, with their bread rations clutched in their hands, and they were laid at his feet. The problem was how to get them buried. For the time being they must be left lying here, side by side; when they thawed they would begin to stink.

Ding-dong ding-dong, rang the bell. 'We will meet here at six for silent prayer,' the pastor told those hurrying by, who couldn't believe that there were dead men and women lying outside the church. News of it went from mouth to mouth.

Peter too saw the old people sitting in the carts, and being lifted down. The carts were already being turned to fetch the rest of the old folk from Mitkau. They couldn't be left to fall into the hands of the Russians. It occurred to Peter that he could go home to Mitkau with the empty carts, pay a quick visit to the Georgenhof and come straight back again. He could give the others who were still there a surprise. The Hesses, Sonya and Jago the dog. Take another look at the family home, see it with new eyes. And then, next day, he could come back here with the last load of old folk.

Perhaps he could bring something from home back as well. Peter thought of the new locomotive he had been given at Christmas for his railway. He'd have liked to have it with him now.

And he thought of his mother's silhouettes. He'd never looked at them properly.

'No, you're staying here,' said Auntie, although the Silesian gentleman tried to persuade her to let him go: Peter could bring some more sausage and ham. He'd really like to taste ham again.

'Good Silesian ham, do you remember?'

Peter was glad to have someone on his side at last, but Auntie insisted, 'No, you're staying here.'

No, he could not go to Mitkau. That chapter was closed. Instead, just for once, he could go to the cinema.

Auntie gave him fifty pfennigs for a seat at the back, and asked afterwards, 'Was it good?' She was still a fan of Beniamino Gigli, whom she had once heard in her youth, and the Silesian gentleman remembered having liked Gigli too.

'Forget me not!' he sang to Auntie, and he did in fact have a good singing voice.

Gigli! That had been ages ago. The Silesian asked Auntie to dine with him at the restaurant in the town hall cellar. You could get meat loaf and potatoes there for fifty grams' worth of meat coupons and a ten-gram fat coupon, and Auntie agreed to provide those. Heil Hitler. She put on a different jacket specially, because she couldn't be seen out in public in this dress, which was in urgent need of ironing. Her good clothes were in Vladimir's cart. She put on her gold brooch with the golden arrows pointing in every direction. It was a long time since she had been asked out by a gentleman. To be honest, she had never been asked out by a gentleman before.

Auntie came back late in the evening, and she was upset.

When Peter asked, 'Was it good?' she snapped, 'Leave me alone!'

Nothing was easy.

Dr Wagner was sitting quietly in his study when he heard about the evacuation of the monastery. A large number of the old people had already been taken away, and now it was the turn of the rest.

He was sitting at his desk with the marble inkwell in front of him. There had always been plenty of ink in it, but the poems he owed it to himself to write were slow to flow out from his pen. Rilke and Stefan George kept getting in the way, so he had thought: let's leave it at that.

Sad to say, his mother had never really supported him. Now and then he would put sheets of paper on her work basket, but she glanced at them only fleetingly. And never said a word about them.

*

He looked at the album in which he had stuck the photos of his students, and put crosses beside the pictures of those who had fallen.

He counted the number of students who had passed through his hands. He saw a long grey line before him, their heads bowed, and he thought of many a bright head, but also of dullness that couldn't be carried away on the wings of grace and dignity.

And he thought of the endless hours he had devoted to them. He calculated the hours of his knowledge like the beads of a rosary, day by day and hour by hour. Always the same, year after year. He had not been granted release.

Tearing himself away from his thoughts, he put on walking shoes and trousers, wrapped his gaiters round his legs and then, wearing his good outdoor coat, set off along the familiar road to the monastery: down Horst-Wessel-Strasse, across the marketplace and past the church. The church organist was coming towards him in the marketplace. He quickly turned up his collar. Meeting that woman was all he needed! She had denied him access to the church when his mother had just died, and he had wanted to lose himself on that instrument playing his variations: in E flat minor, then by way of G flat major to B.

But she wouldn't let him, so he had been obliged to turn to the shimmering sound of his piano, with his dead mother in the room next door.

He passed the town hall, and the little prison. Second floor, the second window from the left? He could make out a pale face there. Someone was waving. But Dr Wagner wasn't looking. He went over the big new bridge that hadn't been paid for yet. Sappers were putting explosives in place on it. He passed the never-ending processions of refugees. They walked on, not with hair flying in the wind, not stealing over borders under cover of night and fog, no, they marched past with their packs, keeping the correct distance apart. Military police showed them the way. Far below them lay the grey, icy surface of the river, with frozen landing stages on which women would beat their washing in the spring.

The carts were standing outside the monastery, fresh straw in them. Old people were being lifted in, little old men and little old women separately, all in black; they were pushed in, laid down and shoved into position. Each with a few possessions, many holding apples, the gift of the Red Cross. They looked like imperial orbs, and the old people's crutches like sceptres. When they were all sitting or lying in the carts, more straw was brought and placed over them. Now they could leave.

'What about it?' the man in charge of the transport asked Dr Wagner. 'Want to come? You could take over the second cart.'

And he made up his mind: yes, he would leave at once, come what may! Did he want to see the town burning, buildings collapsing, *soldateska* running wild, going from house to house, showing off jewellery hanging between their fingers? And perhaps being assaulted by a Russian himself.

All that was to be avoided.

So he climbed up into the cart, and as it had to wait not far from Horst-Wessel-Strasse until the gate was opened to let them through, he paid a quick visit to his apartment and threw his shaving brush into the air-raid shelter bag where he kept everything that mattered to him: money, papers, and the picture of his mother as a young woman, taken at the Imperial Palace in Goslar, sitting on a wall with her wide skirt spread out round her.

Also the picture of his father, a man he had never seen and of whom he knew nothing.

Out, out into the countryside! A last look – he snatched the quilt off his bed, put the key through the letterbox and he was off.

Yes, he would rather have gone with the Globigs. But that wasn't to be. He had not been invited to join them, and that was that. Hadn't a family relationship developed between them? Didn't they belong together?

'But perhaps it's better this way,' he said out loud. 'Perhaps it really is better this way.'

He craned his neck when he was passing the Georgenhof. The soldier beside him said, 'That's the Georgenhof over there.'

There was no sign of Drygalski, or the foreign workers at the Forest Lodge, once a good place to visit in summer for coffee and cakes, when the weather was warm. Carts on the trek stood in its yard, and strangers were going in and out.

'I've spent many happy hours at the Georgenhof,' he quietly said to himself, as the first yellow icicles were already showing under the car. The Baltic baron's chronicle! He suddenly remembered it; the history of the man's native place ... he rushed into the house and retrieved it. It must be saved. Heavens, if he'd forgotten it! Wasn't he a man of his word?

Peter was strolling around. White-painted tanks with Waffen-SS men in white camouflage clothing were driving along the high street, which was named after Adolf Hitler. 'Right turn!' someone called, and the horses pulling the carts began to climb.

The brave German soldiers were going towards the Russians. Were the reserves of manpower inexhaustible? They stopped in the open outside the town, in a field where the traces of a funfair could still be seen, and friendly SS-men gave the children sweets. One boy was in luck; he was even allowed to climb into the turret of a tank.

Then the tanks, those heavy, shapeless things, drove away. The area into which the Germans were crowded was small, and getting ever smaller. All the easier to defend it, said the newspapers. Never fear!

The blue diesel vapour of the fighting machines lingered over the high street for a long time.

Now the remaining shops were giving away their wares free.

Maybe this was the right moment to move on. Auntie reported to the police officer, who wished her good luck. As soon as he heard anything about that Vladimir, he said, he would let her know. At the moment he had a lot on his hands: all manner of thefts had been reported – there were people going from house to house, looting – and there had even been a murder.

Next morning French POWs were led through the town, with scarves round their necks and hands in their pockets. In the thick, driving snow the scene looked a little like 1812. They marched all in time, quietly, in the middle of the road, and the guard with his long rifle brought up the rear, keeping in step with them. One of them, in front and on the left, carried a lantern to let cars know that a troop of Frenchmen was coming, please don't run them down, they're decent fellows, we have nothing against them.

The women with their net shopping bags watched them go. An old man was trying to keep up with them; he wanted to tell them that he had been a prisoner of the French in the last war, and he took cigarettes from his pocket and held them out.

No, they had plenty of cigarettes. They were even sharing them with the guard. He should keep his cigarettes.

'Bonjour!' he called after them. He had worked for farmers in 1917, at the foot of the Pyrenees, and there had been red wine for breakfast. In itself, that had been a good time.

Peter had seen the Frenchmen in Albertsdorf, when they had been drinking vermouth with Vladimir. Should he ask if they knew where Vladimir was? Stealing the cart in cold blood. Peter hadn't even been able to say goodbye to the two bay horses.

While Peter was still thinking of asking the Frenchmen about it, they disappeared into the snowy twilight.

Auntie said, 'So there you are. We won't be staying here much longer.'

The Silesian gentleman was nowhere to be seen, and it wasn't easy to get the gelding back. He was already sold, she was told. Herr So-and-so had sold him yesterday. And at the moment they couldn't lay hands on the key to the fire station.

Auntie was about to go to the police when they told her that she could buy the horse back; they'd let her have him at a special price.

So Auntie paid the money and went off with the grateful animal. He swished his tail and looked straight ahead.

That man was a bastard, Auntie told Peter. He didn't even come from her beloved Lower Silesia, he came from *Upper* Silesia, a place that was teeming with Polacks.

'Nothing's easy.'

They said goodbye to the neighbouring vehicles on the football field, Heil Hitler, and to the Party man who had been so impressed by the coat of arms on the coach door, even if he didn't show it. Heil Hitler. And then the cry was 'Gee up!' and the gelding pricked up his ears.

She would never, ever let herself be taken in like that again, said Auntie out loud. 'What a wretch!'

She had said the same to the men at the fire station, but they told her that if she repeated that remark there'd be consequences.

*

In the high street, they met the first treks coming from the west. Go back, go back, they said of Elbing. No one can get through that way. If they'd known before, said the people on their way back, they'd have stayed put here. Women driving the carts leaned down to Auntie, who was still persistently driving west. 'Go back! You can't get through that way.'

But Auntie didn't want to go to Elbing; she had other plans. And many people, like her, were going neither east nor west, but hoped to find safety at the Frisches Haff, and go on from there over the ice to the spit of land known as the Frisches Nehrung.

Perhaps she would be able to sell the rest of the ration coupons for soldiers on leave at the Haff?

She could not have known that at the same time Uncle Josef and his party were going through Harkunen and back east home, home again! Home to Albertsdorf, where they had spent so many happy years. With his wife and three daughters. No more would ever be heard of him.

21

On the Road

They were trotting slowly along under the grey veil of snow. Now that the gelding had been fed plenty of oats, it was hard to control him, but anyway there was no chance of overtaking the long line of carts ahead of them. Why they were making such slow progress was a mystery. There were dead bodies lying by the side of the road, and some were sitting against trees frozen stiff: the bodies of old people who could go no further and of small children.

Peter was very tired. 'It comes of all that fresh air,' said Auntie. 'Lie down in the back of the coach.' She could manage on her own, she told him. 'If we've made it this far we'll get to the Frisches Haff.'

She uncorked a bottle, put it to her lips and took a couple of gulps, posing as if for a photograph. 'Auntie in Action'. No one would have expected her to be so enterprising.

Peter lay in the straw, covered with rugs and coats. He was tired, in fact almost unconscious with exhaustion, alternately hot and cold. And when he moved because a suitcase was pressing against him, it made him even more exhausted, and he immediately lay back and forgot where he was.

Now and then they stopped to let military trucks driving the opposite way go by. Then the procession went on again. You could hear people cursing and shouting. Auntie was cursing too, swearing roundly, and now and then taking a mouthful from her

bottle. Across the Frisches Haff and then along the Nehrung –
that way to the west was still open.

Auntie on the box of the coach. She imagined Vladimir being
caught, tied up and brought to face her – *On the redoubt in
Strasbourg*, like the deserter waiting for execution in Mahler's
song – and she thought what she would say about him. 'Yes, he
made careful preparations, but he let us down in the end.'

Then she began running through the list of what had been on
the cart. But hard as she thought about it, what she mainly
remembered was how Vladimir had taken a heavy chest of drawers off the load again at the last minute, just before they left the
Georgenhof. The Georgenhof, the crows roosting in the oak tree
and the finial of the spiked mace that didn't stand up straight.

She thought of what Katharina would say some day: 'Auntie did
it all on her own . . . she excelled herself.' Deep down inside, she
was rejoicing. 'How quick off the mark Auntie was!' Eberhard
would say. 'She saved Peter's life.' She'd saved the briefcase of
papers and photographs as well.

The photograph album from the Ukraine: Eberhard and his
comrades out riding in white uniforms. A group photo, with an
arrow added in ink to the deckle-edged photograph (the ink had
run), pointing to 'Our general'.

If I'd had to set off in the farm cart I wouldn't have made it,
thought Auntie, what with the weight of the cart and *two*
horses – even harnessing them up would have been a problem,
and all those reins to be disentangled.

She was glad that, at her age, she could still drive the coach
through the countryside. In these circumstances, too.

As she reined in the gelding, keeping behind the cart ahead,
she even had time to glance at the landscape, the frost on the trees
and the few crows.

When all this is over I'll go back to Silesia, she thought. Some day I'll eat poppy-seed cake in Silesia again. Here we've been on the run from the Devil.

They were now approaching a village with a small church, a Neo-Gothic church built of Prussian brick, and above the porch a cement figure of Christ was giving his blessing.

A solitary aircraft came slowly flying above the road and the long line of carts on the trek. It was moving erratically from side to side as it dropped bombs on the column of vehicles; you could see the bombs come sailing down. One of them fell beside the little coach containing Auntie and the sleeping Peter. The gelding reared up, neighing, and slumped over the shafts. What was left of the animal stretched flat on the ground. The coach toppled over, throwing Peter out into the open air.

The plane came back once more; the pilot probably wanted to see what hits he had scored. Did he make marks on his notepad? One, two, three, four, five horse-drawn carts full of fascist murderers and incendiaries finished off?

To make sure, he fired the plane's machine gun along the column. Then he flew a loop above the fields and went to get more bombs.

The bomb had hit Auntie. Helene Harnisch was dead. Born 1885, died January 1945, unmarried. Two months before her sixtieth birthday. It had smashed her chest open.

Traffic was building up into a jam behind the coach. Other carts were lying on their sides, and lamentations filled the air. At last men came along to push the wrecked vehicles off the road and make way for the great trek that wanted to get past them.

Women laid the dead, including the body of Auntie, in the

ditches at the roadside. Now, for heaven's sake, the other carts could go on.

Peter sat down beside Auntie. One of her arms had been blown off. There were two gold rings on its hand. Red blood stained the snow. Ought he to pray an Our Father? 'Nothing was easy . . .'

The carts went on past him, one after another. He saw them all, and they all saw him: the boy with the binoculars round his neck and the air pistol stuck in his belt. He sat there sprinkled with washing powder that had been blasted into the air.

After a while a man arrived from the village, the local pastor coming to take the dead away. He helped Peter to roll Auntie into a blanket, and put the arm that had been torn off, her left arm, into the blanket with her. It had come right away from her shoulder joint, and was broken as well.

They carried the old woman to the church and laid her in the vestibule, beside the offertory box and the frame that held the numbers of hymns to be sung. On the wall was a plaque bearing the names of the dead who had fallen in the wars of 1870-71 and 1914-18.

There were already several other bodies in the church – a number of them still bleeding – arranged in order of size, among them children; one was a girl with long brown stockings. Part of her skirt had gone, exposing the suspenders holding the stockings up, and some bare skin. Weeping people lingered by the corpses, but they couldn't afford to stay for long.

'When are you coming?' their companions asked. 'We have to go on.'

While the pastor spread a blanket over Auntie, Peter went into the cold church and out again by another door, round the church and back through the main doorway. Then he sat down at the front of the church, under the pulpit. Later, he would be able to say, 'When Auntie died I sat in the church and stayed there for a long time.'

Auntie was dead, her life extinguished, as if a blanket had been smoothed out over it. The blanket is pulled taut, thought Peter. Gone and forgotten? He thought of fortune-telling at Christmas time, when you gradually melted a lead coin, saw it losing its original shape, and then dropped it into cold water to take new shape.

When he offered the rooster a few extra grains of corn, she used to tap on the window up in her room. It meant there was no need for him to feed the rooster, the poultry had plenty to eat, and the rooster got his rightful share every day.

When he thought about what to do next, and went back to the road, the contents of the coach had already been looted. People near it retreated, like vultures flying up when a coyote comes along. He stood beside the wreck undecided, one hand clutching his binoculars. A friendly woman stopped for a moment when she saw him standing there alone, and told him to jump up and get on the back of her cart, quick! She was already reaching her arms down to him.

But no, he thought, he couldn't go with her and leave everything lying around like this, could he?

Then the French prisoners of war came marching up. Left, left, left . . . they didn't stop. As they marched past they looked at the ruined coach. Left, left, left, two, three, four! They knew about this kind of thing: dead horses, a coach on its side. But like Napoleon's Old Guard in 1812 they stuck together, marching all in step. The soldier guarding them did stop for a moment. 'Are you on your own?' he asked in kindly tones. It was difficult for Peter to hide the tears that this question brought to his eyes. Should he go with the Frenchmen?

He collected a few things: Auntie's big suitcase, his rucksack and the microscope.

As for Auntie's lute, a cart had run over it and smashed it to pieces.

As he was retrieving these things, he was asked by a Volkssturm reservist – Heil Hitler – what he was doing there. Was he looting or what? He'd better make himself scarce or the reservist would report him! The crest of the von Globigs on the door, which had fallen off the coach, meant nothing to the man.

Peter stowed some bread and sausage away in his rucksack, put the microscope under his arm, and went away, pulling the suitcase after him.

A couple of lines of verse went through his head, from the *Evening Song* by the hymn-writer Matthias Claudius. *We smile at such illusions, believing them delusions* ... It was funny, he hadn't even heard the bomb going off.

'You must see to getting that dead horse out of the way,' said the reservist. 'It can't stay lying there.' Then he went off over the snow.

The parsonage was behind the church. The pastor's name was Schowalker; he had hair cut very short, although it curled profusely at the nape of his neck.

He had carried the dead bodies into the church, and now he took Peter into the parsonage kitchen with him.

Everything was neat and tidy here, no crumbs lying around. A moderate fire was burning in the stove, and pots and pans were hanging side by side on the wall. You could hear cartwheels crunching over the snow on the nearby road, and the drivers of the carts calling out, but in here everything was quiet and pleasant.

The pastor fetched soap and nailbrushes, and they washed

Auntie's blood off their hands. Peter had put his hand to his mouth, and some of her spilt blood had reached his lips. He wondered: am I connected to her now?

Peter also had a bloodstain on his coat. It could always be washed off when he got the chance.

The pastor asked for Auntie's personal details. Helene Harnisch, born 1885 ...

He wrote the information down on a piece of card and put a length of string through it. He would tie it round the woman's wrist. The wrist that she still had.

They sat at the kitchen table. The pastor placed a glass of hot elderberry juice in front of Peter, and then they ate some of his sausage. 'There's no one left in the village,' said the pastor. 'All the carts went away yesterday.' He rubbed his hands; they were blue with cold. He had sent his wife and daughter off to the Ruhr in autumn, after the Russians broke through at Gumbinnen, he told Peter. But he hadn't had any news of them for a long time. Were there air raids in the Ruhr? He didn't know whether they were still alive.

He'd always thought he must stay where he was, but now he wondered what there was left for him to do here.

He asked Peter's advice: should he, the pastor, go away too?

He pointed to a photo of his wife and daughter pinned to the wall above the kitchen table. A perfectly normal woman and a perfectly ordinary girl. He unfolded a brightly coloured road map from a tourist company, and showed Peter just where they were. 'We're here, and over there is Danzig.' The Frisches Haff was only a few kilometres away. And he showed Peter how the Russian tanks had come from the south, by way of Allenstein, and gone right through to the coast.

*

The map depicted famous sights in colour: the Crane Gate in Danzig; Marienburg Castle on the Nogat; Frauenburg on the Vistula Lagoon; Braunsberg. Above the Baltic coast there was a picture of a wickerwork beach chair, and a young woman wading into the sea with a rubber animal under her arm.

After supper they looked at the contents of Auntie's suitcase. Right at the top was Katharina's gold locket, and under it were handkerchiefs, panties, vests, blouses, along with letters and photographs. The photo of the Silesian donkey cart. And three silver teaspoons. When the pastor saw the teaspoons he said, 'We had teaspoons just like that at home, when I was a child. They came from our great-grandparents, thin silver, because of the bad times.' *Three* of them? He picked up one of those fine, thin, slightly dented spoons. Could he have one? he asked; it would make him so happy. They'd had spoons just like that at home. They ate greengages with them, greengages as dessert every lunchtime. Semolina pudding with greengages.

Peter took his microscope out of its box and set it up. What did Auntie's blood look like? He scraped it off his coat and looked at it. It was a crusted substance with nothing mysterious about it.

When the pastor heard that Peter's name was von Globig and he came from the Georgenhof, he was astonished. A young woman had been here two days ago, a violinist. She had mentioned the Georgenhof, saying she'd been given nothing to eat there and had been thrown straight out. The people there were unfriendly, stupid, miserly aristocrats.

Didn't that give Peter something to think about, asked the pastor. He welcomed the boy here with hot elderberry juice, and there was a bed ready for him, while a few days ago his family at the Georgenhof had sent a lonely girl packing.

No, said Peter, it wasn't like that at all. They'd given her fried potatoes and blood sausage, and gooseberry compote afterwards.

The pastor didn't believe him, judging by the little smile on his face, which clearly meant: I understand you, my boy, you don't want to foul your own nest. And he stuck to his version. It would make the basis of a good sermon.

So Peter talked about the Georgenhof, and the hospitable welcome given there to other refugees. He told the pastor about the finial over the gable in the shape of a spiked mace; the tea-house on the banks of the River Helge; parties in the park with Chinese lanterns; and his sister's white mausoleum. 'It has seven steps leading up to it, and a path to it through the forest.' He talked about suites of rooms in the Georgenhof, and the crystal chandeliers. And there was the chamber organ in the library, but no one had played it since his grandfather's death . . .

'Does it have one manual or two?' asked the pastor at this point, but Peter was at a loss for an answer. However, he said it was a strange thing, but sometimes it seemed to him as if someone were playing the instrument in the night. And a deliberately dreamy look came into his eyes. When he was sitting under the light in his room, reading or looking through his microscope, he had thought he heard the organ playing loud and clear down below.

He was using the past tense, but at that moment he really did seem to hear the instrument that had never existed.

This time he didn't tell the story of the hunched figures, brown as earth, who had scurried past him. He kept it to himself.

*

The pastor knew Mitkau. He had once preached there. 'My colleague Brahms in that city was a German Christian; do you know what that means?' A German Christian? You had to go cautiously with those. Yes, Brahms had been a German Christian, swore loyalty to Hitler and then changed his mind. *Awake, awake, thou German land, too long hast thou been sleeping . . .* When St Mary's Church was reconsecrated after its renovation, he had given the Hitler salute. Heil Hitler, arm in the air and so on . . .

Some people had very flexible consciences.

And now he'd been arrested on some dubious pretext, nothing precise was known about it. A matter of morality, maybe?

The violinist . . . the pastor was enthusiastic about that young woman. She had taken her instrument out of its case, he said, and played it in the church. All the people who were going on the road again next day had streamed in to hear her. It was standing room only, she played so well. The notes might have come from the world beyond! Such music had never been heard in his church before.

The audience had been rooted to the ground. They knew, at that moment, that it was time to say goodbye to their own country. *Now fare thee well, my native land . . .* Imagine turning a sweet creature like that away from your door! 'Did your family stop to think what they were doing?'

'Well,' said Peter, 'she played hit songs too, with a one-armed soldier accompanying her on the piano, and she had two helpings of blood sausage.'

'One-armed?' said the pastor. 'You mustn't exaggerate like that, my boy. A one-armed man can't play the piano.'

His thoughts were still with his violinist. Shaking back her blonde hair, and then playing so powerfully. At the first note, the eternity of German music – however you like to put it – had filled the church.

'Many of the local farmers' wives came to me later,' he said, 'and said they'd never heard anything so beautiful.'

There was a harmonium in the pastor's study. The pastor pulled out the enamelled stops and played a hymn. *So take my hands and lead me / to my everlasting rest.* There was something about the eternity of German music here too. The left-hand bellows of the harmonium was torn, and the pastor could work only the pedal for the right-hand bellows, which made the tune rather jerky, but you could tell what it was.

'Shall we pray, my boy?'

This was very odd. Sitting at a kitchen table in front of a glass of elderberry juice, and praying?

Peter thought of his mother's gold locket at the top of Auntie's suitcase. He had put it in his pocket, and the chain lay in his hand like a rosary.

In the evening Peter went over to the church where the dead were lying. There were more of them now, including two babies. He wanted to look at the girl with the suspenders again.

Auntie didn't belong to him any longer. She lay under the blanket with her legs twisted, and snow drifting round her. The snow had drifted in under the door, covering the dead bodies. The arm that had been blown off lay beside her, with the rings on her finger, and her twisted legs.

He searched the wreck of the coach again by the light of the electric torch. He noticed the little wreath of flowers on the oval back window, and took it with him.

The gelding lay on his back, legs outstretched, entirely covered by snow.

At this moment Katharina was sitting in the overheated room occupied by the police officer – Heil Hitler – wearing her white

Persian lamb cap, with her black trousers tucked into her black riding boots. She had a packet of sandwiches on her lap. Someone had sent them. The officer wasn't allowed to say who it was.

He was looking at the file in front of him. It was a thin one, with only two or three sheets of paper in it. *Frau von Globig has admitted to sheltering a Jew*, said one of them. She had signed it.

'And you also tuned in to foreign radio stations, Frau von Globig? That's what Head Trustee Drygalski said.'

No, she had not, and she hadn't signed anything saying so either. Copenhagen, yes, but not the BBC.

Questions went back and forth. She did not ask, 'What will become of me?' It was more as if she wanted to say: oh, leave me in peace.

Perhaps the police officer was thinking: what will become of *me*? How am I going to get out of this situation, with the Russians at the gates? How can I reach safety? With the whole place full of criminals – they'll get the upper hand if things go wrong, and then they'll cut my throat!

The whole city was getting out, and here he was stuck with twenty-seven prisoners. People who could make short work of you.

He had noticed what nice fillings Frau von Globig's sandwiches had.

Could he have soup that was rather more nourishing given to everyone tomorrow morning, and then go out of town on police business?

Could he fix that somehow?

Katharina wasn't thinking of Peter – he would be all right, she was sure – or of Auntie either. And certainly not of Herr Hirsch, who had climbed the old rose fence to her room. Should she ask how he was? Perhaps he was only a few cells further away. She remembered his scratched hands; she had put sticking plaster on them. And his fingernail clippings on the rim of the washbasin.

She would have liked to talk to the police officer about something else entirely, about that single day at the seaside. But it was nothing to do with this case, and the police officer wouldn't know about it. She would have liked to tell him. Who else could she talk to? Who took any interest, now, in the fact that the mayor of Mitkau had sat in a wickerwork beach chair with Frau von Globig?

A great many things went through her mind. She thought of the water in the cellar and the foreign workers in the Forest Lodge.

How would Eberhard take this? His own wife in prison? Would he pick fluff off his uniform tunic and say, 'It can't be true'?

The police officer took the key and stood up. 'Come with me,' he said. Then he went out into the yard. Stood in the doorway with her, watching the snowflakes floating softly and steadily down in front of the wall. Voices came from the cells. Was that someone laughing?

He opened another door, and they were standing in the marketplace. People were passing by, and didn't even look up. From the north-east the long line of the trek was moving over the marketplace, like Katharina herself, and then it disappeared through the Senthagener Tor again.

A few carts began assembling in the marketplace as if forming a stockade. They were preparing to spend the night there.

The officer was letting her have a little fresh air. And allowing her to walk a few steps up and down.

Doesn't anyone here know me? Katharina wondered. But she knew none of the passers-by. There was a man over there in the town hall who knew her very well. A friend? But there was no sign of him.

The police officer pointed to the church. 'There,' he said. 'You can thank his reverence Pastor Brahms for all this. A fine sort he is!' He stood with her for a few long minutes, letting her breathe in and out. And he thought of the black-haired Jew they had shot in the cellar: he had crumpled at the knees before he slumped sideways.

I'm dancing to heaven with you,
To the seventh heaven of love.

Katharina thought of Felicitas. Just fifteen minutes' walk, past the cinema and the post office, and she would be with Felicitas . . .

But she'd never persuade the police officer to go on such an expedition. Her friend's chatter, and her laughter, and story after story. In fact by this time, as Katharina was not to know, Felicitas was far away. She had thrown in her lot with the refugees billeted on her, who turned out to be resourceful. They had eaten Katharina's hare together, and that had paid off. 'We'll stick together,' Felicitas had said to the refugee woman, who was happy to agree.

'There it is,' said the police officer, 'you can't rely on anyone. The pastor was not an innocent. You've no idea of all the stuff we found at his place.'

Forming an alliance with a man like this, she thought, would be playing with fire. But what did he want? she wondered when she was back in her cell. Did he want to let her go? Was she supposed to console him?

*

Peter spent the night in the pastor's bed. He had put the two teaspoons, the little dried-up wreath of flowers and the gold locket on its chain on the bedside table, and then went to sleep at once.

The pastor himself had got up several times in the night to look out of the window. Was he thinking of his violinist? Were his thoughts with the church?

The pastor thought of what he had told Peter about the German Christians. And he had spoken so disparagingly of them ... this boy was bound to be a Pimpf, in the junior branch of the Hitler Youth. Hadn't children denounced their own parents for an incautious word?

But *von* Globig? Weren't all those aristocrats against Hitler? 20 July and so on?

Imagine if he did something stupid at the last moment. He'd survived the local rural district leader, who had always been sitting under the pulpit listening carefully to his sermons, even making notes, and now was he going to be handed over to the executioner by a child?

It would be best to get out at once. He should have gone with the villagers, they'd offered to take him. His superintendent had allowed him a dispensation, although his Catholic colleague in the next village showed no signs of leaving.

Would he have to knock the figure of Christ off the porch with a hammer and take it with him? Could he leave the beloved image that had accompanied him for so long to be destroyed by the Bolshevist hordes?

He opened Auntie's suitcase. What on earth would the boy do with all that ladies' underwear? Panties and vests? Handkerchiefs with little red bows? Peter had already taken two of the silver spoons, but he had the third safe. I coaxed that one out of him, thought the pastor. He would keep it as a talisman. No hallmark, but it was certainly silver.

He picked up a packet of handkerchiefs. One more or less surely wouldn't be noticed?

Why, why had he let himself be carried away into talking about the German Christians? 'You're so trusting,' his wife had always told him. 'You'll talk yourself into trouble some day.'

But hadn't the boy himself said something that could be used against him if necessary? 'Nazi.' He had mentioned Drygalski 'the Nazi'. Yes, that was it. He could strike back with that. This Drygalski was evidently high up in the Party.

Nazi . . . didn't anyone using a word like that incriminate himself? Hadn't he given himself away?

He sat down at the harmonium and tapped out a tune on the keys, but he didn't tread on the pedals to works the bellows.

I long for my eternal home,
No longer in the world to roam.
Ah, might I pass through heaven's door
To gaze on God for evermore.

He was so tired of everything.

22

Alone

Next morning the pastor looked out of the window and said to Peter, who was washing himself in the kitchen, 'Snow, snow, snow . . .' He tapped the barometer and said, 'It's rising.' On the outdoor thermometer he read fifteen degrees below zero. 'Snow, snow, snow. Those poor people, how will they ever get through? There'll be snowdrifts a metre high.' He went out and threw the birds a little food. But then he shook out the entire contents of the bag, as if sowing the seed broadcast, and birds came from all directions. Why keep any of the bird seed back when all was lost anyway?

Peter returned to the road, where carts were still driving along – or were driving along again – one after another, with a rumbling, crunching sound. 'Where are we going?' someone called. The dead gelding was already buried under the snow, his mouth open and showing his teeth. But he couldn't just leave the animal like that, could he?

Carts that had fallen over lay in the road, bodies among them. And more bodies in the ditches, the bodies of children.

Peter thought of the gelding. He had always blown the chaff away from the oats, clever creature that he was. When Vladimir had lifted him up on the great horse's back, the gelding used to nuzzle his leg affectionately. And hadn't he even once spent the night beside him?

How was he to dispose of the body? At the front of the trek, crows flew up from other horses that had died.

Peter went through the empty village. Not a soul in sight.

A war memorial. The village pond, a lime tree and an inn. Ducks and geese must splash about here in the summer. Now crows were roosting in the lime tree, and you could have skated on the pond. The doors of houses and barns had been left open. Paper was blowing out of them, and net curtains billowed from the windows.

There was a chair in the middle of a room, an old man sitting on it, babbling. When he saw Peter he raised a hand. Peter backed out of the room. What could he do about a babbling old man whose family had left him behind? Sitting there talking nonsense.

A jeep was standing outside the village inn, and Peter heard voices in the building. Three SS men were sitting there. They had fried themselves some bacon and were drinking schnapps with it. The soldiers had stopped for a rest and were discussing what to do next. You could see from their collars that they had won the Close Combat Clasp and the Iron Cross. Two older men, and a younger one who looked like a schoolboy.

When Peter came in – Heil Hitler – the young SS man grabbed his hand, said, 'White bread or black bread?', held it tightly and screwed it round until he screamed.

'White bread,' said the man contemptuously, screwing it even more. Peter trod on his foot as hard as he could. The others laughed; that was the right thing to do. 'Don't take it lying down, boy!'

Couldn't a German boy like Peter stand up to a strong hand-shake, asked the young SS man. 'Made of cotton wool, are you?' Fancy being unable to take a good squeeze of his flipper! He was surprised, said the young man, he supposed Peter was a mummy's boy, was he? Liked to sit in the warm by the stove?

Wasn't he a Pimpf?

Let's see his papers. Oh, only just twelve.

They invited Peter to sit down with them and pushed a slice of bacon over to him.

Did he come from this village? No, said Peter, his own village was already occupied by the Russians and all his people were dead … Then he said he was the only one left alive, he had hidden and then one evening the Russians were there, hunched figures as brown as earth scurrying past his hiding place. And he took his air pistol out of the waistband of his trousers, as if to say: I'd have sold my life at a high price …

The men had stopped listening; they knew at once that Peter's stories were lies, and didn't want to listen to any more. 'Keep your mouth shut,' they said. They could have told different stories; they all wore the ribbons of their orders.

> *When the golden evening sun,*
> *With its last bright rays was going down, going down,*
> *One of Hitler's regiments,*
> *Came to a little town, a little town …*

one of them sang, as if he were making fun of the song, and he beat time to it with a beer bottle.

Yes, those had been the days! Austria, the Sudetenland … Flower wars, they'd been called, because the Austrians welcomed them so enthusiastically! After Austria the Sudetenland, then put a stop to it, that would have been the thing. Now they were in the shit, and had no idea how to get out of it.

While they were sitting there, playing a game of chance with spent matchsticks, several freezing figures came limping up, and after a moment's hesitation one of them came into the inn. He was a Russian POW. He called the soldiers 'comrades', and said they had been left behind. What should they do, where should they report?

Could they help him? the Russian asked in his own language,

which was hard to understand – and then he saw the SS runes on the soldiers' collar patches and turned pale.

'You bet we can help you,' said the young SS man, laughing. 'Come with me!'

There was a bowling alley behind the inn, and he made the Russians stand against the wall and shot them out of hand.

He came back in, putting the pistol away.

The others did not laugh, they just nodded. That was life.

'How do you think they'd have acted let loose on German women?' they said to Peter. 'How do you think your figures as brown as earth will carry on when they get here?' And they went back to their game of chance with the matchsticks.

But soon they had had enough of sitting around. They were going on, now that they had finished here.

'What are you going to do next?' they asked Peter, who shrugged his shoulders.

'Well, we can take you with us,' they said. Perhaps they thought he could be a kind of drummer boy for their unit?

They drove to the parsonage, Heil Hitler. It was entirely surrounded by fluttering birds, tits, woodpeckers and finches. The pastor was just emptying the last bag of bird food. He felt weak at the knees when he saw the SS men, Heil Hitler. So the boy has given me away after all, he thought, and now they'll arrest me . . . But Peter had only come to say goodbye and collect his rucksack and the microscope, which he tucked under his arm. He left the suitcase behind; he didn't need all those women's clothes.

'Are you leaving me, then?' said the pastor. 'I'd just made us some soup.' He didn't shake hands. 'We could have gone together . . .' Going closer to Peter, he whispered, 'Are you going with the SS men?'

Yes, Peter was going with the SS men, but first he looked in at the church. There were many more bodies now. Where was Auntie? He pulled the blanket back, and saw that the two rings were no longer on the finger of her torn-off arm.

Then he got into the jeep, and they were already turning into the road where the great trek of carts was moving along. The driver hooted his horn like mad, the farmers stopped their carts, and then they were racing along through them. Their back wheels spun, and they were away. Once they were stopped, by a woman who placed herself in the middle of the road. Could they take her old mother with them and get her to hospital?

'Sure, we can do that,' said the soldiers, and the old woman was lifted into their vehicle, Heil Hitler, covered with blankets, and off they went again.

But in the wrong direction! It was some time before they realized that Peter wanted to go the other way. Then they stopped and let their drummer boy out. 'Can't force anyone to see when he's in luck!' they said. Heil Hitler. They'd happily have kept him with them, a nice fair-haired German boy like that. Then again, they were beginning to find him something of a nuisance.

The old woman put out a hand to him from under all those blankets. Ought he to stay with her?

Peter didn't know where to go. Left or right? He wanted to reach the Frisches Haff, where Auntie had planned to go. 'Anything else is useless,' she had said. Go to the Haff, yes, but what way was that? It took him a little while to work it out. Then he knew. I must go back to where I was this morning, he told himself.

But he was reluctant simply to turn round and trudge back along the road that the SS men had taken, walking into the wind and the snow, maybe passing the dead gelding again.

He watched the carts going along for a while. I ought to find a short cut, he thought, and he walked away from the column of carts and went uphill, over the snowfield and along a narrow path.

Behind him, the trek wound its way along the road, cart after cart and going slowly. No one noticed him leaving the long line of vehicles.

Soon he had reached a sparse wood of spruce trees. He could just hear the snorting of the horses, the clink of chains, the grinding of the heavy cartwheels as they went along. But then he was going through the little wood, and there was no noise at all.

Finally he came to a house; it was a village school. The door was ajar, and a dead man with vomit round his head was lying in the corridor. He must have been the teacher. Snow had blown in through the crack in the door, dusting the man's body. The table and chairs in the kitchen had fallen over and broken china lay on the floor, with pots and pans. The embers in the stove were still glowing, and Peter carefully fanned the flames. Obviously this little house had only just been abandoned.

He found a few pickled gherkins in the mess on the floor, and a bowl of pickled eggs in the larder.

He stood the chairs up and ate the gherkins. There wasn't any bread; where could he find bread?

He spent a little time looking round. A door led from the kitchen to a classroom. The authorities had placed this little school between two villages. They had done it for practical reasons, to kill two birds with one stone.

Benches were pushed up against the wall of the classroom, and there was straw on the floor. People had spent the night there. He might be able to sleep there too – but what about the dead man in the corridor? The straw was dirty, and stank of piss and shit.

*

He climbed the stairs. A dead woman lay in the bedroom, with a little girl close to her, also dead. The little girl had been clinging to the woman, who had her arm round the child. The wind blew through the broken window.

Don't look, Peter told himself, but he stayed in the doorway. A gilt-framed picture of a guardian angel hung over the rumpled bed. The angel was leading a little boy over a narrow bridge.

The Drygalskis had a picture like that in their house, too.

The living room of the house contained a sideboard with glasses on it, and a picture of a moorland landscape on the wall. There was a bookcase in the study, full of books – *The Teacher's Treasury*. The desk drawers had been pulled out and searched. The teacher and his wife had believed that mankind was basically good and 'nothing will happen to us', but they had taken rat poison in the end. And now they were lying dead in their own vomit.

Or perhaps the teacher had heard his wife's screams and the little girl whimpering, and then it was all over for him too.

He had spent his life explaining the points of the compass to the schoolchildren, and what 'horizon' means. East and west. Mental arithmetic, good handwriting. An old man with a watch-chain over his paunch. The Russians had been here in the First War too, and had behaved decently.

Peter sat down at the desk. Shall I tidy up a bit? he wondered. The official seal was missing; its inkpad lay open on the table. Perhaps someone had liked the look of the seal . . . a royal eagle? It might seem impressive as a means of certification.

You can't stay here, Peter told himself.

But he sat on at the schoolmaster's desk, staring at the scene.

He was roused by the smell of a cigarette. There were two men in the house, he could hear them talking in the kitchen. Soldiers?

They went away as quietly as they had come. There was nothing for them to take here. Peter wished he had gone with them, but they were out of sight.

He read the school register, which showed who had been late, when, and the timetable. There were piles of exercise books. A list of punishments. 'For telling lies: three strokes of the cane.'

Then he rose to his feet. You must get away from here, he told himself, and he followed the trail left by the two soldiers. They'd have known which way to go. Others had also been here, and he could even make out the tracks of cartwheels, all going one and the same way.

After he had walked for two hours, he came out into open fields, and then he saw the trek again, cart after cart. He could hear people talking and calling to each other. His short cut had not saved him much time.

He soon reached the road. No one was surprised to see a boy coming down the hill on his own. They hardly even looked up; their eyes were elsewhere.

Fallen carts lay on both sides of the road, dead animals with bloated bellies, and dead people: old men and women, children. Many children. They were half covered with drifting snow.

A large, solitary oak tree stood beside the road. Some people were hanging from a spreading branch, a couple of soldiers with their coats unbuttoned and their heads bare. Were those the two soldiers from the school? They had notices hung round their necks saying, WE WERE TOO COWARDLY TO FIGHT. And beside them hung a man and a woman. The man wore a rectangular Polish cap on his head, and had a bandaged finger. The woman was Vera. The notices hanging from their necks said, WE WERE CAUGHT LOOTING.

Peter had once seen someone make the sign of the cross, and

he would have liked to make it now. He wanted to stand under the tree and make the sign of the cross. But he wasn't a Catholic. He took off his cap as if he needed to scratch his head; he had to be careful, because there was a vehicle by the roadside with military police in it. Heil Hitler. The dead dangling from the tree swayed back and forth.

The 'watchdogs' stopped several wounded men walking past the carts to check up on them. Heil Hitler. Was a shot in the arm really so bad? Couldn't the man fire a gun all the same, or at least keep watch? They had paper bandages drenched with blood, and labels on their coats saying that yes, their wounds were genuine, and how bad they were. They held up their injured limbs as proof. Heil Hitler, yes, that's in order.

No cowards, no one simply work-shy? Unwind that bandage, will you? Right, that passes muster.

A little further on there was a youth hostel built in the Lower Saxon style, a big place. A notice outside told you that it was the Johann-Gottfried-Herder Youth Hostel. Peter went over to the large building. Two long swastika banners blew in the wind outside it. This was probably the assembly area where the young people met for roll-call. German young people had looked up to the banner with shining eyes and jumped over bonfires here.

> We'll show faith and love
> For our native land,
> And the powers above.

The assembly area was surrounded by a wall of medium height, as if by two arms. The masons had made a wheat-sheaf out of bricks and placed it on the gable end of the main part of the building, with the date 1936 under it. The whole thing reminded

Peter of the Albert Leo Schlageter fountain on the housing development opposite the Georgenhof, although that was much smaller than this magnificent building.

The military police drove up and got out to report to their superior officers: two cowards strung up along with two Russian looters.

'Good,' said the superior officers. They had commandeered the office of the youth hostel, which gave them a view of the road so that they could see whether the long line of vehicles was flowing smoothly. At the slightest disturbance they could have intervened to restore order. However, from their vantage position they couldn't see the beautiful view from the youth hostel, cleverly incorporated in the whole design by the Reich architect Witterkind. That was the view from the back of the building, where the road swung round in a wide loop to the valley, with the trek winding onward towards it. And in the distance was a small town with two churches and a castle.

Discipline and good order reigned in the youth hostel. The washrooms were tip-top quality, and every group of refugees had been given a place in the great meeting hall. They sat close together in families, with their suitcases and rucksacks, and the horses were stabled in the gymnasium. Members of the National Socialist Nurses' Association went round giving out food parcels. Peter had to show his papers, Heil Hitler, and he got a food parcel too. There was even hot soup at twelve-thirty. That was probably what kept the people here.

A single lance corporal tried to get a food parcel for himself, Heil Hitler, and was immediately sent to the military police in the office. He didn't come out for a long time.

'It's come to this, has it? Leaving your unit and then trying to get hold of food!'

And what had the man done with his gun?

He'd been sent off, Heil Hitler, to report three dead Russians that he had discovered in a village.

Oh, well, that was different.

Some two hundred people, large and small, were waiting for soup here under murals illustrating the life and work of the philosopher Herder. As well as soup, they wanted to know how things were going. They listened to the latest news, on the radio and as it was passed from mouth to mouth. How far away were the Russians now? They hoped to find out whether the road to the Frisches Haff was still clear. Every detail was passed on in an undertone. Children ran about among the adults, playing catch.

Up in the gallery, a sailor hoping to cheer everyone up brought out his accordion:

Homeland, see thy stars
Shine in the firmament.

He was surrounded by refugees, small and large, some with tears in their eyes. The sailor was part of an anti-aircraft unit. He hadn't expected life in the navy to be like this. As far as he was concerned, his homeland was one of the old tubs now at the bottom of the sea.

And here in this place, built by the Party to encourage young people to go hiking, in a youth hostel of the Greater German Reich and under a picture of Herder's voyage to the west, it so happened – because the world is nothing but a big village – that Peter came upon his tutor, Dr Wagner the schoolmaster, who was clad in walking trousers and coat and gaiters.

Which of them saw the other first?

Dr Wagner joyfully hugged the boy, and they immediately began exchanging news.

'Mitkau is burning, my dear boy,' said Wagner, 'and the Russians are probably in the Georgenhof by now.'

And Peter told him about Auntie and Vladimir and Vera.

'Oh no!' exclaimed Dr Wagner. 'Hanged? The woman too? They didn't deserve that.' At first the schoolmaster had said only, 'Really?' because he assumed the boy was telling his stories again. But he was shocked by this. 'Hanged?'

'All wrecked,' said Peter, 'the coach too. I drove it all by myself,' he added, 'with Auntie in the back.' He claimed to have made her very comfortable there, with straw packed round her. And that, he said, had been her downfall – the horse and coach done for, and he, up on the box, had got away without a scratch. He fell to the ground, yes, but not a scratch on him. A miracle!

'A miracle,' whispered Wagner. 'To think you were able to drive a coach!' And he thought that Auntie had never been very nice to him. She spoke sharply when he was teaching Peter irregular verbs – *fero, tuli, latum*.

'And do you know who else is here?' he said. 'Come with me.' He went ahead in his old-fashioned walking trousers and his gaiters, which dated from the 1914 war, and led Peter to a back room, but they were sent straight out again, because a woman was having a baby there. It was Felicitas, and half an hour later mother and child were both dead.

'She was always so funny,' said Peter.

'Yes,' replied the schoolmaster. 'Death takes us all just as we are.'

Peter said nothing for a while. 'I expect you're thinking of your mother, my dear boy,' said Wagner. But Peter wasn't, he was thinking of the Georgenhof and the penknife with the four blades that his father had brought back for him last year. He wished he had brought it with him. And he was also wondering what 'opake' meant. The schoolmaster had just said the situation was opake.

His trouble, said Wagner, was having to drag that damn suitcase of the baron's round with him. Heavy as lead, with all those chronicles inside it. He'd been tempted several times to leave it behind . . . and there was a tale to be told about that, too, and how difficult it had been to retrieve the case in the first place. The things the people there had said to him.

What with Drygalski asking, in irritation, what that was supposed to be . . . and Sonya wanting to know what was in it.

And incidentally, Drygalski had left the Settlement too, simply abandoning his wife.

Katharina's situation had changed considerably. The police officer who allowed her a breath of fresh air had not reappeared. She had been left alone in her cold cell with her white fur cap on her head. Were the guards still here? Much as the banging of doors and the sound of a key turning in the lock had alarmed her, this sudden silence was uncanny.

But then, very early in the morning, the cell doors were opened and everyone was told to come out. 'No talking!' They were herded into the yard, and given half a loaf of bread each. 'And bring your blanket with you.'

Almost at once an unshaven man on crutches made his way to Katharina's side. He had a great gash on his forehead, like a sabre wound. 'Dear lady . . .' he whispered. It was Schünemann the political economist, who had been picked up with a bag full of forged papers and ration cards.

'Dear lady . . .' he said. Did he want to pour his heart out to her? Or ease his conscience? Tell her why he had taken the envelope with the military postmark on it?

None of that mattered any more. 'Shut up!' a guard called, and the gate was opened and they had to march out.

They marched through the town, thirty prisoners, and at the Senthagener Tor they were joined by another thirty concentration camp inmates.

'Where are we going?'

'Shut up. There's going to be some shooting.'

They were led westward, and just as they were passing the Georgenhof the big green bridge, Mitkau's pride and joy, exploded. The trek stopped, and the carts were taken over the ice of the River Helge. More and more carts went on to the ice, and there was a jam because it was difficult for the horses to pull the heavy carts up the sloping bank. Then the ice broke and carts sank, and the screams of the people in them sounded, from a distance, like a great sigh.

Katharina kept her head bent. Like the others, she looked neither to right nor to left. Schünemann swung himself along on his crutches beside her.

'Dear lady . . .' he kept saying. Was he trying to tell her how good life used to be, and how he too had seen better days?

'Shut up!' shouted the guards, and then they pulled him out of the group by his coat and hit him. A man who had helped to destabilize the will of the German people to resist, shooting his mouth off. They began beating him in earnest.

Katharina had thought that Lothar Sarkander might get her out of this. Would drive up in his car at the last moment, waving a white cloth out of the window. Reprieved! Reprieved! And then he would get her to climb in as he once did before, holding the car door open, and racing away with her.

'This woman is a very special person ...'

The sea! They had stood on the landing stage at the seaside. Seagulls, and the waves lapping at the wooden breakwaters, her hat like the sun behind her head. And in the restaurant that evening, he had blown cigarette smoke over the candle. Acting the part of a Hungarian café violinist – '*Avant de mourir?*' It had made them laugh so much. He had burrowed his way into her heart with that violinist act ... And the view over the sea from their room. Had the sea shone that night? Had billions of little luminous fish made the sea glow? And when the time came she had brought the little girl into the world.

Katharina thought he might come to her rescue. At the last minute?

But it didn't happen, and she had to take care that no one trod on her heels. The concentration camp inmates from the brickworks were crowding round her. 'Lady ... bread,' they said, and Katharina gave them all the bread she had. These men formed a phalanx against the others who also wanted her bread, and would let no one else near her, a woman who still had bread ... Only when she had no more to give did they move away.

'*Votre coeur* ...' said one of them. Was he an educated man?

The bell in the Johann-Gottfried-Herder Youth Hostel went at six in the morning. 'Stand in line for coffee!' There were people brushing their teeth in the washroom, and Dr Wagner was shaving. You felt different after shaving.

Then they collected their coffee from the Red Cross, and everyone had four slices of bread and margarine. The watchdogs stood at the counter, Heil Hitler, to see if anyone was trying to get into the queue without proper papers. And they filtered out all men aged from fifteen to seventy. They should go and defend their country, damn it all! One woman screamed and clung to her husband, but they took him away no matter how helplessly he looked Around him.

Wagner and Peter passed muster. 'My boy,' said Wagner, 'I think we should stick together. Fate looks kindly on us.'

Peter with his lightweight rucksack, the microscope under his arm, and Wagner with the baron's heavy suitcase.

Outside the youth hostel, there was a keen wind blowing round the corner into their faces. The sun was shining but the wind was keen.

A small hand-sledge stood outside the door, its rope lying in the snow like a snake.

Dr Wagner put his case on it, looked round and said, 'Come on, my boy, quick, before someone takes this away from us.' And they ran as fast as they could. It was a stroke of luck, after all, and as the phrase to remind you of musical notes goes, Every Good Boy Deserves Favour. Dr Wagner even thought it was funny. 'We cocked a snook at them!' he cried. Then they were part of the human crocodile winding its way in wide curves through the trodden snow, between wrecked carts and dead bodies, towards the nearby town.

Peter pulled the sledge and Dr Wagner pushed it. 'Look around you, boy,' said Wagner. Up there stood the Johann-Gottfried-Herder Youth Hostel, banners waving in the wind, with human beings pouring out of it. It was an impressive sight. But the cry was 'Go on!' again.

Dr Wagner held his suitcase down on the sledge like an organ-grinder holding his barrel organ. It bothered him that he couldn't remember anything by Herder. He was racking his brains for literary references. Weimar, that was no problem. Goethe and Schiller. But he couldn't remember anything by Herder, nothing at all. *The Cid*, he thought, but what did that amount to? What did it mean? He used to remember things so well. He would read a poem two or three times, and then he could recite it from memory. *You come again, you strange, you swaying figures . . .* that was Goethe's *Faust*. He knew half of *Faust* by heart, but now the poetry in his mind was ebbing away. He and his mother used to go for long walks and played at capping each other's quotations. *In my boyhood a god would often save me . . .* Hölderlin, yes, but these days his memory played him false, and sometimes wouldn't cooperate at all.

Didn't Herder have something wrong with his eyes? Maybe an ulcer? That was all he could remember about him just now.

On the other side of a lake – the drooping branches of weeping willows lay frozen in the ice – stood a solitary house, broad and comfortable-looking. A bronze deer in front of it was crowned with snow.

BEWARE OF THE DOG, said a notice.

The double door of the terrace stood open, its two halves swinging in the wind. Three dogs, shot dead, lay beside the door.

No one down below took any notice of the house. Why bother to climb the hill? they must have thought. On, go on was the watchword, reinforced by rumour: 'The Russians are coming.'

But the two of them pulled out of the convoy, curious. A house on the banks of a lake? With a bronze deer in front of it? The sun was strong, and Peter pulled the sledge uphill. They tacitly agreed to give themselves a moment's rest.

The procession crawled along the road through the white landscape below. They could hear the cartwheels, the voices, people coughing. But all was still up here. A child's loud cry broke the silence – it had probably lost its mother. The white house looked like the home of an artist. Would they find more dead bodies here?

*

Was it the house of a painter? A sculptor? No, a writer had lived here. His typewriter was still standing on his desk, with an empty coffee cup beside it. From his desk you looked along an avenue leading to a pavilion on the bank of the lake. It was probably a nice place to sit and write.

There was a landing stage beside the lake, and a boathouse. Beyond it were the towers of the town towards which the long line of people were moving. The inhabitants of this house must have seen beautiful sunsets. And at this moment the sun was shining brightly.

They both looked around them. Sunlight fell on the crystalline snow on the terrace, making it sparkle in the spectrum of rainbow colours. What a sight!

There were family photographs on the desk: the writer himself in thick-lensed glasses, his wife and two small children holding a teddy bear and a doll. There was a mourning ribbon on the wife's picture.

A photograph of Hitler hung on the wall above the desk, with the sun shining on it. An inscription could be made out under this photo.

> *To the highly esteemed author*
> *Gotthardt Baron von Erztum-Lohmeyer*
> *on his 50th birthday.*

> Adolf Hitler,
> Führer and Chancellor of the Reich

Should they turn it to the wall to keep it from fading?

The library was next to the study. Its doors were open. When the writer wanted to look something up in a book, he had only to put down his pen and stroll into the room next door. It also held a couch on which he could recline. All very attractive.

And all very tasteful. The walls were covered with clear, bright pictures, ranged side by side. Young people in many different positions, turning towards the future. The young people looked like Peter.

It was a pity that the writer had fled, and was not here any more. He could have looked out of his window at the proud youth hostel down below, and the long line of people in the shining snow spilling out of the hostel to follow the curves of the winding road. What an impressive sight.

From that image, a writer could have been inspired to write a great epic on human nature. When humanity suffers, it should be recorded in literature. The great tales of the Thirty Years War. Verdun. The Children of Israel, always crossing the Red Sea.

Wagner shielded his eyes with his hand. He felt badly shaken.

No one had yet interfered with the books, although the glass panes of the bookcases had been smashed. Why? Perhaps the writer had done it himself, in a moment of despair.

Sucking air in through his teeth, Dr Wagner looked for Herder. The owner of this house, the writer, must surely have the works of Herder on his shelves. He would have kept the classics always at hand. Goethe, Schiller and Körner stood there side by side – but nothing by Herder.

But I myself, Wagner thought now, have no books by Herder on my shelves. Shame on me! He had to smile, and resolved to buy himself Herder when all this was over. Good heavens, he hoped he would survive if only to do that.

Surely it must be possible to get away with his life? Was he to die without ever reading Herder? Didn't culture contribute to the perfection of humanity?

Meanwhile Peter was looking for something to eat. He walked through suites of rooms with pictures on all the walls.

There was indeed half a loaf on the kitchen table, just where it had been left. But it was as hard as a rock. Peter appropriated it, and a jar labelled SUMMER 1944. HERTHA'S BLACKCURRANT JAM.

He tipped oatmeal into a bowl and sprinkled sugar on it. Then he called Dr Wagener, and they ate heartily.

Peter thought of giving the schoolmaster one of the silver spoons he still had in his pocket. Wouldn't that be a bond between them?

Peter opened the baron's suitcase. At the very top was the booklet on *Roads and Footpaths in the Baltic States,* and inside was his father's name, Eberhard von Globig. Well, thought Peter, so the baron helped himself to that.

There was no chamber organ in the writer's house, but there was a grand piano. Wagner sat down at it and tried to play his E minor variations. But the piano was badly out of tune. All the same: 'Listen,' he told Peter. 'E minor – G major – enharmonically changing to F major . . . can you hear that?'

Peter put his microscope on the piano.

The schoolmaster laughed. 'You won't get any further with a microscope.' From F major it wasn't far to B flat major . . . and then the whole world was open to you! But exactly how had he done it before? How did it go? And how had he managed to infuse the whole thing with melancholy? He played so loud a flourish that Peter shushed him. For goodness' sake, someone might hear.

At this moment Katharina was being marched along the road down below. In her white Persian lamb cap she could easily have been seen among the prisoners. Perhaps she was looking up at the house. A lakeside villa with a bronze deer on the terrace, and now piano music?

Her black boots had already been taken away from her, and she was trudging along in a worn-out pair of men's shoes. Whenever she slipped, the guard beside her told her to watch out.

From all sides, onlookers shot the prisoners hostile glances. It's the fault of people like that, they thought. They stirred everyone else up against us, they fanned the flames setting the world alight.

A farmer even reached out towards her with his whip. He had tied little knots in the lash, to make it sting more, and it caught Katharina's cheek.

Wagner was seeing the boy as he never had before: the black grand piano, the bright pictures on the wall, and the fair-haired boy, still a child, with his thin, grave and merry face. Why hadn't he taken better care of him when there was still time?

He would have liked to take Peter hiking, as he used to go hiking with his students in the valley of the Helge.

Now it was too late.

Although, come to think of it, he was hiking with the boy at this moment. He had him all to himself now.

'I tell you what,' he said. 'We'll go on now.'

They left the baron's suitcase behind. The chronicles would be all right here, thought Wagner. If the master of the house came back, the first thing he saw would be the suitcase. 'What's this?' he would say. 'Old papers? Chronicles?' A writer could do something with those. He thought of Adalbert Stifter, *My Great-Grandfather's Portfolio*, or maybe it was in the works of Gottfried Keller or someone – who was it who wrote about finding a case full of old writings in the attic? Was there anything like that in Herder?

Peter thought: I'll build myself a house like this some day, light and airy, not at all like the dark, gloomy Georgenhof. He sat on the sledge and slid downhill, and the old man ran down after him, laughing and holding on to his hat. His own father had never run after him. He had stood in the doorway wearing his white jacket with the Cross of Merit (no swords). Once he had come up to his room after a ride, bending his riding crop into a semicircle. 'Well, you have a kingdom of your own here,' he had said, and he looked out of the window and added, 'But you must tidy up. What a mess it is in here!'

23

A Museum

The little town was full of farm carts. They stood in every street, and more and more kept crowding in. Refugee women went into the houses begging. If the people living in those houses had already fled, they took them over. One house was burning, with flames hissing as they shot out of the windows; no one took any notice.

In the marketplace, surrounded by pretty little gabled houses with the town hall to the north, carts stood packed close together, but the people had gone off to be 'transported' according to regulations. The horses had just been taken out of the shafts, Heil Hitler, they would be handed over to the army. Party officials went up and down between these rows of carts with their shafts tilted upright. They were all being registered, and had numbers chalked on them for the refugees' return journey.

For the time being, everyone was camping on straw in a cinema wondering what next. Apparently they were to board ships. If so, they hadn't needed to come all this way, so far from home, with all their worldly goods. Could he just go and collect his briefcase from the cart? someone asked. No, that wasn't allowed.

'I have to see to my horses . . .'

The Volkssturm reservists stood outside the cinema, and wouldn't let anyone out.

*

A man appeared on the balcony above the porch of the town hall, behind the clock that had been shot to pieces. His name was Lothar Sarkander. He was leaning on the balustrade, looking out over the empty carts, and delivering a speech, making large gestures and hoarsely calling out slogans that no one could hear properly. He seemed to be urging his audience to repent and mend their ways, something of that sort.

> *If I'd known what I was missing,*
> *If I'd known who I was kissing,*
> *That midnight at the lido . . .*

Someone took him by the sleeve and pulled him back into the building. The man had obviously lost his mind. He would have to be taken away.

A Wehrmacht truck stood in a side street. The former bailiff's residence, a very old, squat building that had served as a museum, was just being emptied. The back hatch of the truck's load area had been let down, and soldiers were carefully carrying old chests and paintings out to the vehicle. Demolishing the bailiff's residence had been suggested in the nineteenth century, but then the townsfolk decided that they could still make use of it as a museum.

While Dr Wagner went looking for a pharmacist selling ointment for his piles, Peter entered the old building. 'Wait for me, I'll be back in a minute!' A huge First World War cross full of nails hung in the entrance hall. It represented help rendered by the home country to the men at the front; black nails had cost five marks each, gilded nails ten marks. The idea had been to raise money for arms and munitions, not for the dead. It bore witness to better times.

*

A framed document hung on the wall. In it, on the occasion of his fiftieth birthday, the German author Gotthardt Baron von Erztum-Lohmeyer declared that, in grateful thanks for the freedom of his native town now bestowed on him, he was leaving it his library and all his manuscripts after his death.

The museum curator, Heil Hitler, an old gentleman wearing pince-nez and a Party symbol, watched the building being cleared. He went from one man to another, wringing his hands. 'For God's sake go carefully!' he cried. But there were no outbursts of anger; they could easily have been misinterpreted.

In one large hall – it had probably been a law court; iron yokes hung from the wall – glass showcases had already been emptied. They had held rare books on display, and, coins, seals and charters. Querns weighing several hundredweight each and dating from the pre-Germanic period were lined up along the corridors. After all, they bore witness to the meagre lives of our ancestors: grinding corn into flour, mixing gunpowder for firearms. They were to be left behind, however valuable they might be, because of their weight, but the round pestles used with them were taken away. If anyone looted the querns they wouldn't be much good without the pestles.

The chandelier made of antlers hanging from the ceiling was left behind as well. It was probably seventeenth century; its day was past.

But the curator anxiously told the soldiers not to forget the majolica ware. 'Go carefully with that!'

Paintings were carried out one by one, tiny flower pieces, small pictures on rural subjects, and *The Battle of Tannenberg*, a large battle scene that would probably have been described anywhere else as a frightful daub. It showed mounted messengers on rearing horses, soldiers in spiked helmets firing at the enemy, grenades exploding at regular intervals. Dead Russians and wounded Germans. Two field marshals could clearly be seen in the foreground, one pointing to a map on a table in front of him, the other agreeing with whatever he was saying. Rumpler-Taube aircraft flew against the background of a sky sprinkled with shrapnel, taking part in the battle whenever possible. You could tell which were the enemy planes because they were crashing to the ground. There was a tear in the canvas. 'We didn't do that,' said the soldiers carrying the pictures out. 'It was already there.'

To the left of the door hung the portrait of a plump princess in a sky-blue dress, a fur collar, and with many medals on her breast. She was to become the Tsarina Catherine the Great, insatiable in her thirst for love but a good friend of Prussia. She had travelled through this town on her way to St Petersburg, and the people were still telling risqué stories about her.

That portrait was also taken down, wrapped in a blanket and taken away, although it might have been advisable to carry it in procession to face the furious Russians: 'Look at her, the German nation's great friend!'

The snag there was that she had been German herself.

The soldiers left *The Coming of the Holy Ghost* where it was as well. It was a huge panel from the old parish church that had been demolished in the Middle Ages. The disciples had little flames on their heads and a dove hovering over them. 'We might as well leave this thing,' said the soldiers. The curator wasn't so sure. It went against his instincts, but perhaps this or that could be retrieved later.

They left the stained-glass windows where they were, too; they would probably break in transit anyway.

*

Peter helped to carry things out. The documents in the town archives were to be preserved as well, in a whole series of folders, and with many boxes containing archaeological finds. Didn't one of the boxes have the name Hesse on it? That country teacher with his Stone Age stuff had had the right idea. Wouldn't those items help to show that East Prussia was an ancient German land?

The curator with the Party symbol stood at the exit from the museum, saying, 'Careful, careful, all this is irreplaceable!' every time the soldiers carried anything past him. He was holding a little box containing the municipal seal. 'This is particularly valuable, don't let it out of your sight.'

He didn't even notice how cold he was. Why, he wondered, am I shivering like this?

'I think that's everything,' he said in the end. 'Now we can set out.' He would just go to fetch his wife and daughter . . .

Wife and daughter? How old was his daughter?

'Sixteen.'

'Sure, we can find room for her.'

Peter was asked what he thought he was doing, hanging round here. And what was that box under his arm? A schoolboy's microscope? Why didn't he say so before, for heaven's sake?

When at last they were ready, the curator of the museum got into the cab of the truck with his wife and daughter. 'We'll just have to squeeze up a bit,' said the driver.

The soldiers jumped up on the load area, and Peter, coming to a quick decision, swung himself up too. Then they were off. The box containing the municipal seal was left behind on the museum steps, but Peter's microscope was jammed under his arm.

Hooting, they drove past the farm carts standing in the streets. Peter looked back over the load area at the long line of carts.

I wonder, he thought, whether anyone will ever paint *that*?

Local police officers stood at the town gate, to check that everyone who wanted to go through it had the right papers. And to stop anyone trying to run away. Heil Hitler. They had heavy pistols in their belts, and badges on chains round their necks. They let vehicles through one by one. When the truck had finally been through this procedure and could go on, and the driver was putting it into first gear and accelerating, Dr Wagner came running along, gesticulating and shouting, 'Stop, stop!' Peter knocked at the driver's cab, asking them to pick the gentleman up, but in vain; there was no time. With one last effort, Dr Wagner jumped up to the back hatch of the load area but missed it, slipped off and fell into the street, where a heavy vehicle ran over him.

'Oh no!' cried Peter, falling backwards on the load area.

Was that what Dr Wagner had meant by perfection?

Outside the town, going down the road lined with wrecked cars, corpses and looted luggage, they were driving past more carts trekking towards the town. When they went round a bend Peter threw his weight against the angle of the truck, to keep the pictures from falling over. The pestles belonging to the querns rolled about on the load area in semicircles, sometimes colliding with each other and setting off sparks.

For a while Peter counted the carts they were passing. Were there thousands of them? How long had they been on the road? It was always the same, everyone intent on getting away over the ice of the Haff to the spit of land that was the Nehrung, and from there home to the Reich.

Is Pomerania our fatherland?
Is Swabia our fatherland . . .
All Germany's our fatherland.

And they would surely be welcome there.

After a few kilometres, an untidy column of prisoners joined the main road, soldiers guarding it left and right. The prisoners were dragging themselves unsteadily along with the last of their strength. They had wrapped themselves in blankets to keep off the cold.

'Who are that lot?' asked one of the soldiers in the truck.

'The children of Israel,' replied a guard.

'They should be made a head shorter!' And if the speaker had had stones he would have thrown them, but he couldn't be bothered to pick up the pestles rolling about at his feet.

It took some time for Peter to understand what kind of prisoners these really were, and then it occurred to him that his mother might be with them. He looked more closely at the women. Her white fur cap . . . could he see it?

Did he see the white fur cap?

He took the half-loaf out of his pocket, thinking he should break some off and throw it to the prisoners, like the parents in the fairy tale throwing bread to their children. But the half-loaf was a block of ice.

That was the last time that Peter saw his mother, although he hadn't really seen her at all.

The truck stopped at the Frisches Haff, their journey's end. There was nowhere else to go. The land and brackish water of the Haff were frozen over. Hundreds of carts were waiting. They were led out separately on to the surface of the ice. The wounded were taken out first, Heil Hitler, and then the vehicles went back. You had to keep your distance – fifty metres apart or the ice would break. Fir trees and bushes showed the path where it was safe to stand. It was risky to stray from it. Horses' heads looked out of the ice where carts had fallen in.

The drivers of farm carts had tried and failed to overtake the trek.

The museum curator was looking for the local commandant. He wanted to tell him that there were all kinds of valuable cultural artefacts on the load area of the truck. Heil Hitler!

Cultural artefacts? What did he mean?

The officer in command of the escort party was fetched, and said they could be accommodated elsewhere.

The old gentleman with his wife and young daughter stood beside the truck, their coats blowing in the wind. Paintings! Charters! Folio volumes! The truck was taken away. The curator was told that they would be careful with the cultural artefacts, of course they would. Then the daughter took over and helped her parents out on the ice. They must go on on foot. Perhaps they would be lucky.

The half-frozen Haff. Peter took his mother's little locket out of his pocket. He had been holding it in his hand, and now he opened it. Maybe it contained a picture of him? Or of Elfriede? Or his father in his white jacket?

No, Katharina had kept a picture of herself inside the locket. Peter closed it again. And at that moment, far away in Italy, his father picked up his service pistol and shot himself.

Peter ran out on the ice after a farm cart. A woman was sitting on the box. She had come a long way, and she had put feather beds round her children to keep away the cold.

Peter jumped up to hitch a lift on the back of the cart, and let it carry him over. Water lay on the surface of the ice and spurted up.

24

The Launch

In other lands and here
We live in great despair.
We pray the Lord to heed
Our misery and need.

Some time later, early in May, Peter was standing on the quay in a harbour, scanning the horizon through his binoculars, with his air pistol in his waistband.

The sea! Gulls, and the waves lapping against the wooden break-waters. *'Avant de mourir?'*

Large vessels lay at anchor in the roadsteads, gradually filling up with refugees and then steaming away. Motor launches full of people went out to them from the quayside in the harbour, plying out and back again. And ship after ship steamed away. Was there a painter somewhere, recording the magnificent scene for ever?

Peter was not in any hurry. He slept in abandoned apartments, went to the cinema, got pea soup from a field kitchen, played with a stray cat and ran along the beach. Once, in a back yard, he listened to someone playing the violin. He thought he knew the tune. He meant to go into the building, but it was locked.

There was an apple tree in blossom in front of the house, and behind it the echo of that violin music.

He wandered along the streets with their front gardens in

flower, and when there was an air-raid warning he went into a cellar to join the people with their cases and bags in the shelter. He listened to the anti-aircraft guns and the dull thump of bombs as they dropped, and when it was over he went back to roaming through the streets. He saw sailors with hand grenades in their belts – dating from Kiel in 1918 – and old Volkssturm reservists – *Alas, you have destroyed / this lovely world* – and SS men too, with their boots as shiny as if they were on parade. *If all should turn disloyal, yet we will still prove true.*

A swarm of deaconesses in white caps, holding the hands of children from an orphanage. 'Where are you going? Where are you going?' This way or that, forward or back?

Amidst all the coming and going, Peter saw a hat – a woman with a hat that he knew on her head. It was one of his mother's hats, black with a red feather in it, and the woman was Frau Hesse. Eckbert and Ingomar were trotting along behind her. She was holding tickets for a ship, waving them in the air. Maybe we will all get lucky some time in our lives.

Peter took cover in a gateway. He didn't want to meet these people.

Among the farm carts where they had been left after the trek, he saw a girl in white knee socks. She was perched on the shafts, rocking back and forth. Later, when he came back looking for her, she had gone.

Was it Elfie? he wondered, and counted on his fingers; she would be eight now. He remembered his mother running after the howling Elfie. A lot of screaming, all long ago. Had it been like that? Running upstairs. And then one day his sister was lying in bed, not moving, and his mother had not shed tears.

He would have liked to tell the girl with the knee socks about those hunched figures, brown as earth, and the chamber organ and the crystal chandeliers. And he would have liked to give her the last silver spoon. Had he lost it? And where had the girl gone? He found the dried-up wreath of flowers from the coach in his trouser pocket, and crumbled it to pieces. Only when he had destroyed it did he remember that those were the flowers from the coach.

> *If I'd known what I was missing,*
> *If I'd known who I was kissing,*
> *That midnight at the lido.*
> *If I'd known who it was there*
> *That midnight at the lido . . .*

The Isabelle, a white hotel on the promenade now painted in camouflage colouring. One last deckchair still stood on the terrace. Peter sat in it, and watched the fast motorboats and launches taking passengers out to the big ships in the distance. But weren't they always full?

Many old-fashioned steamships had been sunk in the bay. You could just see their masts under the surface of the water, like the horses' heads in the ice of the Haff.

Once Peter also went to see the foreign workers playing the mandolin and dancing. They had been housed in a gymnasium, cooking themselves fry-ups and waiting to go home.

Was Marcello, the Italian from the Forest Lodge, one of them? And the Romanian who could make money disappear as if by magic? And the Czech with the leather cap? A troop of Frenchmen came marching up as well, and they were all loaded into an open barge. 'Come with us!' one of them called to Peter. No, he didn't want to. He was still waiting.

Wounded men were taken to the barge as well. Peter hadn't noticed before that there was a group of concentration camp prisoners in it. They had to crowd close together in the bows, and the soldiers with their blood-stained bandages spat in front of them.

When Peter was watching a revue film at the cinema, an air-raid warning sounded again, and bombs fell almost at once. The barge had been hit out at sea, and sank at once.

Next day the bodies floated ashore. The wounded men were surrounded by the paper bandages from their injuries; they had come adrift and were floating round them like garlands in the waves. Was there a white cap lying on the beach? White, and made from the skin of a Persian lamb?

So far Peter had not been in any hurry. But now there were many more people standing on the quayside in the harbour, waiting to be taken out to the ships, and there were no more ships in sight. The town was empty, but they still stood on the beach waiting. A torpedo boat came past to see if there was still anyone left, and even a U-boat put in an appearance.

Peter went through the empty streets one last time, and then down to the harbour. He passed the football field, which was full of household goods: furniture, sewing machines, grandfather clocks, all sorted according to size, as well as a solitary goat tied to a baby's pram.

Busy Party officials made notes of all these things – how many pianos there were, how many armchairs – and checked up on occasional passers-by: Heil Hitler, what did they think they were doing here?

Soldiers were ordered around. They were given guns. 'In your own time, quick march!' they were told, and then they were sent off to fight the Russians. There were even members of the Hitler Youth among them, putting a brave face on it.

Many glances were cast at Peter. Couldn't that fair-haired boy handle a weapon too? After all, it was a matter of defending the country. Hey, you, come here! It's a matter of life and death.

Now men, stand up, and let the stormclouds break! Rise up, my friends, the flames send signals out . . .

No, Peter was rejected. He might have fair hair, but he was still too young.

A rampart of silent humanity stood by the harbour, waiting for a miracle: for another boat to come and take them out to the very last ship lying at anchor in the roadstead: a grey silhouette as if cut from grey cardboard. Everyone was hoping for that miracle to happen for himself alone, and they were all surging down to the water to make the miracle come true for themselves. On board a ship to cross the sea! To Denmark. Perhaps we'll be lucky? Strawberries and whipped cream, why not?

They stood as if they were lined up for the Last Judgement, awaiting the verdict.

Peter forced his way through the crowd, his microscope under his arm and with his binoculars and air pistol, and he gradually managed to get closer to the front.

'It's no use, my dear boy,' a woman with children holding both her hands told him. 'You won't get through.' But Peter wasn't giving up, and at last he was on the very edge of the waterside.

One last launch was coming along the quay. It was crammed with people standing close together, the tips of their toes clinging to the side of the craft.

It passed by, its wash creating a semicircle. Then Peter saw Herr Drygalski standing in the boat in his brown jackboots, right at the front beside the sailor steering the launch. At that moment Drygalski also saw Peter. He pointed to him, and said something to the sailor. Sure enough, the sailor steered the launch very close to the quay. Drygalski jumped out, right into the crowd of people – they flinched back, shouting 'No!' It all happened very fast. Drygalski pushed Peter into the launch, and stayed behind on the quay himself.

Did he wave to Peter?

Was everything all right now?

SWANSONG 1945

A Collective Diary from Hitler's
Last Birthday to VE Day

Translated from the German by Shaun Whiteside

**A monumental work of history which brings
to life the final days of WWII**

Collecting together letters, diaries and eyewitness accounts, *Swansong 1945* chronicles four significant days in the endgame of WWII: 20 April, Hitler's last birthday; 25 April, when American and Soviet troops first met at the Elbe; 30 April, the day Hitler committed suicide; and 8 May, the day of the German surrender.

Side by side in these pages, we encounter the voices of civilians fleeing on foot to the west, British and American POWs dreaming of home, concentration camp survivors, loyal soldiers from both sides of the conflict and national leaders including Churchill, Hitler and Mussolini. A monumental account of survival, suffering, hope and despair, *Swansong 1945* evokes the complex reality of a conflict whose repercussions are still felt today.

'Each extract is a revelation ... The best history
writing doesn't simplify a reader's understanding of the past, it
complicates it. It adds layers, draws out contradictions and sharpens
them, digs down into complexity, presenting a narrative that is rich
and not simple at all. *Swansong 1945* does all these things
supremely well' *Independent on Sunday*

'A gripping accumulation of documents brought together by
a leading post-war German writer' *Jewish Chronicle*

'Kempowski is a master of form and proportion. [This is]
a puzzle of voices, of the defeated and the victors, that opens
into panorama ... The end of the war has never before
been depicted like this' *Der Spiegel*